CHAIN OF EVIDENCE

CHAIN OF EVIDENCE

GARRY DISHER

First published in Australia in 2007
by Text Publishing Company Pty, Ltd.

First published in the United States in 2007 by

Soho Press, Inc.
853 Broadway
New York, NY 10003

Library of Congress Cataloging-in-Publication Data
Disher, Garry
Chain of evidence / Garry Disher.
p. cm.
ISBN: 978-1-56947-461-7 (hardcover)
1. Police--Victoria--Melbourne--Fiction. 2. Child molesters--Fiction. 3.
Melbourne (Vic.)--Fiction. 4. South Australia--Fiction. I. Title.
PR9619.3.D56C47 2007
B23'.914--dc22
2006035723

10   9   8   7   6   5   4   3   2   1

For Dan Reed

Down here in Victoria he was the Rising Stars Agency, but he'd been Catwalk Casting up in New South Wales, and Model Miss Promotions in Queensland before that. Pete Duyker figured that he had another three months on the Peninsula before the cops and the Supreme Court caught up with him again, obliging him to move on.

'Gorgeous,' he said, firing off a few shots with the Nikon that had no film in it but was bulky and professional-looking, and emitted all of the expected clicks and whirs. For his other work he was strictly digital.

The mother simpered. 'Yeth,' she said, reminding Pete of that old Carry On movie, the doctor with his stethoscope saying 'Big breaths' and the tarty teenager in his consulting room saying, 'Yeth, and I'm only thixteen.' He fired off a few more shots of the woman's five-year-old. The brat's lank hair scarcely shifted in the breeze on the top of Arthur's Seat, the waters of the bay and the curve of the Peninsula spreading dramatically behind her, the smog-hazed towers of Melbourne faintly visible to the northwest. 'Just gorgeous,' he reiterated, snapping away.

She wasn't gorgeous. That didn't matter. Plenty of them *were* gorgeous, and had factored in to his plans over the years. This one had skinny legs, knobbly knees, crooked teeth and a ghastly pink gingham outfit. It hadn't taken Pete very long to figure out that a mother's love is blind, her ambition for her youngster boundless.

'Golden,' Pete said now, fitting a wide-angle lens from one of his camera bags, the bag satisfyingly battered and worn, a working photographer's gear. 'That last shot was golden.'

The mother beamed, a bony anorexic in skin-tight jeans, brilliant white T-shirt, huge, smoky shades and high-heeled sandals, her nod to the springtime balminess here on the Peninsula. Hers was the ugly face of motherhood, the greed naked. She was seeing a portfolio of flattering shots of her kid and the television work that would flow from it, all for a once-only, up-front charge of $395 plus a $75 registration fee. In about a week's time she'd start to get antsy and call his mobile, but Pete had several mobile phones, all of them untraceable clones and throwaways.

He looked at his watch. He'd led her to believe that he had to rush back to Melbourne now, to update a client's portfolio, the kid who played little Bethany in that Channel 10 soap, 'A Twist in Time'.

'You'll hear from me by next Friday,' he lied.

'Thankth,' said the mother as the kid scratched her calf and Pete Duyker drove off in his white Tarago van, erasing them from his mind.

The time was 2.45, a Thursday afternoon in late September. The primary school in Waterloo got out at 3.15, so he was cutting it fine. There was always Friday, and the weekend, but the latter was risky, and besides, the impulse was on him now, fine and urgent, so it had to be today.

He drove on, heading across to the Westernport side of the Peninsula, winding through townships and farmland, many of the hillsides terraced with vineyards and orchards. Not entirely unspoilt, he thought, spotting an ugly great faux-Tuscan mansion, and here and there whole stands of gum trees looked dead. Pete racked his brains: 'dieback' it was called. Some kind of disease. But the thought didn't dent his equilibrium, not on such a clear, still day, the air perfumed and the Peninsula giddy with springtime growth all around him:

orchard blossom, weeds, tall grass going to seed beside the road, the bottlebrush flowering.

He reached the coastal plain and soon he was in Waterloo. Pete was a bit of a sociologist. He liked to get the feel of a place before he went active, and he already knew Waterloo to be a town of extremes: rich and poor, urban and rural, privileged and disadvantaged. You didn't see the wealthy very often. They lived in converted farmhouses or architectural nightmares a few kilometres outside town or on bluffs overlooking the bay. The poor lived in small brick and weatherboard houses behind the town's couple of shopping streets, and in newer but still depressing housing estates on the town's perimeter. You didn't see the poor buying ride-on mowers, reins and bridles, lucerne hay or $30 bottles of the local pinot noir: they ate at McDonald's, bought Christmas presents in the $2 shops, drove huge old inefficient V8s. They didn't cycle, jog or attend the gym but presented to the local surgeries with long-untreated illnesses brought on by bad diets, alcohol and drug abuse, or injuries from hard physical labour in the nearby refinery or on some rich guy's boutique vineyard. They were the extremes. There were a lot of people who ticked over nicely, thank you, because the state or local governments employed them, or because rich and poor alike depended on them.

Earlier in the week Pete had driven into town via the road that skirted the mangrove flats, but today he drove right through the centre of Waterloo, slowly down High Street, reflecting, spotting changes and tendencies, making connections. He wouldn't mind betting the new gourmet deli might flourish, but wasn't surprised to see For Sale signs in the camping and electronic shops, not with a new K-Mart in the next block. It made him mad, briefly. His instincts were to support the little man.

He drove on, passing a couple of pharmacies, a health food shop, bakery, ANZ bank, travel agency, Salvation Army op-shop, the library and shire offices, and finally High Street opened onto the foreshore reserve: extensively treed parkland, picnic tables, skateboard ramps, a belt of mangroves skirting the bay, and an area given over to the annual Waterloo Show, not busy today but all of the rides and sideshows would be in full swing on the weekend.

Pete passed the Show, making for the far end of the reserve, where he parked beside a toilet block that he'd scouted out earlier in the week: grimy brick, odiferous, no disguising what it was. He went in, checked that he was alone, and changed into a grey wig, grey paste-on moustache, white lab coat and black horn rims with clear lenses. Then he drove to Trevally Street and parked where the sunlight through the plane trees cast transfiguring patterns over himself and his van. He wasn't a smoker, but had been known to toss other men's cigarette butts at a scene, to throw off the cops.

Now Pete waited. He waited by the van's open door, a clipboard in his hand. Time passed. Maybe she had detention, or after-school care, or was dawdling on the playground. He walked to the corner and back. Surely she'd be along soon, dreamily pumping the pedals of her bike, helmet crooked on her gleaming curls, backpack bumping against her downy spine.

Of course, she might not come, but twice now he'd watched her take this detour after school. Rather than ride straight home she had made her way along Trevally and down to the waterfront reserve, to the magic of the Waterloo Show, with its dodgem cars, Ferris wheel, the Mad Mouse ride, the Ghost Train, fairy floss on a stick. The Show was a magnet to all kinds of kids, but Pete had chosen only one kid. He paced up and down, the van door partly open, listening to the bees in some nearby roses.

But then she appeared. Just as he'd imagined. He stood and waited as she approached.

Finally she was upon him and he stepped into her path, saying, 'Your mum was taken ill. She wants me to take you to her.'

She gave him a doubting frown, and quite rightly, too, but his lab coat spelt doctor, nurse or ambulance officer, and he was counting on her natural impulse to be at her mother's side. 'It's all right,' he said, glancing both ways along the street, 'hop in.' If necessary, he'd show her the fish-gutting knife.

She dismounted prettily from the bike and her slender fingers played at her arched throat, undoing the buckle of her helmet. Pete was overcome. When she got into a fluster with the helmet, her backpack and a small electronic toy she had hanging from a strap around her neck, he itched to help her get untangled.

'Would you like a drink?' he said, when she was buckled into the seatbelt and bike, bag and helmet were on board. They'd both forgotten the toy, which lay on the grassy verge alongside a crooked brick fence. 'Lemonade,' he explained, shaking an old sports drink bottle. 'Do you like lemonade?'

She took the bottle. He watched the motions of her throat. 'Thirsty girl,' he said approvingly.

He started the engine. He could see that she would start to fret before the Temazepam took effect. She'd want to know where her mother was and where he was taking her.

But, astoundingly, that didn't happen this time. 'Oh, what a cute puppy,' she gushed.

Puppy? What puppy? Pete followed her gaze, and sure enough, some mutt of a dog lay curled on the old sleeping bag he kept in the back, one drowsy eye on the girl. It beat its tail sleepily, gave a shuddering sigh.

Must have jumped in when my back was turned, Pete thought. He assessed things rapidly. If he ejected the dog now, he'd upset the girl. The dog would ease the girl's mind. Ergo…

'Where are you taking me?'

'To see your mum.'

Frown. 'But she went up to Melbourne,' the kid said, as if she'd only just remembered it. 'To the races. She'll be back late.'

'She had an accident on the freeway,' Pete said.

The girl didn't buy it. 'Let me out,' she mumbled, already feeling the Temazepam.

They were clear of the leafy grove by now and on the access road, with cars, kids wobbling home on their bikes and a knot of people yarning and eating ice creams at the bench seats outside the only corner shop in this part of Waterloo. Pete concentrated. The girl, fading rapidly, turned heavy eyes to her side window and mouthed 'Help me' at Mrs Elliott, the library aide at her school, who had stopped by for a litre of milk. Mrs Elliott gave her a cheery wave and disappeared, and soon Pete had, too.

That was Thursday.

Friday was Sergeant Ellen Destry's first morning stretched out in Inspector Hal Challis's bed. Challis wasn't in the bed, but she lay there convinced that some trace or imprint of him lingered.

Six o'clock, according to the bedside clock, and sufficiently light outside for her customary walk, but to hell with that. She closed her eyes, giving herself up to daydreams and fugitive sensations, and the real world retreated. Challis's house was an old-style Californian bungalow on two acres of grass along a dirt back road a few kilometres inland of Waterloo, and he'd asked her to mow the grass while he was away, for the spring growth was particularly rampant this year, but the mowing could wait. The final summations in the Supreme Court trial of Nick Jarrett were expected later, but not until early afternoon. And so Ellen Destry lay there, barely moving.

The next thing she knew it was 8.30 and she was awakening from a dream-filled, stupefying sleep. Her limbs were heavy, head dense, and surroundings alien. She groaned. When she moved it was sluggishly, and she couldn't figure out how to adjust the shower temperature. She dozed under the stream of water, and then remembered that Challis's house ran on rainwater, not mains water, so she cut the shower short. 'Stop the world, I want to get off,' she said to the misted mirror. Her neck wound looked raw and nasty, even though it had happened months ago, a graze from a hired killer's 9 mm Browning.

Her first breakfast in Challis's house was scarcely any easier. The coffee came too weak from his famous machine and she couldn't make sense of how he'd arranged his cupboards and drawers. Finally, as she spooned up her muesli—organic, from High Street Health, two hundred metres down from the police station in Waterloo—she realised that she missed the sounds of human habitation. She'd had neighbours when she'd lived in Penzance Beach, the next town around from Waterloo. She'd lived with her husband and daughter, for God's sake. They'd created a comforting background murmur of voices, slammed doors and morning radio. But that house was sold now, she was estranged from her family, and reduced to this, housesitting for her boss.

Standing in for him at work, too. Challis, head of Peninsula East's Crime Investigation Unit, was away for a month, maybe longer. Family business. He seemed to think that she was perfectly capable of coping until he got back, but, in her worst moments, Ellen found herself biting her bottom lip. She felt an ever-present, low-level anxiety. Her everyday work as a CIU detective often involved up to a dozen cases at a time: some small, some middling, none very large, but the point was that she managed. But as temporary *head* of CIU, the job seemed enormous. She just knew that her male colleagues expected her to fail. Maybe I'm depressed, she thought. She should speak to the naturopath who gave free consultations in High Street Health, go on a course of St John's wort.

She glanced at Challis's wall calendar, hanging next to a cork pin board, hoping that its rows of unmarked days might give her a sense of security. False security. She moved her gaze to the photos pinned to the board. They showed Challis with the old aeroplane he was restoring. A weird hobby. Still, it was a hobby. What interests did she have, outside of work?

Sometimes it's the little things that set the world right again. She moved her breakfast things out onto the deck, where the morning sun drenched her. Presently the wood ducks wandered into view, a male, a female and seven ducklings—down from ten ducklings, owing to a fox, according to Hal. They paid her no mind but foraged through the flowering grasses that passed for a lawn out here, far from town.

Another reason not to do the mowing yet. She stretched, wondering if Challis liked to breakfast in the sun. She tried to picture it. She saw toast, coffee and a newspaper. Curiously, she didn't see a woman. There had been women, but he sat alone, and she was thinking about that when the phone rang. It was Scobie Sutton, one of the detective constables under her command. 'Ellen? We've got a missing child.'

Ellen wanted to say, 'So?' Kids went missing every day. It was a job for uniform, not CIU. Instead she said, 'How bad is it?'

'Katie Blasko, ten years old, missing since yesterday.'

'*Yesterday?* When were we notified?'

'Uniform were notified an hour ago.'

Ellen closed her eyes. She would never fathom how careless, vicious or stupid some parents could be. 'Be there as soon as I can.'

Katie Blasko lived in a house on Trevally Street in Waterloo, a few blocks from the mangrove flats and the yacht basin. The house was small, a yellowish brick veneer structure with a tiled roof and rotting eaves. Ellen met Scobie at the front gate. The detective was wearing one of the funereal suits that exaggerated his earnestness and awkward, stick figure shape. Two uniformed constables, Pam Murphy and John Tankard, were doorknocking in the distance.

'What can you tell me?' Ellen said.

Scobie flipped open his notebook and began a long, sonorous account of his findings. Katie Blasko had attended her primary school the previous day, but hadn't been seen after that. 'There was some mix up. She was supposed to stay at a friend's house last night.'

Ellen copied the relevant names, addresses and phone numbers. She glanced at her watch. 'Head over to the school, check with her teachers and classmates. I'll catch up with you as soon as I've finished here.'

'Sure.'

Ellen stepped through a little gate and up to the front door. The woman who answered was thin, nervy, dressed in jeans and a T-shirt. She looked wrung out and pleaded, 'Have you found her?'

Ellen shook her head. 'Not yet, but you mustn't worry, it's only a matter of time. Why don't we go inside and you can fill me in.'

'I already told the police everything. A guy called Scobie.'

Her voice was peevish and distraught, not that Ellen was blaming her, exactly. 'If you could just go over it again, Mrs Blasko,' she said gently.

Like, why did you wait so long before reporting your daughter missing?

Donna Blasko's sitting room was a pokey space dominated by a puffed up sofa and a wide-screen TV. A six-year-old girl sprawled on the floor, stretching tiny, rubbery dresses and pants over the unresponsive plastic limbs of Polly Pocket dolls, alternately humming and talking to them. A cat twitched its tail on the carpet under a chunky coffee table. And, as Scobie had said, there was also a man, Donna Blasko's de facto, Justin Pedder. Ellen wasn't the least bit surprised to see that he was stocky, dressed in jeans and a T-shirt, with a shaven head to complete the picture. If you're a blue-collar male aged between twenty and forty in Australia, that's how you cloned yourself. You had no imagination at all. Nor did your parents, who named you Justin, Darren or Brad.

God I'm in a sour mood today, Ellen thought.

Donna sat beside Pedder, saying gracelessly, 'This is Justin.'

Ellen nodded. She'd be running his name through the databases as soon as she got back to the station. As if he saw that in her eyes and wanted to deflect her, he scowled. 'You should be out there looking for Katie instead of questioning us again.'

He might have been expected to say that. It was in the script. Ellen stared at a yellow lava lamp on an empty shelf and said, 'I have constables doorknocking the area at this very moment. Now, according to Constable Sutton, you were both up in the city yesterday afternoon, correct?'

'Spring carnival,' said Pedder.

Horse racing. 'Back any winners?'

Pedder gave her a humourless smile. 'You want to see our betting slips, right? To prove we were there?'

Ellen went on. 'Katie has her own key?'

'We work, except for Thursdays,' Pedder said. 'Katie always lets herself in.'

'She makes herself a snack,' said Donna, 'does her homework and watches TV until we get home. The TV goes off then. She's not allowed to watch it after dinner. She's a good girl.'

And we're good parents, thought Ellen. 'And last night?'

'Me and Donna like to do stuff together on Thursdays,' said Pedder. 'Shopping up at Southland. A movie. The races. If we're going to be late, we arrange for Katie to stay at a friend's house. It's like her second home.'

Gets more love there than here, thought Ellen. She referred to her notes. 'The friend's name is Sarah Benton?'

'Yes.'

'And that's what you'd arranged for last night?'

'Yeah.'

'What time did you get home from the races?'

'About seven.'

'Seven in the evening. And you didn't call to see that she was all right?'

They shrugged as if to say: Why would we?

'But you did call this morning?'

'Yes,' said Donna, suddenly wailing, her face damp and ravaged. 'Sarah's mum said Katie wasn't there and hadn't been there and she didn't know anything about it.'

'But I thought you'd arranged it?'

Donna squirmed. 'Katie was supposed to ask Sarah if she could stay. She must of forgot to.'

Ellen liked to change tack swiftly. 'Do you live here, Mr Pedder?'

'Me?'

Ellen gazed about the room for other Mr Pedders. 'Yes.'

'Sure.'

'But this is Donna's house?'

He gazed at her bleakly. 'I get where you're coming from. Yeah, I've got a place of my own that no one knows about and I took Katie there and did her in.'

'Justin!' wailed Donna.

'Aw, sorry, love, but it's so fucking typical. Blame the bloke.'

'We wouldn't be doing our job if we didn't examine every avenue, Mr Pedder.'

'I know, I know, sorry I said what I said. Look, I was renting a flat until I met Donna.'

'You always spend your nights here?'

'You interested in my sex life now?'

'Answer the question, Mr Pedder.'

'He *lives* here,' asserted Donna. 'He's here every night.'

Ellen turned her gaze to Donna. 'Did that bother Katie?'

'No. Why should it? Justin's good to Katie, aren't you, Jus? Never hits her or anything. No funny business, if that's what you're on about.'

They were both staring at her hotly now. 'We have to ask these questions,' Ellen said.

According to Scobie Sutton's brief preliminary investigation, the neighbours considered Donna to be a reasonably good mother, but there had been a few boyfriends over the years. The police had been called to noisy parties a couple of times. Sarah Benton's mother claimed there was no point in trying to phone the Blasko household after about seven in the evening, for Donna and Justin were probably getting quietly stoned and never answered the phone. You'd leave messages but they'd never be returned. It was a common picture, in Ellen's experience. No real cruelty, just ignorance and benign neglect—and mothers putting their partners first, ahead of their children, afraid of being single again.

'Maybe Katie's little sister knows something?'

'Shelly?' said Donna, amazed. 'Shelly was next door, weren't you, love?'

The child continued to play. Ellen said, 'Next door?'

'Mrs Lucas. She likes to baby-sit Shell, but Katie can't stand her.'

Ellen was watching Pedder. Apparently struck by the cuteness of the child playing on the floor, he reached out a flash running shoe and poked her tiny waist. The child battered his foot away absently. No fear or submission, Ellen noted. The child hadn't been introduced to her. Ellen had always introduced her own daughter, even when she was a toddler. It was good manners. Had she been taught good manners by her own parents? She couldn't recall. Then again, good manners were a matter of commonsense, surely.

I am sour today. She said pointedly, 'When you realised that Katie hadn't slept at Sarah's last night, what did you do?'

'Made a couple of calls.'

'Who did you call?'

'My mum,' said Donna. 'She lives up in Frankston.'

'You thought Katie was there? Why?'

Pedder exchanged a glance with Donna. 'Look,' he said, 'she sometimes runs away, all right?'

'Ah.'

'She always comes back.'

'She runs away from *you*?' Ellen demanded.

'No,' said Pedder stiffly.

'We usually track her down to me mum's or another of her friend's, but this time no one's seen her,' said Donna, tearing up swiftly and dabbing her eyes with a damp, crumpled tissue. There was a box of them beside her, a cheap, yellow, no-name brand from the supermarket.

'And so you called the police?'

'Yeah,' Pedder said.

'How many times has Katie run away before?'

'Not many. A few.'

'Do you fight with her? Argue? Smack her when she's naughty?'

'We've never smacked her.'

'Fights? Arguments?'

'No more than any other family.'

'How about Wednesday night, Thursday morning?'

'Nothing happened.'

'Does she ever spend time on the Internet?'

'When she's got a school project and that,' said Donna.

Pedder was quicker. 'Are you asking did she spend time in chat rooms? You think she met a paedo, a paedo's got her?'

'Is that what you think?'

'I'm asking you.'

'We'll need to look at any computers you have,' Ellen said. 'We'll give you a receipt.'

'Oh, God,' said Donna.

'We'll also need a list of all Katie's friends and acquaintances.'

Donna was sobbing now. 'You think she met some pervert on the Internet, don't you?'

'Very unlikely,' said Ellen soothingly. 'Has she ever wandered off before?'

'We already told you she does.'

'I don't mean running away; I mean is she a dreamer? Maybe she likes to explore creeks, the beach, farmland, deserted houses.'

'Not really.'

'Not the beach? I know I did when I was a kid.'

She hadn't done anything of the kind. She'd grown up in the hills. She meant that her own daughter had liked to explore the beach, back when she was little, back when Ellen and her husband and Larrayne had been a happy family.

'Maybe with her friends of a weekend, but she has to ask permission first,' said Donna, the responsible mother.

'You think she drowned?' said Pedder.

Donna moaned. Ellen gave Pedder a look that made him go pale. 'What about the area between here and the highway?'

'Katie's scared of snakes,' said Donna.

Larrayne had been, too.

They'd all run out of things to say. Ellen gathered her notes together and got to her feet.

'What do you think happened to my baby?' whispered Donna.

That was in the script, too: the words and the whispered voice. 'Kids go missing every day,' said Ellen warmly. 'They always turn up again.'

She glanced at Justin Pedder as she said it, warning him not to say the obvious.

3

It was now 11 am. Ellen was due at the Supreme Court by early afternoon. Saying goodbye to Donna Blasko and Justin Pedder, she called Scobie Sutton's mobile, and met him outside Katie Blasko's primary school. 'I'll have to leave it in your hands for a few hours,' she told him. 'It's possible that Katie simply ran away, but why would she stay away for this long? To be on the safe side, continue the doorknock, check with hospitals, contact family and friends. I'm going to see Kellock. We need more uniforms.'

'Thanks.' He shivered. 'Missing kid. I hate it, Ellen.'

Scobie Sutton was nuts about his own child, Roslyn, who was also aged ten. He could be a bore about it. 'Stay in touch during the day,' Ellen told him. 'Call or text me if you find anything.'

The police station was by the roundabout at the head of High Street. She parked at the rear and entered, heading first for her pigeonhole, where she collected a sheaf of letters and memos. She found Kellock, the uniformed senior sergeant in charge of the station, in his office. He was a barrel of a man, his head a whiskery slab on a neckless torso. There were cuts on the hunks of flesh that were his hands. He tugged down his shirtsleeves self-consciously and scowled, 'Been pruning roses.'

She was about to say that she should have been mowing Hal

Challis's grass, but stopped herself. She didn't want to broadcast the fact that she was staying in Challis's house. Just then Kellock's desk phone rang. 'Be with you in a minute,' he said.

She sifted through her mail while he took the call. Most of it she'd bin; the rest was bound for her in-tray. One item enraged her. It was a memo from Superintendent McQuarrie: 'Owing to budgetary constraints, all of Peninsula Command's forensic testing will henceforth be carried out by ForenZics, an independent specialist laboratory based in Chadstone. Not only are ForenZics' fees significantly lower, their laboratory is closer and their promised turn-around time quicker than the state government's lab.' Ellen shook her head. She'd never heard of ForenZics. She and Challis had always worked with Freya Berg and her colleagues in the state lab.

Just then Kellock snarled, 'They're all scum.'

Ellen glanced at him inquiringly. He put a massive hand over the receiver and said, 'It's Sergeant van Alphen. He's in the courtroom, says Nick Jarrett's family's been heckling and jeering.'

'Doesn't surprise me,' Ellen said.

Kellock ignored her, barking into his phone: 'I want a car stationed outside their house all night, okay?'

He listened to the reply, grunted, replaced the receiver and said to Ellen, 'If the jury acquits, the Jarretts will come home and celebrate. If they convict, the Jarretts will hold a wake. Either way, it's not going to be much fun for us. Now, how can I help you?'

'Katie Blasko, aged ten, been missing since yesterday.'

She wasn't sure that Kellock had heard her. His face was like bleak wastes of granite, revealing no emotions, but under it he probably continued to be furious and vengeful about the Jarretts. Then there was a subtle shift. He twisted his mouth. She supposed it was a smile. With Kellock you couldn't be entirely sure, not until he spoke. 'You want some uniforms to help search?'

'If you can spare them.'

'You already have Murphy and Tankard. I can spare a couple more, maybe a probationer or two.'

Ellen grimaced. The perennial shortage of available police on the Peninsula affected them both. 'Thanks. If we don't find her soon, we'll need more bodies, more overtime.'

He nodded. 'I'll square it with the boss.'

He meant Superintendent McQuarrie. It was said that he was McQuarrie's spy, but that could be a good thing if he was also able to drum up support when it was needed. 'Thanks, Kel.'

'We'll find her, Ells, don't worry.'

Kellock was bulky and confident. Ellen felt a little better about everything.

Finally she headed up to the city, striking heavy traffic. It took her ninety minutes to reach Melbourne and then find a car park near the Supreme Court. It was two o'clock by the time she entered the courtroom, and she was dismayed to see McQuarrie there.

'You're late, sergeant.'

'Sorry, sir,' Ellen murmured, sliding onto the bench seat, her movements stirring the air, arousing faintly the odours of floor wax and furniture polish.

McQuarrie sniffed: a good sniffer, Ellen thought. He was a neat, precise, humourless man who professed a glum kind of Christianity, like many ministers in the federal government. She darted a glance past his costly dress uniform at Sergeant Kees van Alphen, who with Ellen had arrested Nick Jarrett all those months ago, and helped put the case together for the Office of Public Prosecutions. He winked; she grinned.

Finally she gathered herself, willed her racing pulse to settle. It soon became clear that she hadn't missed much of the prosecutor's final summation to the jury. He droned on, a man with almost no presence, when the trial of Nick Jarrett surely required prosecutorial outrage. Eventually, with a weak flourish, he finished.

Nick Jarrett's lawyer leapt to his feet, placed his hand on his client's shoulder, and said, 'Reasonable doubt, ladies and gentlemen.'

Ellen snorted. McQuarrie glanced at her sourly. So did the judge. She ignored them. Reasonable doubt? Nick Jarrett was twenty-four, a wiry, fleshless speed addict, his skin jumping today in a suit that might have come from the Salvation Army op-shop in Waterloo. Barely literate, but cunning, driven by amphetamines and base instincts, not intellect. Young men like Nick Jarrett passed through the courts every day of the week. Owing to the drugs and the alcohol, they were vicious and unpredictable. They hurt people, and got hurt. They made stupid mistakes and got arrested. But not all of them ran over cyclists for sport.

One day in May, Nick Jarrett and his mate, Brad O'Connor, had been engaged in their latest enterprise, carjacking. They'd done it six times since March, and had developed a taste for it. What you did was, you hung around a car park, like the dusty overflow area of a hospital, somewhere there are no security cameras, and some woman comes along, blinded by tears because her husband's dying in intensive care, or joy because she's newly a grandmother, and you shove a blood-filled syringe in her face before she can buckle her seatbelt. Sometimes, for a laugh, you take her for a little ride to the middle of nowhere, and shove her out of the door.

The cars from the first five carjackings had never been found. Ellen suspected they'd been stolen to order by Nick and Brad, taken to a chop-shop or straight onto a shipping container, but that wasn't the issue before the court today. The issue here was vehicular manslaughter, and the police had impounded the sixth car, which had yielded some—admittedly not very compelling—forensic evidence.

What young Nick Jarrett liked to do, while driving his carjacked vehicle to who-knew-where, was play chicken with cyclists and pedestrians. He'd got pretty good at it, pretty deft with the brakes and the steering wheel. To give his victims an extra thrill, he liked to open his door at the last minute, watch those schoolkids and old ladies duck and weave, throw themselves down on the bitumen. He'd always liked mucking around with cars. Never meant no harm by it.

But on 13 May he'd crossed a median strip and misjudged things a little. A lot, really. Tony Balfour, aged fifteen, on his way home from school. Everything to live for, said the newspapers. A young life cruelly snatched, etcetera. Not only that, he was the son of a popular civilian clerk employed at the Waterloo police station.

Ellen and van Alphen had gone for murder, but the OPP had reduced that to criminal negligence. After all, Nick had been driving under the influence of amphetamines and alcohol, to which he was addicted.

Now his defence lawyer had the nerve to argue reasonable doubt, and was doing a pretty good job of it, too, Ellen realised. She stiffened to see thoughtful nods on the faces of the jury. It had barely registered during the trial, but now the testimony of Nick's mate, Brad O'Connor, was looking pretty shaky. Yes, Brad had testified against his friend, but had he really done that to assuage his guilty feelings and see justice done? 'I don't think so,' Nick's lawyer thundered. 'Mr O'Connor was driven by malice and greed: malice because his de facto wife had developed a relationship with my client, and greed because he wanted the fifty thousand dollars reward offered by the victim's family. Put that together with the fact that no forensic evidence places my client in the car that struck the particular blow, and you have no alternative, ladies and gentlemen of the jury, but to find that a reasonable doubt exists, and find him not guilty.'

'I thought the forensic evidence proved it,' snarled McQuarrie from the corner of his mouth. 'I thought this was sewn up, Sergeant Destry.'

'It links the vehicle with the victim but not to Jarrett, sir, but even so...'

McQuarrie gestured for her to shut up. A chill went through her. She risked a glance over her shoulder. The dead boy's mother and sister were weeping on one side of the courtroom; the Jarrett clan was taking up three rows of seats on the other. Rowdy and ever-present during the trial, they were now flashing grins at the prosecution team. They clearly thought a reasonable doubt had been shown to exist. The only exception was the clan's patriarch, Laurie Jarrett. Aged fifty, a hard, motionless presence, he was staring at Ellen as though he'd never had a thought or a feeling in his life.

4

The jury retired to consider its verdict, and now it was a waiting game. Hours. Days. Ellen left the court building and glanced at her watch. Mid-afternoon, but it was Friday, so the traffic would be hell wherever she went now. She bit her lip indecisively: return to Waterloo and the search for Katie Blasko, or catch up with her daughter?

She pulled out her phone. 'It's me, Scobie. Any news?'

'Not yet. What about you?'

'The jury's out. Look, I'd like to see Larrayne, since I'm in the city.'

He was silent; she could imagine his sombre face. 'I guess that's okay.'

She wanted to say that she didn't need his permission, then wondered if he were judging her for not racing back to help find Katie Blasko. 'I'll be back before five o'clock. I want to have another go at the parents.'

'All right.'

The man irritated her. She made another call. 'Hi, sweetie. I'm in the city. Would it be okay if I popped in to say hello?'

Ellen's daughter was nineteen, a health sciences undergraduate who shared a house in Carlton with two other students. She was always prickly these days. She blamed Ellen for splitting the family up. 'I should be studying, Mum. Exams soon.'

'I won't stay long, promise.'

Larrayne sighed heavily. 'If you like.'

A ringing endorsement. Ellen retrieved her car and skirted around the glassy office towers of Melbourne's central business district, fighting the traffic to the inner suburb of Carlton. Workers had lived here in the boom years after the 1850s gold rushes. In the early decades of the twentieth century much of Carlton had been a slum, then home to the waves of Italian and Greek immigrants after the Second World War, and was now sought after by yuppies, who paid half-a-million dollars for the little brick cottages along the side streets, either living in them or renting them out to students like Larrayne Destry. Ellen could see the appeal: Melbourne University, RMIT, Chinatown and the downtown boutiques and cinemas were only a short walk or tram ride away.

She parked on a hydrant, hoping she wouldn't get booked. Owing to the lack of off-street parking, small European and Japanese cars crowded both kerbs. These days, in this place, it was difficult to tell if the Audis and the Subarus belonged to student renters or yuppie owners, but there was no mistaking her daughter's 1991 Toyota Camry. It was a first car, a student car, through and through.

Ellen banged the iron knocker on the front door. After a long delay, Larrayne answered, and Ellen picked up conflicting clues. Her daughter looked flustered, her pinned-up hair escaping in wisps, her T-shirt wrinkled, but she also looked studious in the elegant reading glasses she'd been prescribed a year earlier.

Mother and daughter kissed and hugged briefly. 'I won't stay long,' Ellen said again.

'Okay.'

The façade of the house, unchanged since the colonial era and preserved by council regulations, gave way to a short hallway of closed bedroom doors and then a large, airy living room. Typically, some interior walls had been knocked down and skylights, a mezzanine floor and a rear sundeck put in. The furniture was a mismatched collection of op-shop armchairs, Ikea stools and bright, cheap floor coverings and cushions. A kid of about twenty leapt from one of the armchairs. He was skinny, with earrings and chopped-about hair. 'Hi, Mrs Destry. I'm Travis.'

The boyfriend? A new tenant? Ellen glanced at Larrayne, who said expressionlessly, 'Tea? Coffee?'

'Coffee.'

Ellen stayed for thirty painful minutes. Her daughter was unresponsive; the boy overcompensated with chatter. Finally Ellen glanced at her watch and said, 'I have to get back.'

Larrayne leapt to her feet and took her to the front door. 'Thanks for coming, Mum.'

Ellen said brightly, 'Is Travis your boyfriend?'

'So what if he is?'

'Just wondering, sweetheart. How are your studies?'

'All right.'

'If you need peace and quiet in the lead up to the exams, come and spend a few days with me.'

'You must be joking, me in lover boy's house,' Larrayne said, and Ellen saw that nothing had changed. It might have been bearable if Hal Challis *were* her lover boy.

She felt heat rising inside her and turned away before she said something she'd later regret. Twenty minutes later, as she headed southeast on the freeway toward Waterloo, her mind was still stewing. If criminals can be granted the benefit of the concept of reasonable doubt, why couldn't she? Instead, her daughter and her husband had examined the 'evidence' against her—she'd walked out on her marriage, she'd always worked closely with Hal Challis, she was now living in his house—and found her guilty of adultery.

I wish, she thought.

I *think* I wish.

The freeway was choked with traffic, moving at a walking pace down a broad channel between seas of tiled roofs, home to middle

Australia. The routes in and out of Melbourne had never coped and never would, not when the satellite areas like the Peninsula offered cheap, high-density housing but no jobs.

Beside her a siren whooped, highway patrol, festooned with antennas and decals, motioning at her mobile phone. She showed them her badge through the window. They shrugged and shot away down the shoulder of the freeway, looking for other mugs who were driving while talking on a mobile phone.

It was inevitable that thinking about her own daughter—and love, protection and responsibility—would lead Ellen to thinking about Katie Blasko. A ten-year-old, missing for—she glanced at her watch—twenty-four hours now. Was Katie at a friend's house? Getting off the bus in Sydney, where she'd be swallowed up in the fleshpots of Kings Cross? Twenty-four hours. Twenty-four hours of heaven or hell.

Her phone rang. It was a text message from a Supreme Court clerk.

Jarrett acquitted.

All she wanted to do was call Hal Challis. She had him on speed-dial. But he had a family crisis to contend with. It wouldn't be fair. She had to do this alone.

5

Detective Inspector Hal Challis was one thousand kilometres away, in the far mid-north of South Australia, crossing a barrier of stony hills on a hazardous switchback road at a point known as Isolation Pass. Drivers had been killed on the Pass. Challis knew to take it cautiously that Friday afternoon, climbing the upward slope in his rattly old Triumph, braking for the downward.

Before long he caught sight of Mawson's Bluff, his glimpses of the little settlement interrupted by guardrails, then rock face, one alternating with the other. Complicated feelings settled in him. The Bluff was a drowsy wheat and wool town on a treeless plain, a place where they knew the cost of everything but the value of nothing. It was named for Governor Mawson's son, who, in 1841, had set out from Adelaide to survey the range of hills that now sheltered the town and the merino stud properties, but failed to return, and was found a year later with a spear pinched between the bones of his ribcage. Challis had been taught that at the Bluff's little primary school. He hadn't been taught that it marked the beginning of a doomed Aboriginal resistance to rifles, horses and sheep. No one in Mawson's Bluff wanted to know that. He was only going home because his sister had called him.

Home. He still called it that. He visited from time to time but hadn't lived there for twenty years.

The road levelled out and he accelerated. Before long he could read MAWSON'S BLUFF painted on the roof of the pub, a landmark for the buyers who flew in from the sheep stations of New South Wales for the merino stud ram sales. And there was the cemetery, a dusty patch of gum trees and gravestones on a rise beyond the stockyards. Challis swallowed. He'd attended a funeral there last year, and if things followed their course, he'd soon be attending another.

He slowed at the outskirts of the town. An old sensation went through him, of emptiness and isolation. He'd felt it as a child, Broken Hill lying far to the east, Adelaide far to the south, and nothing between them. He shook off the feeling and looked for changes. Nothing had changed. The houses were the same, low, slumbering, walled in local stone, protected from the sun by broad verandahs, gum trees and golden cypress hedges. TV antennas fifteen metres high. The Methodist church in a square of red dirt, where the ants were always busy. The returned servicemen's hall where he and Meg had dumped empty bottles for the annual Legacy drive. The stone school with the steep, faded red corrugated iron roof. The old women watering their geraniums and staring as he passed. The cars with their coatings of powdered dirt. Not mud. This was a dry spring, of a dry year, of a dry decade. Nothing had changed.

But he'd spoken too soon. He spotted changes in the little main street. There was a café now, a craft shop, and a place selling collectibles. Every façade had been renovated in late colonial styles. Then Challis saw a sign on a picket fence, and understood: Mawson's Bluff Community Preservation and Historical Society.

But the grassy plains still stretched on forever, the droughty bluffs loomed over the town and the sky was a cloudless dome above.

Challis had slowed to no more than a walking pace. The town was airless and still. No one moved. Curtains were drawn. Presently a farmer emerged from the post office, nodded hello as if Challis had never left the town, and drove away in one of the battered white utilities that populate the outback. Challis recognised him as Paddy

Finucane, from an extensive clan that lurked on forgotten back roads, married into similar struggling share-farming families and drove trucks for the local council. There had been dozens of Finucanes in the convent school and the football team when Challis was a boy. There always had been and always would be. Some, he remembered, had been done for stealing sheep, diesel fuel, chainsaws or anything else that hadn't been locked away in a shed. Paddy was one of them.

He came to the northern outskirts of the town and turned down a rutted track toward a more recently built house. Young wives of the prosperous 1960s had eschewed the cool old stone houses of the mid-north of South Australia and insisted on triple-fronted brick veneer houses with tile roofs—houses indistinguishable from those in the new suburbs and satellite towns of the major cities. Challis's own mother had got her dream home. Challis's father had been happy to oblige her: the love was there, and the money. In those first few years, Murray Challis had been the only lawyer in a one hundred-kilometre radius, drawing up wills, contracts and occasional divorce settlements for everyone from the mail contractor to the local gentry. Now, forty years later, the house he'd built for his wife still hadn't accommodated itself naturally with the landscape. Like the old stone buildings of the region it came complete with an avenue of pines, a garden of roses and shrubs, rainwater tanks and a kelpie beating his tail in the dust, but it didn't quite belong. Nor had the Challises, quite, and at the age of twenty Hal Challis had left for the police academy. Perhaps it was wanting to belong that made him apply for a posting back 'home' when he graduated. Certainly that had been a mistake. You can never go back. A couple of years later he'd left the state, and now was an inspector in the Victoria Police.

Challis braked at the head of the driveway, angling his car into the shade of the pepper trees. He got out, stretched his aching back and looked north over the struggling wheat flats that merged, in the far distance, with arid country, semi-desert, a land of pebbly dust, washaways, mallee scrub and hidden gullies. Men had died out there.

They called it 'doing a perish', and many in the district believed that that's what had happened to Challis's brother-in-law, five years ago now. Gavin Hurst's car had been found abandoned out there. No body. He'd been the district's RSPCA inspector, a difficult man. Challis had never liked Hurst, but his sister had married him, had loved him, so what can you do?

'The conquering hero returns.'

Challis wheeled around with an answering grin. Meg, two years his junior, was smiling tiredly at him from the verandah. A moment later she was embracing him, a round, comfortable shape. 'Driving the same old bomb, I see,' she said fondly, beating the flat of her hand against the chrome surround of his windscreen.

'Hey, don't mark my pride and joy.'

She snorted, throwing her arms around him again. 'It's so good to see you. You're a sight for sore eyes.'

When she released him he saw that her eyes were, in fact, sore looking. 'How is he?'

'Sweetie,' Meg told him gently, 'he's dying.'

Well, she'd told him that on the phone earlier in the week, and so he'd hastily arranged a month's leave. What she meant now was, how else did Challis *expect* their father to be? It was faintly reproving, and Challis couldn't blame her. Their mother had died a year ago, and their father had immediately declined. Meg, who lived on the other side of the Bluff, near the tennis courts, had been the one to nurse both of them. Their mother would have been undemanding, but Challis guessed that their father, an exacting man even in good health, was making hard work of dying. There rose between Challis and his sister a knot of unresolved feelings: Challis had escaped, Meg hadn't. 'I'm sorry.'

She brightened. 'You're here now.'

Challis had asked for a month, but McQuarrie, his boss, a superintendent in regional command headquarters, had clearly thought that excessive. As if he wants my father to hurry up and die, Challis had thought at the time. 'I have several weeks of accrued leave owing to me, sir,' he'd said. 'And Sergeant Destry is perfectly capable of holding the fort until I get back.'

McQuarrie, a small man who disapproved of many things, said, 'Your father, did you say?'

'He's dying, sir.'

'Very well.'

The super, who knew more about meeting procedures than catching bad guys, would give Ellen a hard time, but Challis couldn't do anything about that now. Besides, Ellen knew how to look after herself.

He followed Meg along the path to the verandah steps. 'Where's Eve? She inside with Dad?'

Meg shook her head. 'Studying. Always studying.'

Challis's niece was in Year 12. He'd last seen her a year ago, at his mother's funeral: tall, lovely, and absolutely desolate. He hated to think of Eve in pain. First her father, then her grandmother, and now her grandfather.

'You'll see her eventually,' Meg said.

Challis stepped into the house behind her, into rooms unchanged from when he'd been a boy, into sluggish air laden with the odours of a dying man. For a brief mad instant, he looked for his mother to come bustling from the kitchen, ready to wrap him in loving smiles and hugs. The grief hit him like a punch to the heart: he stopped, swayed, breathed in and out.

'Hal?'

Challis swallowed. 'Nothing, sis, I'm okay.' He paused. 'Mum.'

Meg looked fleetingly unimpressed. This wasn't a competition, but she'd been closer to their mother than Challis had, and she'd had to cope with their father's decline. Then, relenting, she gently touched his arm and called, 'Dad! Look who's here.'

She'd set the old man up in a brightly upholstered cane chair in the screened-in back porch. Here the sun penetrated for the greater part of the day. It was a cheerful room, furnished with other cane chairs, a pair of glass-topped tables on cane legs, flowery curtains pulled back on the windows. White walls, a couple of vaguely Turkish rugs on the terracotta tiled floor. Challis took these things in first, a way of delaying the inevitable. Then, his heart hammering, he said, 'Hello, Dad.'

His father stirred feebly, a bony hand fluttering out from under the tartan rug that enclosed him. Pathetic white ankles above carpet slippers. A food-stained blue dressing gown with shiny lapels revealed his sunken chest and throat. His face was sharp and fleshless, his hair a few wispy white tufts. Finally, the eyes that had always had the power to unnerve Challis. They were unchanged.

'My boy,' the old man said.

Overcome, Challis crossed the short distance, knelt, and hugged his father. A hand beat feebly on his back. 'That's enough, that's enough, I'm not dead yet.'

Challis stood back, blinking. His father wasn't easily comforted. He was too powerful for that. 'Sorry to see you like this, Dad.'

His father gave him a ghastly smile. 'It happens to all of us.'

Challis returned the smile.

'I'll make tea,' Meg said, and presently began to bang around in the kitchen. Domesticity settled over the house. Challis and his father talked. Challis even held a papery old hand for a while, until his father gently removed it. They had never been ones to embrace. They had never kissed.

'So, what are the bad guys up to in your neck of the woods?'

Challis went very still, calculating madly. Was this the lead up to a confrontation? His father had always said, 'You've got a good brain. Why the hell did you go into the police?' Challis thought he understood: Murray Challis had been born in the 1920s and seen his family suffer during the Great Depression. The Second World War had been his way out. He'd met educated men in the Air Force. Education was the key. It didn't matter that his son had completed a bachelor degree at night school in recent years: it was the fact that his son hadn't done anything with it but remained in the police force. 'Your average criminal is stupid,' was the refrain. 'He brings you down to his level. He certainly doesn't elevate you.'

'Yes, but putting him in jail, and getting justice for the victim, elevates me,' Challis would reply.

He could feel his asthma starting up. He found himself telling his father about a lawyer he'd arrested a month earlier. The man had a cocaine habit. He'd stolen two million dollars from clients who'd invested their life savings with him. 'Picked him up boarding a plane to Bangkok,' said Challis challengingly.

His father patted his wrist. 'I'm a family solicitor, son, not a lawyer.'

Meg came in with a tray: blueberry muffins, teapot, mugs, milk and sugar. They ate, and presently the old man fell asleep. Challis and Meg chattered. Their father awoke and said, 'How long are you staying, son?'

Challis didn't know what to say. *Until you die?* He coughed. 'They've given me a month off, Dad.'

So please don't die after *that time?*

Meg rescued him. 'Be glad he's here, Dad.'

Their father winked. 'She thinks I'm dying.'

Challis barked an uncomfortable laugh.

Then the old man entered one of the mood swings that had always kept Challis and Meg on their toes. 'Which way did you come?' he demanded.

'Dad,' said Meg warningly.

Challis didn't visit very often, making the two-day car journey from his home on the Mornington Peninsula in Victoria to Mawson's Bluff only once every two or three years, generally at Christmas time. He would break the drive in Adelaide or, if he'd set out late, in Keith or Bordertown. There had been only two exceptions to that in the past decade: when his mother had died last spring, and when Meg's husband had disappeared on a winter's day five years earlier. On both occasions, Challis had flown to Adelaide and driven up in a hire car the same day.

He considered lying now. It was his father's fierce contention that Challis should always skirt Adelaide and detour via the Barossa Valley, which was beautiful wine-growing country settled by German immigrants in the 1800s. The old man's mother, Lottie Heinrich, had been born there. But Challis couldn't lie to him, and began to describe his route: through Adelaide, up into the wheat and sheep country of the mid-north, and eventually to Mawson's Bluff, in marginal country near the Flinders Ranges.

His father began to shake his head. If he'd had a walking stick he'd have thumped it on the floor.

'How often have I told you,' he said, 'avoid Adelaide, go through the Barossa. It saves time and petrol, and it's safer.'

It was an old refrain, but it still had the power to churn Challis up inside. He had trouble breathing. He was having an asthma attack. He coughed and gasped, 'Be back in a sec.'

He collected his bag from the hallway and took it through to his old bedroom. The inhaler—rarely used these days—was in a plastic zip case together with his comb, razor, toothbrush and painkillers. He took a hit from the inhaler, eyes closed, holding it in for a few seconds before gently exhaling.

Miraculous.

What he couldn't tell his father was that a feeling of wretchedness had settled in him as he'd driven the long kilometres 'home'. He'd cut himself off from his family, not been there to help when misfortune had come to them. And so, resolving to do more, he'd stopped in Adelaide to consult the South Australia police file on Gavin Hurst's disappearance. He couldn't tell his father that he'd done that. The old man firmly believed that Gavin had simply left his car at the side of the road five years ago and walked out into the badlands to die. He'd loathed Gavin. Gavin was dead. Enough said. But Meg had evidence that Gavin was still alive, and Challis was determined to discover what had happened to him.

6

Kees van Alphen had returned to Waterloo and spread the unwelcome news about Nick Jarrett's acquittal. Pam Murphy and John Tankard, coming off duty for the day, were sitting in his office, commiserating with him. 'It sucks, Sarge,' Pam said. She leaned toward his desk. 'All that hard work down the drain.'

'Yeah,' Tankard said.

Pam glanced at her partner. This was possibly the only time in history that she and Tank were in agreement on anything.

'Who'd believe it?' she asked.

'Yeah,' Tankard said again.

Van Alphen, the lean, wrathful son of Dutch immigrants, leaned his elbows on his desk. 'What have I told you two over and over again?'

'Yeah, yeah, yeah,' Pam muttered. 'Doesn't make it any better, Sarge.'

'Constable,' he said warningly.

'Sorry, Sarge.'

She didn't look or feel sorry but sat upright in one of van Alphen's hard office chairs. She was twenty-eight, precisely put together, tanned from surfing and toned by jogging and the gym. Her mind was keen, too, she'd been told, but she'd never quite accepted that, for her father and brothers were university academics and she'd been the youngest, a girl, mad about sport, average in the classroom.

'I've said it before and I'll say it again,' van Alphen said, 'your job is to help put a case together, help get the bastards into a courtroom. Your job is not to convict. Don't take it personally. It's not your fault Jarrett got off.'

'We had a good case.'

'He had a good lawyer.'

There was silence. Then Ellen Destry was in the doorway, a little breathless. 'I've just got back from the city. I suppose you've heard about Nick Jarrett?'

'Yeah,' growled van Alphen, 'it stinks.'

Then Ellen was nodding at Pam and Tank. 'Thanks for your help today.'

'Sorry we couldn't find her, Sarge,' Tank said.

'I might need you both tomorrow, too,' Ellen said, hurrying away again.

When she was gone, John Tankard leaned forward, lowered his voice. 'Is she overreacting, Sarge?'

Van Alphen shrugged.

Pam, feeling a surge of loyalty for Ellen Destry, glared at both men. 'You guys are incredible. This is a missing kid. What if she's been snatched? Maybe by this paedophile ring.'

Tank turned to her. 'What paedophile ring?'

'On the Peninsula.'

'They snatch kids off the street?'

Van Alphen stirred. 'Guys, it's just a rumour. There have been no reports of abductions.'

Tank ignored him. 'So, if Katie Blasko was abducted, it could have been by someone from outside the area, not a local, not part of this ring.'

'We don't know that there *is* a ring, Tank,' van Alphen said. 'Just drop it, okay?'

Tank looked at Pam. 'Maybe someone with a holiday house down here?'

'Who knows?' she said, wondering why he was so fired up.

'Drop it, okay?' van Alphen said sharply. 'Back to business. We need a car on the estate. The Jarretts could get rowdy.'

Pam and Tank stirred. 'We're off duty, Sarge.'

'We're short-staffed,' van Alphen countered. He leaned toward Pam and said, almost nastily, 'Do you good, some ordinary police work before you go off to holiday camp.'

She flushed. She hadn't told Tank yet. Tank went on full alert, his chair creaking under his agitated weight as he turned to her. 'What holiday camp?'

Pam gestured. 'Just some training thing I enrolled for.'

'What training thing?'

'Criminal investigation procedures, stuff like that.'

Tank wasn't buying it. His overheated face got hotter. 'Detective training? You're becoming a dee?'

His tone said, *You're leaving me behind?*

'Probably won't lead to anything,' Pam said. 'No vacancies.'

'Bull *shit*,' said John Tankard, spittle flying. 'You've got bloody Destry mentoring you. You've been brown-nosing for years, don't deny it.'

'Can it, Tank.'

'Children, children,' van Alphen said.

DC Scobie Sutton had given Ellen Destry an update, and now he was heading across town to the Community House on Seaview Park estate. His wife volunteered there. Beth had once *worked* there, paid by the shire, but then the bastards had retrenched her. *Sacked* her in order to come in under budget, the budget blowing out because the shire's various managers had voted they be outfitted with a fleet of Ford Territories, one of the thirstiest four-wheel-drives on the market.

Meanwhile Beth and Scobie were down to one car, a tired Magna station wagon. They couldn't afford to run two cars now, so Scobie was forever running his wife and daughter around the Peninsula, trying to fit in Roslyn's school and social activities, his wife's volunteering and his own CIU work. Scobie Sutton felt a kind of low-level indignation these days. Until his wife's sacking he'd been like most decent churchgoing folk and never thought about social justice issues.

A different kind of indignation took him on a detour into the blighted part of Seaview Park where the Jarretts lived. News of Nick Jarrett's acquittal had been all over the station and Scobie just wanted to sit and stare for a moment, as if that might cure him. He idled at the kerb: there were three cars crowding the patch of dirt that passed as the Jarrett's front lawn, and he could feel the percussive force of a sound system at full volume. The Jarretts were celebrating. That usually meant escalating noise, violence and calls to 000.

A couple of neighbours came out to stare at Scobie with mingled appeal and reproach. The Jarretts had made their lives a living hell, and what good had the police ever been?

The Jarretts had once lived in Cranbourne, but their Housing Commission house had burnt to the ground—suspected arson, probably payback by someone they'd cheated—and the Commission had relocated them to Seaview Park estate, in Waterloo, which had no view of the sea and no park, only a hundred cheap houses elbow to elbow along bewilderingly curved streets or huddled together in blind culs-de-sac. This was a region of older cars, weedy front yards behind a range of mismatched fences, washing lines visible in back yards, and the occasional Australian flag hanging limply from a stubby pole. Families struggled on the Seaview, but it was generally an honest struggle. Unemployment was high, and the police were often called, but most residents did not rely on welfare or attract the attention of the authorities.

Unlike the Jarretts. At last count there were twelve of them, an extended clan that included cousins, live-in girlfriends and boyfriends, half brothers and sisters, the odd uncle or grandmother. Scobie had never been able to sort them out. If they worked, it was 'at this and that'. The children were more often shoplifting than attending school. Sons and husbands would disappear for a stretch of jail time and come home to find someone else in their beds. Ex-boyfriends and girlfriends, remembering some old insult or unpaid debt, would come around with a carload of mates to smash windows and kneecaps. Neighbours were burgled; there were drunken and drug-crazed arguments and brawls; hotted-up, unroadworthy cars performed burnouts in the narrow streets and ploughed over lawns, fences and letterboxes. Scobie had once been called out when a boyfriend or husband, making an access visit to his kids, had been attacked by his ex-wife, who'd come storming out of the house with her new bloke and proceeded to bash the guy and his car with steel bars, the kids screaming, 'Don't kill my dad, don't kill my dad.' Which didn't mean the kids were little angels. In fact, they scared Scobie the most. They were knowing and cold, and if not the sexual playthings of the adults, or addicts, they surely witnessed the adults having sex or out of their skulls on booze or speed.

All in all, you didn't dare meet the eye of a Jarrett: you crossed the street or stayed indoors if a Jarrett was around. You didn't complain: It was never proven but they'd firebombed the house of a woman who'd got up a petition against them.

It hadn't taken long for public opinion on the estate to turn against the police. Scobie was sympathetic. The Jarretts should have been evicted long ago, but the Waterloo cop shop was understaffed, like many on the Peninsula, the Jarretts were cunning, and the younger constables found excuses to respond late, or not at all, to callouts to the Jarrett house. Meanwhile the Housing Commission bureaucrats lived in the city, not on the estate, and liked to say that they worked for a government that stood for the battlers in society. In their view the Jarretts paid their rent (more or less), hadn't trashed the house (much), and were a struggling family deserving of charity, not criticism, from those who were luckier than they were. Besides, it was argued, the Commission's resources were stretched to the limit.

Did they have a fleet of brand-new, fuel guzzling four-wheel-drives too? wondered Scobie.

If Nick Jarrett had been convicted, he thought, we could have made a start on dismantling the whole clan. Pursued charges against the others, found decent homes for the kids, weakened Laurie Jarrett's power base.

Now they'd have to start all over again.

Just then a marked patrol car pulled up behind him and tooted. He glanced in the mirror: Pam Murphy and John Tankard, here to watch the Jarrett house. Scobie waved and drove on to the Community Centre and there was his wife. 'Hello, love,' she said, taking him away from all of the badness for a while.

On the other side of Waterloo, Ellen Destry was asking Donna Blasko how she was coping.

'I'm a wreck,' Donna told her, 'all this coming and going.'

'It must be hard,' Ellen said. 'Have you thought any more about where Katie might have gone?'

Donna shook her head. 'We've both been out searching.'

'Yeah,' said Justin Pedder, 'doing your job for you.'

Ellen ignored him. 'No one's seen anything? Heard anything?'

Donna shook her head. 'Maybe Katie's trying to ride her bike to my mother's place.'

Ellen went very still. Bike. Why was she only just learning about a bike? Why hadn't it occurred to her that there would be a bike? 'Katie rides to school?'

'Yeah.'

'Can you describe the bike for me?'

'Just a bike.'

'A Malvern Star,' said Justin. 'Gears, a pannier. I keep it in good nick for her.'

'And Katie would have been riding her bike when she left school yesterday?'

'Yes.'

'Did she also have a helmet? A school bag?'

Donna nodded wretchedly. 'We looked everywhere. She can be a bit careless sometimes, you know how kids are, she's coming home from school and meets a friend and just dumps her stuff on the ground while she has a play, then comes home empty-handed. But no way would she leave her Tamagotchi on the footpath, it was her favourite thing in the whole world.'

Two streets away, Sasha was home. A cross between a Shi-Tzu and a Silky Terrier, with a squashed-in face and adenoidal breathing, Sasha was small, guileless and hairy. She didn't discriminate between humans, for all humans adored her. She sought them out. She sought warmth—human and sun. When she'd jumped into the Tarago van yesterday, it wasn't the first time she'd done something like that. Last year she'd travelled all over the Peninsula in the back of an electrician's van, asleep under the guy's spare overalls. When called on his mobile phone by Sasha's owner, he'd sworn black and blue that Sasha wasn't with him. The poor owner had gone out of his mind looking for Sasha, phoning the dog pound, the RSPCA, all the vets in the local phone book. Then, at the end of a long day, he'd received a sheepish call from the electrician: 'Got your dog here, mate. Sorry.'

Everyone knew the story, and so, when an elderly woman who lived on Trevally Street saw Sasha jump out of an unfamiliar white van that Friday afternoon, she smiled indulgently and watched Sasha race home. The stories she could tell if she could talk, thought the old woman fondly. What adventures has she had this time?

If Sasha had been able to talk, she might have revealed that she hadn't been fed for twenty-four hours. She also hadn't been *loved* for twenty-four hours. Her instincts had told her to cuddle up to the child, but the child had been asleep for most of the time. At one point Sasha had bared her teeth in protection of the child, had even drawn blood, and been kicked clear across the room for her pains.

7

Sitting in the patrol car outside the Jarrett house, John Tankard was thinking about life after Pam Murphy.

He felt betrayed. Sure, he knew that he'd often rubbed her up the wrong way, and she hadn't appreciated his clumsy attempts to get her to sleep with him over the years, but he'd always counted her as an ally, one of the gang, us against them—them being ordinary citizens, crooks and senior police officers.

Now she was leaving him behind, stepping over a line that would take her into the ranks of the enemy. He didn't know if he could work with anyone else. Would a new partner put up with his bullshit, or report him? Would a new partner watch his back? Console him when things got a bit rough, personally speaking?

He shifted in his seat, half closed his eyes and gazed at the Jarretts' wreck of a house. Three cars crowded the front yard: a rusting Toyota twin-cab, a little black Subaru and a lowered silver Mercedes with smoky windows. Just then, four Jarrett kids came out, boys, one of them sauntering over to the front gate, where he turned and swiftly dropped his jeans. Pale, skinny shanks. Tank was furious. 'We can arrest him for that.'

Murphy said wearily, 'Leave it, Tank.'

'Yeah, well,' said Tank uselessly.

Who at Waterloo did he like and trust apart from Pam? Some of the other constables were okay, guys you could have a beer with, but they came and they went. The plain-clothed crew, like Challis, Destry and Sutton, were a bit up themselves. Kellock and van Alphen were okay, old-school coppers crippled by the kinds of procedures and regulations that made it hard to do your job properly. Yeah, John Tankard had plenty of time for Kellock and van Alphen.

Pity they were a lot older than him. Pity they were senior in rank. He couldn't see either of them becoming his best pal when Murph left. He respected them, that's all. Looked up to them. Thank Christ he had that in his life.

Two girls aged about ten walked past, beating their knees with tennis racquets. Sweet kids, friends, not a care in the world. Then they saw the Jarretts and veered away, suddenly afraid, and John Tankard acknowledged what was at the back of his mind: an image of Natalie, his kid sister, and how awful it would be if anything ever happened to her.

The radio crackled. Sergeant van Alphen was replacing them. Apparently Sergeant Destry had called an urgent briefing.

Pam was glad of the reprieve. It was close in the patrol car; even closer, with big, sweaty John Tankard behind the wheel, overheated from watching the Jarretts and from learning that she might be leaving the uniform behind. Even so, she couldn't see any harm in raising the temperature a little. 'Are you going to miss me, John?'

She usually called him Tank. He scowled and muttered, reading 'John' as an insult, and pressed hard on the accelerator pedal.

'Sorry, I didn't catch that?'

'Think your shit doesn't stink.'

'Charming as ever.'

She looked away at the run of tyre outlets and engineering firms that lay between the estate and the Waterloo police station. He *is* going to miss me, she thought. He's always been half in love or lust with me, I don't let his bullshit get to me, and he's afraid of being left behind. 'It's no big deal, Tank. It's just a training course. Doesn't mean there are any detective positions open once I've completed it.'

'A training course for a select few,' he said. 'Who did you suck up to? Challis? Destry?'

'I'm not going to honour that with an answer, John.'

They rode in silence. The shadows were lengthening, pines and gums striping a roadside field that would soon be crammed with new housing. Plenty of traffic, people returning home from work, heading for the pub, the Waterloo Show—or just cruising, Pam thought, as a lowered Falcon utility roared up behind them, two kids on board, nervous about passing a police vehicle but itching to all the same. Pam, her window down, could hear the hotted-up motor.

'Tank,' she said, 'is everything okay?'

After a pause he said, 'I'm working a "one-up" tomorrow night.'

A 'one-up' was a lone patrol, just you in the vehicle, owing to a shortage of police on the Peninsula. Pam herself had made several lone patrols in the past few weeks. Nothing bad had happened to her, but you heard stories. 'Take it easy, okay?' she said, meaning it.

His voice lightened, welcoming the concern in hers. 'No worries.'

Pam daydreamed. Then she heard him say, 'Katie Blasko. I've got a bad feeling.'

'Me, too.'

'It's no bullshit, there really *is* a paedo ring on the Peninsula?'

'I've heard rumours, that's all.'

He shook his head. 'I've got a sister her age. I was at her birthday last weekend. It makes you think. Makes you…' He rolled his hand, searching for the word. 'Makes you feel how vulnerable they are.'

He'd never mentioned a kid sister before. 'What's her name?'

'Natalie. Nat. My parents had her late in life.'

'Pretty name.'

He shrugged. He'd revealed too much, and gave a blokey squaring of his shoulders. 'I'm picking up a new set of wheels tomorrow.'

Until recently he'd driven a real shitheap, a barge-like Falcon station wagon, in which he'd hauled the local kids to and from football matches, but the motor had seized on it and he'd given up coaching the Waterloo Wallabies at the end of the season. 'What kind?' said Pam.

'Mazda RX, one of the scarce series.'

She had no idea what that was. 'Where from?'

'Caryard up in Frankston. I saw it in the *Trading Post*. Thirty grand,' he said proudly.

'Thirty grand? Jesus, Tank.'

He said defensively, 'Low kilometres, one owner. I beat him down from thirty-five.'

Pam gazed out of her side window, not wanting to talk about cars or let him see that she thought he'd done a stupid thing. They reached the station, parked at the rear and got out, but instead of heading inside, Tank walked off into the shadows with his mobile phone. 'Oi, we're supposed to be at the briefing,' Pam said.

'I'll be there in a sec. Gotta make a phone call.'

Shrugging, Pam entered the station and climbed the stairs to CIU.

8

The evening light was drawing close in Waterloo. Ellen stood at the head of the incident room's long table, waving around a small plastic object clipped to a narrow woven neck strap. It resembled a flattened purple egg with buttons and a screen. 'This is a Tamagotchi,' she said. 'A pink one resembling this was found on Trevally Street, not far from the foreshore reserve, and identified by Donna Blasko as belonging to her daughter, Katie.'

She'd sent the original Tamagotchi to the new lab, ForenZics. This one belonged to Scobie Sutton's daughter, Roslyn. He'd gone home for the day, but she'd called him in again. You don't get time off when a kid's missing.

Just then, John Tankard hurried in. 'Nice of you to make it, Constable.'

Tank went red and sulky. 'Sorry, Sarge.'

Her face tight, Ellen said, 'To continue, Donna Blasko found her daughter's Tamagotchi lying on the footpath near her home and—'

Kees van Alphen raised a lazy hand. 'What the hell's a Tamagotchi?'

Scobie said indulgently, 'It's a little electronic toy. You give it a name and a personality. My Ros spends all of her free time—'

Ellen had to cut him short before he bored the pants off everybody.

'I was there for an hour before Katie's mother mentioned the damn thing.'

'Nothing else?' asked van Alphen, bored, picking nuggets of Styrofoam out of the rim of a disposable cup. 'No signs of a struggle? No witnesses?'

'No.'

'No sign of the bike, helmet or school bag?'

'Correct.'

'So what are you saying?'

They all looked bored, this was just a missing kid, but, in her bones, Ellen was afraid for Katie Blasko. She wanted to act swiftly. There were three whiteboards behind her: photographs of the girl, and headings and notes in her neat hand. 'Here are the obvious alternatives,' she said, using a pointer. 'One, Katie Blasko ran away.'

'Exactly,' said van Alphen heavily.

Ellen ignored him. 'She has a history of it, always returning home of her own accord or being discovered at a friend's house. But she's never stayed away as long as this before, and none of her friends have seen her. Second scenario: she's had an accident, possibly on her bike, possibly while running away or exploring waste ground somewhere. If that's the case, she'll be found eventually, but if she requires urgent medical care we need to send out search parties at first light tomorrow morning. Uniforms have already begun searching the mangrove flats, the tip and the quarry.' Here Ellen nodded an acknowledgement to Kellock. 'Third alternative, her classmates, or older children, have done something with her. Locked her in a shed, perhaps. An abandoned house. Again, we need to search thoroughly. Four, this is revenge for something. Does the family have any enemies? Five, the mother's de facto, Justin Pedder. He had access to Katie. She'd go with him willingly. He has an alibi, however, and I didn't really get a feeling that there was anything amiss in the home situation. But what if his mates are involved? Six, she's been abducted by a stranger or strangers. She might be found alive, or dead, or never found. For years now there have been rumours of a paedophile ring on the Peninsula.'

'Rumours, that's all they are,' said van Alphen.

Ellen ignored him. 'Trace, interview, eliminate,' she said. 'That's what police work boils down to in cases like this. Friends, family, neighbours, teachers, everybody. But we don't have a lot of time. According to statistics, most kidnapped or abducted children are killed in the first twenty-four hours. If a paedophile ring is involved, they'll abuse her for a few days and then kill her. We can't sit around worrying about our shift entitlements, childcare arrangements or overtime. This is too important for that. She could be in a car or house on the other side of the country by now. This is the worst kind of case: no body, no obvious crime scene, and no clear place to start.'

She hoped she wasn't communicating her performance anxieties and doubts to the room. Of course she wasn't Challis, but how would Challis handle this case? Would he move swiftly, too, and hang the criticisms? She visualised the way he liked to stand at briefings, either propping up a wall, pacing at the head of the long table or tapping wall maps or displays of surveillance and arrest photographs. There were always coffee cups and plates of scones and apricot Danish on the table, but her table was bare, apart from reams of paper. She didn't want him to hear whispers about her. She didn't want the officers now watching her expressionlessly to smirk, roll their eyes, look bored or later go bolshie on her because they didn't think she was up to the job.

Friday, early evening. They'd all rather be at home. She glanced out of the window at the darkening night. She could see flags and streamers curling lazily outside, lit by the streetlights, advertising the Waterloo Show. A perfect weekend coming up.

'The mother and the boyfriend told you she's run away before?' van Alphen asked.

'Yes.'

'Then she's run away again.'

'Leaving her favourite toy behind?'

He shrugged as if the whole thing was beneath him.

'Kees,' Ellen said exasperatedly, 'tell us what you really think.'

He pushed away the ruins of his cup and looked at her finally. 'She has a history of running away, right? And she's a kid—kids have short attention spans. She dropped her stupid toy and forgot about it. As for running away, maybe she's reacting to tensions at home; maybe she's trying to throw a scare into her mother. Note she didn't leave the bike behind, a bike's too precious for that. She'll turn up. They always do.'

'We've tried all of her friends,' Ellen said, feeling defensive.

'Yeah, but have you tried her *enemies*? Her friends are bound to lie, to protect her.'

'And her enemies are bound to tell us the truth?' said Ellen, cocking her head at him, even though she knew his idea was sound: an enemy will lie to hurt, just as a friend will lie to protect, but an enemy might also reveal those things a friend will want to conceal—not that she thought little girls of that age had confirmed enemies.

Van Alphen shrugged. 'It's just a thought,' he said, meaning that she hadn't covered all of the bases yet.

'Prints on the Tamagotchi?' Scobie asked.

Ellen turned to him with relief. 'Too soon. It's being tested.'

They watched her, and waited. 'I've had a few hundred flyers printed,' she said, her voice sharp. 'Van, I'd like you to muster up some uniforms and start distributing them tonight and tomorrow, all around town, especially along her bike route and at the showgrounds. I want a thorough canvass: flyers in shop windows, on bus shelters and light poles, etcetera, a saturation doorknock. The main Melbourne newspapers will run stories tomorrow, and TV and radio this evening. But we do not make public anything about an abduction or a paedophile ring. It's too alarmist. It's also too soon.'

Senior Sergeant Kellock hadn't said a word as yet. He'd sat there, a massive, brooding presence, signifying disapproval, as though she'd gone too far. She sighed inwardly. 'Senior Sergeant?'

He stirred, his huge head lifting and turning to take in Ellen, the room and the men and women around him. 'This is a kid, just remember that,' he growled, and Ellen could have embraced him.

That's what she wanted them all to remember. This was a kid. A kid was missing. 'Scobie, you can be incident room manager. If this gets any bigger we'll want data inputters, a receiver and an analyst, so plenty of computers and phones, please.'

'Okay.'

The briefing had taken ninety minutes. Before Ellen could wrap it up, her mobile phone rang. She took the call, tried not to show how thoroughly it disturbed her, and crossed to the TV set in the corner. 'Behold,' she said sourly, 'the mother and the boyfriend.'

'Evening Update', Channel 5, five days a week from 7.30 until 8 pm. As Ellen watched, it occurred to her that grief, stress and anxiety have many faces: numb, teary, expressionless, defeated. But sometimes—awfully—grief wears a smiling face. The voices coming from the TV were a little hoarse and broken, but Katie's mother and her boyfriend were smiling for the cameras.

The segment was live, the reporter in Donna's sitting room. 'The police fear that little Katie's been abducted,' he said. 'Have you a message for her abductors?'

'We hope you'll return Katie to us unharmed,' said Justin Pedder, showing his teeth. Reptilian teeth, thought Pam.

Ellen Destry whirled around. 'I never said a word to those two idiots about abduction. How did the media get onto this?'

They looked at her blankly.

'If I find that anyone in this investigation has been leaking information, I'll come down on them like a ton of bricks. Understood?'

'Sarge.'

Ellen scowled and turned to the TV again, where the question of victims-of-crime compensation was being raised. 'Yes, we think we should be compensated for our suffering,' Pedder was saying.

'How do you put a dollar amount on that?' the reporter asked rhetorically.

'Katie is priceless to us.'

The reporter nodded, full of feeling, and said gravely, 'Tell us how you're feeling right now.'

'Like I want to rip your wig off,' snarled Ellen.

'We feel just devastated,' said Katie Blasko's mother.

'Afraid?'

'Yes.'

Gently now: 'You fear the worst?'

'Yes,' the mother and the boyfriend said with their blinding smiles.

'How would you deal with the monster or monsters who have taken little Katie from you?'

Justin Pedder showed his teeth and gums and mimed hanging from a tree.

'Where's the public interest in this?' Kellock demanded.

Ellen was angry, but a part of her was also thinking that the public interest would quickly move on, leaving behind Justin Pedder and Donna Blasko, who surely felt ravaged to the core, even if they hadn't the means to express it.

She closed the briefing and returned to the paperwork in her office. Thirty minutes later, she had an inkling of what Challis often went through.

'I understand we have an abduction, Sergeant,' said Superintendent McQuarrie from her doorway.

'Sir, I—'

'I have that on good authority, of course. The media, no less.'

'Sir, someone must have—'

'This station has always leaked like a sieve,' McQuarrie said.

He began strutting back and forth before her desk. She didn't know what the protocol was. Should she come out from behind the desk? Should she be standing while he bawled her out? She decided to stand. That made her taller than McQuarrie, who was slight, dapper, a bloodless little man. Was it correct protocol to be taller than your boss?

He scowled at her resentfully. 'I've called a press conference. What do you suggest I tell them? That "Evening Update" got it wrong?'

Ellen sat again. Headlights flickered outside. Waterloo was bopping tonight. She could see all the way down High Street to the waterfront and the showgrounds, the Ferris wheel and the wilder rides lit up like Christmas trees. 'It's beginning to look like an abduction, sir.'

'Beginning to look like,' said McQuarrie flatly.

A snide little turd. She wondered what he was overcompensating for. His size? His total lack of coppers' instincts? His years of administering rather than policing? The fact that his Rotary pals were company CEOs while his occupation was largely blue collar? She badly needed to go home, pour a gin-and-tonic, soak in a bath.

'I realise we're talking about a small child, for God's sake, but it's surely too soon to state categorically that it is an abduction, and too soon for teary parents to be making a public appeal. Do you have compelling evidence one way or the other?'

'No, sir.'

'Then you see my dilemma.'

'Sir.'

'Are you up to this, Ellen?'

So now she was Ellen, his best pal? What a prick. 'I am, sir.'

'Because Inspector Challis is only a phone call and a plane ride away.'

Ellen clenched and felt herself blush, the heat and the colour coming from shame, defiance and anger. When she found her voice she said, 'That won't be necessary, sir.'

'Glad to hear it,' her boss said, turning briskly and striding out of the station to address the cameras. He loved the cameras and believed sincerely that they loved him.

Ellen stared gloomily at the wall. Presently she got a call from a technician at ForenZics. His name was Riggs; the voice was the kind that sniffed disapprovingly. 'That toy you sent us. We found prints and partials from the child and the mother, no one else.'

Ellen sighed. 'Thank you.'

Riggs said, 'Hours. The state lab sometimes takes *days* to furnish results.'

Was he after praise? 'Thank you.'

'At your service,' Riggs said, closing the connection with a brisk click.

Ellen stared at the wall again, then picked up her desk phone and dialled.

Fielding occasional calls from journalists, and referring them to the media office, she worked until 10 pm. Without the benefit of daylight or fresh leads, there was no point in hanging on later than that. She'd be of more use to Katie Blasko tomorrow morning, with a clear head, and so she clattered swiftly down the stairs and out into the car park at the rear of the police station. More than once on the drive along the moonlit back roads did she think about turning back and doing an all-nighter at the station. She wanted to be in her office, not in Hal Challis's unfamiliar bath, kitchen or bed, when the body was found.

For she was sure there'd be a body, crammed into a culvert somewhere, or tossed onto waste ground. Katie Blasko would be torn and bruised, internally and externally. Ligature marks on her wrists and ankles, maybe her neck. Things organic and inorganic would have been inserted into her. She'd have been photographed and videoed by the creep or creeps who abducted her, the images transferred onto compact disc and sold overseas or stored on computers and e-mailed all over the world, catering to a range of perverts: those who liked pre-pubescent girls posed in their cottontails, those with rape and incest fantasies, sodomites, all the way up to those who got a kick out of killing children or seeing it done.

Challis's house was dark, her footsteps a lonely series of slaps on his floorboards. It was a house to her, not a home. Without Challis there, it was just a house she'd be living in for the next few weeks. None of the angles were friendly, even with all of the lights on.

She'd collected Challis's mail and rolled copy of the *Age* from the letterbox at the foot of his driveway. Now she poured herself a gin-and-tonic and tried to free the *Age* of the plastic film that wrapped it, but couldn't find the join. Frustrated, she got one of Challis's kitchen knives and cut and sawed at the plastic, tearing the paper here and there. She could cry.

Instead she did a stupid thing and picked up the phone.

'Al? It's me,' she said in a small voice.

Her husband didn't know how to read it. 'Oh, hi,' he said neutrally.

He was renting a flat in Frankston now. She didn't know what his life was like. 'How are you?'

'All right.' He was wary. 'Is everything okay, Ells?'

He hadn't wanted her to leave him. She heard from his voice that he was a little encouraged that she'd called. 'I'm fine,' she assured him hastily.

'You don't sound it.'

'No, honestly, I'm fine.'

'I heard on the news they acquitted Nick Jarrett.'

'Yes.'

'Bad luck.'

Ellen tried to detect satisfaction in her husband's voice. Like her, he was a cop, but he was also liable to be pleased by any reversal that came her way. She changed the subject. 'I saw Larrayne while I was in the city.'

'She told me.'

'Oh. She had a boy with her.'

'Travis.'

'So you know him. You could have told me. Are they living together?'

'Why don't you ask her? She's your daughter.'

'No,' said Ellen, feeling hurt and nasty, 'she's her dad's daughter.'

They were silent. The past and the present sat heavily. Ellen sipped her drink and said, 'I wasn't sure you'd be home.'

He was attached to the accident investigation squad. He rarely had Friday nights free. 'Meeting up with a friend later,' he said.

Code for a female friend, a lover? Ellen wondered if he was telling the truth. It hadn't occurred to her to think about his love life, for she hadn't wanted to sleep with him again. Now she felt a faint twinge of something she hoped wasn't jealousy. Was it jealousy because he had a love life, or jealousy because *he* had a love life and she didn't? There was a world of difference between the two.

'Oh yeah? Who?'

'Are you jealous, Ells? Lover boy's gone away and you're all on your lonesome?'

'Go to hell.'

She almost cut the connection, but found herself telling him about Katie Blasko. There had been a time, long ago, when they'd talked over their day's work, the hassles and triumphs. That was before she'd become a sergeant and he'd failed the sergeant's exam. That was before he'd decided she was sleeping with Challis.

'I might be able to help there,' he said, when she'd finished.

She sipped her gin-and-tonic. Challis's sitting room began to take on warmer configurations. She liked its plain furniture and simplicity, the mix of wood and leather, the CD collection under the rows of books along one wall. 'How?'

'I don't know, Ellen,' he said impatiently, as though she'd doubted his abilities. 'Check speed cameras in the area, infringement notices, stolen vehicle reports.'

'Thanks,' she murmured, oddly touched.

'Yeah, well…'

Into the pause that followed, she said, 'Don't be late for your date.'

'Oh, okay,' he said mutedly, and she didn't know if he'd been hinting for an excuse to break his date, or keeping up a pretence to make her jealous. She felt about sixteen again.

As she was getting ready for bed the phone rang, and Hal Challis said, 'Burnt my house down yet?'

Relief flooded her. There was no cluttered history, he was rock solid and he'd be able to help her. Then, just as instantaneously, complications took shape in her mind. Her boss was a thousand kilometres away. He had troubles of his own. He'd left her in charge.

She cleared her throat, trying to rally 'Burnt the toast,' she said.

He laughed. 'How's the grass?'

'Long, getting longer.'

He said apologetically, 'Get someone in to mow it for you. I'll pay you back.'

They were far apart in the night, the staticky murmurs of the atmosphere sounding on the line between them. 'Bad news,' she said. 'Nick Jarrett was acquitted.'

'Hell.'

'Tell me about it. McQuarrie's steaming.'

'I'll bet. Look, don't beat yourself up about it. We'll get Jarrett on something else.'

'Yeah, something minor, no jail time.'

They were silent, acknowledging the frustrations of the job. 'Hal, there's something else,' Ellen said, and told him all about it: Katie Blasko, Katie's home life, the delay, the indifference of van Alphen, McQuarrie's grandstanding, and, more than anything, her doubts and fears.

56

'You're right to treat it as a worst-case scenario,' Challis assured her. 'When it's a kid, you can't afford to take chances.'

'But I *did* take chances, Hal. Instead of sticking around this afternoon and mounting a proper search, I left Scobie in charge and swanned off to the city. What if she's dead because I didn't take it that one step further?'

'But you have to cover the obvious bases first,' he said soothingly, 'and that's what Scobie was doing.'

'I know, but I feel guilty.'

'And you've made up for it.'

She laughed without humour. 'Now everyone thinks I'm overreacting.'

'You've got good instincts,' Challis said. 'Better instincts than I have.'

Did she not believe him, or not believe that he believed it? She was about to reply when he said, 'Get Kellock and van Alphen on side. They'll look out for their own interests first, but they're straight and they're canny. Above all, don't let McQuarrie stage-manage everything.'

'I know. It's just that I keep imagining Katie Blasko somewhere dark,' she said. 'She's hurt. She's scared. I know you have to take a step back and not get involved, but it's hard.'

'Actually,' Challis said, 'I don't think you can be a good investigator if you *don't* feel something. Feelings are an essential part of imagination and intuition. You can't do those things cold.'

They'd never talked like this before. Perhaps it was the phone. She liked it. 'You think so?'

'Positive.'

'Thanks, Hal.'

They lingered on the line. Eventually she heard him say, 'Goodnight. Call me if you need me.'

'How's your dad?' she said, because she wanted to know, and to prolong his voice in her ear.

9

Early on Saturday morning, Ellen was back at Katie Blasko's house, acting on the firm principle that you always examine the home situation first. In this case she wanted another look at Justin Pedder, the mother's de facto. His alibi for Thursday afternoon was sound, but that didn't mean anything. For all that Ellen knew, he'd been sharing Katie with his mates, only this time something went wrong and they'd killed and dumped the girl. Or he'd stoked them with photos and fantasies and they'd decided they wanted some of that action while he was away at the races.

Or he was completely innocent. Certainly he was unknown to the rape squad, the child exploitation unit and the various government agencies like Children's Services.

But Ellen was thinking of the six-year-old, Shelly. Was she next? Would Pedder groom her, too, and discard her as easily as he'd discarded Katie? *Had* Katie been discarded—too old?—or had something gone wrong, she'd been smothered to shut her up, or strangled because someone failed to control himself?

Wanting answers to some of these questions, Ellen knocked on Donna Blasko's door at eight o'clock. Donna answered, blotchy from weeping and sleeplessness, stale smelling, a tissue in one hand, wearing a grimy towelling robe over men's pyjama pants and a green T-shirt.

The air was laden with odours: breakfast toast and bacon, and older, fuggier layers that Ellen automatically sifted through, identifying cigarettes, beer, marijuana and perspiration. She wanted to open up the house, every door and window. A TV set droned in the background: cartoons.

'Have you found her?'

Ellen shook her head. 'Sorry, Donna, and sorry to call so early. May I come in?'

'S'pose,' said Donna reluctantly.

They moved through the sitting room to the kitchen at the back, skirting a pizza box, a bra, empty DVD case, the Saturday *Herald Sun*, toys, and the little sister, Shelly, sprawled in front of a wide-screen TV. 'Excuse the mess.'

'You should see my place,' said Ellen, then wondered why she'd said it. She didn't have a place. Her old place had been tidy, with Larrayne no longer living in it. Donna looked at Ellen in astonishment, either because she thought the police were neat or she didn't expect kindness. 'Cuppa tea?'

'Thank you.'

Ellen sat, touched the sticky tabletop, withdrew her hand into her lap. The sink was piled with breakfast dishes, the fridge noisy, the floor grimy, linoleum tiles lifting here and there. And apparently the cat liked to move its food from the bowl to the floor. Ellen itched to get a scraper out.

'Justin still in bed?'

Donna shook her head. 'Out with his mates.'

Ellen's disapproval must have been apparent, for Donna added aggrievedly, 'They're looking for Katie.'

Ellen got her notebook out. 'Bright and early. Their names?'

'They're looking for Katie, I'm tellin' ya.'

'I don't doubt it. We need to speak to everyone who's had contact with your household in the past few weeks and months.'

'I thought Katie was snatched off her bike?'

'We're not absolutely sure what happened,' Ellen said. 'But let's not jump the gun.' She paused. 'I saw you on television, Donna. At no point did I state categorically to you that we thought Katie had been abducted.'

'No, we had to hear that from the "Evening Update" guy.'

Ellen sighed. 'There are other scenarios.'

'So? She's still missing, no matter what happened to her. Are the police actually doing anything to find her?'

'Search parties went out at first light. From eight-thirty this morning an incident caravan will be parked at the entrance to Trevally Street. Officers will be on standby to hand out leaflets, answer questions and take statements. After school on Monday we've arranged for a model to trace Katie's movements.'

Roslyn Sutton, in fact, Scobie's daughter, the same age, build and height as Katie Blasko. 'Do you have a photo of Katie on her bike? Wearing her helmet? We need to match bike and helmet.'

'Somewhere.'

'And a spare school uniform we can use?'

Donna was looking alarmed and confused. 'Yeah, but what do you mean, a model?'

'A child who resembles Katie will ride slowly from the school gates to this house, taking Katie's usual route home. Then we'll do it again, taking alternative routes. Several police officers will follow her, handing out leaflets. We'll use a megaphone to explain what we're doing. The purpose is to jog people's memories, either of last Thursday or of other days when something out of the ordinary might have occurred.'

'Like what?'

'Perhaps Katie spoke to an adult along the way, a stranger or someone she knew. Or an unfamiliar vehicle was seen in the area. Anything at all. You'll be surprised how well it works.'

Ellen held no hopes whatsoever that it would work, but couldn't say that, and in fact Donna didn't look gladdened. Her face crumpled.

'You think she's dead.'

'We mustn't give up hope.'

'I wish Justin was here.'

'A bit callous of him to leave you alone,' Ellen said carefully.

'I'm not alone,' said Donna hotly, pointing in the direction of the TV in the other room. 'Plus he's not far away. He's doing more than you lot to find Katie.'

Guilt? Smokescreen? Genuine concern? 'How well did—do—he and Katie get along?'

Donna sniffed. 'Not bad. Argue a bit.'

'What about?'

'Oh, you know, the usual stuff, noise, TV watching, homework, stuff like that. Katie's always saying, "You're not my dad". She's got a temper on her.' A sudden change came over Donna's face. 'You think he done it, don't you? Well, he was with me on Thursday and I can prove it. And if he was abusing her regular, or at all, would she shout and yell and give him cheek? I don't think so. My uncle done stuff to me and I tell you now, it makes you quiet and sad.'

Ellen blinked away sudden tears. 'I'm sorry, Donna.'

'Yeah, well, so you should be.'

Ellen said carefully, 'What about his relationship with the little one. Shelly.' She held up a placating hand. 'I have to ask, Donna, to get it out of the way. If I don't, someone harder and more senior will come along and ask,' she added, feeling nasty and small.

'Shelly? Shell adores him.'

'She doesn't say, "You're not my father"?'

Donna was disgusted. 'Justin *is* her father. God. Get your fucking facts right, why don't you.'

Ellen blushed. 'Forgive me, Donna, I should have checked. Are you Shelly's mum?'

'No. God. When we first met, I was alone with Katie and he was alone with Shelly.'

Ellen bent her head to her notebook to hide her face. She should have been told all of this. She should have checked.

'Justin's not involved, take it from me. His mates aren't, either. They've all got kids of their own; we're always in and out of each other's houses. Yeah, they're rough, they've got tattoos, a couple have even been done for minor stuff, but they're not into anything sick. It's a stranger, I tell ya.'

Ellen nodded, closing her notebook, glancing at the crowded refrigerator, where drawings, cards and photographs jostled. *Peninsula Plumbing*, the cards read. *Mr Antenna. Waterloo Motors. Rising Stars Agency.*

10

The Seaview Park kids were notorious for surging and flickering about the town like a dangerous organism, appearing, disappearing, dispersing, merging again. On Saturday morning they were first spotted forming inside the main entrance to the estate, eight of them, mostly Jarretts and Jarrett acolytes, aged between six and eleven; a moment later they were outside it, throwing eggs at passing cars. They were gone well before the police arrived. 'So what else is new?' sighed Pam Murphy, taking witness statements from irate motorists in between doorknocking and handing out flyers.

Over the next hour she tracked them by their crimes. They lifted packets of LifeSavers from Wally's milk bar and spray paint from High Street Hardware. All along High Street they went, like quicksilver, terrorising the law-abiding. T-shirts from Hang Ten Surf Wear, sunglasses from a rack in the pharmacy, cheap jewellery from a couple of the $2 shops. Their movements were obvious: they were heading straight down High Street to the parkland on the waterfront, to the dodgem cars, shooting galleries, Ferris wheel, ghost train, flower, jam and cake displays, pony rides, outdoor art show, sound stage and food stalls that denoted the annual spring show in Waterloo. Pam didn't know what they'd do there, but did know they'd do more than merely gawk or spend any money they'd stolen or cadged. It wasn't in their nature to *give* to the community but to take. That was the Jarrett way, and there were plenty of takings at the Waterloo Show.

They had the Show sussed out within five minutes. The eleven-year-old said, 'You like it up the arse?' to a young woman pushing a pram. The nine-year-old snatched a purse. The twins pushed and shoved an old geezer who went red and breathless and an ambulance was called. They grabbed a fistful of *Have You Seen Katie?* leaflets from Donna Blasko and dumped them in a rubbish bin. On flowed the estate kids, untouchable, undetectable until the last moment, which was when their victims recognised that distinctive estate/Jarrett look, something quick and soulless.

'Where you from?' they demanded at one point.

Four kids visiting from Cranbourne, thirty minutes away. Outsider kids. The Jarretts knew all of the local kids.

'Nowhere,' the Cranbourne kids said.

'Gotta be from somewhere.'

'Over there,' said one of the Cranbourne kids, meaning a few hundred metres up the road.

'Liar.'

They crowded the outsiders, poked and jabbed. Wallets were taken. A knife was pulled, flashed once, leaving a ribbon of blood. Miraculously, an opening appeared. The Cranbourne kids ran for their lives. Whooping, the estate kids chased them, herded them, out of the showgrounds and back up High Street.

'Save us!' cried the visitors.

'Get out,' said the local shopkeepers, recognising the pursuers.

'Youths hospitalised,' said the next edition of the local paper.

While that was going on, Alysha Jarrett climbed over the fence at the rear of Neville Clode's house, trampling the onion weed as it lay limp and dying, and knocked on his back door. When it opened she stood there wordlessly, looking at but not seeing the doorsill or his bare feet, the left foot with its birthmark like the remnant of a wine-red sock, the nails hooked and yellow.

'Don't remember inviting you,' he said, smirking.

She said nothing. He made room for her and she passed him, into the house. She breathed shallowly. He never aired the place, but that wasn't uncommon in Alysha's experience. She came from people who kept their doors and windows closed and abhorred the sun. She could detect cigarettes, alcohol and semen. She knew those smells.

'Can't keep away, can you?' he said. She was thirteen and would soon be too old.

She shrugged. She never talked, never looked him in the face. Never looked at him anywhere if she could help it. She never used her own hands and mouth on him but pretended they belonged to someone else. Everything switched off when she came here. In fact she was never entirely switched on when she was away from here. She floated. She was unmoored. Her body had nothing to do with her.

'Here you go,' he said afterwards, giving her twenty dollars. Sometimes it was smokes, lollies, a bottle of sweet sherry. At the back door he sniffed, holding a tissue to his nostrils; he often got a nosebleed from the strain of labouring away at her body. Giving her what he called a cuddle, he peered out into his yard like a nervy mouse. 'The coast is clear,' he said, giving her bottom a pat. He'd washed her in the spa. She felt damp here and there. Alysha floated away with her $20, which she later spent on pills and went further away in her head.

Meanwhile Tank had the morning off. He'd been slotted for a grid search of Myers Reserve later in the day, followed by night patrol, so the morning was his one chance to take delivery of his Mazda. He went by train, getting off one station past Frankston, where the road that ran parallel to the tracks was used-car heaven, yards stretching in either direction, plastic flags snapping joyously in the breeze from the Bay. He set out on foot for Prestige Autos.

It was good to be decisive. Last weekend he'd driven all the way up to Car City, on the Maroondah Highway, and been told, at more than one yard, 'It's no good taking this car for a drive unless you mean to do business today.' Tank couldn't believe it. 'How do you sell cars if you don't let anyone test drive them?' The salesmen would gesture as if they didn't care. Perhaps they didn't. Perhaps there were plenty of idiots with money to burn. 'Do I look like a tyre kicker to you?' Tank had demanded. Another indifferent shrug. 'Don't you want my business? Do you think I'm broke?' And they'd said, 'Are you prepared to do business today, or are you "just looking"?'

Tank shook his head now at their stupidity and the obscure shame he'd felt. Anyhow, last weekend he'd also stopped off here in Frankston, and in the third caryard visited he'd found the Mazda. Sleek lines, as new, Yokohama tyres, the paint still glossy and unmarked. The guy there had no problem with Tank taking the car for a burn: 'Go for your life, mate,' he'd said. Luckily, the freeway was close by, and Tank was able to really test the car. In the blink of an eye he was doing 140 km/h on the straight. Effortlessly. The car sat straight and true, braked well, the exhaust snarling so sweetly it got him in the pit of the stomach. Tank, being canny, had even run a fridge magnet all over the bodywork. Not a trace of filler anywhere.

'I'll take it,' he said, moments later. As he'd told Murph yesterday, he'd negotiated the guy down in price by $5000. What he hadn't told her was he'd arranged a loan through the caryard's finance company.

'We haven't had time to register the car in Victoria,' the guy had said last weekend, 'it's only just come in, but the Northern Territory registration is still current, so you can drive it around.'

'No problemo,' Tank had said. All he needed to do was get a roadworthy certificate from Waterloo Motors, then register the car at the VicRoads office in Waterloo.

He strolled into Prestige Autos now, and there she was, gleaming in the sun.

11

The long day passed. At 3.30 that Saturday afternoon, Pam Murphy uncovered a lead. Given that her detective training was due to start on Monday, this was possibly her last act as a uniformed constable. Katie Blasko had been missing for forty-eight hours.

'This was when?' she asked the woman in Snapper Way.

'After school.'

'On Thursday?'

'I think it was Thursday.'

Pam gazed at the woman, said politely, 'Could it have been yesterday?'

'Let's see, yesterday was Friday. No, it wasn't yesterday I saw her. I don't work on Fridays. It must have been Thursday. Or Wednesday.'

Pam was door knocking in an area bounded by Katie Blasko's house, her school, Trevally Street and the Waterloo foreshore. Some of the houses were fibro-cement or weatherboard holiday and weekender shacks owned by city people, but most were brick veneer houses dating from the 1960s and '70s, their old-fashioned rose gardens pointing to leathery retirees who walked their dogs on the nearby beach and collected sea weed for fertiliser, and their bicycles, plastic toys and glossy four-wheel-drives pointing to young families who probably had no cash to spare after paying off their gadget, car and home loans. Pam met many women aged around sixty that afternoon, and many aged around thirty, like this woman, Sharon Elliott, the library aide at Katie Blasko's primary school. Short, round, cheery, anxious to please, dense—and, Pam decided, blind as a bat without her glasses.

'If you could tell me *where* you saw her, it might help jog your memory.'

'Near the shops.'

'In High Street?'

'Well, no,' Elliott said, as though that should have been obvious to Pam. 'Of course, I do my main shopping at the Safeway, but if I run out of bread or whatever I nip across to the corner shop.' She pointed vaguely. 'You pay more, but if I drove over to Safeway every time I wanted bread or milk, what I spent on fuel would outweigh the money I saved.'

Pam felt her eyes glazing over. 'And you bought something in the corner shop last Thursday?'

'I'm pretty sure. No. Wait. Yes, it *was* Thursday. I needed the latest *Trading Post*. I placed an ad to sell a mattress, and wanted to see if it had appeared.'

Pam knew that the *Trading Post* was published every Thursday. She beamed. The air was briny from the sea, the afternoon sun benign. The Peninsula had erupted with flowers, too, drawing the bees. It was a lazy, pleasure-laden Saturday in spring, and you were apt to forget that children could be abducted or murdered regardless of the season.

'Good,' said Pam encouragingly. 'And you're sure this was the girl?'

They examined the flyer again. 'It *looks* like the girl I saw.'

'Do you know her? Have you taught her?'

'I'm just an aide at the school. Almost five hundred children go there. I know quite a few by sight and many by name.'

'Yes, but did you ever have anything to do with *this* girl?' Pam asked, wanting to beat the woman around the head with a damp fish.

Sharon Elliot gazed at her blankly. 'What do you mean?'

Not for the first time, Pam realised that suspects and witnesses alike looked for traps behind your questions. They anticipated, evaded, lied, glossed the picture, told you what they thought you wanted to know, or got needlessly defensive. Or they were stupid. 'I'm wondering,' she said, trying to conceal her irritation, 'if you recognise this likeness of Katie Blasko precisely because you'd encountered her at school recently, helped her find a library book, perhaps, comforted her because she'd been crying about something, *or* because you saw her outside the corner shop between three-thirty and four this past Thursday afternoon.'

'Both,' said Sharon Elliott promptly.

'I see.'

'She was a bit noisy during quiet reading. Mrs Sanders had the Preps that session so I was taking the Grade 6s, and had to ask Katie to keep the noise down, except I didn't know her name was Katie, this was earlier in the week, so I was surprised when she waved to me.'

Pam didn't try to sort through the account. Her feet and back ached. She'd welcome a cup of tea or coffee, but Sharon Elliott was keeping her there on the front verandah, beside potted plants that were leaking water onto the decking. Above her the roofing iron flexed in the heat. 'She waved to you?'

'Like this,' said Sharon Elliott, gesturing.

'Was it a cheerful wave? Did she smile? Or might it have been a gesture of some kind?'

'A gesture?'

Pam didn't want to lead this witness, but really, the woman was dense. 'A beseeching gesture, for example, as if she needed help.'

Sharon Elliott gave her a blank look. 'I don't know. It was just a wave.'

'Did you get a good look at the driver?'

'No. I just assumed it was her dad.'

'But it was a man?'

'I *think* so. It could have been her mother.'

Did teachers' aides ever become teachers, Pam wondered. She waited a beat and said, 'What can you tell me about the vehicle.'

'It was just a car.'

'A car? I thought you said it was a van?'

The woman's face crumpled. 'Car, van, I don't really know much about that kind of thing. My husband's the driver in the family.'

'Let's see,' said Pam, glancing up and down the street. 'Was it the shape of that silver vehicle over there?'

A bulky four-wheel-drive. 'Not really.'

'Like that blue one?'

An old Nissan sedan. 'Now that I think about it I'm sure it wasn't small like that or have a lot of windows and big wheels like that silver one. More of a boxier shape.'

A van or a panel van, thought Pam. 'Colour?'

'Oh, now, white, I think.'

'And what time did you see this vehicle?'

'After school.'

'Yes, but three-fifteen, three-thirty, quarter to four?'

'Before four, anyway.'

'And we're not talking about separate things here, you're saying the vehicle and the girl who waved at you are part of the same incident?'

'I think so,' said Sharon Elliott.

Pam made a note.

'She might have been saying "Help me",' said Sharon Elliott into the pause.

As Sergeant Destry had mentioned at last night's briefing, witnesses often save the best till last. And not because they're artful or mischievous, either. '"Help me"?'

'I can see her mouth saying it.'

'We may need to speak to you again, Mrs Elliott.'

'Glad to help.'

12

At five that afternoon, Tank and the team finished the grid search of Myers Reserve. Tank showered and changed in the station locker room, and then slipped away to the car park behind KFC, where the producer of 'Evening Update' slipped him an envelope containing $500. Tank had hoped for more than $500 but the 'Evening Update' producer—bearded guy, lots of white teeth and a hint of makeup—reckoned there would be more dosh down the track, depending on the quality of the information that Tank could pass on. Tank put it into perspective: $500 was a year's registration on his new car. The cash was burning a hole in his pocket, though, Saturday night, Waterloo Show, the district humming. Too bad he was on duty. Could have been having a glass of suds with his mates.

He went home and crashed for a couple of hours. At eight o'clock he returned to the station, yawning his head off, and logged on for his solo patrol.

The long night unspooled. First up was a radio call: would he respond to an agitated citizen, 245 Bream Street, who'd phoned in a complaint, not making much sense. Bream Street—plenty of marine names in Waterloo, owing to the fishing industry in Westernport Bay—hugged the mangrove flats and was one of the main routes into the foreshore area, where the Ferris wheel revolved prettily and overweight families gorged on popcorn and fairy floss. John Tankard was overweight, too, but despised it in the common herd. He pulled up outside number 245, a featureless brick veneer from the 1950s. Just down the road from it was a police presence, plenty of lights and traffic cones glowing in the dark: a booze bus and a roadworthy checking station. We cops can be pricks sometimes, Tank thought, grinning. The local citizenry out for a good time at the Show, and bang, they're breathalysed and a roadworthy infringement notice is stuck onto the windscreen of the family rust bucket. He knocked on the door of 245.

'Who are you?'

'Constable Tankard, ma'am. You called the station?'

'I can't go out.'

She was about sixty, fierce and aggrieved on the other side of her screen door. 'Sorry?' said Tank.

She came out and pointed. 'Look.'

He followed her finger, which was quivering at the booze bus and the constables flitting about in the misty evening light. 'What?'

'Don't say "what". Where are your manners? Why do they have to set up so close?'

He understood finally. 'Have you been drinking, madam?' he asked, trying hard to keep the grin out of his voice.

'How dare you. I'm teetotal.'

'Then you have nothing to worry about from a breath test.'

'My car,' the woman said.

There was a new Corolla in the driveway. 'Are you sure it's unroadworthy? Looks new to me.'

'Not fair,' sulked the woman.

Tank pushed back his uniform cap. 'Tyres?'

'That's a new car. It's not fair.'

'You have nothing to worry about.'

'But I love to drive down to the Show. Too far for me to walk.'

'Then drive,' said Tank irritably.

'But they'll make me unroadworthy.'

John Tankard made the necessary leap and nodded slowly. 'It's not their job to *make* you drunk or unroadworthy. If you're neither then they'll let you through.'

She was sceptical. 'What if there's a quota?'

'Doesn't happen,' said Tank emphatically. He cocked his head. 'I think that's my car radio. Sounds urgent.'

He peeled out of Bream Street, reporting to base that he'd resolved the matter. On through the night he roamed, a lone ranger and liking it, issuing warnings, taking in the occasional abusive drunk or cokehead. He always checked them for concealed weapons or drugs before bundling them into the divisional van, always checked the cage for discarded drugs afterwards. At one point he answered a call to Blockbuster Video and nabbed a guy well known to the Waterloo police for a string of offences proven and suspected. The guy had four new-release DVDs stuck inside his underdaks, and, enjoying himself hugely, began admitting to all kinds of shit—rape, assault, burglary—before Tank could read him his rights. Tank knew how it would go: once in the interview room and cautioned, he'd clam up, not even admit to his name or even to being in a police station.

And Joe Public thinks we're corrupt or incompetent? Fuck Joe Public.

Finally there were the pull-overs. Typically you had kids in a lowered or hotted up Falcon or Holden, driving erratically, going too fast, not wearing seatbelts, music too loud, tossing a can or a butt out on the street, busted tail light, etcetera, etcetera. Some of the Waterloo police cars were fitted with an MDT, a moving data terminal, meaning you could get a rapid readout of a vehicle owner's address, licence status and criminal history, but Tank's divvy van was your basic model, cracked and faded plastics, stained upholstery and an odour suggestive of takeaway food, sweat and poor digestion, and so he was supposed to radio in the registration details and wait for a response before approaching a driver. But radio traffic was heavy that night, so he compromised, radioing in the registration request and approaching the driver *before* the answer came back. He usually had an answer in less than four minutes.

There was always plenty of movement in a pulled-over vehicle. It was as if the occupants were in a dark street, fucking in the back seat, but when it was a pull-over you could be sure they were getting rid of evidence, tucking joints, speed or ecstasy under the seat cushions. Or pulling out a weapon. John Tankard always had butterflies in his stomach, waiting for that to happen. That's why you approached from the rear, your hand on the butt of your .38. You didn't want to see a back window winding down. You didn't want a door opening. You didn't want a driver getting out.

And then, at about 1 am—the Showgrounds, the video joint and the restaurants long since closed, little kids and their mums and dads tucked up in their beds, High Street deserted, just an occasional bleary car making its way homewards—John Tankard took a last call from the dispatcher: unknown suspects had been seen climbing over a back fence, not on Seaview Park estate itself but one of the leafy crescents across the road from the estate, there where the outskirts of Waterloo faced farmland, there where no streetlights burned. Rain clouds had built up, shredding the moon; shards of glass glittered in the roadside grasses; the wind came in low from the distant mudflats. A road junction, broad, dark, and empty but for a black WRX idling on the verge, brake lights hard and red in the night. Tank could see the little Subaru throbbing. It was a popular car with your boy racers and drug dealers. He pulled in hard behind it, called in the plate number, and got out. He could smell the sea, and the Subaru's exhaust. Suddenly the driver cut the engine and now Tank heard the moaning empty wind, a ticking engine block, the faint static of the radio in the van far behind him as he approached the car, static speaking no doubt of crimes and misery in far-off corners of the lonely stretches of the night.

He reached the rear passenger door, leaned forward and tapped on the driver's window, straightened again. The window whined down a crack. 'Your licence and registration papers, please, sir,' said Tank.

'Why?'

A hoon's voice, pumped up, sour and uncooperative. 'Why?' repeated Tank. He could think of a million reasons why. Because you're out here in the middle of nowhere. Because you're a young dickhead yet you can afford this car. Because Pam Murphy gets to be a detective and I'm stuck driving a stinking divvy van. Because causing people grief is about the only thing that makes me feel better. He didn't hear the other car until it was too late.

The tyres alerted him, gently crunching the gravel at the side of the road. He swung around: a silver Mercedes, not new, running only on sidelights, came purring in from the intersecting road. Lowered, alloy wheels, smoky glass all around. It stopped and waited, and then Tank wasn't surprised when all of the doors opened. He began to back away from the Subaru. He backed right up to the divvy van and sped away from there, trying to swallow. Sometimes there was weird shit going on at night and he was better off out of it.

The dispatcher's voice cut in then. 'The registered owner of the Subaru is a Trent Jarrett of Seaview Park estate.'

'Tell me something I don't know,' muttered Tank.

And the guy driving the Merc had been the killer, Nick Jarrett.

John Tankard went home and didn't sleep.

13

One thousand kilometres northwest of Waterloo, Hal Challis had spent a long Saturday caring for his father. He felt inadequate to the task. At the same time, he couldn't concentrate fully. Being 'home' again had put him into a dreamlike state, brought on by old familiar objects—like his mother's jacket.

It was heavy cotton, faded navy, with a cracked leather collar, still hanging on a peg by the back door, and, in his mind's eye, Challis could see his mother on one of her solitary rambles. He'd quite forgotten that she liked to do that, yet she had always done it, right through his childhood and adolescence. He'd taken it for granted back then. It had simply been his mother out walking. Now he wondered if it had signified more than that. She'd been a big-city girl. Had she been lonely out here? Had she yearned for more? People had always said that Challis resembled her—olive colouring, dark hair, narrow face—but had they also meant character? His mother tended to be silent, watchful and withholding. She'd tolerated Gavin for Meg's sake. She'd adored Eve. She hadn't judged or prodded Challis. She'd stood up to the old man's nonsense. The coat brought a lump to his throat.

To throw off the dreaminess, he began to make notes about his brother-in-law. Gavin Hurst had suffered extreme mood swings in the months leading up to his disappearance. He'd become paranoid, argumentative, suspicious and belligerent. RSPCA regional headquarters had received dozens of complaints. Then his car had been found abandoned in dry country several kilometres east of the Bluff. Suicide, that was the general verdict, but, four months later, Meg had begun to receive unusual mail. *National Geographic* arrived, followed by an invoice for the subscription. She complained, and was faxed the subscription form, filled out in her name. An Internet service provider sent her a free modem, part of the two-year package deal she'd 'signed' for. She received catalogues, mail-order goods, book club samples, and applications for life insurance policies naming her husband as beneficiary. Challis had to ask himself: Was Meg capable of setting something like this up—maybe with the old man's help? Or had Gavin staged his disappearance, then begun to taunt her out of malice?

He was relieved when Meg arrived, as arranged, to cook dinner. 'You don't have to do this, you know,' he told her.

She was already clattering about in the kitchen. 'I know.'

'Eve couldn't come?'

'Give the girl a break. It's Saturday night. She's going out with some of her friends.'

Challis helped. Soon a stir-fry of onions, garlic, ginger, soy sauce and strips of chicken was hissing and crackling in a wok. 'I didn't know Mum had a wok.'

'There are a lot of things you didn't know about Mum.'

'Ouch.'

Meg looked mortified and touched his forearm. 'I didn't mean to sound so harsh.'

'Probably deserved,' Challis said. Meg had carried the burden of the last couple of years. She'd been closer to their parents in all respects, yet the family dynamics had always demonstrated, very faintly, the sense that he was the favoured one, the first-born.

Challis glanced guiltily through the archway at his father, who was slumbering in one of the sitting room armchairs. He'd rarely given much thought to the South Australian compartment of his life: his mother, when she was alive, his father, Meg and Eve, their individual heartaches and vulnerabilities. Partly distance, and partly that he was a bad son? Certainly self-absorption wasn't a factor, for he rarely considered his own heartaches and vulnerabilities but lived inside the crimes and criminals he dealt with. Now, here, he had things to face up to.

'I didn't tell you why I came through Adelaide.'

Meg was busy at the wok, but cast him an inquiring glance.

'Do you remember Max Andrewartha?'

'The sergeant here when you were a probationer?'

'Yes. Well, he's head of the missing persons unit now.'

'Oh, Hal.'

'I read their file on Gavin.'

Meg seemed distressed. 'Why would you do that?'

Could he tell her that a sense of responsibility was growing inside him, threatening to swamp him?

'Hal?'

'Sorry, miles away.'

'Forget about Gavin. That's what I'm trying to do.'

'The case is still open. Nothing can change that.'

Meg breathed out exasperatedly. 'Did you learn anything new?'

'No. I thought I'd ask around while I'm here.'

'Please don't.'

'Low key, sis, low key.'

She gave him a shove. 'Out of the kitchen. You're in my way.'

Challis went through to his father, woke him gently, and read to him from *Mr Midshipman Hornblower*. When Meg called, 'It's on the table,' he helped the old man through to the dining room. Three plates steamed on the table, one of them minuscule and plain, chicken without soy sauce, cut into tiny pieces, adorned with a spoonful of rice and what looked like overcooked carrots and peas. Dad's dodgy digestion, Challis thought.

'Wine, I think,' he said, and went to his bedroom, returning with a bottle he'd packed before leaving Waterloo.

'You read my mind, son.'

'Dad,' warned Meg.

The old man ignored her, waggling his glass at Challis, who poured a tiny measure.

'Jesus Christ, son. A bit more wrist action.'

'You shouldn't have alcohol, Dad,' Meg said, tucking a napkin into the old man's collar.

'Too late.'

Challis said 'Cheers' and they toasted each other and began to eat and talk, their conversation punctuated by peaceful silences. Early evening, the sun settling, darkening the room but not removing its essential warmth. Now and then the old man tore a knuckle of bread from the white slice on his side plate and masticated slowly. The wine, and the presence of his children, rallied him in contestable ways. Challis found it exhausting, and was relieved when his father fell asleep.

Meg smiled. The light was soft all around them and encouraged release and harmony. They murmured into the night, sipping the wine. Meg examined the bottle. 'This is good. Elan. Never heard of it.'

'A small winery just up the road from where I live,' Challis said.

'I guess it doesn't really matter if Dad has a glass now and then. You know…'

'Yep.'

Their father continued to sleep, diminished by age and illness.

'What are Eve's friends like?'

'Nice.'

This led by degrees to a discussion of their own late teens: the heartaches, rituals, mating and courting indiscretions, and, above all, the waiting.

'*Weeks* would go by and nobody would ask me out.'

Challis laughed. 'Weeks would go by when I didn't have the nerve to ask anyone out.'

Meg said slyly, 'Except Lisa Acres. You didn't have to wait long for her.'

Challis shifted ruefully in his chair. 'No one did.'

He was being unfair. Lisa Acres—'Acres' because the first thing she asked you was how many acres you owned—hadn't really been free with her affections. But she was the daughter of the local publican and had ambitions to settle down with a rich man. Challis hadn't been rich, so she must have seen something else in him. It had been heady fun while it lasted and had broken his heart.

'Do you ever see her?' he asked.

'Oh, she's around. Still stunning to look at, in a brittle kind of way. The husband's an alcoholic. She virtually runs the place. They'd go bankrupt if it wasn't for her.'

She'd married a man named Rex Joyce, who came from old money in the district. Rex had been sent away to boarding school, Prince Alfred College in Adelaide, at the age of five. He'd suddenly reappeared one day, in a red Jaguar given to him by his father when he turned eighteen. Rex, that car, and the acres that came with them, had offered Lisa more than Challis ever could.

'Any kids?'

Meg shook her head. 'Some unkind people say she didn't want to ruin her figure, others that she's been too busy keeping the property intact. A lot of farms have gone under in the past few years.'

Meg toyed with her knife, turning it to catch the light. 'Are you seeing anyone, Hal?'

Was he? At once he was visualising Ellen Destry, the way her fair hair would swing as she walked, her intensity when she was working, her sly humour, above all her beauty. She wasn't straightforwardly beautiful. You had to know her for a while to see it. She'd once said her looks were 'average', 'girl next door', but they were more complicated and alluring than that.

He wanted her, but was he seeing her? 'Not really.'

Meg sighed. 'Nor am I.' She paused. 'The kids go out as groups of friends these days, rather than as couples, like we did. It's healthier, I think.'

'Do you think Eve's, you know…'

Meg cocked her head. 'Sexually active? I don't know about active. We've talked about it. She's not a virgin. She knows she can have a boy stay overnight if she really cares about him and he's nice to her.'

'Not like our day.'

Meg shook her head vehemently. 'God, no.'

They glanced at their father again; how terrifying he'd seemed when they were young. He'd wanted Challis to go out into the world rather than marry a local girl—which he'd said would lead to stunted opportunities, bawling babies and debt. On the other hand, he hadn't wanted Meg to leave, or get an education, but marry locally and raise a family. She'd mostly obliged, marrying Gavin Hurst and producing a daughter with him.

Challis brooded down the years. He remembered the country-dances of his youth, often in far-flung town halls or football clubrooms. It hadn't been unusual for him to drive his father's Falcon station wagon two hundred kilometres on a Saturday night, Lisa Acres at his elbow, her hand on his thigh. He'd take her home, pull into the shadows behind her father's pub, but not get further than that before the light went on above the back door and she'd say in a rush, 'Dad's awake, I'd better go in.' It went beyond birth control: it was desire control.

He could see now that it wouldn't have worked with her anyway. He had a history of choosing the wrong woman. In fact, Angie, the woman he'd married, had conspired with her lover—a police colleague of Challis's—to murder him. She'd gone to jail for that. She'd killed herself there.

As if reading his mind, Meg said, 'We both made mistakes, didn't we?'

They glanced at their father again, wondering if he was to blame, not wanting to believe that they might shoulder some of it, or that many marriages simply ran their course and ended.

'Gavin has stopped messing with your head?' Challis asked.

Meg nodded. 'Nothing in the past couple of years.'

'Where do you think he is?'

She shrugged. 'Sydney?'

'Why would he want to hurt you like that?'

It was a rhetorical question. Meg shrugged again, then leaned forward, dropping her voice. 'You won't tell Dad about the letters?'

He shook his head. He'd promised years ago that he wouldn't. Their father being such a difficult person, one simply knew not to tell him everything. But now Challis was curious about Meg's motives. 'Is there a reason why you told Mum but not him?'

'You know what he's like. He wanted me to stick around and marry and have kids, but didn't want me to marry Gavin. It gave him a sense of satisfaction to believe Gavin had committed suicide. Confirmed what he thought of Gavin. But if he'd known Gavin was still alive, and taunting me, I'd never have heard the end of it.'

Challis gave a hollow laugh of recognition. They were silent for a while. Meg said, 'Rob Minchin is still sweet on me, you know.'

Rob Minchin was the local doctor, and one of Challis's boyhood friends. 'And?'

'And nothing. He calls in to check on Dad, and that's about it.'

'I remember he was pretty jealous of Gavin.'

'Rob in the grip of passion,' said Meg, shaking her head.

They stared at the tabletop, too settled to move. Their father snored gently. Soon they would put him to bed, Meg would go home, and Challis would toss sleeplessly on his childhood mattress.

14

Bucketing rains came through overnight, preceded by thunder and lightning that seemed to mutter around the fringes of the horizon, then approach and encircle the house where Ellen Destry slept, and retreat again. Dawn broke still and balmy, the skies clear, as though nothing had happened. Spring in southeastern Australia, Ellen thought, glancing out of Challis's bedroom window. The bedside clock was flashing, indicating that the power had gone off during the night. She glanced at her watch—6 am—and went around the house, resetting the digital clocks on the microwave, the oven, the DVD player. Then, pulling on a tracksuit and old pair of Reeboks, she set out for her morning walk.

And immediately returned. Rainwater had come storming down the dirt road and roadside ditches outside Challis's front gate, carrying pine needles, bark, gravel and sand, which had formed a plug in the concrete stormwater pipe that ran under his gateway. The ditch had overflowed, scoring a ragged channel across the entrance. She should do something about it before the channel got too deep.

Hal had told her the grass would need mowing regularly. He hadn't told her what a storm could do.

In his garden shed she found a fork, a five-metre length of stiff, black poly agricultural pipe, and a long-handled shovel. She hoisted them over one shoulder and returned to the front gate. There were signs of the overnight storm all about her: twigs, branches, ribbons of bark and birds' nests littered the road; water-laden foliage bent to the ground; the air seemed to zing with promise.

Ellen forked and poked at the blocked pipe, shovelled and prodded. Suddenly, with a great, gurgling rush, the stopper of matted leaves and mud washed free and drain water flowed unchecked toward the...

Toward the sea? Ellen realised that she knew very little about life out here on the back roads.

Finally she walked. She passed a little apple orchard, the trees heavy with blossom despite the storm. Onion weed, limp and yellowing at the end of its short life, lay densely on both sides of the road, and choking the fences was chest-high grass, going to seed. Sometimes her feet slipped treacherously where the dusty road had turned to mud. The blackberry bushes were sending out wicked new canes and the bracken was flourishing. Now and then she passed through air currents that didn't smell clean and new but heavy with the odours of rotting vegetation and stale mud revitalised by the rain. Everything—the sounds, the smells, the textures—served to remind her of Katie Blasko, abandoned, buried, merging with the soil.

She walked slowly up the hill, stunned to see huge cylinders of hay in one of the paddocks, freshly mown and wrapped in pale green polythene. When had that happened? She rarely saw or heard vehicles, and yet here was evidence of the world going on without her.

Without warning she heard a sharp snap and felt a stunning pain in her scalp. Her heart jumped and she cried out in terror. Only a magpie, she realised soon afterwards, swooping her because it had a nest nearby—but she'd hated and feared magpies ever since a long-ago spring day when she'd been pecked and harried across a football field as she'd taken a short cut home from school on her bicycle. Magpies sang like angels but were the devil.

Windmilling her arms wildly about her head, and trying to make eye contact with her tormentor, Ellen trotted home. She missed her morning walks on Penzance Beach with Pam Murphy, where the world was reduced to the sand, the sea, the sky and a few gulls. Out here on the back roads there was too much nature. All around her ducks sat like knuckly growths on the bare branches of dead gums, and other birds were busy, calling out, making nests, protecting their young, and in the paddocks ibis were feeding. A strip of bark fell on her, scratching her neck. Challis's ducklings were down to six, she noticed, as she entered his yard, and she wanted to cry.

At nine that same Sunday morning, Scobie Sutton was at the little Waterloo hospital. He was entitled to a day at home with his wife and daughter, a quiet time, church and Sunday School, a spot of gardening after lunch, but the station was short staffed. He'd be working the Katie Blasko case later—and it *was* a 'case' in Scobie's mind: his own daughter was Katie's age, and if she went missing for even thirty minutes he'd be calling it a case—but right now he was the only CIU detective available to interview the victim of an aggravated burglary.

'How are you feeling, Mr Clode?'

'I'll live,' Neville Clode said.

Extensive bruising to the head and torso, a cut lip, cracked ribs. Clode was swaddled in bandages and lying very still in the bland, pastelly room. The place was overheated and so he'd thrown off the covers, revealing skinny legs and the ugliest feet that Scobie had ever seen: yellowed nails and a blotchy birthmark. No flowers, fruit or books. I'm possibly his first visitor, Scobie thought. 'You took quite a beating last night.'

The voice came in a strained whisper, 'Yes.'

'Did you recognise the men who attacked you?'

'No.'

'Do you know if they took anything?'

'Cash,' whispered Clode.

'Cash. Do you know how much?'

'Six…seven hundred dollars.'

Scobie whistled. It was a lot. It would also grow when Clode submitted his insurance claim. 'Do you always have that much cash on you?'

'Won it at the horses yesterday. Emu Plains.'

It was the spring racing carnival everywhere, metropolitan racetracks and regional, including Emu Plains on Coolart Road, just a few kilometres from Waterloo. No security cameras, though. 'Do you think you were followed home from the track?'

'Could have been.'

'Were you alone?'

'Yes.'

'And nothing else was stolen?'

'No.'

Clode hadn't once made eye contact but stared past Scobie at the TV set bolted high on the wall, so high it was a wonder hospitals didn't get sued for encouraging neck strain in their patients. Scobie dragged the visitor's chair around; Clode slid his eyes to the beige door. Scobie said gently, 'Are you telling me everything, Mr Clode? Was this personal? Did you owe money to anyone? Is there anyone who would want to hurt you?'

Scobie had visited the crime scene before coming to the hospital. Clode lived in a brick house along a secluded lane opposite the Seaview Park estate. Like its neighbours, it was comfortably large and barely visible from the road, a low, sprawling structure about ten years old, the kind of place where well-heeled tradesmen, teachers and shop owners might live, on largish blocks, screened by vigorous young gum trees, wattles and other native plants. Residents like Clode were several steps up from the battlers of Seaview Park estate, and several steps down from the doctors and real estate agents who lived in another nearby enclave, Waterloo Hill, which overlooked the town and the Bay. Clode himself was some kind of New Age healer, according to a sign on a post outside his house.

Letting a forensic tech dust and scrape, Scobie had done a

walk-through of the house. It was evident that a woman had once lived there—a woman slightly haunted by life or by Clode, judging by the face she revealed to the world in the only photograph Scobie found, a small, forgotten portrait in a dusty cream frame, the woman unsmiling in the front garden of the house, Clode with his arm around her. No signs of her in the bathroom cabinet, bedside cupboard or wardrobe. The rooms themselves were sterile, a mix of mainly worn and some new items of furniture, in careful taste, neither cheap nor costly, with here and there an ornamental vase or forgettable framed print. A couple of fat paperbacks, several New Age magazines, some CDs of whale and waterfall music. It was the house of an empty man. The only oddity was a small room taken up with a spa bath, bright wall tiles and cuddly floating toys.

And the damage, of course—the overturned TV set, rucked floor mats, splintered chair and broken glass. And blood.

'Did you injure any of your assailants, do you think?' Scobie asked now. 'There seemed to be a lot of blood in the sitting room.'

Clode put a hand to his cut lip and winced. 'Don't know.'

Scobie watched him for a while. 'Are you telling me everything, Mr Clode?'

Signs of anal penetration, according to the doctor who'd examined Clode. No semen present. 'Were you raped?'

Clode's eyes leaked and he shook his head minutely. Scobie waited. Clode swallowed. 'A bottle.'

There had been no bottles at the scene. 'Before or after they beat you?'

'It was part of the whole deal,' Clode said.

'You were also kicked?'

'Yes.'

'What were they wearing?'

'Jeans. T-shirts.'

'What about footwear?'

'Runners.'

Scobie had scouted around the house: lawn right up to the verandah, so no shoe prints, and none in the blood. 'You didn't recognise them?'

'Happened too quickly, plus I covered my face to protect it.'

'When did it happen?'

'About midnight.'

'Yet you didn't report it until six this morning?'

'Unconscious.'

'I don't understand why they didn't take anything else—your DVD player, for example.'

Scobie watched Clode. The man's face was bruised and swollen, but evasiveness underlay it. 'Don't know.'

'I think this was personal, Mr Clode.'

'No. Never seen them before.'

'Are you married?'

'My wife died a couple of years ago. Cancer.'

'Grandchildren?'

'Yes.'

That explained the spa bath and toys. 'How old were these men?'

'Don't know. Youngish.'

'You're almost sixty?'

'What's that got to do with it?'

'What about their voices. Did you recognise anyone? Anything distinguishable, like an accent?'

'They didn't say much. Didn't say anything.'

'What about names, did they let any names slip out?'

'Nup.'

'Did they address you by name?'

'No.'

'Have you got any enemies, Mr Clode?'

'No. I'm in pain.'

Pam Murphy, conditioned by years of police duty and triathlon training, was also up and about.

According to the surf report, Gunnamatta Beach was too big and turbulent today, Portsea had messy onshore waves, Flinders onshore waves to 1.5 metres, and Point Leo a fair, one-metre-high tide surf, so she settled on Point Leo. The surfing conditions were right. It was also her closest surf beach and she'd learnt to surf there.

It was uncanny the way certain memories and sense traces hit her the moment she drove past the kiosk and over the speed bumps. Sex, mainly, together with the taste of salt—human and marine—and the sounds of the seagulls, the offshore winds, the snap of wetsuits, kids waxing their boards. Desire flickered in her. The guy who'd taught her to surf had been scarcely seventeen years old, she in her mid twenties. A disciplinary offence, maybe even dismissal from the police force, if it had ever come out. But it hadn't, and they'd both moved on and no hearts had been broken or psyches damaged. It had been a tonic to her, that summer. She'd never been desired quite like that before. She'd scarcely felt desire herself, or desirous. Her body had always been a beautiful, flexible instrument whenever she swam, ran or hit a ball around, but sexual desire had been its untapped dimension. A male colleague like John Tankard, commenting on her tits in the confines of a police car, was hardly going to awaken her.

She parked on a grassy verge beside a cluster of familiar roof-racked panel vans and small cars, pulled on her wetsuit, and trudged over the dunes with her surfboard, passing the clubrooms, a poster of Katie Blasko pinned to a noticeboard. The beach curved slowly to the west; a few solitary people walked their dogs; gulls wheeled above the sea; surfers—tiny patient dots—rose and fell, rose and fell, as small waves rolled uneventfully to the shore. Pam felt a surge of feeling for the lost summers of her life and for the end of her years in uniform.

Unless she blew it. 'You have the right instincts,' Ellen Destry would often tell her, 'but becoming a detective also means writing essays and passing exams.'

Things that Pam had never been good at.

15

'Thank you for coming in,' said Ellen Destry, late morning. 'I know it's Sunday, and you've all clocked up a lot of overtime, but we can't afford to drop the ball.'

They shrugged good naturedly, all except John Tankard, who looked tired and edgy, and Superintendent McQuarrie, who glanced at his watch and said, 'Let's get on with it, Sergeant.'

Why was he here? Ellen could sense his impatience. Maybe he was supposed to be meeting his pals on a golf course somewhere. 'Yes, sir.'

He'd always treated Challis with impatience, too. McQuarrie was a pen-pusher, a man who resented the competence and usefulness of street cops, for they made the kinds of decisions and intuitive leaps that left him bewildered—and so he took it out on them. More so, if a female officer was calling the shots. He was the kind of man who'd want her to fail so that he, or a male appointee, could step in. Sure, he probably wanted Katie Blasko found, but a corner of him didn't want *Ellen* to do it. Meanwhile the other men in the briefing room, particularly Kellock and van Alphen, were reserving judgement. If she revealed emotions or doubts, they'd roll their eyes, put their arms around her bracingly, and tell her how things should be done.

So she acted hard and fast, assigning tasks to the CIU detectives and to the uniforms. 'We've interviewed many of these people before,' she said, 'but I want you to do it again, and given that it's a Sunday, you should be able to catch up on those who were not at home yesterday or on Friday. Teachers, shopkeepers, neighbours, school friends, enemies. Grandparents, aunts, uncles, cousins. The Show finishes today, everyone's packing up and moving on to another town, so I want ticket sellers, roustabouts, drivers and hangers-on interviewed and checked before they disappear into the never-never. Search their vehicles.' She paused. 'Public transport. Did Katie take a train to the city? Dump her bike and hail a taxi? Go into a shop, accompanied by someone, a friend or a stranger? Check security camera footage again. Re-interview everyone on the sex offenders' register. And don't rule out other children: check Children's Services for local kids who have a record of violence and inappropriate sexual behaviour.'

The acknowledgement, 'Boss,' went raggedly around the room.

'Justin Pedder. So far he checks out, but keep an open mind. All of the open land in and around Waterloo has now been searched, without result, but broadening the perimeter is not warranted yet, there's just too much of it on the Peninsula. It's eyewitnesses we want. Hopefully tomorrow afternoon's bike re-enactment will help.'

'Boss.'

'Has Katie turned up in Sydney or Brisbane or Adelaide, giving a false name? Is she sleeping rough somewhere? Is she in a homeless shelter? Check empty and condemned buildings. Make sure every detail is entered in the computer for cross-checking.'

She let her gaze settle on each of them in turn, encouraging but firm. McQuarrie stirred, looking irritable. 'I hope you realise how much all this is costing, Sergeant Destry.'

Ellen flushed. He had no right to carp and criticise her in front of her colleagues. 'I think a missing child warrants it, sir.'

He seemed to realise that he might make enemies here rather than be admired for leadership qualities. 'Very good, carry on.'

'Thank you, sir.'

They all began to file out. McQuarrie went first, John Tankard last. She stopped him. 'Everything all right, John?'

His eyes were bloodshot. He'd shaved badly. When he answered, she caught a whiff of negligence and carelessness in his life: 'Just a bit tired, Sarge. I was on patrol last night.'

Ellen regarded him carefully, then smiled. 'Why don't you help Scobie manage the incident room today? Let others do the door-to-door.'

He managed a smile. 'Thanks, Sarge.'

With a nod, Ellen gathered her notes and returned to her office. The phone rang immediately; a reporter from the local newspaper was in the foyer. Ellen trudged down the stairs and out through the security door beside the front desk. The reporter was aged about thirty, jittery looking, hectically dressed in a swirling peasant skirt, purple singlet top, ropes of coloured beads and clanging bangles. Her smile was vivid. 'Hi! Thanks for seeing me!'

Ellen nodded non-committally and took her through to an interview room. The *Progress* was pretty much a weekly broadsheet of advertising, sporting results and flower-show photographs, but it couldn't afford to ignore a big local story. 'I have a child of my own,' the reporter said, when they were seated. 'I've been walking around the town, listening to what people are saying. There's a lot of concern out there, a lot of fear.'

Into the expectant pause, Ellen said, 'The police are doing everything possible. Search parties...'

'The word is, she was taken by a paedophile.'

'We have no evidence of that.'

'Come on, give me a decent quote.'

'The police are doing everything possible and welcome any information the public can give us,' said Ellen flatly.

The reporter rolled her eyes.

'You'll be at our re-enactment tomorrow?' Ellen asked.

'For what good it will do.'

They went to and fro for several more minutes, and then Ellen showed the woman out. Donna Blasko was there, sitting forlornly in the foyer. The reporter leapt on her. 'A quick word, Mrs Blasko?'

'Leave her alone, please,' Ellen said. 'Have some decency.' She happened to glance through the glass doors to the street outside. 'Look, there's Superintendent McQuarrie. He'll give you a statement.'

The reporter hurried out with small cries. Ellen turned to Donna, who was wringing her hands, and said gently, 'Donna, can I help you?'

'Any news?'

'Not yet, but we're hopeful.'

'I feel I should be doing something.'

You're doing more than enough, spreading alarm about abductions and paedophile gangs. Ellen took her to a quiet corner of the canteen. They sipped the awful coffee. 'The best thing you can do is maintain things at home, Donna. For your sake and your other daughter's. And Justin's,' she added. 'I understand why you wanted to come in for an update, but we all need you to be strong, at home.'

'It's hard,' Donna Blasko said.

In an office just along the corridor, van Alphen and Kellock were looking out at Superintendent McQuarrie, who was standing on the forecourt of the police station, talking to a reporter. A photographer was snapping away discreetly. Kellock exchanged a wry grin with van Alphen and returned to his seat. 'Close the door,' Kellock said.

Van Alphen complied and sat too, resting his heels on the edge of Kellock's desk, 'Destry got what it takes, you reckon?'

Kellock shrugged. 'She's all right. Covering all the bases.'

It was almost lunchtime. They had a few minutes before getting back to Katie Blasko. 'I saw Nick Jarrett in the street yesterday,' van Alphen said.

Kellock gazed at him bleakly. 'And?'

'The prick grinned at me.'

They thought back to Jarrett in the Supreme Court on Thursday afternoon, the crime that had put him there, the fact that he was a killer and roaming free again. 'I wanted to wipe it off him,' van Alphen continued.

Kellock nodded. He and van Alphen went back a long way. 'The Jarrett name cropped up last night. John Tankard ran a plate number.'

Van Alphen stared at him. 'The Jarretts were out and about, committing burglaries.'

'Probably.'

'Let's get Tank's version.'

John Tankard had almost fallen asleep over a pile of folders when Senior Sergeant Kellock called him. He made his way downstairs to Kellock's office, the bad feelings of last night's creepy encounter on the back roads still on his mind. Kellock's door was wide open, Sergeant van Alphen sprawled in the office chair across from him. Tank could tell from the way their faces shut down that they were cooking up something.

Kellock spotted him. 'Come in, John.'

'Sir?'

'You were on duty last night?'

Where was this going? Tank hadn't made a formal report of his encounter with the Jarrett clan. He darted his gaze from Kellock to van Alphen and back again. 'Sir.'

'Anything out of the usual happen?'

'Not really, sir.'

They watched him, expressionless but fully disbelieving and barely civil, a cop's gaze. After a while, Kellock said, 'The collators have been looking at a spate of recent burglaries.'

Tank nodded. The civilian collators charted chronologies, friendship networks, incident patterns. He knew where this was going. 'Sir?'

Van Alphen spoke for the first time. 'Look, John, don't fuck us around, all right?'

Tank went wobbly inside. Of course his numberplate requests last night had been noted by Kellock and van Alphen. 'Sir, the Jarretts.'

'That's better,' Kellock said. 'Where?'

Tank told them. 'They weren't doing anything at the time.'

'That's because they'd just done it,' said van Alphen, 'an aggravated burglary a couple of kilometres from where you saw them.'

'Oh.'

'It was only a matter of time,' Kellock said. 'The occupant was home, and they beat the shit out of him, older bloke, put him in hospital.' He paused. 'Was Nick Jarrett among these guys you encountered?'

'Yes, sir.'

Van Alphen gave his sharkish smile. 'You didn't log it in.'

'Sir, there was no crime being committed and—'

'Our collators depend on that kind of intelligence gathering, John.'

'Sorry, sir, won't happen again.'

There was a pause, and then something happened, a silent communication between Kellock and van Alphen that John Tankard couldn't decipher.

'That will be all, constable,' said Kellock. 'Go home, put your feet up. Big day tomorrow.'

16

In Mawson's Bluff, Hal Challis was feeling seriously housebound. At mid-afternoon, his father said gently, 'Take yourself off for a walk, son.'

'But what if—'

'What if I die?'

'Cut it out, Dad.'

'Vital signs are in good shape. Heart, lungs, liver, bowels, bladder. Well, enough said about the bladder.'

Challis had heard him at night, slipper-shuffling to and from the bathroom. Several times.

'If you're sure.'

'I'm sure.'

And so Challis walked around Mawson's Bluff for a couple of hours. The town was laid out in a simple grid, with side streets branching off the main street, which was part of the highway. It felt good to get his legs and heart pumping. He was curious to see that no one was about. There were clues to the presence of humans—cars parked in driveways and out in the street—but everyone was inside, spending a dutiful Sunday with relatives. Curtains were drawn over every window. Here and there a lawn sprinkler hissed, a cat arched its back, a dog wandered out from a driveway. Challis heard TV sport at a couple of the houses. The town was low, flattened, almost asleep, and all along the drooping telephone and power lines were the small-town birds, waiting.

He wandered into the grounds of the primary school, crossing dry grass and red dirt, stopping long enough to try the hip-hugging playground slide with an antic joy before continuing among the gum and pepper trees, drawing in their scent. And then, pushing through a cypress hedge behind the school, taking a short cut he remembered from his childhood, he came to the town's sportsground: football oval, tennis courts, lawn bowls rinks and a tiny enclosed swimming pool.

And there was his niece. Eve wasn't doing anything, just watching four other teenagers as they hit a tennis ball on one of the courts, a raucous game of doubles without a net. Like Eve, they wore cargo pants, T-shirts and trainers. They called to him, 'Hi, Hal!' He had no idea who they were.

Eve spun around, startled. He'd last seen her at his mother's funeral last year. Back then she'd been wearing a sombre dress, tall, slim and striking but utterly grief-stricken, her face raw with it. He saw that an underlying sadness still lingered, even as she ran at him like a delighted kid and hugged him fiercely.

'Hi, gorgeous,' he said.

She rested her jaw on his shoulder. 'It's so good to see you, Uncle Hal.'

'Same here.'

She let him go. 'I've been meaning to drop in. How's Gramps?'

'Cranky.'

She cocked her head, amused, but also half serious. 'He's never cranky with me.'

'That's because you're perfect.'

'True.'

They sat on a bench and watched her friends play. The sun washed over them and Challis felt easy, some of his cares evaporating.

'Are you staying long?'

'As long as it takes,' he said.

Eve sighed and edged closer to him. He couldn't be a father to her, or even much of an uncle, but did she want something like that from him? He scarcely knew her, and wondered if the things he might say to her, or the very act of saying them, would perplex her. He put his arm around her and they chatted inconsequentially. 'Mum really needed a break,' she said at one point. 'Thanks, Uncle Hal.'

'Well, he is my old man.'

'But not easy.'

'No.' Challis reconsidered his reply. 'Look, your grandfather was never mean to us, he never hit us, he was a good father. It's just that he was...stern, inflexible.'

'Uh huh.'

They were silent. Eve said, 'He didn't like Dad much.'

'I know.'

Challis guessed that so long as Eve didn't know where her father was, or what he'd done, or even if he was alive or dead, she couldn't say a proper goodbye to him. The parents of Ellen Destry's missing kid would be feeling that too, only more acutely. How could he broach it with Eve, that he'd been thinking of Gavin, been doing some digging? Maybe Eve, like her mother, didn't want him to do that.

Eve sighed. 'I wish it was the end of the year.'

It seemed to Challis that her words were loaded with meaning. On an immediate level she was saying that she should be at home studying for her final exams, not mucking around with her friends, even if it was a Sunday. She was also saying that her grandfather's decline was bad timing—not that she was blaming him. And finally she was saying that the future was huge and beckoning. What were her dreams? Why didn't he know? He thought back to the culture of the high school and the town when he was eighteen. It had been assumed by teachers, parents and the kids themselves that you would marry each other and remain in the district. You didn't leave—or certainly not to attend a university.

He found himself saying, 'What will your friends do next year?'

She was sitting so close to him that she had to scoot away to gauge his face. She shrugged. 'Nursing. Teachers' college. Home on the farm.'

'You?'

'Not sure yet. I'd love to travel, just fly overseas and move around, stay in youth hostels and get waitressing jobs for a while, you know?'

She was wistful and it was heartbreaking. 'Do it,' Challis said fervently.

'I don't know. I can't. What about Mum, here all alone?'

'*Do it!*'

He'd startled her. 'Yes, sir,' she said, snapping him a salute.

'You'll come back refreshed,' he said, moderating his tone, trying to be a wise uncle or father. 'University will be a breeze.'

A white Toyota Land Cruiser with police markings pulled up. A policeman got out, tall, heavyset and scowling in a crisp tan uniform. A sergeant. 'Oh shit,' said Eve, and one of the boys grew wary and still.

'What?'

'It's Sergeant Wurfel. He's super anal.'

They watched Wurfel advance on the boy. 'Who's your friend?'

'Mark Finucane.'

A Finucane. Challis wanted to say, 'That figures.' Then the sergeant clasped the boy, who went rigid and shouted, 'Fucking leave off.'

Eve clutched Challis. 'Uncle Hal, stop him.'

Challis had to be careful. He approached, gave his name but not his occupation or rank. 'May I ask what's going on?'

The sergeant gazed at him tiredly. 'No offence, sir, but am I obliged to tell you?'

Eve reached past Challis to put her arm around the Finucane boy. 'Leave him alone. He hasn't done anything.'

Wurfel blocked her. 'Settle down, Eve, okay? We just need to speak to Mark about a couple of things.'

'*Speak* to him? I know what that means.'

Sergeant Wurfel grew very still. 'Eve, if you get in my face, I'll take you down to the station, too.'

Challis said quietly, 'There's no need for that.'

Wurfel looked fed up, and stared at all of them one by one. 'You want to know why I want to question him? Your little pal took the hearse for a joyride last night, okay?'

He paused, staring at Challis. 'You think this is funny?'

Challis straightened his face. One night when he was sixteen he and a couple of others had stolen a ride in a shire tip truck. 'Not at all. Eve, sweetheart, let the man do his job.'

'Yeah, well, it's not fair.'

Her temper was up, her colour high, her eyes flashing, but then it evaporated. They all watched while Wurfel opened the passenger door for Mark Finucane, who gave them a quick grin and a cocky thumbs up.

'Evo,' said one of Eve's friends, 'want a game? Hal, a game?'

'Sure,' they both said.

That evening Ellen Destry called him. He felt a strange relief, realising that he'd been waiting. There was no reason why they should call each other regularly, or turns about, but he had opened that possibility when he'd called her on Friday.

Her mood was flat. 'Is Katie Blasko getting to you?'

'Yes.'

'Tell me.'

'I can't help feeling that I've fumbled the ball. I let myself be blinded by her dysfunctional family, when I should have been concentrating on harm from *outside* it.'

'In most cases it is internal,' Challis said. He found himself telling her about Gavin Hurst, and the effects on Eve.

Ellen grunted. 'Like the poet said, your parents fuck you up.

Larrayne is so prickly with me these days.' She paused. 'And when I'm old and infirm, the poor thing will feel obliged to look after me— or maybe not. Sorry, Hal, insensitive of me, given your current situation.'

He laughed. He wasn't offended. A comfortable silence settled around them. 'What's your next step?'

'Tomorrow we re-enact Katie's bike ride home from school.'

Challis experienced a sudden and intense mental flash of Waterloo and the flat streets near the mangrove flats. He could almost smell them. Then it occurred to him that for a long time after he'd left Mawson's Bluff he'd smelt dust, wheat and sheep. Home is where the nose is, he thought.

'It might trigger something.'

'A lot of false leads, probably.'

17

Monday.

Ellen started the day with Donna Blasko and Justin Pedder, who seemed confused about Katie's bike ('It was a blue bike.' 'No, it was purple.' 'It had a basket on the handlebars.' 'No, that was her old bike.'). Sighing, she drove to the bike shop in High Street and borrowed a purple bike and helmet. The bike shop used to be Café Laconic, and a jeans-and-T-shirt shop before that, so she guessed it would be selling something else this time next year. Ellen missed Café Laconic. You couldn't get decent coffee anywhere in Waterloo now.

As she was wheeling the bike to her car, a voice said, 'Need a hand?'

She turned. Laurie Jarrett, with two teenage boys. Being Jarretts, the boys knew who she was, and smirked. The smirk said, 'We won, you lost.'

'How's it feel, copper?' sneered one of the boys.

Laurie surprised her. He thumped the back of the boy's head, not hard, and said, 'A bit of respect, okay?'

'Ow!' sulked the boy.

Ellen glanced at Jarrett, trying to read him. Despite herself, she was compelled by his looks. She was fascinated by the shapeliness of his hands and head, unnoticed by her before. He was dressed neatly and, unlike the other males—and females—of his clan, he didn't carry scars or tattoos. He wasn't overweight. He didn't smell like a brewery. His eyes were clear. No giveaway facial tics or hand tremors. She'd heard he was a charmer. He lived with two women, sisters, apparently. There was also a daughter, Alysha, twelve or thirteen, with learning difficulties, whom Jarrett doted on.

'Help you with the bike?' he said again.

Why not? She watched him stow it in her car.

'Present for your kid?' he asked.

'For a re-enactment,' she said. 'Katie Blasko, her route home from school. You've got a large network: pass the word around.'

He nodded abruptly and left, the boys trailing him.

What had all that been about?

She returned to the station. By late morning she'd obtained reports of three recent abduction attempts on the Peninsula. In June a middle-aged man had tried to lure a ten year old boy into his car in Frankston South. Two months earlier, a young man grabbed the arm of an eight-year-old girl who was riding her bike to school in Mornington. And during the January school holidays, a nine-year-old boy had been lured out of his front yard by two young men, who had then been chased off by a neighbour.

No worthwhile descriptions. No trace evidence.

The long day passed. At 3 pm, she met Scobie and his daughter outside the gates of Katie Blasko's primary school. A dozen uniformed police were there, too, an open jeep fitted with a public-address system, and plenty of media. Scattered among the spectators and the media pack were plain-clothed officers, who would video and photograph the onlookers.

Roslyn Sutton resembled Katie Blasko in colouring, height and build. Ellen crouched beside her. Roslyn looked very pleased with herself. An unappealing child, Ellen had often thought. She smiled stiffly. 'All set?'

Roslyn immediately planted her foot on the pedal and hunched her shoulders as though to speed away. 'Steady on, not yet, darling,' her father said.

Ellen didn't think she could bear to see all of Scobie's doting love just then, pouring out, and avoided his eye. She smiled at Roslyn again. 'The kids don't get out until 3.15. Wait until we hear the bell, then a while longer for them to appear with their bags. Katie was neither early nor late leaving school last Thursday, so we'll allow time for half the kids to be picked up or start walking or riding home before *you* set off, okay?'

'Uh huh.'

'Your role is very important. We're very proud of you.'

Roslyn Sutton knew it. She couldn't mask it.

'Ride slowly,' Ellen said. 'Apparently Katie rode slowly, too, but we also need time for people to watch you, and perhaps remember something. Okay?'

'Yes.'

At 3.23, the caravan set out, Ellen standing in the Jeep with the microphone. Several times during the forty minutes that followed, she repeated the same message: 'A child has gone missing. Her name is Katie Blasko and she's ten years old. We are re-enacting her ride home from school last Thursday afternoon. Did you see Katie on that day or any other day, either alone or in the company of someone? Did she deviate from her routine or route in any way? Any help you can give us, however trivial it might seem, could be vital in finding her. You may approach any of our officers or phone the Waterloo police station.'

People wanted to be helpful. In the days that followed, they flooded Ellen with useless information.

Operation Calling Card—so-called because their burglar liked to leave an unflushed turd at the scene of every break-in—came together quickly for Kellock and van Alphen. Of course, they could have obtained DNA from the calling card and matched it to Nick Jarrett, but you'd have to be keen. Besides, in seven of the eight burglaries so far, the owners had come home, traced the offending odour to its source, and flushed the evidence away, feeling doubly violated.

So van Alphen and Kellock used a time-honoured method: while CIU and most of the uniforms were out looking for the missing kid, they put the hard word on some of their informants. This led them to Ivan Henniker, who had a speed habit, the speed produced in a fortified laboratory by the Yanqui motorcycle gang and distributed by members of the Jarrett family in the Waterloo area. Henniker feared the Jarretts and wanted to be free of them, but he also needed access to a ready supply. A dilemma, but van Alphen and Kellock helped him to resolve it. Surprising how effective a telephone book can be, in a soundless, windowless back room.

'Your girlfriend works in Waterloo Travel?'

'Yes,' sobbed Henniker. A jumpy, scrawny guy, limp hair owing to the speed he'd run through his system over the years.

'She gives you a list of names and addresses of who's away on holiday? So we should be arresting her, too?'

'No! No, don't do that. She's got this little notebook computer.'

'Brings her work home with her.'

'I access it when she's taking a shower,' said Henniker.

'Lovely guy,' said van Alphen to Kellock.

'A real prince.'

Henniker flushed. 'Do you want the details, or not?'

'Fire away.'

'She's got this file, travel insurance, of people away on holiday.'

'And you pass on names and addresses to the Jarretts.'

'Yeah. They'll kill me for this.'

'Not unless we kill you first,' said Kellock. 'Who in the Jarrett clan?'

'Nick.'

Van Alphen and Kellock beamed at each other.

'Here's what we want you to do,' van Alphen said, proceeding to lay it out for Henniker.

'Nick will kill me,' said Henniker miserably. 'He's a mad bastard. They all are.'

'We'll protect you,' van Alphen said unconvincingly.

18

Why do I do it to myself? wondered Pam Murphy late that afternoon.

Tests, exams and formal challenges of any kind always made her anxious. So why had she applied to do this course?

She'd been up since 5 am, when she'd showered, had breakfast, packed, and driven to the training facility, a converted youth camp in the foothills outside Melbourne. Prefabricated huts, a gym, swimming pool, running track, classrooms, dining hall and firing range. The morning had been aimed at seeing how fit they were. Pam, placed in the top five of her last three triathlons, had made it through without raising a sweat. The afternoon had involved a mock conflict-resolution scenario, which she'd stuffed up. This evening there would be a seminar. All in all, a testing regime of physical and intellectual activities aimed at sorting the wheat from the chaff. Two candidates had dropped out already.

Pam groaned, feeling stiff and sore. She was lying on a hard, monastic bed in a narrow room with flimsy walls. A guy in each of the adjacent rooms, and she wouldn't mind betting that both were snorers. Not many female candidates.

The second week might be better. They would attend further courses at the police academy in Glen Waverley, followed by a final week at Command Headquarters in the city. There had been other two-, three- and four-week courses over the past year, and this was the last round. If she graduated she'd be entitled to apply for detective positions.

If she graduated.

She lay there, needing a shower but too sore and tired to move, and thought about the pressures faced by your average cop, wondering why she stuck it out. Tests, exams, even promotions and transfers—all stress inducing. Malicious civilian complaints, which always had to be investigated and blotted your record. Giving court evidence, especially being cross-examined by snide, flash defence barristers.

And the day-to-day aggravations. Two weekends ago she and John Tankard had picked up a drunken thirteen-year-old girl at three in the morning, driven her home, and been screamed at by the parents for 'interfering' in the family's affairs. This year alone she'd attended five fatalities on the freeway—alcohol, drugs and speeding. Earlier in the year she'd arrested three teenagers from the Seaview Park estate who'd gone out armed with knives and machetes—'Just in case we get attacked by the Jarretts.' A month before that she'd helped social workers remove three children aged under ten from a house in Seaview Park, the children starving and showing signs of years of abuse. They'd kicked and screamed: 'I want my mum, I want my dad.'

Her bedside alarm sounded. She had an hour free to study before dinner and the evening seminar. Stretching, groaning, she told herself to see the following days as an opportunity to learn rather than be found wanting for what she didn't know or couldn't achieve. She took her little transistor radio with her into the shower, turned it to the 6 pm news.

The water gushed, drowning out the first item.

John Tankard was feeling a lot better that Monday. Good sleep last night, new car, Pam Murphy not around to bust his chops, an early finish time. He still burned inside, reliving that night on the back road behind the estate, but sensed that Kellock and van Alphen had a plan in mind.

He finished work at 3 pm, then shot up to Berwick in time to pick his little sister up from school. Nat was full of awe, running her hand over the duco of his new car. 'Cool,' she said. She was skinny where he was fat, olive-skinned where he was fair, quick and darting where he was slow. He hated to think of strangers laying their hands on her.

He took her for a spin. She bubbled over, madly waving at her mates. He felt protective. He felt helpless. How could you have sex with a kid? How sick was that?

On the way back he sent a text message to the woman he knew only as Terri, confirming drinks in the Chaos Bar at 6 pm. He'd met her through an on-line dating service. She sounded hot in her e-mails and text messages, her voice over the phone low, pleasantly husky. She'd sent photos: dark hair, humorous eyes, perhaps a tad round-faced but that often spelt big tits. In just a couple of hours, his laughing gear around a glass of ale, he'd know one way or the other.

You could get lucky and score on a first date. You were desperate, the chick was desperate (that's why you were using a dating service, right?), so hitting the mattress was the logical outcome. But Tank had a secret weapon. He'd read on the Internet how attraction and desire boiled down to the odours released by the body. A bloke subconsciously picks up the scent when a woman is ready to mate. Women are turned on by something virile in a guy's perspiration. Testosterone? Pheromones? Something like that. Or maybe he'd misunderstood the whole thing, the technical side of it, the long words.

Still, he spent late afternoon in the gym and went straight to the Chaos Bar without showering, a touch of healthy, moist heat in his face, hair and neck. Did the women turn their heads as he passed among them? Tank strode tall, that Monday afternoon at one minute to six. Chicks gasping for it, left, right and centre, nurses, receptionists, even a couple of young lawyers he'd seen around the magistrates' court.

To the table in the corner, where Terri waited, a pretty face, yeah, but short, tubby, her butt overflowing the chair. Before he could stop himself, the words popped into his head and straight out of his mouth: 'Looks-wise, you haven't been exactly honest with me, have you?'

She flushed. They stared at each other. Suddenly she recoiled. 'Body odour-wise, you really stink.'

She got up and left.

Well, shit.

He watched her go, his eyes drawn to the street beyond the smoky glass, where his fire-engine-red Mazda was being ticketed by a parking inspector.

Double shit.

His mobile rang. It was the producer of 'Evening Update'. 'I need all you can give me on Katie Blasko.'

'I've already given you everything.'

'Where she was found, who by, was she abused,' the producer said.

'Huh?'

Tank's gaze went to the wide-screen TV on the wall. Later you got music clips—Kylie Minogue's lovely arse, Beyoncé's crotch—but right now it was the six o'clock news, live feed coming in, Waterloo in the background, a reporter in the foreground, the familiar shot of Katie Blasko tucked into the top corner of the screen.

Alive? Dead? He strained to hear.

19

Eddie Tran had come a fair way in life. He'd eventually eased his way out of the Vietnamese gang scene in Melbourne—the co-ordinated shoplifting raids, the drug dealing, 'justice' and revenge enacted with machetes—and married a nice girl who, like him, was the offspring of parents who'd spent time in a refugee camp in Malaysia in the early 1980s and later been allowed to settle in Australia. Eddie and his wife had lived on the Peninsula for five years now. They'd run a $2 shop for a while, but there were too many such shops, and now they were partners in a bakery near the roundabout on High Street, Waterloo. They baked a tray of Vietnamese buns occasionally, but mostly the locals wanted white bread, doughnuts, scones, vanilla slice and apricot Danishes. And freshly made sandwiches at lunchtime.

The women in Eddie's life ran the business, his wife and her mother and sister. There wasn't a lot for Eddie to do, once he'd completed the baking every morning. And so he worked for CleanSwift, a contract cleaning business that called on Eddie and a couple of other immigrants once or twice a week for the shit jobs.

Literally. For example, the shire provided emergency and short-term housing for needy people: single-parent families, alcoholics who'd burnt down their own houses, teenagers who'd been kicked out of home, refugees from northern Africa, the hopeless, the luckless, the disgraced and distressed. Eddie saw people and a way of life that most Australians didn't see. He saw it because he wasn't an Australian, not in their eyes. He'd been born here, but he wasn't Anglo-Celtic. The number of astonished looks he got when he opened his mouth and out came a broad Aussie accent!

So it was usually Eddie and the other guys, a Somali and an Iraqi, who were sent to clean up whenever one of the shire's emergency-housing properties fell vacant. They literally scrubbed shit off the walls, sometimes. Eddie had studied Psychology at Swinburne for a couple of years, before dropping out, and knew that smearing excrement on the walls was a symptom of some kind of psychosis. The emergency houses provided by the shire were very ordinary but maybe felt like prison walls to some poor individuals. The number of times Eddie and the guys had torn up carpets and thrown them out! Eddie, a fastidious man, and luckier than these poor souls, nevertheless found it hard not to despise them. Spend five minutes a day picking up after yourself, he'd think, five minutes going from room to room with a garbage bag, and you wouldn't have to live like pigs. Pizza boxes, dozens of bottles and cans, unidentifiable smears and excretions, mouldy hamburger buns, used tampons and condoms, syringes, the carcasses of cockroaches, mice, rats and family pets, empty foil packets, scratched CDs, overdue Blockbuster videos, bras and knickers, unpaired shoes and earrings, toys, dust balls, skin magazines, hair clips, combs, cellophane wrappers like the husks of strange creatures.

Sometimes it would take days to clean a place. Then the painters would come in, the plasterers to fix holes in the internal walls (fists? boots? heads?), the locksmith, the carpet layer. Big, contemptuous guys, usually, who couldn't see why the shire would want to prettify a house just so another lot of crazies, addicts, immigrants and no-hopers could have somewhere nice to live. What was the point? Eddie sympathised with this view, while trying not to think of the conditions that his parents had lived in before they settled in the lucky country.

De Soto Lane lay at the forgotten end of the little township of

Warrawee, ten kilometres northeast of Penzance Beach. Eddie and the guys parked the van outside number 24, a small brick-veneer house set well back from the road among blackberry canes and rusting cars lost in chest-high spring grasses. A timber yard sat on one side of it, behind a high cyclone fence. Behind it was a market gardener's packing shed. Opposite was a stand of tall pines, black cockatoos clinging to the top branches and squawking softly as they cracked cones with their powerful beaks. Amid the pine trees was a small brick house with drawn curtains. An old woman was pottering about in her garden. Otherwise the lane was sparsely populated, with the only other visible house a new but ugly McMansion, two storeys, red tiles, four-car garage, lots of off-white pillars and columns, a vast landscaped garden under construction. The market gardener lived there, Eddie guessed, or would live there soon, for there were heaps of soil and bricks lying around.

He shivered. He'd hate to live out here. He'd seen from the street directory that there was a Cadillac Court, a Mercedes Terrace, and a Buick Drive. Did they make De Soto cars any more? He didn't think so. He'd asked the other guys, but they didn't know what the hell he was talking about.

Eddie assessed number 24 rapidly that Monday afternoon. 1960s vintage, with only a handful of small, low-ceilinged rooms: living room, kitchen, laundry, bathroom, hallway and two bedrooms. He knew this at a glance. He'd cleaned dozens like it. The lawn needed mowing, he noticed, weeds thrived in the garden beds, scaly mould patches covered the roof tiles. He sniffed experimentally as he approached the front door. Often you could assess the size of the job within by the stench factor.

Nothing discernible.

Eddie went in first.

No furniture, no crud lying about. There was dust, sure, scuffs on the walls, but the place wasn't too bad. The carpet would need a shampoo, but that's all. The smudges would come off the walls okay.

With any luck, they could be out of here by lunchtime tomorrow. Eddie made these assessments as he walked from the front door to the sitting room.

Then he heard a whimper and his skin crept. The other guys went round-eyed and took a step back involuntarily.

'Anyone there?' Eddie called, being the boss.

That whimper again. With a hammering heart, Eddie approached the room that in most of these houses was the smaller bedroom. He tried the door; it was locked. He rapped his knuckles. 'Anyone home?'

More whimpering. Eddie figured it could be passed off as damage caused by the previous occupants if he forced the door, so he went out to the van and returned with a crowbar and splintered the door away from the jamb.

The stench was shocking. She was naked and afraid and lying in her own wastes. She scrabbled away from him on a mattress in a room decorated as a nursery, one wrist tethered to a hook in the wall. Eddie was nominally a Catholic; he crossed himself. 'Little girl, little girl,' he cooed, the other guys coming in behind him then, hovering at his elbow. Who knew the trials, heartaches and torture they had experienced and witnessed in their own countries? Yet they rushed past him with distressed and comforting cries and gathered her up.

20

Challis spent the day chatting with his father, reading aloud from *Mr Midshipman Hornblower*, and preparing simple meals. His childhood home seemed smaller than he'd remembered; stuffier, older, less well cared for. Since his mother's death, his father had lost the will to be house-proud. Had nothing to live for, in fact. It was sad; it broke Challis's heart. He wanted to make things better. He wanted to run away.

'Cup of tea, Dad?' he said at four o'clock, the afternoon sun angling into the back room, lighting the dust motes.

His father reached his right hand across his stomach and pulled his left into view. He examined his wristwatch for a while—as if time had now become a puzzle, where once it had ruled his life.

'I'd like to eat at five, five-thirty.'

Challis said nothing. At five-twenty he'd microwave the chicken soup that Meg had left in the fridge, grill a lamb chop, boil half a carrot, and add a lettuce leaf and a slice of tomato. Would he himself eat at five-thirty? Yes, to be companionable. Besides, being a policeman had accustomed him to snatching dinner at all hours of the night and day. He was adaptable.

But the evening would be long. TV reception was poor this far north. A couple of his mother's opera and ballet videos in the cabinet under the TV set, a short shelf of CDs: light classics, mostly, The Seekers, Welsh male choirs. He couldn't go to the pub and leave his father alone. It was too soon to ask friends around—and what friends, anyway?

There was his laptop. Work on the discussion paper on regional policing that he still hadn't written for Superintendent McQuarrie? Play solitaire? Somehow use the Web to find Gavin Hurst?

Actually, there was one thing he could do. He'd been restoring an old aeroplane before things had got so complicated in his life. It was gathering dust in a hangar on the little regional airport near Waterloo, and he knew, as one did know these things, that his *not* completing the restoration was symptomatic of a malaise, of a life that marked time, that waited when it should act. He'd feel better about himself if he went on-line and searched for missing parts—instrument-panel switches, for example.

The doorbell chimed, the sound bringing back vivid memories of his childhood, when friends had visited this house. The feeling strengthened as Challis made his way along the passageway to the front door, past his mother's framed tapestries of English rural scenes, thatched cottages and haystacks, past the upended shell casing from the Second World War, now crammed with walking sticks and umbrellas.

And continued when he saw Rob Minchin on the doorstep.

'Hal, old son.'

'Rob.'

They shook hands, then embraced awkwardly. 'How's my patient?'

'Cranky.'

'Unchanged, in other words.'

Like Challis, Minchin had gone away, trained, and returned to the town. Unlike Challis, he'd stayed. He was the only doctor in the district, run ragged by surgery consultations, hospital rounds and house calls. He travelled huge distances, attending home births on remote farms, talking through the anxieties of lonely widows, taking the temperatures of sick children, pronouncing death when stockmen ran their mustering bikes into gullies and broke their necks. He was also the on-call pathologist for the region.

And Challis's one-time friend. Time and distance had weakened the friendship, and fine distinctions in ambition and personality had become marked disparities, but, still, history always counts for something, and Challis and Minchin grinned at each other now.

'Wish the circumstances were better,' the doctor said.

Shorter than Challis, Minchin had grown solid over the years. He was fair-skinned and had always looked a little pink from sunburn or embarrassment. His hair was straight, reddish, limp and needed cutting. He'd been married, but his wife had run away with his partner in the little practice he'd inherited from his father.

'It's a waiting game,' Challis murmured.

They went into the sitting room, where the old man was slumped in his chair. Minchin hurried to his side, but then a ripping snore stopped him.

Challis laughed. 'Kept me awake last night.'

Minchin nodded. 'Might as well let him sleep. I'm just checking in. No scares?'

He meant the series of minor strokes. Everyone was waiting for the big one. 'No,' said Challis. 'Offer you a drink?'

'Better make it coffee.'

'If you can call it that,' Challis said, leading the way to the kitchen.

When it was poured, Minchin asked, 'How's Meg holding up?'

The guy's still in love with her, Challis thought. He saw how he could use that. 'Not too bad, given all she's had to deal with in the past few years.'

'Yes.'

'Gavin running out on her like that.'

'Yeah,' said Minchin flatly.

'Rob,' said Challis after a considering pause, 'without breaching patient confidentiality, what sort of state was he in before he disappeared?'

'You asked me that at the time.'

'I didn't take it in.'

Minchin leaned forward across the kitchen table, dropping his voice in case the old man was listening. 'Gavin was veering from one extreme to the other. I prescribed medication to level him out, but I don't know if he ever took it.' He paused. 'He hit Meg a couple of times, you know.'

Challis nodded sagely, but he hadn't known. Just then, Minchin slapped at his solid thigh, leaned to one side and fetched a mobile phone from his side pocket. 'Minchin. Yep. Yep. Oh, Christ, be right there.'

He pocketed his phone again and looked at Challis. 'Do you know Ted Anderson?'

'No.'

'Wife died of cancer five years ago, leaving him with a baby to bring up. He's gone off the Pass.'

'Gone off the Pass'. Everyone knew what that meant. 'Killed?'

Minchin nodded. 'The kid's okay, but trapped in the car.'

'You'd better go, Rob.'

'Tell your old man I'll look in again when I can.'

'Will do.'

Small-town tragedies, Challis thought, watching Minchin drive away. Next week it might be an ambulance officer coming upon his own wife in a burning car. Last year five teenagers had been killed when they failed to beat a train over a level crossing. When he was growing up, a bride-to-be from the next town was killed on her way to her wedding. As a young constable in Mawson's Bluff, he'd attended when a jack-knifing semi-trailer had wiped out a family of five. There was never an end to it.

He was drawn back into the house by the ringing of the phone. 'Hal?'

'Ells,' he said.

And she told him about Katie Blasko.

21

The atmosphere crackled on Tuesday morning, affecting everyone in the Waterloo police station, uniformed officers, detectives and civilian staff alike. It was most evident at the briefing, the mood heightened and expectant as Ellen began to talk. Ellen herself was fierce, dynamic, showing sorrow, disgust and anger. Those seated close to her saw that her eyes were damp as she described the house, the room, the small, abused body.

Then, unwinding, she got down to business. 'As you can see, there are fewer of us today.'

She didn't need to explain why. Word always got around the station quickly. Now that Katie Blasko had been found alive, Superintendent McQuarrie wanted those uniformed constables who had been on the search detail back on regular duties, and was allowing Ellen only a small team to investigate the abduction. Van Alphen and Kellock were not obliged to attend, but had offered their services, arguing that they knew the case and could allocate uniformed assistance from time to time.

'Let's start with the house,' she said. 'Our man was taking a chance, using the shire's emergency housing.'

She looked around the room, inviting reasons for that. It was van Alphen who answered. 'Those houses are sometimes empty for days, weeks,' he said. 'People move on without informing their social workers, parole officers or the shire.'

'You're saying that many people could have known about that particular house, and that it would be empty for a while?'

'Yes.'

Scobie supplied another detail. 'I spoke to the shire housing officer. There's been a sudden increase in demand. The order to clean De Soto Lane came in yesterday morning. Clearly our man wasn't expecting that.'

John Tankard stirred as if making a vital point. 'Meaning he could come back.'

Kellock smiled at him without much humour. 'Unlikely. Have you seen the publicity? But I'm sure we can roster you to watch the place.'

'Senior Sergeant,' Tankard muttered, going red.

'What scenario are we looking at here?' demanded Ellen. 'They keep her prisoner for a few days, dress her up in school uniforms, frilly underwear, nighties, film each other having sex with her, then let her go?'

'Or kill and dump her,' Scobie said.

Ellen made a brief, bitter gesture. 'Meanwhile the neighbours can't tell us a thing.'

She'd examined the house last night and again early that morning. It was well chosen, for there were no neighbours to speak of. The builder erecting the market gardener's new house had recently gone bankrupt and so no one had been working at the site. The few workers employed in the timber yard and the market garden had seen nothing, owing to trees, shrubbery and high fences. The elderly couple living in the little house opposite were used to seeing cars come and go at 24 De Soto Lane, and had paid no attention to recent activities there. 'So long as they aren't noisy and aren't going to murder us in our beds, we leave them be,' the old woman had told Ellen.

'But didn't they *think* about what they were seeing?' Scobie Sutton demanded now. 'Didn't they *hear* anything?'

Because of his height, he sometimes sprawled like an arrangement of twigs, but this morning he sat stiffly upright, as if too distressed to concentrate. Ellen didn't want that. 'Scobie, take Constable Tankard and question everyone again. Are there surveillance cameras on the timber yard or the packing shed? Did the mailman deliver to the house late last week and again yesterday? Track down anyone who bought timber or fruit and vegetables in De Soto Lane over the past several days—go back prior to the day Katie was abducted. Did the old couple have visitors during the past few days? All right?'

Scobie stared at the coffee rings on the incident room table. He gave a shuddering sigh.

'*Scobie!*'

He blinked and jerked. 'Yep. Sure.'

Ellen saw Kellock and van Alphen watching her appraisingly, the former built like a wrestler, the latter slender and hawkish and surprisingly like Hal Challis. Then van Alphen dropped his scrutiny, the narrow planes of his face relaxing into a slight, commiserative smile. 'Forensics, Ellen?'

She shook her head bleakly. 'Not as much as I'd hoped for. We've got a handful of prints and partials, but most of those will match people who have recently lived in the house, some of whom will be in the system for a range of unrelated offences—mothers jailed for dealing, kids for burglary, etcetera, etcetera. But all will have to be eliminated, which will take time. On the other hand, the cleaners do a pretty good job between tenants, and the last tenant, a battered wife, says she cleaned pretty thoroughly after herself, so we might pick up fresh prints.'

'Only if our guy didn't wear gloves,' Kellock said.

'True.'

Van Alphen was watching her again but not seeing her. 'What is it, Van?'

'He might have got careless.'

'How?'

'When he's finished with her, is he going to kill her? Take her somewhere and release her? Either way, he's not going to leave her in the house, is he?'

Ellen nodded. 'You're right. He knew the house would be vacant. He knew he had a few days. Whether he released her alive, or killed and dumped her, he would clean up after himself, with the obvious benefit of the cleaners coming along afterwards and accounting for anything he overlooked. It means he knew about the house and the emergency housing scheme. It was bad luck for him that the cleaners came along sooner than expected.'

'Yes.'

'An insider, someone who works for the shire or social services,' Ellen said. 'Scobie, can you look into that?'

'Yes.'

'Thank you. Now, forensics. We have a blanket, towels, a mattress, a chain and manacle, a range of clothing. And dog hairs.'

'Dog hairs,' Kellock said, throwing down his pen. 'Could have come from anywhere. She patted a dog on the way home from school. A friend took a dog to school. The neighbours have a dog. Maybe it's cross contamination: the cleaners carried dog hair in on their clothing or shoes. Can we get DNA? Do we have a dog to match it to? Dog hairs,' he said in disgust.

'Look,' Ellen said, 'I know we're all frustrated by this case. But we don't have much to go on, and the dog hairs were found at the scene and have to be accounted for.'

'I heard there was blood, Sarge,' John Tankard said.

'Yes, but it might all be from the child.'

Of course, they were hoping otherwise. They were hoping their abductor had been scratched by Katie, or suffered a nosebleed. If his DNA was in Crimtrac, the national database of DNA, fingerprints, palm prints and paedophiles, then they could make an arrest and move on. In the best-case scenario, Crimtrac would give them a specific name, face and record, but Crimtrac was also proving itself helpful in solving cold cases, where identities were unknown, for most crims were repeat offenders, and most graduated from low-level to serious crimes. They cut themselves on glass pulling a modest burglary, and years later found themselves arrested for leaving DNA at a rape or murder scene. And Crimtrac was national, which helped in a country where the population was highly mobile. Twenty per cent of fingerprint inquiries lodged through Crimtrac led police to crimes committed hundreds, even thousands of kilometres away.

'Semen?' said Scobie. A good churchgoing man, it was a word he tiptoed around.

'The techs ran a black light over the whole house but didn't find any.'

'He used a condom.'

'Or washed everything. Bathed the girl afterwards,' van Alphen said. 'Ask her, Ellen.'

Ellen winced. She was not looking forward to that.

22

Katie Blasko had been taken to the Children's Hospital in the city. Ellen waited through the long morning. When the call came to say that Katie was well enough to be interviewed, Ellen was in the CIU tearoom, rinsing her coffee mug and trying to think of ways to further deface the sign that read: 'Don't expect someone else to wash up after you—you're not at home now.' She shook the water off her hands, flipped open her mobile phone. 'Scobie, we've got the okay. Meet you downstairs in five.'

She encountered Kees van Alphen on the stairs. 'Take me with you,' he said.

Ellen shook her head. 'I need your eyes on the records, Van. Sorry.'

He scowled, stalked away, unaware of Ellen's real reason for not wanting him with her when she interviewed Katie Blasko. Van Alphen was a prohibitive-looking man, and long estranged from his wife and teenage daughter: quite simply, Ellen felt that he would frighten the child.

She drove. Scobie Sutton could be an appalling passenger, given to outlining the daily inanities of his home life, but an even worse driver: slow, talkative and easily distracted. She was prepared to ask him to shut up if he got started, but he rode in silence that afternoon. He's still shocked, she thought. He's conflating Katie Blasko and his daughter.

She headed along the old Peninsula highway to Frankston, where the road widened, three lanes in and out, a ribbon of black bisecting hectares of low brick houses with tiled roofs. Frankston is Australia, she thought, with its modest, usually disappointed expectations and achievements, its anxieties and conservatism. We admire rapist footballers, own plasma TVs we can't afford, grow obese and vote to keep out strangers. Our fifteen-year-olds get poor educations and move on to senseless crimes, addiction, jail time or death behind the wheel of a stolen car, and if they make it past fifteen they can't find work. A great, banal sameness defines us, making us mostly soporific— but nasty if cornered. We're vicious with paedophiles, probably because we produce them. Ellen felt sick and sour and an atmosphere built up in the car, as if they both felt it.

She made an effort. 'It's a pity Pam Murphy can't be assigned to this. Good experience for her.'

Scobie stirred in the passenger seat. He wore old-fashioned aftershave, stale and dense in the confines of the CIU car. She watched out of the corner of her eye as he struggled to cross his long legs under the glove box.

'Yes.'

Ellen sighed and drove on, through the endless suburbs, and then finally along the river, the glassy office buildings of the city centre now clearly visible. The traffic raced and darted, unnerving her. She edged across to the outer lane, took the exit that would lead her to the hospital.

They were shown to a suite intended to comfort children whenever the authorities were obliged to step in with questions, intervention orders or counselling. The surfaces were soft, the colours cheery, the light muted. There was a TV set, a sound system, plenty of books and toys. Donna Blasko was seated on a sofa, cuddling Katie. A paediatric nurse, smiling, bouncy, like a big sister, sat in the corner. Scobie joined the nurse, leaving the interview to Ellen.

The first thing Ellen did was separate mother and daughter. 'Donna,' she murmured, 'I'd like you to sit with the others. That way Katie can concentrate for me, but know that you're still in the room.'

Looking doubtful, Donna complied. Katie immediately reached out, alarmed, but Donna reassured her, saying, 'It's all right, sweetheart, I'm right here.'

Out of Katie's direct line of sight, fortunately. Ellen smiled encouragingly at both of them. Katie swallowed, fighting down her panic, lost in a vast stretch of flowery upholstery. Donna said from her chair next to Scobie, 'If Katie can't hack it, I'm terminating. Terminating.'

'Of course,' said Ellen gently.

'Sweetie, the police just need to ask you some questions, okay?'

'Okay.'

Ellen smiled at Katie. 'My name is Ellen. That kind man is Scobie. He's got a daughter your age. And you know what? Yesterday she pretended to be you. We dressed her up like you, put her on a bike like yours, and she rode home from your school for us, to help jog people's memories.'

Katie, mouth open, in awe as she grasped the significance of the police effort and her notoriety, risked a meek smile at Scobie. Scobie returned it, a huge, transfiguring smile, one of great sweetness. Katie relaxed further and turned her attention back to Ellen.

'We want to catch the man who hurt you.'

'Catch *all* the men,' Katie said.

Ellen said carefully, 'How many were there?'

'I think four.'

Ellen closed her eyes briefly, opened them again. Her voice cracked a little. 'Four men. Can you describe them to me?'

Katie grimaced, wiping her palms on her thighs. She wore a striped hooded top over a pink T-shirt and yellow cargo pants, the colours pastelly and new. Red canvas shoes. Pink ankle socks. Her fingernails were bright red, but chipped, and Ellen realised with a shock that the men had probably painted them for her.

'They had grey hair and moustaches,' Katie said. 'And glasses.'

'All of them?'

'Yes.'

Disguises, Ellen thought. 'Anything else?'

Katie tossed in distress. 'I was so sleepy. I could hardly keep my eyes open.'

Temazepam had been found in her system. 'Let's concentrate on something else,' Ellen said. 'After school on Thursday you set out on your bike to ride home.'

'Yes,' whispered Katie.

'What route did you take?'

Katie looked hunted. She swallowed and said, 'I went past the Show.'

Donna attempted joviality, tut-tutting in the background. 'Oh, Katie, we told you not to do that.'

The interruption had an unintended effect. Katie's face grew stubborn, as though she were tired of being nagged, and this small rebellion made her stronger. Ellen stepped in, taking advantage. 'I used to do that, when I was a kid. Did you ride past the Show every day after school?'

'Yes.'

'During those rides, did you ever see the man who kidnapped you?'

'No.'

'Did you ever see a white van driving or parked nearby?'

'I can't remember. Don't think so.'

But the abductor and his van would have been nearby, Ellen was convinced of that. 'Did you ever go into the showgrounds? Spend your pocket money on the rides, for example, or just wander around?'

With a look at her mother, Katie whispered, 'Yes.'

Ellen nodded. She would make a public appeal asking Show visitors to hand in their photographs and video footage. They might get lucky and spot Katie, particularly Katie being followed or watched. 'Describe what happened after you left the Show last Thursday.'

Katie took a deep breath and matter-of-factly described the man who had abducted her and the circumstances of the abduction itself. 'Then I woke up in a strange house,' she said. 'I don't remember getting there.' She swallowed once or twice. 'I hardly remember anything,' she wailed. 'I felt woozy all the time. My tummy was really sore, I was bleeding.'

Donna uttered an inarticulate cry; Scobie and the nurse murmured reassuringly. Ellen, trying hard not to weep, said, 'But you're sure that only one man put you in the van? There were no passengers inside it?'

'I'm sure.'

'Did you recognise him?'

'You already asked me that.'

'No,' said Ellen gently, 'I asked if you'd seen that man in the days leading up to Thursday.'

'I didn't know him,' said Katie. 'He said my mum needed me.'

Again Donna wailed. Ellen said above it, 'What can you tell me about the van?'

'It was white.'

'That will help us very much. Thank you. What about the inside of it?'

Katie cast her mind back. 'It was white. There were these boxes and stuff, and plastic bags.' Her mind cleared. 'And this cute little dog. Sasha.'

Ellen beamed. 'How do you know it was called Sasha?'

'It was on her collar, this tag thing.'

'Any other name?'

'I don't remember.'

'An address, or phone number?'

'*I don't remember.*'

'That's all right, you're doing extremely well. That man made a big mistake, letting you read his dog's collar.'

Katie gave an almost comical look of dismay. 'Sasha wasn't his. He was really surprised. Sasha must have jumped in when he wasn't looking.'

There goes one line of inquiry, thought Ellen gloomily. 'Did he let her out again?'

'No. She came with us. We cuddled each other. She stayed in that room with me.' Katie started to wail. 'Then next day she was gone.'

Ellen knew she'd not get much more out of the child. 'Perhaps she ran away.'

'She was scared. They hurt her.'

'Poor Sasha.'

'Once she knocked over the tripod for the camera. Another time she bit one of the men when he touched me.'

She was deeply distressed now, suddenly gulping, and reaching for Donna. Donna shook off Scobie and hugged her daughter, too late to avoid a jet of vomit, but not caring about that at all, just as Ellen didn't care.

23

The death of Ted Anderson on Isolation Pass, the earlier death of his wife from cancer, and the survival of their little daughter resolved themselves into the kind of small-town tragedy that on a slow news day will go national. The story was an ABC news item on Monday night and in the Adelaide *Advertiser* on Tuesday morning. Challis's father took a gloomy interest in it, seated in the sunroom with a blanket over his knees, the newspaper in tented sections on the floor, the sofa, and the coffee table. 'Suicide,' was his verdict, gloomily expressed, as though he wished for the ways and means to speed his own death.

Challis privately agreed, for the town's gossips claimed that Ted Anderson had been despondent in recent months. But Challis was feeling contentious, a reaction to the past few days spent cooped up with his father. 'The Pass is a dangerous stretch of road, Dad.'

'The poor man lost his wife to cancer. He wasn't coping.'

'That was five years ago.'

'Still,' his father said.

Challis felt a twinge of guilt. He hadn't been here to see what his mother's death had done to his father. Like Ted Anderson, the old man wished for death, his body obliging him slowly, but Ted Anderson's method had been quicker and more absolute.

That afternoon, Challis wandered down to the police station, a small brick building behind the shire council offices. The walls and floor were a pale, institutional green, the reception desk high and laminated, the noticeboards rustling with wanted posters, a faded gun amnesty notice, and pamphlets regarding home security and driving offences. A civilian clerk said, 'Help you?'

She was young. He didn't know her. 'Is Sergeant Wurfel in?'

Her jaws snapped. 'Yeah.'

Challis said patiently, 'Then may I see him?'

Her face cleared. 'Okay.'

She disappeared through a door and returned with Wurfel, who gave him a flat cops' look and jerked his head. 'Come through.'

Wurfel took Challis along a short corridor to his office. 'Take a seat. I asked around about you.'

Challis shifted a little in his chair. 'I'm here as a civilian.'

'Fair enough.'

Carl Wurfel was a familiar type to Challis: large-framed, a heavy drinker but not a drunk, tough and pragmatic but not necessarily a bully, probably divorced. He scared people and got the job done. He wouldn't respond to cop talk from Challis.

'If you know about me then you know that my brother-in-law disappeared out east a few years ago.'

Wurfel nodded.

'I'm looking into it,' Challis went on.

'It was looked into at the time.'

'You checked the file?'

'Soon as I knew who you were.'

'May I see it?'

'Why?'

Challis eyed him carefully. 'I need to see if there is anything in it that's not in the Misper file at police headquarters.'

'They gave you access?'

Challis nodded. 'Last Friday.'

'Wait outside,' Wurfel said. 'Let me make a call.'

Challis waited in the corridor; Wurfel beckoned him back a minute later. He was frowning. 'I'll let you see our file. But I thought your brother-in-law committed suicide?'

'Most of the locals think so. He was a bit unstable.'

'Your mate in missing persons told me your sister's been receiving strange mail, as if he's still alive.'

'Yes,' said Challis levelly.

Wurfel was about to say something more, then shrugged and went to his filing cabinet. 'Here's the file. You can read it here. No copying.'

'Okay. Thanks.'

Wurfel remained in the office, ignoring Challis. He raced through his in-tray in a kind of habitual fury and made several abrupt phone calls while Challis tried to concentrate. The file was brief and told him nothing he didn't already know. There was no mention of the letters that Meg had received, only a brief, handwritten update made several months after Gavin's car had been found abandoned at the side of the road: 'Suicide scenario not favoured by Mrs Hurst. Says her husband ran away.' But there were two unrelated reports in the file. One a domestic disturbance callout to the residence of Gavin and Meg Hurst, another an interview with Meg following a report that she'd been assaulted by Gavin: 'Mrs Hurst declines to press charges.'

Challis pushed the file across the desk to Wurfel. 'Thanks, sergeant. I appreciate it.'

Wurfel grunted. 'We gave the kid a verbal warning.'

Challis blinked, then understood. 'Mark Finucane?'

'He's not a bad kid, considering the family he belongs to.'

'I know all about the Finucanes,' Challis said.

He returned to the main street and wandered, his mind drifting, but after a while the town began to impinge on him. People kept stopping to say hello, ask after his father and reminisce about the old days, when he'd been just another town kid and later, for a short time, one of the town's three policemen. They didn't dwell on this latter aspect of his past, and Challis was thankful for that, but, as he walked, he wondered what he'd gained and lost by moving away. Professional advancement, sure, broader horizons, but at a cost. Did he have a family now, or a community? He was remote from the former, and despite his years on the Peninsula, and in the police force, he inhabited the margins, not the centre. How much that owed to his not fitting in, and how much to not wanting to, he really couldn't say.

He walked on. Small things—a voice, a gait, the hot-wood smell of a verandah post in the bright springtime sun—aroused in him powerful memories of his school days and weekends in Mawson's Bluff, a time of idle, harmless vandalism, boredom and longing. He even found himself feeling the same hostility or indifference toward some people, the same affection for others.

And the same desire. He'd slipped into the Copper Kettle for coffee, and was standing at the cash register, when a lithe shape pressed against his back, arms encircled him from behind, and a voice breathed, 'Guess who, handsome?'

He knew at once. He felt his body yielding, arching, his head tipping back and inclining toward her mouth, which reached up and pecked him on the hinge of his jaw. He turned around then. 'Lisa.'

She grinned and released him.

'Lovely to see you,' he said.

She continued to grin. He was a little discomposed. A part of him meant what he'd said, for she was as lovely as he'd remembered, still slight, nimble, direct, her dark hair cropped short, her dark eyes bright with affection. Another part of him remembered her directness and how uncomplicated and selfish her ambitions had been.

'Join me?' he said.

'What are you having?'

'Coffee and a muffin.'

Another customer was already waiting, but Lisa, smiling apologetically, called to the counter hand, 'I'll have the same. *Strong* coffee.'

'Yes, Mrs Joyce.'

'You have to tell them to make it strong, Hal.'

Challis forked out more money and they found a table beside a window. There had been nothing like the Copper Kettle when they were growing up. The décor suggested sidewalk café bohemia, and you could consume anything from a soy latte to a smoked salmon baguette. It was evident that the locals patronised it, too: he saw shopkeepers, farmers, housewives, visiting salesmen, kids on their way home from school.

'Sorry to hear about your dad,' Lisa said.

'Thanks.'

'Is he, you know…'

'Meg thinks he'll go soon, but he's so pigheaded he could rally for a few weeks or months, or even go on like this forever.'

Lisa nodded. 'My parents are still going strong. Rex's are barely hanging on.'

Her wealthy husband's parents had retired to the town, signing everything over to their son. Challis wondered if Lisa had been behind that. Rex Joyce's parents had seemed old and frail twenty years ago. As Lisa said, they must barely be hanging on now.

'How is Rex?'

Lisa told him. He scarcely took it in, finding attractive—all over again—her fine, animated features and gestures. She was very alive there, on the other side of the little table. Their knees touched, and their shoes, once or twice. But he did take in the fact that Lisa was disgruntled. Rex Joyce was a drinker. He remembered that Meg had told him that.

'And you?' she asked. She gave him a lopsided look. 'Are you over all that…business?'

She meant the fact that Angela, his late wife, had tried to have him killed. Lisa's voice and manner suggested that despite everything else she had or might have done to him, she would never have wanted to kill him. He nodded, feeling tired suddenly. It was as if he was being confronted by past mistakes—mistakes in matters of the heart, first with Lisa and then with Angela. He said bluntly, 'It would never have worked, you and me.'

She wasn't disconcerted. She patted his wrist. 'In fact, it *didn't* work. But it was fun.'

He grinned. She returned it, and said lightly, 'Involved with anyone at the moment?'

Her gaze was direct, amused but merciless. He met it, thinking rapidly. Lisa was acting on him; the old chemistry was still there. But old instincts were kicking in, too. He remembered that Lisa Acres was not someone you confided in. If she listened it was to store information that she might use one day—against you, or to her advantage, or both.

'Cat got your tongue, Hal?'

That tugged at his memory, too. He'd often been mute with her, back when he was eighteen, mainly out of simple astonishment: he'd never met anyone so vain, unreliable, bored and easily distracted. All those careless, shrugging explanations for missed appointments and unreturned phone calls. Reproaches never worked because she was unaccommodating, unconcerned about hurting him and unable to make concessions. But her sauntering walk, sleepy smile and softly rounded, flawless brown skin had made up for all of that, over and over again.

She saw all of this passing across his face and a brief, peevish expression flickered on hers, as if she was like everyone else and wanted to be loved. Her gaze slipped to the table.

He sipped his coffee and said inanely, 'How's the drought affecting you and Rex?'

'The *drought*? For God's sake.'

The tightness persisted between them. Presently Lisa said, 'I see Eve in here sometimes. A whole gang of them. Nice kids.'

'Yes,' said Challis, relieved.

'I feel sorry for her.'

'Eve's okay.'

Lisa reached across and placed her hand over his and it felt hot and alive there. 'On the surface, maybe.'

He withdrew his hand. 'Did you know Gavin?'

Lisa sipped her coffee. 'This is all froth. Gavin? Not really. He was not someone you got close to.'

Challis had to acknowledge the truth of that.

'Well, I'd better go,' Lisa said, getting to her feet and bending over to kiss him. She swept out of the place as though she owned it, as she'd always done.

He sat for a while, reluctant to return to his father, and checked his phone, which had been turned off. One message. He dialled, mood lightening, and said, 'Only me, returning your call.'

Last night Ellen had been elated: Katie Blasko had been found alive. Today the elation was still apparent in her voice, but Challis also heard resolve. She now knew what sort of crime and criminals she was investigating. 'Hang on,' he told her, 'I'm in the local café, and I don't want to upset the natives.'

Smiling thanks as he passed the front counter, he stepped outside. 'I'm back,' he said.

They talked for a while about the possibility that a paedophile ring operated on the Peninsula. Like her, he'd heard the rumours. 'Or it was an isolated incident,' he said.

'Which makes it harder to investigate,' Ellen said. She paused. 'Such a brave little kid. I hated interviewing her, making her dredge it all up.'

'I know.'

Challis did know. Sad, broken and fearful children walked through his dreams sometimes. In many cases he'd avenged the harm done to them, but not nearly often enough.

He walked, listened, made suggestions. Talking like this, about work, and its logical steps, was a blessing, an antidote to the fog he was feeling here in the Bluff. 'You're a tonic,' he said, after she'd kidded him about something.

There was a pause. 'Am I?'

Then, as he was beginning to think he'd gone too far, she said, 'You are, too, Hal.'

24

Operation Calling Card.

While Ellen Destry had been interviewing Katie Blasko, van Alphen and Kellock found their ambush site, a house behind the fitness centre. It belonged to Kellock's wife's cousin, who worked on a Bass Strait oil rig and was therefore away for several days at a time. They fed the details to Ivan Henniker, and he fed them to Nick Jarrett. To cover themselves, van Alphen and Kellock obtained three other addresses, of people who were genuinely away on holiday, and arranged for each location to be staked out that night. Ivan Henniker was not told those addresses. 'We might get lucky and catch Nick Jarrett in the act,' van Alphen and Kellock told the stakeout teams in one of the little briefing rooms behind the canteen, later that afternoon, 'or we might sit on our arses all night. It could be weeks before we trap the bastard.'

'So Jarrett's been fed four potential locations to burgle?' asked John Tankard, who was highly motivated. He'd spent a fruitless morning in De Soto Lane with Scobie Sutton, and still cringed inside at the memory of his fear last Saturday night, encountering the Jarretts on that back road behind Waterloo.

'Yes,' lied van Alphen. He glanced at his watch. 'Take the rest of the afternoon off. Meet you back here at eight tonight.'

John Tankard hurried out of the station. Four o'clock. He was anxious to grab this small window of opportunity to do something about his new car. He'd shown it to a few mates at work, and their reactions had ranged from envy to ridicule (which Tank read as envy), but he'd not had a chick in the passenger seat yet—not counting his little sister—and the Northern Territory registration would run out soon.

And so he drove around to Waterloo Motors and booked it in for a roadworthy test. He wouldn't be able to register the car in Victoria without it.

'I can fit you in early next week,' the head mechanic said, flipping through the grimy pages of his desk diary.

'But the rego runs out on Friday,' Tank said. He cursed that he'd changed out of his uniform. The uniform gave him authority. In jeans and a T-shirt he was merely bulky.

He'd had a shower though.

The mechanic made *tsk* sounds and ruminated on the problem. 'Get it privately, did you?'

'A dealer,' Tank said.

'Dealers are supposed to provide a roadworthy certificate.'

'The car's from Darwin, just traded in, not much registration left, so the guy discounted the price if I'd buy it as it is,' said Tank in a defensive rush.

The mechanic said nothing but was unimpressed. Electric tools whirred and clattered beyond the door that led to the workshop area. Someone whistled, another dropped a spanner, and the air was laden with the odours of oil and grease. Everything was satisfying to John Tankard, except this hitch regarding the mechanic's busy diary.

'I could do it first thing tomorrow,' the guy said eventually.

'Awesome,' said Tank.

'Seven-thirty?'

Tank intended to be still in bed at seven-thirty tomorrow, what with working late tonight on Kellock's and van Alphen's operation to nab Nick Jarrett. 'You couldn't make it later?'

'Nope.'

Tank thought about it. 'How about I give you the car now, you lock it up overnight, and start on it first thing in the morning.'

'No problem.'

'Got a loan car?'

'Sorry, mate, none available,' said the mechanic glibly.

What he meant was, he didn't intend to loan Tank a car to compensate for a measly thirty-minute roadworthy test. So Tank walked home to his flat. It didn't feel right, walking. It put him too close to the populace, some of whom he'd arrested over the years, and all of whom knew him as a bully.

His mobile rang. 'I'm waiting,' said the producer from 'Evening Update'.

That same afternoon, Pam Murphy was trying to do things by the book. 'Excuse me, sir,' she said.

Confronting a guy who looked young, about twenty, and indistinguishable from other guys his age: baseball cap, loose T-shirt, baggy jeans, bulky, expensive trainers on his feet. And hostile with it.

'I'm Constable Murphy,' Pam said. One day she'd be able to say Detective Constable, but not yet. She stood about four metres away from the kid, and to one side, the side he'd try for if he wanted to make a run for it. On his other side was a chain-link fence, behind him a brick wall.

'So?' said the guy, showing plenty of attitude, reminding her of a Jarrett hoon from the Seaview estate.

'How long have you been standing here?'

'What's it to you?'

'Answer the question, please, sir,' Pam said.

'Couple hours.'

'Alone?'

'Yeah.'

'You haven't moved from here in two hours?'

'Nup. What's this about?'

'There's been a report of a robbery near here.'

'Yeah? So? You sayin' I done it?'

'Don't you want to know what kind of robbery? Perhaps you already know?'

'Listen, bitch, I done nothin' to no one.'

'You're in the vicinity. We have a witness description that matches yours.'

The guy getting edgy now, looking for a way out, even prepared to use violence. 'Yeah? Who?'

'If I could see some ID please, sir.'

Last night's seminar had involved conflict resolution, a visiting American lecturing to them for three hours on how to use speech to deflect or negate threatening situations. 'The gun you're carrying isn't the most dangerous thing about you,' he'd said. 'Neither is your ability to use a baton or your fists or your boots. It's your tongue.'

'Tongue = danger,' Pam had written on her A4 writing pad, feeling a little absurd.

'It's your tongue and how quickly you use it to show anger or contempt,' the lecturer continued, 'how quickly you use it to say the wrong thing or take the wrong tone. In certain situations it can be like throwing a match into a gas tank.'

John Tankard's approach, Pam had thought, listening to the lecturer drone away. He'd gone on to explain how you should avoid 'conflict phrases' such as 'What's your problem, pal?' and use 'peace phrases' like 'May I help you, sir?'

Pam had scribbled dutifully: *conflict phrases*, *peace phrases*.

'It's all about sublimating ego and anger,' the lecturer continued. 'Try to read your customers. What they say and what they mean can be two entirely different things.'

Customers? Jesus Christ. Sometimes Pam could sympathise with the likes of John Tankard. She'd raised her hand last night, the lecturer giving her plenty of lecture-circuit teeth. 'Yes, young lady?'

'And when words fail?'

'Then you kick ass,' the lecturer said.

So now Pam was trying the softly, softly approach with this twenty-year-old would-be gangster. 'Perhaps you have a driver's licence you can show me, sir?'

'Got no pockets.'

'You don't carry a wallet?'

'Nah.'

'Your name and address, then, sir.'

'Why should I tell you my fucking name? This is bullshit. I done nothin' wrong.'

'Sir, I'm obliged to investigate. I'd like to be able to eliminate you from our inquiries, let you be on your way, so if you could just give me a name...'

'Fuck you!' the kid screamed.

He had a knife. It seemed to materialise in his hand. He was wild-eyed, waving it around, there in that alley that smelt of cat piss and mouldering cardboard.

Just as suddenly, Pam had her .38 centred on his chest. 'Sir, put the knife down, please. I don't want anybody to get hurt.'

'I'm not goin' back to jail! I didn't steal nothin'!'

'Then you have nothing to worry about. Just put the knife down, please, sir.'

The tension left the kid's face. It was gone in an eyeblink. He tossed the knife aside, said cockily, 'There. Satisfied?'

Pam holstered her .38 warily. 'Thank you, sir. Now, if you could just step away from the knife...'

The kid snatched the knife from the ground. He lunged, the blade winking in the dim light, flicking cruelly past her unprotected stomach. Any closer and her guts would have spilt out. She'd relaxed too soon. She might fumble getting her revolver out again, drop it, have it snatched by this quicksilver kid, something she'd never live down—if she lived.

She had a fallback position, her capsicum spray. Before the kid could take another swipe at her, she let him have it full in the face.

'Yeah, yeah, yeah, overkill,' he said, wiping water from his eyes.

She grinned, handed him her handkerchief commiseratively.

'Not bad, Constable Murphy,' the training officer said. Behind him the other trainees applauded ironically.

'Thank you, sir.'

'But you know where you went wrong?'

'Yes, sir. Didn't shoot him, sir.'

The other trainees cheered, and the 'kid', a senior constable, gave her the finger.

Scobie Sutton got home at six that evening to a house full of cooking smells, but something else registered in his senses, too, an atmosphere. Maybe Beth had been yelling at Roslyn. She did that sometimes. She hadn't used to, before she was retrenched from her job with the shire—via e-mail. Scobie came to the back door, as usual, removed his shoes in the little space they called the mud room, as usual, and walked in his socks to the kitchen, where the fluorescent light was merciless, showing up the essential tackiness of their out-of-date cabinets and bench tops. They'd had plans to renovate the kitchen, back when Beth still had her job. The atmosphere: it wasn't frustration or anger, it was guilt.

'Hello, my darlings,' Scobie said, wondering if his tone alone would tip the balance toward harmony.

Beth was brushing oil over an uncooked chicken. Cubes of potato and pumpkin ringed it. She hardly dared to glance at him but kept her face and eyes averted as she accepted his kiss. She felt stiff in his arms.

Scobie turned to his daughter, who was absorbed with her homework. She liked to do her homework here. The kitchen was at the centre of things. The cheap pine desk in her bedroom wasn't. He ruffled her hair and kissed her bent neck. She squirmed delightedly before saying 'Daddy!' and throwing her arms around him. He couldn't get enough of that.

'How was everyone's day?'

'Fine,' his wife muttered.

His had been miserable. That poor, poor child.

Presently Roslyn wandered into the sitting room to watch 'The Simpsons'. Scobie turned to his wife. 'What's wrong?' he said, his tone a little sharp.

'I've done something stupid.'

'Such as?'

They kept current bills, letters and junk mail in an old in-tray beside the fridge. Beth took out a brochure. 'I paid for this,' she said, her face furiously red. 'My own money.'

Scobie scanned the brochure. It said *Rising Stars Agency* in bold type, with a list of the agency's accomplishments, including modelling contracts in Sydney and New York, and young actors placed in several films and TV shows. 'I thought it would help our finances if Ros got picked,' Beth said.

Scobie was pretty blind when it came to his daughter. His co-workers could have told him that—and some did. But even he didn't think it likely that Roslyn would be hired to model little dresses and tops for the Myer or Pumpkin Patch catalogues, or get picked to play someone's kid in a TV serial. 'When was this?'

'A month ago,' said Beth in shame.

Scobie dimly recalled it. He'd been embroiled in a murder inquiry at the time, obliging him to spend long hours away from home, and had thought his daughter was having her photograph taken at school. He felt stricken: poor Beth. All she wanted was to help ease the family's financial situation. But to do it like this! The world must be full of hopeful mothers, he thought, who believed their children photogenic enough to be models and actors. 'Oh well,' he said gently, 'these sorts of things are bound to be a long shot.'

'It's not that,' Beth whispered. 'They promised they'd deliver the photos within seven days, but it's been weeks now and they still haven't arrived. I called the number on the brochure and got a recorded message, "Please check the number and call again".'

Scobie frowned down at the brochure. No address, not even a post office box. Only a cell phone number.

'You've been conned, sweetheart.'

Beth's face crumpled. 'Oh, Scobie, I'm so sorry.'

'No harm done,' Scobie said. He'd pass it on to the fraud squad. The guy's prints might even be on the brochure.

'You don't have to go out again, do you?' Beth said, wringing her hands a little.

Scobie shook his head. 'I'm staying home all night.'

25

The darkest hours, well past midnight. Inside the ambush house, a roomy weatherboard cottage on a quiet street behind the fitness centre, van Alphen examined the expensive gear, the highly polished floorboards. The owner clearly made good money on the oil rigs. A tasteful place, if you discounted the Harley Davidson pennants and Grand Prix posters—which van Alphen didn't.

A night spent in silence in an unfamiliar house is a long night. From time to time Kellock and van Alphen took turns to prowl through the dark rooms, but otherwise they were still, and rarely conversed. They pinpointed which floorboards creaked, which leather armchair crepitated under their weight. Van Alphen was a smoker but he couldn't smoke tonight; Kellock badly wanted a drink. They didn't touch a light switch, rarely used the torch.

At five minutes to four on the morning of Wednesday, 2 October, van Alphen whispered to Kellock, 'We have a visitor.'

They waited. They tracked the glow of a torch as it passed one window and then another. Nothing happened for ten minutes. Finally there came the sounds of a window being forced. They were in the sitting room. A short hallway led from it. They moved to the hallway, listened again.

The spare bedroom.

Still they waited, allowing time for the guy—Nick Jarrett?—to boost himself through the window and into the room. They heard a soft thump, as though someone had jumped down onto a carpeted floor. 'Now,' whispered van Alphen.

Kellock moved first, a torch in one hand and his .38 Smith and Wesson service revolver in the other. 'Police, don't move!' he shouted. 'Police, don't move!'

A retired forklift driver lived next door. Owing to his years of shift work at the oil depot on Westernport Bay, he often woke at four in the morning. He heard Kellock's shout. 'I heard it twice,' he told investigators, in the days and weeks that followed.

'And then?'

'Nothing for a while, then I heard a couple of shots.'

'Two shots?'

'Yes.'

'How long after the shouted warning?'

'Hard to say, really. Could have been two minutes, could have been five.'

So much for Scobie Sutton's vow to stay in all night. He got the call, beating the ambulance, in fact. Kellock and van Alphen met him at the door. He'd always been intimidated by them. They were big men, in size and in the way they carried themselves, and had always treated him with faintly amused contempt, as though he were not a man, as though decent men, churchgoing men, were a joke. It couldn't be contempt though, could it? What sorts of upbringings had they had? What values had their parents instilled in them? Scobie couldn't work them out and was afraid, as they stood there in the doorway, not letting him in.

Somehow he found the nerve to say, 'Unusual for a sergeant and a senior sergeant to be on a stakeout together.'

Kellock made a wide, lazy gesture, snideness in his sleepy eyes.

'Staff shortages, Scobe old son. Plus I had uniforms watching three other houses.'

Scobie swallowed. 'Can I come in?'

Both men pantomimed are-we-stopping-you? Scobie edged past them, then paused, looking at Kellock's arm. 'You've cut yourself.'

'Defensive wounds,' van Alphen said matter-of-factly. He was right behind Scobie, practically breathing in his ear. 'The little cunt pulled a knife on him, didn't he, Kel?'

'Yep.'

'Who shot him?' Scobie said, backing away from them.

'I did,' Kellock said.

'Where is he?'

'Along here.'

They took him to the spare bedroom. Nick Jarrett had apparently stumbled backwards, collided with the bed, and then fallen crookedly beside it. He wore overalls and had been shot twice in the chest. Gloved hands, his left clutching a knife. 'Good riddance, eh, Scobe?' said Kellock, crowding him there in the doorway.

'What happened?'

'Told you, he pulled a knife.'

Scobie said stupidly, 'That one?'

'No, a huge Japanese samurai sword that we put back over the fireplace. Of course that fucking knife.'

'I have to be sure,' said Scobie defensively. 'So, he cut you?'

'No, he gave me a haircut,' said Kellock, clutching a handkerchief to his forearm.

'Kel,' admonished van Alphen mildly.

'Sorry. Sorry, Scobie.'

Scobie didn't believe it. 'Can I see?'

Kellock proffered his arm. Three shallow cuts, parallel to the watchstrap. 'Defensive wounds.'

Too shallow, too neatly arranged, for that. Scobie swallowed again. 'That's what your report will say?'

'Why? You think I'm lying, Detective Constable Sutton?'

'I'm just here to note what was said and done, that's all,' Scobie said.

'Mate, you're a real character.'

They were creeping him out. He heard a vehicle arriving, a heavy motor. 'That will be the ambulance,' he said, relieved.

He was gone about a minute, greeting the ambulance crew and showing them to the body. Soon the little room was crowded, and Scobie's view of the body obscured. 'Weak pulse,' one of the paramedics said. 'We have to get him to the hospital pronto.'

Scobie saw van Alphen and Kellock exchange a complicated glance. Were they relieved? Worried? He couldn't say.

'I need to bag the knife,' Scobie said, pushing through to Nick Jarrett's body, taking an evidence bag from his jacket pocket. He paused. He could have sworn the knife had been in Jarrett's left hand. He could have sworn that Jarrett had been wearing gloves. Jarrett gasped then, drawing a painful, rattling breath. His hands fluttered.

'Mate,' an ambulance officer said, elbowing Scobie, 'we have to get him out, now.'

Scobie bagged the knife wordlessly, using his last few seconds to run his gaze over Jarrett. There was a cut above one eyebrow, signs of swelling on one cheek.

'Mate?'

'Okay, okay, just remove his overalls first.'

He stood back while it was done. Finally Jarrett was carried out to the ambulance, which tore away, sounding the siren once it had reached the main road.

'We've got a situation,' Scobie said.

'No we don't,' said van Alphen emphatically.

Scobie trembled and his voice wouldn't come. There were procedures to follow. But van Alphen and Kellock were his police colleagues. At the same time, he didn't exactly mourn Jarrett, who was a killer, a man prone to violence. Scobie didn't doubt that a tox screen would show large amounts of speed in Jarrett's system. Jarrett would have been volatile, vicious and unpredictable, so it could have happened as described by van Alphen and Kellock.

'Headquarters will have to look into this.'

'We know that.'

'There will be a coronial inquest.'

'In about a year's time,' Kellock said. 'A lot can happen in that time.'

'Boss, I need to bag your weapon,' Scobie said, his voice not holding up. 'I also need the outer clothing of both of you.'

'Well, sure,' said Kellock, not moving.

'I have to do this by the book,' gabbled Scobie.

'Wouldn't have it any other way.'

'I have a couple of forensic suits in the back of my car.'

'Not a problem.'

Van Alphen and Kellock said nothing more but stared at him. He could feel their eyes at his back as he left the house.

One hour later, dawn light streaking the horizon, Scobie called in at McDonald's for breakfast, a guilty Big Mac with fries because his nerves were shot. Then he called the hospital, learning that Nick Jarrett had died in the ambulance, and finally called Ellen to report the shooting—a clumsy conversation on his part, he felt. Finally he drove up to the city and delivered the knife, gloves, bagged clothing and .38 to the ForenZics lab, arriving as the doors opened for the day. A guy called Riggs, young, abrupt, irritable, took custody of the evidence, the irritation growing as he removed the items one by one. 'Jesus, pal.'

'What?'

'Cross contamination.'

'I was rushed,' said Scobie, feeling sulky. 'It's clear enough what happened.'

'Not to me. Gunshot residue and blood evidence are easily

transferred. You've got the clothing of several people here.'

'Three: two police officers and the victim, a burglar.'

'Oh, well that's all right, then,' said Riggs snidely.

'One officer was slashed with the knife. He then shot the burglar.'

'Don't you have procedures for collecting evidence? My findings will be meaningless.'

Scobie felt like weeping. None of this was his fault. 'Please see what you can do.'

When Ellen arrived at work that morning she found people congregated in corridors and doorways, whispering, murmuring. It was partly elation, partly awe, partly apprehension about the fallout that would follow now, not only for Kellock and van Alphen but for all of them. Nobody was very sorry about Jarrett. Some were almost pleased that he'd been shot dead, although they could not have done it themselves. Feelings were complicated, uneven, hard to pin down.

She walked past Kellock's office. The door was open. He beckoned her in, saying, 'You heard?'

'Yes.'

He looked exhausted. 'Van and I have been limited to desk duties until it's sorted out.'

Ellen nodded. It was to be expected.

'But feel free to call on us if you need help with the Blasko investigation.'

Ellen blinked. 'Really?'

'No problem,' said Kellock evenly.

Scobie was waiting for her upstairs. He hadn't shaved; his thinning hair was awry. 'Ellen,' he said, relieved.

She took him into her office. He wouldn't sit but paced in agitation. She waited, eventually prompting him: 'The Jarrett shooting.'

He continued to pace.

'*Scobie!*'

He jumped. 'What?'

'It's clean, right?'

He was silent for some time. 'I got there about five this morning.'

'And?'

'I was tired. I wasn't taking everything in.'

Ellen closed her eyes, opened them again. 'Are you saying there are anomalies?'

He considered that. 'There's an explanation for everything.'

'You did it by the book, Scobie, tell me you did it by the book.'

He sat finally. He twisted in his seat. 'I can explain.'

The explanation was disjointed, and at the end of it she said, 'Was the knife Jarrett's?'

Scobie stared at the carpet, then lifted his sorrowing face. She heard the fretfulness as he asked: 'Was he left or right handed? Was he or wasn't he wearing gloves? I went back there just now: the carpet's been shampooed already.'

Ellen watched him.

'I got a bad vibe, Ellen,' he said, not meeting her gaze.

She wondered if he'd ever uttered the word 'vibe' aloud before. It didn't sound right in his mouth. 'What kind of knife was it?'

'Generic kitchen knife. Could have come from anywhere. Could have come from the house.'

'He always wore gloves?'

'According to the collators, yes. His girlfriend wouldn't confirm or deny. Nor would his family.'

An image of Laurie Jarrett came to Ellen. She coughed. 'God, Scobie, I don't want a dirty shooting.'

'It's not yours to worry about,' Scobie said sourly. 'It was a uniformed operation, and the police shooting board will be stepping in.'

'Still.'

Into the pause that followed, Scobie said softly, 'They threatened me.'

'Who? The Jarretts?'

'Van Alphen and Kellock.'

'They're just a bit macho, that's all. They like to intimidate.'

'It was more than that. When I arrived just now, Kellock said, "How's that daughter of yours going?" A clear threat.'

'Doesn't sound like one.'

'You weren't there,' Scobie muttered.

Ellen had barely started work when a call came from the front desk: Laurie Jarrett was in the foyer, angry, distraught. 'He wants to see you, Sarge.'

'Me? The stakeout was a uniformed operation, not CIU.'

'He says his nephew was set up, ambushed. He'll only speak to you.'

'Put him in a conference room. Have a uniform outside the door.'

'Sarge.'

Wondering what she'd done to earn Laurie Jarrett's regard, Ellen went downstairs, a part of her thinking that Nick Jarrett had got what he deserved, another part hoping it had been a clean shooting.

She found the patriarch of the Jarrett clan in the foyer conference room, two nervous constables standing beside his chair. He'd come storming into the station, according to the officers on the front desk, but now looked calm and unreadable. 'Thanks for seeing me,' he murmured.

Ellen got down to business. 'You're saying the police set your nephew up?'

'I know they did,' Jarrett said.

The man's low tone and steady demeanour spelt barely concealed fury. 'We're sorry for your loss, Mr Jarrett, but—'

'You cunts set him up and bushwhacked him.'

Ellen flushed. 'Mr Jarrett, I know you're upset, but I find your language offensive.'

'So charge me.'

It was 9 am. She'd brought her coffee mug with her and toyed with it now, idly noticing the words printed across it: *Our day begins when yours ends.* She looked up; Laurie Jarrett was staring at her bleakly across the conference room table. 'I want a face-to-face with the officers who shot Nick,' he said.

'There's no way that's going to happen.'

'I want a full inquiry.'

'All police shootings are rigorously examined,' she said.

He snorted. 'Words.'

'Like I said, the shooting will be—'

'You've always had it in for my nephew. You've had it in for all of us.'

She wasn't going to take that lying down. 'Our officers are called to your house at least once a fortnight, Laurie. Legal searches of the cars and bedrooms of your sons, stepsons and nephews have regularly uncovered drugs and stolen goods. The younger kids are caught shoplifting almost weekly. You yourself have a record for burglary and assault. Did we fit you up for all of those crimes and charges? I don't think so.'

'*This* time,' he snarled, stabbing the table top with a slender finger, '*this* time you did.'

Ellen shifted uncomfortably, compelled by his looks again. She didn't want to admit that it was a form of attraction. In response, something shifted in his gaze. He'd sensed the alteration in her body, and almost but not quite smiled. Then, to her astonishment, his eyes filled with tears.

'It wasn't a clean shooting.'

'Laurie, he attacked two officers with a knife.'

A kitchen knife, possibly from a set found in the kitchen of the house. Ellen made a mental note: how did Nick Jarrett enter the house? Which rooms did he enter before being accosted? Did he go to the kitchen?

'He was lured, Ellen,' Laurie Jarrett said.

It was a shock, his using her first name, and quite out of order. 'He was a burglar, Mr Jarrett. We've found burgled items in his girlfriend's flat from time to time. He burgled to a pattern. We identified that pattern and intercepted him. He took drugs and was prone to violence. It was always going to be a matter of time before something like this occurred.'

Jarrett gave her a look, a man with a permanently unimpressed mind. It was a cops' look, frankly. Eventually he said gently, 'You're a sore loser.'

'If that's all,' Ellen said, standing, 'I have work to do.'

'Just the beginning, sweetheart,' Jarrett said, uncoiling gracefully from his chair.

'There will be a coroner's inquest in due course.'

'You mean a coroner's whitewash.'

Ellen lost it, just a little. 'Look, we've just had the abduction and sexual assault of a young girl. She's lucky to be alive. I am yet to find the man, or men, responsible. Meanwhile, the shooting of your nephew will be given full attention, but it's not my concern.'

Laurie Jarrett, a slender, shapely, dangerous man, a man who had her number, smiled. The smile didn't reach his eyes. 'Katie Blasko is not the only one,' he murmured.

Ellen stiffened. 'What do you mean?'

He ignored the question and got to his feet. 'I have a lot to do, a grieving family, a funeral to arrange.'

Ellen returned to the CIU incident room and waded through reports and witness statements until mid afternoon. It was all fruitless, until Riggs, the technician from ForenZics, called. 'We have the results on those Katie Blasko samples.'

Ellen was impressed: she'd expected the results much later. Maybe Superintendent McQuarrie had done the right thing in contracting CIU's forensic testing to the private lab. Not that the situation in any way matched the ideal, the ideal being one of those American cop shows like 'CSI', where a detective walks down a flight of stairs with a blood or fibre sample, and there is the lab, and the lab is full of experts who process evidence on the spot with state of the art equipment—and who also go out and make arrests. Even so, ForenZics had processed the samples from the Katie Blasko abuse house quickly. In Ellen's experience, the state lab was often running weeks, even months behind. Not only had successive state governments failed to fund it adequately, but it was also swamped with work, for defence and prosecution lawyers had come to believe that forensic evidence could prove or disprove everything. Even the privately owned labs like ForenZics were overworked in testing samples—giving second opinions, confirming the state lab's results or throwing them into doubt. Consequently judges and prosecutors were putting pressure on the police to find additional, better and more irrevocable evidence.

'That was quick,' Ellen said. 'Thank you.'

'Just doing our job,' Riggs said.

Ellen swivelled in her chair. She gazed at the perforated ceiling battens, then unseeingly through the window that overlooked the car park and its scattering of police and private cars. 'So, what did you find?'

'The bad news first. Plenty of fibres, but they're generic to all kinds of cotton and synthetic clothing.'

'DNA,' said Ellen firmly, 'that's what I want.'

'Don't rush me. We found blood, other fluids and skin traces that are a DNA match to Katie Blasko.'

'As expected. I want to know who else was there.'

'Don't rush me,' said Riggs again. 'For your information, we did find traces of someone other than the victim.'

'Enough for DNA?'

'Yes.'

Ellen felt her skin tingle.

'*And* he's in the system,' Riggs said. 'Neville Clode. He lives in Waterloo.'

Ellen left her office and found Scobie Sutton in the incident room, examining the doorknock canvass sheets, studiously ignoring Kees van Alphen, who was thumb tacking a wall map of the Peninsula. Ellen paused. 'Heard about the shooting, Van,' she murmured. 'Bad luck.'

'Or good luck. Depends how you see it.'

'Quite.' She pointed at the map. 'What are you doing?'

'Since I'm desk bound, I thought I'd help CIU. I'm mapping sex crimes. The blue pins are the home addresses of known sex offenders.'

There were not many of these, and most lived in the main population areas: Waterloo, Mornington and the coastal strip from Dromana to Sorrento. 'The red and yellow pins?'

'The red pins show the locations of sexual assaults on children by strangers, the yellow pins show the locations of related offences.'

'Good work,' Ellen said. And it was, painstaking and probably pointless. A lot of police work was like that. 'What do you mean by "related offences"?'

'Women, and young girls, have reported flashers along here,' van Alphen said, indicating a couple of popular beaches. 'This woman—' he indicated another yellow pin '—was walking her dog and a man grabbed her breasts from behind. She screamed and he ran. She followed him to a nearby house, then called the police, who promptly arrested him.'

Ellen shook her head. Most crimes were stupid. Most criminals were stupid. 'This pin,' van Alphen went on, 'indicates reports of men seen lurking near public toilets and schools.'

'Fantastic, Van, thank you. We're stretched for resources.'

'No worries.'

'But broaden what you've been doing. In addition to incidents that are clearly sex related, I want everything you can find about abductions, abduction attempts, unsolved disappearances and murders, particularly of children and young people.'

'Peninsula wide?'

'Australia wide, Van. Our guy could be very mobile.'

Van Alphen scowled. 'I guess that will keep me out of trouble, but I'd rather be out in the field, kicking down doors.'

Ellen patted him on the shoulder. 'That's my boy. But right now I want everything you can give me on a Neville Clode.' She gave the details. 'A full background check,' she urged. 'Criminal record, vehicles registered in his name, circle of friends, his relatives, work colleagues, acquaintances, you know the drill.'

Van Alphen gave her an unreadable look and nodded abruptly. She crossed the room and said, 'Scobie? We have a suspect.' She told him about Neville Clode and the DNA.

'Neville Clode? I questioned him a few days ago, that ag burg, guy ended up in hospital.'

Ellen nodded slowly. 'Interesting.'

'He was knocked about pretty badly, wouldn't give straight answers. A falling out with his pals?'

'Or maybe it wasn't an ag burg. Maybe he has a history, and one of his victims got revenge.'

'He didn't seem the type.'

Scobie Sutton was easily, and often, impressed by the people he dealt with. He was a churchgoer, a decent family man, and perhaps the police would have a better press if more officers were like him, but the police also needed officers who could step over the line and inhabit the minds of the bad guys. 'Tell me about him.'

Scobie perched his bony rear on the edge of the main table while

Ellen sat attentively. 'He works from home.'

'As?'

'Some kind of counsellor or healer.'

'Psychologist? Physio? What?'

'Can't recall.'

'What *can* you recall?'

'His place was trashed. A real mess. He was beaten pretty badly.'

'Anything else?'

Scobie searched his memory. 'There's a kind of spa room in his house. Spa bath and toys.'

'Toys? Does he have children? A partner?'

'He's almost sixty.'

'Scobie, does he have children or a partner?'

'No sign of either.'

'Let's go and rattle his cage,' Ellen said, rattling her car keys at him.

27

Thirty minutes later, Ellen and Scobie were in an unmarked silver Falcon from the motor pool. Ellen drove. Scobie stretched his stick legs and yawned. The interior was stuffy, for the car had been sitting in the sun. Bird shit streaked the windscreen: trees ringed the car park behind the station and the birds were busy now, building nests. Scobie sneezed. Presently Ellen sneezed. Spring on the Peninsula brought a special kind of hell to hayfever sufferers. The air was laden with pollen. People suffered through it and their eyes itched.

'Roslyn can't stop talking about it,' Scobie announced after a short period of blessed silence.

'About what?' said Ellen before she could stop herself. At least the poor kid's bowel movements had ceased to matter to her devoted father. Now it was how she coped with maths, friendship crises and the scary bits in Harry Potter.

'About riding her bike, dressed up like Katie Blasko.'

Ellen stirred, irritated. What mattered was what had happened to the real Katie Blasko, not the pretend Katie's moment of fame. She didn't say any of this to Scobie Sutton. He'd be crestfallen, offended or bewildered, and Ellen didn't feel like coping with any of his reactions. 'Left or right?' she said at the next intersection.

'Straight ahead, then the second on the left.'

He directed her past the fenced boundary of the Seaview Park estate to a low, newish-looking house set behind a screen of trees. Ten years old, Ellen guessed, assessing the architecture and the height of the trees. Not long after she'd settled on the Peninsula with Alan and Larrayne, several streets had been carved out of what had been farmland on the outskirts of Waterloo. Alan had been interested in buying a plot and putting up a house, but Ellen had been adamant that as a copper she was not going to live where she worked, and so they'd bought the old fibro holiday house ten minutes drive away in Penzance Beach. And now that house had been sold and she was marking time in Challis's house.

She braked the car. A small sign, burnt into a polished board mounted on a low concrete pillar that doubled as a letterbox, read *Wellness Centre*. 'Oh, for God's sake,' she muttered.

Scobie knew what she meant. A hypochondriac, he was defensive. 'Don't knock it, Ellen. Our naturopath has really helped my arthritis and Beth's depression.'

Naturopaths were probably the acceptable face of what bugged Ellen. It seemed to her that on every back road, side street or strip of shops on the Peninsula, a 'healer' of some kind could be found. They set up 'wellness boutiques' and read palms, Tarot cards and probably tea leaves, offered massage, crystal therapy or ear candling—whatever that was—and taught certificate courses in automatic writing and angel visions—whatever they were.

If you wanted to awaken your life-force, then a powerful and ancient Tibetan modality was available in Mornington. A woman in Penzance Beach offered Sandplay and Expressive Therapy. There was a Holistic clinic next door to a shoe shop in Waterloo, and even an Inner Balance Master a few hundred metres along the dirt road past Challis's house (yeah, she could just see Hal checking in for a treatment). Quacks came through lecturing on 'Thought Field Therapy' at $500 a pop, or sold books and CDs that showed you how to become animal spirit intuitives, so long as you forked out $89.99

for a shamanic field guide that offered insight into the wisdom of Mother Earth's natural creatures.

The practitioners and devotees of this alternative Peninsula gave their children weird names, wore flower-power and vaguely Indian clothing and entered wispy, inept paintings in the local art shows. Ellen was pretty sure that the intelligence quotient of the Peninsula was lower than anywhere else on the planet.

She ignored Scobie and got out. There was a small wooden rack mounted to the wall beside the front door. She took out a brochure and read that Neville Clode's Wellness Centre specialised in wellness for children, promising to cure their irritability, hypertension, nervousness, fears and phobias. 'Let me unlock the feelings, emotions and hidden belief systems that block the journey process to true maturity,' he offered.

Scobie stood beside her. He pushed the bell. She thrust the brochure at him. 'Jesus Christ, Scobie—he works with kids.'

Scobie read. Time ticked by. Here on Clode's street the houses were silent and far apart from each other, separated by trees and high paling fences. No witnesses, in other words. 'I'm checking around the back,' Ellen said.

She prowled down the side of the house, passing a carport hung with grapevines that sheltered a Saab. A moment later she rounded the corner onto a broad yard and a scattering of fruit trees. There was a small aluminium garden shed. Two children, a girl and a boy aged about twelve, were disappearing over the back fence. They looked gleeful, panicky and hard-eyed, as if they'd been in trouble with the authorities for all of their short lives and weren't about to reform. Even so, they were children, and they should have been in school.

Ellen shouted futilely, then turned her attention to the rear wall of the house. Scobie was coming around the corner, still reading the brochure. The back door opened and a man stepped out, moving stiffly. Facial bruises were vivid on his face; blood streaked the whites of his blackened eyes; his top lip carried a couple of stitches.

'Mr Clode? My name is Sergeant Destry and you've met Constable Sutton.'

'Did you get the little buggers?' Clode said, his voice melodious, as though remembering that he was supposed to be a healer, a man who brought comfort to people. He approached Scobie warmly and shot out his hand. The two men shook. Then he offered his hand to Ellen and she ignored it. 'Do you know those children, Mr Clode? Were they visiting you?'

Through the damage to his face she could see a bleak, scoffing expression. 'Kids from the Seaview Park estate,' he said. 'Surely no strangers to the police.'

'Do you think they're the ones who attacked you, Mr Clode?' said Scobie.

'Could well be.'

Ellen wasn't having this. She'd read Clode's statement. 'I thought you said that men attacked you, not children.'

'Youngish men, I think.'

'All right, did you recognise those children just now?'

'No. I told them to clear off.'

'Would you recognise them again?'

'I only saw their backs.'

Ellen stared at him, unconvinced. But she doubted she'd recognise them, either. 'Are you in the habit of inviting children to your home, Mr Clode?'

He flushed. 'I didn't invite them.'

'But you treat children.'

'That's different. And their parents bring them to me for therapy.'

'May we come inside, please?'

He looked uncertain, but took them through to his sitting room. 'Has a parent made a complaint against me?'

'Are the parents present when you treat their children?' Ellen responded.

'No way. It destroys the energy.'

Ellen supposed that it probably did. 'Can you tell us what you were doing between Thursday afternoon last week and Monday afternoon this week?'

'What's this about?' said Clode, appealing to Scobie.

'Just answer the question,' Ellen said.

'I was in hospital for two days.'

'And the other two days?'

'Here.'

'Can you prove that?'

'I live alone, so no, I can't,' said Clode, irritable now.

'Your appointment book might hold the answer.'

Clode coughed and shifted about. 'Actually, I didn't have any appointments. I'm retraining.'

'Retraining? As what?'

'A thought field therapist.'

Ellen smirked.

'Look, why do you want to know my movements? What am I supposed to have done? I'm a *victim*, remember.'

'Do you own a white van?'

'No, why?'

'Do any of your friends or family?'

'Don't think so. How would I know?'

'I understand you have a spa room, with toys in it.'

To cover his confusion or apprehension, Clode threw up his hands. 'What's that got to do with anything?'

'Is it part of children's therapy?'

'No. It's for when my granddaughter visits.'

Ellen watched him for a long moment. He didn't waver. 'Is your wife with you, Mr Clode?'

'She died.'

'Oh, I'm sorry,' Ellen said unconvincingly. 'How many children do you have?'

'My wife had a daughter from her previous marriage. Her name's Grace.'

'Oh.'

'I rarely see them.'

'Them?'

'Grace is married. Husband and one daughter.'

'They live some distance away?'

Clode shook his head. 'Just on the other side of the Peninsula.'

'But you rarely see them.'

'I'm not related by blood,' said Clode.

'How old was Grace when you married her mother?'

Clode thought about it. 'Early teens.'

'How old is her daughter?'

'About seven.'

'An address, please, Mr Clode.'

'Why? You haven't told me what this is about.'

'Whose white van did you borrow last Thursday?'

Clode was ready. 'I didn't borrow a white van. I didn't rent a white van. I don't own a white van. I don't know anyone who owns or drives a white van.'

Ellen sneezed and her eyes itched. She fished a damp tissue from her pocket, feeling obscurely undermined by her hayfever.

'Satisfied?' said Clode. 'I get beaten up and you lot treat me like I'm a suspect in some crime.'

'We were thinking the assault on you might have been personal,' Ellen said. 'I understand they also trashed your house pretty badly.'

The signs were still apparent in the sitting room: the remains of a chair in the corner and a crooked print on the wall. Clode shook his head. 'They would have been high on drugs. They stole a digital camera and a coin collection.'

Scobie frowned. 'You told me they hadn't taken anything.'

'I've had time for a proper look since then,' Clode said. 'This is just a junkie burglary.'

'More than that, Mr Clode,' Scobie said. 'You were beaten up pretty badly.'

Ellen was watching Clode, and saw him go very still. 'I'm fine. I don't want to make a fuss,' he said. 'It hardly seems worth bothering about.'

Now, why is that? Ellen wondered. Muttering about briefings and deadlines, she nodded goodbye to Clode and hurried Scobie out to the car. 'So, what do you think?'

Scobie swung his mournful face toward her. 'About what?'

'Scobie, wake up. What did you make of Clode?'

He seemed to make an effort. 'Er, it's hard to tell.'

His head was all over the place. 'Forget it,' Ellen said. Hal Challis had always been her sounding board, but he wasn't here.

28

This was his routine now, to leave the house for a couple of hours in the afternoon while his father napped. Meg was usually sitting with the old man when Challis returned. A freelance bookkeeper who worked from home, she had the freedom to come and go.

That Wednesday Challis made for the little library, briefly pausing on the footpath for a road-train as it headed north with huge bales of hay to where the drought was most acute. He crossed the road and went in. The library opened on Wednesday and Friday afternoons, and he was the only borrower. He selected three talking books for his father and took them to the desk.

'How's your dad doing?' the librarian asked.

Retired now, she'd been Challis's English teacher twenty-five years ago. 'Fine, Mrs Traill.'

She sighed. 'And Meg? I bet she needed the break.'

Did Mrs Traill know how demanding the old man could be? Challis smiled neutrally. Nothing was sacred or secret in the Bluff.

Arms went around him from behind and his first thought was: Lisa. Even the words were the same. 'Guess who!'

More exuberant than Lisa. He turned and kissed his niece. 'You wagging school?'

'As if I'd come here—no offence, Mrs Traill.'

'None taken, dear.'

Eve wasn't in school uniform, a liberty allowed the senior students, Challis supposed. She was returning a couple of books. 'Research?'

'Exams soon, Uncle Hal.'

'Have you seen Mark?'

Eve nodded. 'They gave him a ticking off, made him pay for petrol.' She paused. 'Sorry I overreacted on Sunday.'

'You were sticking up for your friend,' Challis said. 'That's important.'

She gave him a brief hug. 'Thanks. Wurfel's okay, I suppose. A bit law and order, friends with the local gentry.' She beamed at him challengingly.

Challis glanced at Mrs Traill, who was seventy years old, round, comfortable and powdered, an old grandmother who had a perspective on everything and a sense of humour. She gave them both an enigmatic smile, as though she understood many of the things that happened in the town but kept them to herself. 'Let me take those books from you, dear.'

Eve handed them over. 'How's Gramps?'

'The same,' said Challis.

'Tell him I'll try to pop in later.'

'I will.'

'Have to go,' she said, looking at her watch.

Challis glanced through the window. An old car, two girls and a boy in it, bopping to music. 'See ya,' he said.

'See ya,' and she was through the door and into the car.

Mrs Traill smiled fondly after her. 'She's often in here. She studies hard, that girl.'

Challis nodded.

'A tragedy.'

Challis gazed at her. 'Did you know Gavin very well?'

'He wasn't from around here.'

Challis gave her a half smile. 'But did you know him?'

'I was one of your mother's best friends. She told me about the strange mail Meg was getting.'

'Mum and Meg didn't tell Dad about any of that.'

'Who can blame them? A lovely man, your father, but some things are best kept quiet.'

'Yes.'

'Anything else?'

It suddenly occurred to Challis: the weekly *Northern Herald* would have covered Gavin's disappearance. Unfortunately it was based in another town. 'Do you keep back issues of the local paper?'

'Of course.'

'Going back five years?'

'Gavin?'

'Yes.'

'Stay there.'

She was gone for some time. After a while, he strolled idly around the shelves, peering at book titles, and then heard the main door open and close. He peered through a gap in the books and saw a woman enter shyly, scurry to one of the little tables, remove a book from her cane basket and begin to read, all of her movements painfully slow and defeatist.

'You can use the back room,' said Mrs Traill behind him.

He jumped. 'Thanks.'

She led him behind her desk to a storeroom, where she'd dumped dusty bound copies of the *Northern Herald* on a table. 'That woman who came in,' he said.

'Alice Finucane, married to Paddy. She's here every Wednesday and Friday, her only escape.'

Challis remembered a story that Meg had told him, of how Paddy had been reported to the RSPCA for mistreating his dogs. Gavin had investigated and been kicked and punched off the property.

'Poor thing,' said Mrs Traill.

Challis smiled non-committally and sat at the table. 'I'll leave you to it,' said Mrs Traill reluctantly.

When she was gone, Challis began to read. Gavin's disappearance had been covered in fair detail, but there were no hard facts beyond the abandoned car and a faint hint that Gavin Hurst's job had been 'demanding', which Challis read as meaning Gavin had been unpopular. He wiped dust from his hands, thanked Mrs Traill and left the building.

The library was next door to the shire offices. Parked outside it was a dusty new Range Rover with tinted windows. One window whirred down and Lisa said, from the front passenger seat, 'Afternoon, handsome.'

Challis glanced automatically at the heavy glass doors of the shire offices. 'Rex is in there making a nuisance of himself,' Lisa said.

'What about?'

'Council rates. It happens every year.'

Challis stood by her door for a while and they chatted. Life had slowed right down, to this, gentle walks around the town and idle conversation. He half liked it. At the same time, he missed the Peninsula, and catching killers.

Rex came out, looking angry. He wore the uniform of the successful grazier who doesn't like to get his hands dirty: tan, elastic-sided R. M. Williams riding boots, R. M. Williams moleskin pants, Country Road shirt, even a wool-symbol tie. Then Challis could smell the man: a heavy aftershave, tinged with alcoholic perspiration. Blurry red eyes, heightened red capillaries in his cheeks, dampness under the arms.

Rex edged between Challis and the passenger door of his Range Rover. He placed a pale soft hand on his wife's forearm, which rested on the windowsill. Everything about him said: I got the girl. The girl chose me, not you.

'Sorry to hear about your father, Hal,' he said, probably not meaning it.

Challis nodded.

'Well, mustn't keep you.'

Challis nodded again and stepped away from the Range Rover, which sped away soon afterwards, voices muffled inside it.

That same Wednesday afternoon, John Tankard sloped off work to pick up his car. He intended to take it to the VicRoads office in Waterloo, wave the roadworthy certificate under their noses, and pay for a year's registration. But the head mechanic at Waterloo Motors said, 'Bad news, pal.'

'What?'

'I'm pretty sure your car was a grey import that was subject to rebirthing.'

'Explain,' Tank demanded.

'Your car was never sold in Australia. It came in as a grey import and was fitted with compliance plates and VIN number from a written-off vehicle. There's no way it complies with Australian design rules. Even if you did spend the thousands and thousands of dollars necessary to make it compliant, there are no parts available locally, and service costs would be high.'

Tank snarled, 'I'm a police officer.'

'I can see that,' the guy said, taking in Tank's uniform. 'As a policeman you know we have to abide by the regulations. Your car is missing many of the items necessary for registration here: side intrusion bars, child restraint mounting points, for example.' He was reading from a list. 'The seatbelts don't pass, the cooling system is insufficient for Australian conditions, the speedo is only graduated to one hundred and eighty kilometres per hour, the exterior mirror on the driver's side is convex...I could go on.'

Tears of rage and disappointment pricked Tank's eyes. He felt a black cloud hovering. 'You're just loving this.'

The mechanic was unmoved. He handed Tank the keys. 'There's no charge. I could see immediately what was wrong.'

'Why didn't you call me?'

'Busy,' said the mechanic.

'I'm going to see what VicRoads has to say about this.'

'I've already informed them. Sorry.'

'You're not sorry.'

Tank shot around to the VicRoads office in High Street and asked what could be done. He was hot and blustery and it did him no good at all. 'I'm afraid we've already black-flagged your car,' sniffed the guy behind the counter, the sniff owing a little to hayfever and a lot to superciliousness. He had very red lips, dampish eyes and nose. John Tankard wanted to thump him.

'What do you mean, black-flagged?'

Tank had slipped away from work for five minutes. He could see that he'd need five hours.

'Just what I said. You can't register that car in Victoria, or anywhere in Australia. We've black-flagged it.'

'But I bought the car from a dealer fair and square.'

'But not with a roadworthy certificate, apparently. That should have alerted you.'

'You're saying it's *my* fault?'

'Sorry, sir, but you're a policeman. Go back to the dealer and get him to return your money.'

The dealer, then the finance company, thought Tank miserably, and neither one is going to want to know me.

Evening, the light outside setting toward full darkness as Ellen sat with a scotch in one of Challis's armchairs. The fact that it wasn't her own armchair, glass or scotch served to underline her estrangement from her old life. She'd had foundations back then—her own house, family life—and now she was living alone in temporary accommodation. She took a gulp of scotch: seeing her situation in those terms was too depressing for words. For a start, it rendered Hal Challis as some kind of remote landlord who might turf her out at any moment. She needed to hear his voice. That would banish the image.

She called him. No answer.

She immediately called Larrayne. 'Everything okay, babe?'

'Yes, for the ninetieth time.'

Larrayne's voice was muffled, her tone distracted, as though she was engaged in some other activity, like painting her nails, taking notes from a textbook or fondling her boyfriend. Ellen didn't know. Larrayne had a new life now, new daily habits.

'Just checking.'

'Yeah, yeah,' Larrayne said, and Ellen wanted to slap her.

'Mum,' said Larrayne suddenly, her tone focussing, 'are you working on this paedophile thing?'

'Yes,' Ellen said. Maybe she'd get some respect, some acknowledgement.

But Larrayne failed to follow through. Ellen heard chewing. 'It's a nasty one,' she went on.

'Don't tell me, I don't want to know,' Larrayne said, Ellen sensing a shudder of distaste in her daughter. A creature cried in the night. Maybe a fox, maybe after the ducklings.

The call finished, Ellen turned to 'Evening Update', which told her that Katie Blasko had been abused and kept dosed with Temazepam. Now, that information could have been leaked by a hospital worker, but just as easily by a member of her team. Shit, shit, shit.

30

Just before lunch on Thursday, Ellen Destry learnt a great deal more about Neville Clode, owing to a visit from a Children's Services psychologist.

'I don't understand why you didn't come to us as soon as Katie disappeared,' Ellen said.

'What good would that have done?'

Jane Everard was about forty, with a cap of pale fine hair, and wore a sleeveless white shirt over a dark blue cotton skirt. Her glasses, costly and fashionable, glinted contemptuously, an impression reinforced by her mouth, half open with a sardonic twist to it. Her teeth were a little crooked, which Ellen found oddly reassuring. In all other respects, Dr Everard was forbidding.

They were in Ellen's office on the first floor of the Waterloo police station. 'We would have investigated,' Ellen replied.

'Yeah, sure, males investigating males, just like last time.'

Ellen stared at Everard, blinked, then leaned back from her desk, telling herself to be conciliatory, start again. 'I'm sorry if you got no satisfaction last time,' she said. 'But this is all new to me, so please be patient.'

The psychologist evidently weighed it up and returned Ellen's smile. 'I hadn't realised that a woman was in charge of the abduction until I saw a story on the TV news,' she said. 'I came forward, hoping you'll be more amenable than a man. I'm hoping you're not a part of the masculinist culture of the police.'

Careful, Ellen thought. It's not your place to point that out to me—even if I do agree. 'Why don't you start at the beginning, Dr Everard?'

After a moment, Everard said, 'Call me Jane.'

'Jane,' Ellen said. She didn't return the favour. She wanted to keep some distance. Maybe they'd become pals, but not yet.

'It all started eighteen months ago. A couple of teachers from Waterloo Secondary College started hearing rumours that kids from Seaview Park estate had been sexually molested by a man in the town. They went to the police, who seemed unable or unwilling to do anything.'

Ellen made a mental note to check the logs. 'Did they say why?'

'Lack of evidence. The teachers didn't even have names to give them.'

'Well, there's not much that we can do if we don't have possible victims or culprits to interview.'

Again she got a 'So, what's new?' look from the psychologist, who went on to say, 'To cut a long story short, the principal and the welfare co-ordinator at the school contacted us to come in and run some workshops.'

Ellen glanced at her notes, hurriedly scrawled when Everard had first come into her office. 'You are the Child Sexual Abuse Prevention Agency, attached to Children's Services?'

'We are.'

'Go on.'

'We ran several classroom workshops at all age levels, from Year 7 through to Year 12.'

Ellen waited.

'We discussed the forms and levels of abuse, to help kids realise that they had rights, and the protection of the law, and how to avoid certain situations, and when and how to report abuse.'

'And?'

Jane shrugged. 'As expected, it was new and terrifying information to many kids, nothing new to others. Most looked uncomfortable.'

'Embarrassment is a great prophylactic,' said Ellen, immediately regretting her choice of words.

Jane cocked her head. 'You could say that.'

Ellen flushed. 'Did any of them come forward?'

'We encouraged them to write down their concerns and pass those to us.'

'Anonymously?'

'Yes.'

'And?'

'Two girls in Year 7 and one girl in Year 8 asked to speak to us privately. They gave mobile phone numbers. One girl wrote this…'

Jane Everard poked a scrap of paper toward Ellen with a slender forefinger. The nail was blunt, but lacquered a bright red. Out of habit, Ellen prodded the note into position with a ballpoint pen.

'There is this guy Nev Clode in Waterloo,' she read, 'and he does stuff to girls and he tried to do it to me but I run off but one of my friends didn't, I don't want to give you her name.'

Ellen looked up.

Jane caught her expression. 'You know this Clode, don't you? *In*-credible. Absolutely incredible. How is it that he's roaming free?'

'I can't discuss an ongoing investigation with you, Jane, you know that.'

'Oh, bullshit. We have a paedophile in our midst, Katie Blasko was apparently abducted and raped by paedophiles…Are you going to look into this or not?'

She'd cast aside her formal enunciation, showing heat, showing a personality that Ellen could relate to. 'We are.'

'You know this creep?'

Ellen smiled the kind of smile that answered Jane Everard's question.

'Well, Ellen, I'm telling you now, you won't get very far if you're relying on Senior Sergeant Kellock or Sergeant van Alphen.'

Ellen didn't want to hear this. 'Is that why you've come forward now? Because they're in trouble?'

'*In* trouble? They *are* trouble.'

'You'd better explain.'

Glancing at her notes, the psychologist said, 'First, we spoke to the three girls in person. The writer of that note said, and I quote, "Clode tried to kiss me and feel me and he tried to get me drunk. He showed me his dick as well. I ran away but this friend of mine goes back there sometimes."' Everard glanced up at Ellen. 'The second girl gave a similar account, again refusing to name the friend, who turns out to be the third girl. She gave a clear, unprompted account of being abused. Clode would apparently sit her on his lap and reach around and touch her between the legs. On several occasions he raped her. He also took photographs of her.'

'Did she consent?'

Jane said coldly, 'Does that matter? She's thirteen.'

Ellen shook her head irritably. 'What I mean is, she goes back there, according to her friends. Why?'

'Why do you think? He pays her, some cash now and then, marijuana, booze, cigarettes.'

Ellen felt stricken, and it must have shown in her face. Jane smiled kindly. 'I know, I know. She said lots of the estate kids visit him. She herself started going to him when she was eleven, in primary school.'

'Can you give me her name?'

Jane wasn't keen to do that. Eventually she said, 'Only because I trust you. It's Alysha Jarrett.'

Ellen blinked.

'You know who she is?'

'We know the family.'

'Incest?'

'That's never been suggested,' said Ellen carefully. 'They're known to us in other contexts. What did you do next?'

'Contacted the sexual crimes unit in Melbourne.'

'Not the Waterloo police?'

'No. We wanted to act quickly and firmly on this. Big mistake.'

'How so?'

'Melbourne sent down three male detectives. They arrived half a day late. On arrival, they didn't come to see my colleagues or me but went straight to Kellock and van Alphen—mates of theirs? By the time they came to see us, they'd already made up their minds.'

'Did they interview the girls?'

'If you can call it that.'

'Explain.'

'The interviews were a joke, lasting only ten or fifteen minutes. We saw the reports: nowhere do these so-called detectives give any detail about what questions they asked or what the children said in reply. Brief summaries are all you get, and even they are contradictory. I talked to the school's welfare co-ordinator, who was allowed to sit in on the interviews. She said the detectives were rude and intimidating. It was clear to her that they'd prejudged the children. In tone and body language they were accusing the children of being liars, stirrers, troublemakers.'

Ellen closed her eyes briefly. 'Oh, God,' she murmured.

'Then these three esteemed members of Victoria Police went to the pub with Kellock and van Alphen.'

'You saw them?'

'Yes. We tried to talk to them immediately after the interviews, but they warned us off, said it would be all in their report. I was so pissed off I followed them to the pub. They gave me the cold shoulder.'

'I'd like copies of all reports.'

'I'm a step ahead of you,' Jane Everard said, passing a folder across the desk. 'Main summary on top.'

Ellen scanned it quickly, catching the phrase 'on the grounds that no criminal offences were disclosed'. She looked up. 'Did you follow through?'

'We decided to report the matter to the Department of Human Services. They followed it up, then reported back to us, saying they'd elected not to pursue the matter further because the sexual crimes unit and the Waterloo police had told them that a full investigation had been carried out and the children were safe.'

'Safe to be abused by Clode again,' Ellen muttered.

'Are you going to do anything about this?' Jane demanded.

'Yes.'

Jane got to her feet, gathered her things. 'Good luck,' she said, evidently not believing in luck, or Ellen.

Meanwhile Scobie had been assigned to interview Neville Clode's married stepdaughter, Grace Duyker. He was shown into the kitchen of a kit house situated on a sandy track among ti-trees in Blairgowrie, on the Port Phillip Bay side of the Peninsula. The house was vaguely American log cabin and mid-western barn in design, the air laden with a headachy mix of new wood, carpet, plasterboard, paint and wood stain odours. And freshly baked muffins on a rack. Green numerals on the oven gave the time as 13.10. Scobie realised that he hadn't had lunch. He'd been poured a mug of weak tea but not offered a muffin.

He took out a pen and his notebook. 'First if I could have Mr Duyker's work details.'

Grace Duyker was confused. 'What?'

'We'd like to speak to your husband as well, Mrs Duyker.'

Grace Duyker threw her head back with an appreciative laugh. 'Duyker is my mother's maiden name. I didn't take my husband's surname.'

'Forgive me,' Scobie Sutton said, making the alteration in his notebook. He said delicately, 'Is there a reason why you didn't take your father's name?'

'He was never in the picture. It was only my mother and me. Then when I was fourteen, Mum married Nifty Nev.'

Scobie grinned. 'Nifty Nev.'

Grace Duyker grinned back. She was about thirty-five, he guessed. His gaze flickered around the kitchen, taking in further information. There were crayon drawings under fridge magnets, a bicycle abandoned on the back lawn, which was visible through the window above the sink, and four or five photographs of Grace, her husband and seven-year-old daughter. Typical family snaps: plenty of sunshine, grinning teeth and bright T-shirts. But there was also a photograph of a middle-aged woman who looked worn down by life.

'My mother,' Grace said, following his gaze.

He nodded. 'Clode has a similar photo of her.'

'That's not exactly reassuring.'

There was something unbalanced about the composition of Grace's photograph of her mother, as though part of the subject matter had been cropped with scissors. Clode?

'She died last year,' Grace continued.

'I'm sorry.'

'Neville Clode wore her down,' said Grace simply.

Scobie said nothing but waited.

'A real creep.'

'In what way?'

'Oh, nothing overt. He never touched me or anything when I was a kid, but the way he looked at me gave me the creeps. I used to hate taking my daughter to visit. Now that Mum's gone I don't see him. Look,' she said, changing her tone, 'what's this about? I know he was attacked, it was in the paper, but somehow I don't think that's why you're here.'

'We're investigating another matter.'

'And keeping it close to your chest,' said Grace Duyker, scooping up their empty cups and taking them to the sink. Scobie heard the tap run, saw her upend the cups on the draining board. She wore lycra bicycle pants under a shapeless T-shirt that reached her thighs. Her feet were bare. She returned to her chair, a solid, capable woman with a challenging air. The antithesis of her sad-looking mother, Scobie thought.

'He's clean,' Grace said, surprising him.

'Clean?'

'My husband and I tried for years to get Mum to leave him. We looked into him.'

'Private detective?'

'Yes. Nifty Nev's never been in trouble with the law.'

Scobie already knew that. 'But he made you feel uncomfortable.'

'Yes.'

'You didn't want him around your daughter.'

Grace Duyker gave him a lopsided grin. 'Finally.'

'Finally what?'

'Finally you want to know if he's a paedophile.'

Scobie shrugged minutely.

'My instincts say yes, but I have no evidence,' Grace admitted. 'My uncle, on the other hand.'

Scobie stiffened, got his pen ready. 'Uncle?'

'Write it down: Peter Duyker. My mother's brother.'

Scobie recorded it dutifully. His stomach rumbled. Silently Grace crossed to the cooling muffins and placed two before him on a plate. 'They needed time to cool. Enjoy.'

'Thank you.'

He nibbled cautiously: blueberry. Slightly doughy. But warm-centred and delicious. He took another bite, almost cramming it in.

Grace smiled. 'You're enjoying that, aren't you.'

'Delicious.'

She folded her arms. 'A real piece of work is my Uncle Pete.'

Scobie finished chewing, nodding for her to continue.

'Convictions for fraud in New Zealand and Queensland.'

Scobie ran his tongue over his teeth. 'Fraud.'

'He's a photographer, so-called. Offers to produce a professional portfolio, but fails to deliver.' Grace gave him a crooked smile. 'He photographs children, mostly.'

Scobie tingled. 'Do you know what he calls himself?'

'It varies,' said Grace. She reached behind her to the fridge and fumbled under a crayon drawing. She handed him a brochure. 'Rising Stars Agency,' she said.

'I know it,' said Scobie, feeling panicky.

'Are you all right?'

'Fine.' He coughed. 'Fraud. And he photographs children. Anything else?'

Grace Duyker grimaced and rubbed at her forehead. 'I think so but Mum was always cagey about him. Protective, but also embarrassed. I heard rumours in the family that he'd been done for exposing himself, groping schoolkids on a train, something like that. When he was young.'

'How old is he now?'

'About fifty-five.'

Scobie wrote in his notebook and Grace watched him, pleased and avid. He ate the second muffin.

'More?'

Scobie was warming to her. 'What about when your daughter gets home from school?'

'I'll bake another batch. No problem.'

This time she ate one with him. He didn't mind being managed in this way. Even so, he knew he'd have to watch what he said. For all he knew, Grace Duyker might contact Neville Clode and Peter Duyker just to gloat, thereby warning them, or her husband was in on it. Or she was.

'Where is Mr Duyker now?'

'Mr Duyker. That's good. Mr Duyker's too close for comfort.'

'He's here on the Peninsula?'

'He returns every so often—I think when things get too hot for him elsewhere. He rang a few nights ago to say he was back.' She sensed Scobie's frustration and added, 'A shack in Safety Beach. Fibro holiday house. Been in the family for decades.'

Scobie noted the address. 'You haven't seen him this time around?'

'No. He wanted to visit the other day, but I put him off.'

Scobie said carefully, 'What does he drive?'

Grace shrugged. 'Never paid much attention. I'm not good on makes.'

'Van? Sedan? Four-wheel-drive?'

'Oh, a van, to cart his gear around in,' said Grace.

'Colour?'

Again she shrugged. 'There have been two or three over the years. White? One year he had a yellow one but it broke down.'

'Married? Children?'

'No.'

'Does he have friends here?'

Grace was enjoying herself again. 'Oh, Uncle Pete and Nifty Nev have always got along well.'

31

In the mid-north of South Australia, Jim Ely was thinking that the Bluff's forefathers had chosen a well-drained site for the cemetery. On a gentle slope beyond the town's stockyards, it was screened by several old gum trees and was an oddly silent place, especially today, a soft spring day, and a good day for digging a new grave.

Ely arrived just after lunch that Thursday, driving his rattletrap truck, a Massey Ferguson tractor on the back. The tractor came with a bucket on the front, and a backhoe, making it a useful piece of machinery for hire in the district. Ely was always in demand. He'd been digging graves for ten years, but he also contoured paddocks to protect against soil erosion, dug septic lines and carved out drains, dams and swimming pools. He'd known Ted Anderson: they'd gone to school together. He'd known Ted's wife, even dating her a couple of times. With a heavy heart he parked the truck on clear ground near her grave and unloaded the tractor. The funeral was early the next morning, so today was Jim's only opportunity to prepare the grave. The Catholic priest's circuit took in several towns, and he was giving the service at two other funerals on Friday, eighty kilometres apart.

Galahs screeched from the trees, disturbed by the racket Jim was making. They wheeled pink and grey against the balmy sky and settled again as he worked.

The soil above Glenda Anderson's coffin had settled in the five years since her death but soil once disturbed is easier to gouge out than soil compacted or baked hard since the beginning of time. Jim carved away. He knew that Glenda's coffin was two metres down. He wouldn't go that deep, of course, but leave a hand's width of soil above her for her husband's coffin.

The thing is, when Jim made his first swipe at the soil, going down about half a metre, and had swivelled around in the tractor and deposited that first load, and returned for his second, he spotted an anomaly in the loosened earth. He got down and crouched for a better look.

Heavy-duty black plastic, maybe a garbage bag. But the scoop's steel teeth had gashed it open and a putrescent mass was oozing out. The stench was stupefying. Odd place, he thought, to bury offal or a dead pet. He didn't want to think past that.

He climbed aboard the tractor again and manoeuvred the bucket carefully, deftly going in under the plastic and hoisting it out. Soil fell away. The whole oozing mass rolled like jelly.

He swung around and gently trundled to a far corner of the cemetery, where he deposited the putrid bag. Jim's intention was clear: finish digging the grave, nice and tidy, ready for Ted's coffin tomorrow morning, then rebury the rubbish somewhere else.

Still his mind wasn't letting him make the obvious leap. That didn't happen until the bag split open and slime-covered trousers and shoes emerged into the open air for the first time in several years.

32

The child psychologist's accusations were serious, but Ellen wanted more facts before she tackled van Alphen and Kellock. Besides, it was too soon after the Nick Jarrett shooting. She would start by talking to Alysha Jarrett, and phoned Laurie to arrange a time.

High school got out at 3.30. Laurie Jarrett arrived with his daughter at 4.15. 'This had better be good,' he said. He glanced around Ellen's office with contempt. 'I can think of better things to do than share a building with my nephew's killers. You say you want to talk to Alysha?'

'Yes.'

Ellen's gaze went to the girl. Her initial impression was of a pretty child, physically advanced, wearing black leggings and a yellow top that showed her midriff. A typical thirteen-year-old, in fact. But she wore rings in her ears and navel, dark makeup around her eyes, as if she were years older, and knowing.

'About what?'

'Neville Clode.'

'Ah.'

Ellen cocked her head. 'Laurie?'

'Nothing. Ask away.'

Ellen began with a series of gentle questions. It soon became apparent that Alysha's air of knowingness had no foundation: she was a child; her replies in response to Ellen's gentle probing and her father's gentle coaxing were slow, monosyllabic and affectless. But she had clearly been abused by Clode. She hadn't the guile to be a convincing liar, or the ability to read people or situations to her advantage. Ellen was surprised that Kellock and van Alphen hadn't seen that. Instead, they'd demonised her because she was a Jarrett, hated by the police and the good people of Waterloo.

'A word in private?' Laurie said eventually.

Ellen nodded, first arranging for a female constable to take Alysha to the canteen. Alysha went submissively, still vague, inattentive and unaware of the situation she was in. Laurie Jarrett watched her receding back with an expression of grief and tenderness. He caught Ellen's glance as they re-entered her office. 'Some slight brain damage at birth.'

'I'm sorry.'

'Why? Was it your fault?'

Ellen gazed at the man. Again she had an impression of powerful feelings barely kept in check, and again she felt compulsion and repulsion. He was an attractive man, finely put together. 'I have a daughter,' she said.

'Yeah, but is she a victim?'

Ellen found herself telling Jarrett that Larrayne had been abducted several years earlier. Challis would have told her that you never shared personal heartaches and vulnerabilities with the bad guys, so why was she doing it? To impress Jarrett? Get closer to him? Get him on side?

He listened attentively. 'Fair enough,' was all he said at the end, and she sensed that he wouldn't use the information against her.

'Laurie, Alysha was abused by Neville Clode. Clode was attacked in his home on Saturday night. Did you attack him, or order it done?'

'No. Poor guy. Remind me to send him some flowers.'

'You can't take the law into your own hands,' Ellen said, hearing the foolishness of the words in this context.

'Then what are reasonable people expected to do when the law fails them?' asked Jarrett mildly.

Ellen blinked. Jarrett went on: 'You think I'm stupid, uneducated?'

'No, I don't think that.'

He smiled at her tiredly. 'The law did not protect my daughter eighteen months ago.'

'I agree. We should have done more at the time. But—'

'As far as the police are concerned, the Jarretts are scum. Kellock and van Alphen as good as told me that Alysha was a liar, a manipulator. You saw her. Did she strike you that way?'

'No.'

'She kept going back to Clode because he gave her money, cigarettes, clothing, CDs.'

'Did you try to stop her?'

'Yes. As far as I knew she'd stopped seeing him. When you phoned asking me to bring her in, I questioned her. She told me she'd started seeing him again.'

'Did she say why?'

'No. She can be stubborn that way. I assumed she wanted the presents he gave her.'

'Laurie, you'll have to monitor her. Meanwhile I want you to stay away from Clode.'

'Wouldn't touch him with a bargepole.'

Ellen cocked her head. 'Why didn't you do anything about him eighteen months ago?'

'I was in prison. Armed robbery.'

'You could have ordered it done.'

Jarrett merely watched her, but she could see his mind working, as though he wondered what his family had been up to back then. His head was shapely. The light caught the fine blades of his cheeks. He smirked, destroying the effect. 'Laurie Jarrett calling Sergeant

190

Destry...Are you receiving me, over?'

Ellen scowled. She pushed down with her palms as if to rise from her desk. 'Leave it to me. I'll—'

'What about Kellock and van Alphen?'

'What about them?'

'Dinosaurs, aren't they? Time they were pensioned off?'

'Are you making a threat against them, Laurie?'

'I don't know. Am I?'

His face belied the words and tone, for he looked sad and empty. His gaze went to the bullet graze on her neck, and his fingers to his own neck. 'You were lucky,' he said softly.

She touched the scar. 'Thank you.'

When he was gone, she began working on a warrant to arrest Clode and search his house. By themselves, Alysha's allegations would be difficult to substantiate, the word of a simple-minded child, further undermined by the lack of admissible evidence, the reputation of the Jarretts and the recommendations of that earlier investigation. But taken together with the discovery of Clode's DNA at De Soto Lane, the scene of Katie Blasko's abuse...

Her elation was short-lived. Before taking the paperwork a step further, she called Riggs at the ForenZics lab.

'Actually, I was going to call you,' he said.

'About?'

Riggs was apologetic. 'That DNA match.'

Her skin crept. 'What about it?'

'It turns out we already have the guy's blood sample here in the lab.'

'So? You said he was in the system.'

'Yes, but as a *victim*. He's not in Crimtrac. Another sample of his blood had been sent to us *before* the one found with the girl, what's her name, Katie Blasko.'

'You have a *victim* sample for Clode?'

'An aggravated burglary.'

Ellen closed her eyes, opened them again. Scobie Sutton must have taken samples at Clode's house and forwarded them to the lab. Why hadn't he told her? Why hadn't she anticipated that? She had to keep on an even keel. 'Okay, so you have that sample. But you also have his DNA from the Katie Blasko scene, right? That's how we know he was there—he'd been a victim in an unrelated incident. I don't see the problem. He either abducted Katie Blasko and held her for several days while he raped and photographed her, or someone else abducted her and he was invited to join in. Katie told me that a small dog had been present. It attacked one or more of the men who were abusing her. That might account for the blood.'

Riggs was silent. 'It's our procedures,' he offered finally.

Ellen went cold. She understood at once. 'You're saying the evidence is contaminated.'

'I can't...we don't...what I mean is...'

'Spit it out,' she snarled.

'We had several blood samples come in from several jurisdictions and agencies over a short period of time,' said Riggs in a whining rush. 'We're overworked and understaffed.' He paused, coughed. 'Unfortunately victim blood samples were somehow stored with suspect and offender blood samples. If this comes to court, we're not in a position to say for certain which Clode sample is which, or even that there are two separate samples.' He coughed again. 'Procedures weren't followed.'

'You're kidding me.'

'I'm sorry,' said Riggs. 'If it helps, I don't think there *was* a mixup in this particular instance, and there's the presence of mucus in the sample, possibly from a nosebleed, but we've had a few stuffups in the past couple of years, and a good lawyer will cast doubt on our procedures in this case. We can't lie on the witness stand.'

Ellen's head pounded. A few stuffups? Now *this* stuffup. 'I have nothing but contempt for you,' she said.

'There's no need to be like that.'

Wanting to lash out further, Ellen tracked van Alphen and Kellock down to the sergeants' lounge.

'If not for you two clowns, we could have arrested Neville Clode eighteen months ago and Katie Blasko's abuse need never have happened.'

She was rigid in the doorway. Kellock turned his massive head to her slowly, then back to his newspaper, which was spread open on a coffee table. He flicked slowly through the pages, stopping at the crossword. He uncapped his pen, tapped his teeth with it. 'And hello to you, too, Ellen.'

Ellen advanced into the room. 'Just because she's a Jarrett doesn't mean she's a liar. Before he went to prison, Laurie noticed changes in Alysha. Nightmares, inappropriate sexual behaviour.'

Van Alphen was a few metres away, arms folded and legs outstretched in an old vinyl easy chair. He gave Ellen a chilly smile. 'Maybe he was diddling her himself. Wouldn't surprise me.'

'Or it's all bullshit,' said Kellock, rapidly beginning the crossword as he spoke. 'You know the Seaview poverty, poor parent supervision, parents in jail, all leading to kids wagging school, shoplifting, getting their kicks out of gullible punters...'

'I'd like to know where the main file is from that time,' Ellen said. 'Which one of you two characters got rid of it?'

A couple of Traffic sergeants, rocking an old pinball machine in the corner, looked up with interest. 'Lower your voice,' said Kellock contemptuously. 'And act with professionalism.'

'I've looked everywhere in the system,' said Ellen. 'It's missing, and one or two reports have been tampered with.'

'Don't look at us for that,' van Alphen said. 'Plenty of agencies are after the Jarretts: the drug squad, major crimes, fraud...'

'There was nothing to the case anyway,' said Kellock.

'The school counsellor thought there was. A psychologist thought there was. And now, after talking to Alysha, *I* think there's something worth investigating.'

'Get more evidence.'

Her face twisting aggrievedly, she told them about Neville Clode's DNA. Kellock gave her his wintry smile. 'So you can't use it in court.'

'No.'

'He was attacked last weekend?'

'I think Laurie Jarrett ordered that as payback for molesting Alysha.'

'It had nothing to do with the Katie Blasko case?'

Ellen gestured irritably. 'Clode could be part of a loose circle of paedophiles. They don't do everything together. Perhaps Alysha Jarrett was his own project.'

Van Alphen was contemptuous. 'Alysha Jarrett is a little slut.'

'You decided that before you even investigated the complaint,' said Ellen hotly, 'and that's the story you gave the sex crimes detectives from Melbourne. You didn't even bother speaking more closely with the other girls who claim Clode molested them.'

'"Claim" being the operative word.'

'They support her story.'

Now van Alphen got heated. In the little room where the sergeants got their rest and recreation while in the station, she could smell him, his perspiration and stale aftershave. 'If there was anything going on,' he said, 'it was at the Jarrett bitch's hands. I know for a fact she was standing over Clode for favours, demanding money, booze and smokes or she'd go to the police and say he'd raped her.'

'Know for a fact?'

'Yes.'

'The fact being that he told you that?'

'Yes.'

'What amazing insights you have, Van. So you're saying paedophiles don't groom their victims, don't coerce them into abusive relationships. Maybe you even believe that paedophiles are the victims themselves. The children take charge. Is that what you think?'

Kellock interrupted mildly. 'It's not unusual, Ellen. Kids enter these relationships willingly in exchange for gifts, then when they get found out or the supply gets cut off, they claim they were forced into it.'

An unholy alliance, Ellen thought, her gaze shifting from one man to the other. Kellock had flown through the crossword. Van Alphen sipped at a mug of coffee—marked, she noticed, like hers: *Our day begins when yours ends.* 'I can't believe I'm hearing this. In effect, you both let Clode carry on abusing children for another eighteen months.'

'We talked to Mr Clode,' said van Alphen, smooth now, his outburst forgotten. 'Alysha's story was a complete beatup. I'd look more closely at the Jarrett household if I were you.'

Ellen flashed mentally on the Jarrett household and wondered irrationally who Laurie was sleeping with. She sensed all kinds of murkiness, but not father in bed with daughter. But what of the legions of cousins, brothers, stepbrothers, family friends and uncles?

'The attack on Clode,' she said.

Van Alphen shrugged. 'Could be a simple ag burg, could be Laurie decided to get revenge for the kid's false claims, could be anything.'

'Laurie is vengeful,' Ellen said. 'I'd watch your backs if I were you.'

'That prick doesn't scare us,' van Alphen said.

'Is that all, Ellen?' said Kellock. 'We're entitled to unwind without plainclothes coming in and hassling us.'

'Us against them,' muttered Ellen.

Van Alphen smiled. 'That's what policing's all about.'

She felt tired and discouraged, and changed the subject. 'Van, have you found any cold cases of interest?'

'Still looking,' he told her.

That evening Ellen told Challis about ForenZics and the DNA cockups.

He was perplexed. 'Go back a step. You used a private lab?'

She told him about McQuarrie's cost-cutting measures. 'I'll call you back,' Challis said.

She prowled his sitting room, restlessly scanning his CD collection. One caught her eye: k. d. lang, *Hymns of the 49th Parallel*. She supposed it made sense: Challis seemed to like female vocalists: Emmylou Harris, Lucinda Williams, even Aretha Franklin. What did it say about the role of music in her own life that her car radio was set to a news station and she owned very few CDs—and they were in storage? Her daughter liked techno, her husband the edgier kind of country music, but her CD purchases had always been random and sporadic. Did that denote a formless mind, or the pressures and anxieties of her professional life? She felt obscurely that she'd hate to disappoint Challis.

With her slender forefinger Ellen flipped out the k. d. lang, removed the disc and played it. The strong, sad voice filled her up. She played two of the songs again: Neil Young's 'Helpless' and Leonard Cohen's 'Hallelujah'.

What was keeping Challis?

Twenty minutes later, he said, 'I had a word with Freya Berg.'

The government pathologist. 'And?'

'Good and bad. She's lost some highly trained people to ForenZics. They pay a lot more and have better equipped labs. But some of their procedures have been suspect or careless.'

He listed a number of instances. Technicians had transported and stored items of clothing with recently-fired automatic pistols, thus transferring gunshot residue; they had stored victims' clothing with suspects', thus transferring blood, semen and fibres; they had handled the evidence from different cases over a period of time without changing their gloves; they had even contaminated new evidence with old. In one notorious instance, the DNA of a 2003 rape victim had been found on the clothing of a 2005 murder victim.

'Great,' said Ellen. She paused: 'Maybe McQuarrie holds shares in ForenZics.'

It was good to hear Challis laugh. It was good to hear his encouragement. She told him about Peter Duyker. 'He and Clode are close, apparently.'

'If you can't get Clode, get Duyker.'

'That's exactly what I intend to do.'

She'd called his mobile; now she could hear his father's house phone ringing in the background. 'I'd better get that,' he said.

'Miss you,' she said.

33

Challis pocketed his mobile and hurried through to the kitchen before the phone disturbed his father. Then he realised: Ellen had said 'Miss you.' Grinning, he answered the phone.

'Hal,' said his sister. 'They think they've found Gavin.'

She sounded panicky. It was seven o'clock and stars hung in the sky, a vastness of sky above the plains, clearly visible through the window above the kitchen sink.

'Where?'

Meg's voice was tight, barely controlled, as she explained it to him. It was a vivid account: he could see the lonely cemetery and the body coming into view, the latter image coloured by his years as a homicide inspector. He knew what time and certain conditions—water, air, chemicals, earth, and the *lack* of these—could do to a corpse.

'How certain is it?'

'His wallet was in his pocket. And his keys.'

Challis sat at the table. 'They will still need to carry out a proper identification. Dental records, DNA.'

'I know. They told me that. Hal, they said he'd been shot in the head and did I know anything about that and where was I when he disappeared.'

Challis straightened. 'Who are you talking about? Who's asking these questions?'

'Two detectives. They came up from Adelaide.'

Homicide Squad, thought Challis. 'I'll come over. Is Eve there?'

'She's staying the night with a friend. They're studying together. I haven't even had time to tell her.'

Challis checked on his father, wondering what to tell him. 'That was Meg. She—'

'I didn't see her today,' he replied querulously. 'Why didn't she come to see me today?'

The voice and manner were fretful. He had good and bad days, good and bad periods every day. Challis sat on the edge of the bed, where the air was stale, close and redolent of age and illness. 'Dad, they've found a body. They think it could be Gavin.'

The eyes turned sharp. 'Suicide? Out east? He'll be a skeleton by now.'

Challis touched his father's frail wrist. 'Buried, Dad. They suspect foul play.'

The eyes grew sharper. 'They suspect Meg, you mean.'

'Possibly. I'm going over there now. I'll see what I can find out.'

'I'm coming with you.'

'Dad.'

'I'm coming with you.'

It took Challis thirty minutes to get his father ready. They took the old man's boxy station wagon, driving in silence, his father leaning forward as though to speed them through the evening to Meg's house on the other side of the Bluff. It was a ramshackle place, with plenty of small pens and shelters, from when Gavin had rescued orphaned, injured or mistreated animals. The animals were long gone and the garden looked untamed, the spring growth getting away from Meg and Eve. The gravelled turning circle glowed white in the moonlight and the headlights flashed on the lenses of three cars: Meg's Holden, which was in the carport, a police car and an anonymous white Falcon.

Challis braked and switched off the engine. His father fumbled with the door catch, dropping his cane between his seat and the door. 'Let me help you, Dad.'

Before he could do that, Meg was there, opening the door. 'Dad, you shouldn't have come out.' She glanced reprovingly at Challis across the roof of the car as if to say, Are you trying to hasten his death? Challis shrugged.

They went into the house, to the shabby but homely sitting room, where three men waited. All three stood politely, the local man, Sergeant Wurfel, saying, 'Hello, Mr Challis.'

Challis's father gestured impatiently and turned to the other men, who were hard and suited, but weary looking, aged in their forties. Challis recognised the type: they were dedicated, hard working, cynical and exhausted. They weren't about to take anything at face value. They also knew that you start looking close to home when it's a homicide.

They stepped forward expressionlessly and shook hands with Challis and his father, announcing their names as Stormare and Nixon. Stormare was dark-haired, Nixon carroty and pale. Challis needed to get something out of the way immediately. 'Did my sister tell you that I'm—'

'An inspector in the Victoria Police? Sergeant Wurfel told us,' Stormare said.

'May I ask what you have?'

They gave him their flat looks. Nixon jerked his head. 'Let's talk in the kitchen.' He glanced at Wurfel. 'You stay here.'

Wurfel flushed but nodded.

Challis followed them into the kitchen. Here the three men stood tensely for a moment before sitting, mutually untrusting, around the little table. Cooking odours lingered: a garlicky sauce, guessed Challis.

'According to Sergeant Wurfel, you've been asking questions about your brother-in-law.'

'Yes.'

'Why?'

'He's my brother-in-law,' said Challis with some heat. 'My father is dying, my sister and my niece haven't been able to get on with their lives because they didn't know if Gavin was alive or dead. Wouldn't *you* want answers?'

He wasn't reaching them. He knew he wouldn't. Like them, he always treated these situations with an unimpressed mind.

'We don't want you meddling in this.'

'At least tell me copper to copper about the body.'

Nixon shrugged. 'Fair enough. It was found in a garbage bag, which slowed decomposition. Not a pretty sight. Pretty much a soupy sludge.'

Challis nodded. He knew exactly what the body would have looked like. 'What forensics do you have?'

'We'll try to get prints off the bag, but don't hold your breath,' Stormare said.

'We've sifted the soil,' said Nixon. 'Nothing.'

They stared at him. 'That's all we can tell you.'

'What did the autopsy reveal?'

'We're not at liberty to say.'

'But he was shot. My sister told me he'd been shot in the head.'

'We can confirm that, yes.'

Both men were watching him almost challengingly, as if to say: We know our job, pal.

'If there's any way I can help...' said Challis.

'You can't,' said Nixon flatly.

'My sister didn't do it,' Challis said. 'Nor did my father.'

They gave their empty smiles and said nothing. They all returned to the sitting room, where Wurfel sat awkwardly on a stiff-backed chair and Meg and her father shared a sofa, holding hands. Meg looked washed out. The old man looked mulish. 'Dad,' she said warningly.

He shook her off. 'So it's not suicide.'

'Doesn't look like it,' Stormare said indifferently.

The old man smarted at his tone. 'Gavin made enemies. He wasn't himself at the end.'

'Is that so?'

'He rubbed several farmers up the wrong way. He came down hard on anyone who wasn't treating his sheep or horses or dogs right.'

'Mrs Hurst, do you own a gun?'

Meg's hand flew to her heart. 'No. Of course not.'

'Surely your husband owned one, to shoot dangerous animals, put sick and injured ones out of their misery.'

She frowned. 'Now that you mention it, he did. A little .22 rifle.'

'It was found in his car,' muttered the old man.

'It was?' said Meg. 'What happened to it?'

'I handed it in to be destroyed.'

'You didn't tell me that.'

Challis was watching Nixon and Stormare, who were in turn watching the exchange. His sister and his father were asking some of the questions they wanted to ask and getting the answers they wanted to hear. Stormare turned to Wurfel. 'Dig up the paperwork.'

'Sure.'

'Do you have a bullet,' asked Challis, 'or fragments?'

Stormare ignored him. 'Are there any other firearms in the family?'

'No,' snarled the old man, 'but this is a farming area. Rifles and shotguns all over the place.'

'We'll be sure to look into it,' Nixon said, giving a smart clap of his hands as if to say, Time you went home now.

'You treat my daughter with the respect she deserves. All these years she thought he was alive.'

'Dad,' said Meg.

'Find the person who sent her those letters and you'll find your killer.'

The Adelaide detectives went very still. Challis watched their minds working even as they gave nothing away.

'Letters?' said Nixon.

Wurfel coughed. 'I was going to tell you. It's in the Misper file.'

'Dad,' said Meg, 'how did you know? Did Mum tell you?'

He gestured impatiently. 'Doesn't matter. Tell them.'

Meg turned to Nixon and Stormare. 'I thought it was Gavin, mocking me, trying to hurt me. Magazine subscriptions, memberships, credit card applications. I thought it was Gavin.' She swallowed. 'Even a subscription to *Playboy*. That was the hardest to take. We hadn't exactly been intimate for some time.'

The old man rocked a little and closed his eyes.

'Did you keep any of them?' said Stormare.

'No.'

Both detectives turned to Challis with the kinds of clever, assessing smiles that he'd given over the years. 'I don't suppose you saw any of this mail?'

'No. But look at her. Look at the hurt.'

They sighed. 'Perhaps you could come to the station and make a statement, Mrs Hurst. Tomorrow morning, nine sharp.'

Meg glanced anxiously at Challis. 'Can my brother come with me?'

'No.'

Challis's father made some phone calls when the police had left. A lawyer friend from a nearby town agreed to accompany Meg the next morning. The family's dentist confirmed that he'd been asked for Gavin's dental X-rays. The effort exhausted the old man, and soon he was slumped in his chair, apparently asleep. By now it was 10 pm.

Meg glanced at Challis, the tension tight in her face. 'First Dad to contend with, now this.'

'You've got nothing to worry about.'

'I didn't kill him.'

'I know you didn't. I mean, why would you?'

It was a rhetorical question, but Meg looked away and Challis felt his heart thump. 'Meg?'

'He was going to divorce me.'

'And?'

'He was going to rewrite his will, leaving everything to the RSPCA and sell this house.'

Challis knew that people had murdered for less compelling reasons. 'Sounds weak to me, sis.'

'But they'll investigate and think that's why I killed him. I mean, not that I *did* kill him.'

Challis placed his arm around her. 'Come and sit down and tell me about it.'

They talked for an hour, murmurs punctuated by their father's snores and heart-stopping silences when he didn't seem to breathe at all. As Meg told it, Gavin had been subject to violent mood swings for almost two years. Sometimes he was manically happy, but was more often depressed and angry. The mistreatment of animals distressed him deeply, he accused Meg of being unfaithful to him, he became protective and narrow as Eve's body matured after puberty, and he often threatened suicide. 'Threatening to divorce me, sell the house and cut us out of the will was typical of what he was like at the time he disappeared. I mean, was killed.'

'So you had no reason to suspect anything else?'

'Naturally I thought he must have committed suicide, especially when they found his car abandoned out east, but then I started to get that weird mail and thought he'd staged his disappearance and wanted to taunt me. He'd run away because he couldn't cope, but still wanted me to suffer.'

'Tell the police that.'

'I will.'

'When was the last bit of strange mail?'

'Two, three years ago. I hired a private detective. He didn't get anywhere.'

'Why didn't you ask me for help?'

'You're so far away, and so busy.'

Challis felt mortified. He tried to swallow it. 'Tell the police that, too. Show them receipts.'

'Okay. But who sent me the mail? Why would they do that?'

Challis shrugged. 'The killer, I suppose, trying to throw everyone off track.'

Paying attention to his doubts and suspicions, even uncomfortable ones, had always been Challis's main tool in detective work. He couldn't ignore the possibility that Meg, or the old man, or both of them acting in concert, had shot Gavin. The mysterious mail had been a useful bit of misdirection. The rifle that had been handed in for official destruction had been the murder weapon. The desire to find out what had happened to Gavin was fierce in him now.

'Fancy Dad knowing,' Meg said. 'Mum must have told him before she died.' She laughed, brief and rancorous. 'Not that it changed anything. Dad's always been good at holding conflicting beliefs simultaneously. Or his mind's going.'

Challis patted her back, rocked her against him briefly. 'Where were you the day he disappeared, assuming he died the same day?'

'Here.'

'Can anyone vouch for that?'

'God, I don't know, it was so long ago.'

He held her hand. They were not a demonstrative family, but holding her hand felt right to both of them. 'Meg, I saw the file they have on Gavin at the local station.'

Something closed down in her face. 'Did you?'

'Gavin used to hit you.'

She looked at him steadily. 'Only a couple of times. At the end. But I didn't kill him.'

He nodded. 'Did he hit Eve?'

'If Gavin had hit Eve I would have left him, no mistake.'

'Anyone else? Dad, for instance?'

'The whole world would have known about it if he'd hit Dad. As for anyone else, I can't say.'

'But he offended lots of people.'

'God, yes, even before he started going off the rails he was always taking people to court. Paddy Finucane, for example—Gavin brought several prosecutions for cruelty to animals against him.'

They gazed at each other. Challis told her to tell that to the police, too.

She sighed raggedly. 'I have to tell Eve. I want her here with me.'

'Shall I stay?'

Meg looked at him sadly. 'Thanks, but you'd better take Dad home.'

'I'll see you tomorrow,' he told her, and together they helped their father into the car.

Later he called Ellen Destry. 'Only me.'

'Twice in one evening,' she said, sounding pleased. He told her about the body.

'Oh, Hal, I'm so sorry.'

'A couple of homicide guys from Adelaide are sniffing around.'

Ellen was silent. She knew whom they'd be sniffing around. 'Hal,' she said warningly, 'you're not going to…'

'Of course not. Not my jurisdiction.'

'Yeah, right, as Larrayne would say.'

'But I was missing a good murder,' Challis said.

Come tomorrow morning, he intended to go in hard, tracing Gavin Hurst's last days and sworn enemies.

Friday was the morning for the District Nurse and the shire council's Home Helper, and that gave Challis three hours to himself. First he drove across town to wish Meg luck with the police interview. There was a Channel 7 news van parked in the street outside the house, and a couple of newspaper reporters leaning against Meg's fence, smoking, exchanging war stories. They'd come three hundred kilometres north for this story; it involved murder, grisly remains, concealment and buried secrets. Challis, who had perfected reporter brush-off techniques over the years, passed through as if he didn't see them.

Eve answered the door, her face tight and unhappy. He hadn't seen her since Wednesday, and made sure that the door was firmly shut before he hugged her.

'They keep knocking and ringing. I hate it. They're ghouls.'

'They'll go away eventually.'

'Dr Minchin was here earlier.' Eve looked at Challis as though recalling a bad taste. 'He took a mouth swab, can you believe it?'

Challis hugged her again. 'DNA, sweetheart, to help them identify the body.'

'I felt like a criminal.'

'There's nothing to be ashamed of.'

She heaved a sigh. 'Today's going to drag on forever.'

It occurred to Challis that Eve would be alone here while Meg was questioned. 'Want to come around with me this morning?'

'Where?'

He gazed at her steadily. 'Out east.'

She twigged at once. 'Where Dad's car was found?'

'Yes.'

She didn't ask why. It was as if she knew. He found Meg in the kitchen and said goodbye and good luck.

'Thanks.'

She looked tired and bewildered. She'd assumed that Gavin Hurst had been alive all these years, and had grown to hate him because he'd been taunting her. Now this.

'Call me when the police have finished interviewing you.'

'Unless I'm in jail.'

'I'll break you out.'

'My hero. Pity you're my brother.'

'Call me,' he said again.

'I will,' she promised.

'On my mobile.'

'Okay.'

There was a transmitting tower in Mawson's Bluff. In fact, Challis got better mobile phone reception in the wilds of South Australia than he did on the Peninsula. He kissed Meg and then hurried Eve into his car and drove east on a road that had been subject to potholes and bone-jarring corrugations back when he was a teenager driving to outlying sheep stations to pick up a girl and take her to a dance. It was a fine sealed road now, and passed through a rain shadow, leaving the grassy plains of the Bluff behind and rapidly entering stony saltbush and bluebush country—the change so dramatic that God might have thrown a switch when your eyes were blinking. If you kept going you'd reach the vast northeast of the state, a virtually unpopulated region of stone ruins, deep gorges, dry salt lakes and landmarks that named the fate of European settlement: Mount Hopeless, Termination Hill,

Dry Well Track, Blood Creek Bore.

But Gavin's RSPCA station wagon had been found only twenty kilometres east of the Bluff—twenty-one kilometres east of the cemetery. Dry country, sure. Country you could walk out into, never to be found, if you had your heart set on it. A country of hidden gullies and undiscovered rocky caves decorated with ancient Aboriginal carvings and paintings. But country that was still close to town. A daily Trailblazer bus went along that road, before turning southeast to the River Murray towns. Salesmen went along it, livestock agents, local farmers, tourists in cars and buses. Gavin could have abandoned his car and hitched a ride with a stranger, you'd reason, if you believed he'd wanted to stage his disappearance. Or he'd walked out into the dry country to die, you'd reason, if you believed that he'd wanted to commit suicide.

Two reasonable hypotheses, both widely held in the town.

Eve knew where the car had been found, and directed him to pull over fifty metres past the twenty-kilometre post. 'You're getting a feeling, Uncle Hal?'

She said it slightly teasingly. In fact, he often did feel his way into the atmospherics of a place, and the skin and bones of a victim or a culprit. There was nothing supernatural about it. It was merely one man's imagination—albeit an imagination honed by dozens of murder investigations over the years.

'Something like that,' he said.

A warm wind blew, raising a willy-willy on the dusty plain. Two wedge-tail eagles soared above, and bleached, horned rams' skulls gleamed in the reddish dirt nearby. They stood there for some time, thinking, talking, reminiscing. It was not a lonely spot. Several cars and a dirty Land Rover passed by, their drivers raising a hand in greeting.

Eve said, 'I hate to think of him being shot out here.'

'It might not have been here.'

He could see her mind working. 'He was shot somewhere else and they dumped his car here?'

'Yes.'

'That would need at least two people, one to drive Dad's car here, the other to collect the driver.'

'It's one scenario.'

Challis pictured Paddy Finucane with his sad-looking wife. He pictured Meg with the old man. Just then his mobile phone rang.

'Hal?'

Meg's tone was bright but he froze inside. 'Everything okay?'

It was as if all of the cares of her life had evaporated. 'Everything's fine. The lawyer was terrific. He made them promise they'd look at everyone Gavin brought prosecutions against.'

Challis was less enthusiastic. 'But you're not off the hook?'

'Well surely—'

'So long as you're not behind bars, sis,' he said hastily.

She was disconcerted. 'I'd better go.'

'Bye,' Challis said to the empty air.

'That was Mum?'

'She's back home.'

'I should be with her.'

Challis nodded and they drove back to Mawson's Bluff. He ran Eve through the gauntlet outside her house and then drove to the hospital, where he was directed to the cafeteria, an airy, clattering room in the east wing. Minchin sat at a window table, staring out at the scrubby trees that separated the town from one of the adjacent farms. He'd pushed a partly consumed plate of lettuce, spinach, fetta, olives and bamboo shoots to one side and was dreaming over a mug of black coffee.

'Not fond of grass?'

The doctor gave him a tired smile. 'Trying to lose weight.'

'And bound to succeed if you don't actually eat.'

'Yeah, yeah. You're here about Gavin?'

'Is he still in the morgue?'

Minchin shook his head. 'The lab.'

Meaning the forensic science lab in Adelaide, three hundred kilometres south. Challis was disappointed: he'd wanted to view the body. 'But you did the preliminary examination?'

'I pronounced death,' said his friend.

'Very funny.'

'Well and truly deceased.'

'Gunshot to the head?'

'Gunshot to the *back* of the head.'

'Shotgun? Handgun? Rifle?'

'A single entry wound, single exit wound with massive damage, so not a shotgun. And probably not a low calibre handgun or rifle.'

'Gavin apparently travelled around with a .22 rifle. You're saying it couldn't have been the murder weapon?'

'Very doubtful.'

'Any fragments?'

'Hal, I don't have the resources to determine things like that. Contact the lab.'

'I will. But you did match his teeth to his dental records?'

'Yes, and there were a couple of broken ribs, old knitted fractures.'

'Meaning?'

'Gavin was kicked by a horse about ten years ago. I patched him up. Still have the X-rays.'

'In that case you needn't have taken a DNA swab from Eve.'

'Just covering bases, Hal, you know that.'

Challis scowled and they brooded together, two men who'd once been close and had complicated ties to the dead man.

'So he couldn't have shot himself,' Challis said after a while, 'and he couldn't have buried himself.'

'But someone could have shot him by accident and panicked.'

'You're doing my job for me.'

'But *is* it your job, Hal?'

'What do you mean?'

'Those Adelaide detectives.'

'What about them?'

'They asked me about you.'

'What did you tell them?'

'Nothing to tell.'

'Did they ask *you* where you were? And if you own a rifle?'

Minchin opened his mouth, shocked and appalled, then swiftly angry. 'Fuck you.'

'Rob, sit down, I'm only asking questions that you'll be asked sometime or other, by the police or the coroner.'

'Just because I went out with Meg a few times twenty years ago.'

There was more to it than that, Challis thought. 'Yes.'

'Yours is a pretty shitty job, you know that?'

'Yes.'

'Do you know where I was when Gavin disappeared? In the UK.'

'The UK?'

'Medical conference. On providing distance health care.'

'In the UK?'

'Some of those moors towns are several miles apart, Hal.'

Challis grinned. 'True. So that lets you off the hook.'

Minchin was relaxing slowly. 'I could have put out a contract, of course.'

'Let me jot that down.'

They stared out at the drying landscape, some wildflowers here and there, aroused by a short-lived springtime rain before Challis had arrived in the district.

'I have to do my rounds now.'

'They questioned Meg this morning,' Challis said.

'Is she okay?'

'Well, she's not under arrest.'

'Should I, you know, call on her?'

Challis weighed it up, even though he knew the answer. 'Not yet.'

'You know, Hal, not once did I make a move on Meg after Gavin disappeared.'

Challis gazed at his friend. Did Rob want forgiveness, understanding, absolution? Did he want permission to woo Meg now? Meg had once bawdily confessed to Challis that she hadn't wanted Rob as the family doctor, taking pap smears, squeezing her breasts for lumps. And forget about him putting his hands on Eve. She didn't mean that Rob was creepy, just a little inept, a little pathetic, as he'd tried to go beyond first base with her in the backseat of his car when they were growing up. There had always been a kind of gingery, soft-fleshed lack of appeal about Rob Minchin, poor sod. But that didn't mean he wasn't capable of murder. Challis said, 'I think she'll need plenty of time and space, Rob.'

'Point taken.'

35

'Peter Duyker,' said Ellen Destry that same morning.

Faces tired, glum and plain resistant stared back at her. Van Alphen hadn't even bothered to attend the briefing. Kellock was flipping through and annotating a folder of reports and statements unrelated to the Blasko case. She wanted to say: *What is it with you people? Is it because Katie's a child? Is it because she wasn't murdered?* Suddenly irritated, she rapped the display board with her knuckles. 'Neville Clode's brother-in-law,' she explained, her voice sharp and loud.

There was a stir of interest. The photographs were candid shots, taken with a telephoto lens by Scobie the previous afternoon, and showed a fibro shack on stilts, tangled foliage, Duyker carrying groceries into the house, a white van in the driveway. Duyker was nondescript looking: medium height, average build, short brown hair. You wouldn't look twice at him. Then Ellen pinned three booking photographs to the wall. 'Duyker in 1990, 1993 and 1998: fraud and indecent exposure, here and in New Zealand.'

Neither prison nor age had wearied him, Ellen thought, pausing briefly. Duyker was as forgettable looking now as he'd been in 1990. She focussed again. 'The indecent exposure involved minors.'

John Tankard, looking as if he hadn't slept, raised his hand. 'Have you shown Katie Blasko these photos?'

'Yes. I called in there yesterday afternoon as soon as I had copies. She failed to identify Duyker or the van. But the van is common, and the man who'd abducted her was bearded.'

'So Duyker shaved it off or wore a disguise.'

Ellen glanced at Scobie. He also looked tired, distracted, dark circles under his eyes. 'Scobie?'

He seemed to shake himself awake. 'His niece says she's never seen him with a beard.'

'Clode?'

'She's never known him to have a beard, either.'

'Can we get either of them on tape?' van Alphen asked, entering the room at that point. 'The Blasko kid might recognise a voice.'

Ellen was curious to see him avoid the empty chair beside Kellock and sit opposite, beside Scobie Sutton. Maybe Van wanted to distance himself from Kellock after the Nick Jarrett shooting. Maybe he wanted to intimidate Scobie. She shrugged inwardly. 'Katie was doped the whole time,' she replied.

'Bring Duyker in and get heavy with him. He'll fold.'

Scobie Sutton edged his chair away from van Alphen and found the nerve to say, 'The same way you got heavy with Nick Jarrett?'

Kellock snarled, 'Shut the fuck up, Sutton.'

Scobie was shocked.

'Boys, boys,' said Ellen.

It was van Alphen who defused the tension. 'It's okay, Scobes,' he murmured apologetically, 'don't sweat it.'

There were undercurrents. Ellen couldn't work them out. 'We need more and better evidence,' she continued. 'The convictions against Duyker are old. We need to know what he's been doing since 1998, and who his friends are—apart from Clode. What are his interests, hobbies? What clubs does he belong to?'

John Tankard shifted his bulk in his plastic chair and gave her a look of unconvincing alertness and concern. 'Are you thinking Duyker and Clode are part of the same paedo ring, Sarge?'

Ellen kept her face neutral but inside she was tingling a little. Was Tank their leak to the media? 'I won't speculate, John, not without evidence. I especially don't want the media speculating about paedophile rings.'

'Just thinking aloud, Sarge,' Tankard said. He swallowed and wouldn't meet her gaze.

'And your instincts are valid, John,' she said warmly. She included the room in her gaze now. 'You know the drill, people. I want surveillance on Peter Duyker: where he goes, what he does, who visits him, anything and everything.'

'Sarge,' they said, and they filed out disgruntledly, Scobie and van Alphen holding back.

She cocked her head. 'A problem, gentlemen?'

Van Alphen seemed to change his mind. 'It can wait, Ells. Catch you later,' he said, and left.

'Scobie?'

Scobie stared at his shoes as though they might inspire him. 'There's something I have to reveal.'

Ellen felt alarmed. 'What?'

'Duyker's convictions for fraud. He cheated people, right? Promised to provide them with a portfolio of photos, if not modelling work?'

Where was he going with this? 'So?'

'So Beth hired a man to take Roslyn's photo. She paid him but he hasn't sent her the photographs yet.'

'Duyker?'

'I don't know. I'll ask her tonight, get her to ID him from photographs. But what if he had his eye on Roslyn, too? It makes my skin creep.'

Ellen screwed her mouth up in thought. 'We could get him on defrauding your wife, but I need something stronger.' She shook her head, frustrated. 'I'm sorry, Scobie, fraud of a few hundred dollars would be a bullshit charge. Duyker would plead guilty, the magistrate would let him out, and that would be the last we'd see of him.' She paused. 'What does he call himself?'

'Rising Stars Agency.'

'Why didn't you bring this up in the briefing?'

He went bright red. 'I didn't want anyone getting a laugh out of it, Beth being conned by Duyker.'

He sounded like a child. But Ellen thought he had a point. He'd barely left the room when the phone rang. It was Superintendent McQuarrie. He was in regional HQ in Frankston, and said, without preamble, 'I've been speaking to Senior Sergeant Kellock.'

That was quick, Ellen thought. Five minutes ago Kellock had smiled benignly, promising he'd do what he could to find spare officers for her surveillance teams, and then turned around and gone straight to McQuarrie. 'Sir?'

'Your proposed surveillance of this Duyker character. The budget won't allow it, Sergeant.'

'Sir, Duyker's a firm suspect. He has a record for sexual…'

'So, bring him in for questioning.'

'We need more evidence, sir.'

'We don't have the manpower. You know that. Here in Frankston we're sometimes thirty uniformed members *below* the accepted profile for a twenty-four-hour complex. Waterloo is understaffed, Mornington, Rosebud. We can't even respond to some calls for police assistance; others we respond to hours, *days* later. We have *cadets* appearing on staffing rosters. Our members find themselves patrolling solo because we don't have the manpower to partner them, putting them at risk every day and night of the week. Sometimes there are only two patrol vehicles for the whole of the Peninsula.'

Ellen knew all of this. She'd been to the stop-work meetings and read the newsletters. What did surprise her was that McQuarrie would dare to cite the Federation's grievances to support his denial of more backup and overtime. McQuarrie was management, and hated the Federation. What a cynic.

'Sergeant? Did you hear what I just said?'

'Yes, sir.'

'Get yourself some evidence and arrest him.'

'With respect,' Ellen said, 'that's why I want surveillance.'

'Like I said, we don't have the resources.'

'Fine, I'll do it myself,' Ellen said, feeling childish.

'Sergeant,' he said warningly.

'Thank you for your time, sir,' Ellen said, putting the phone down and wishing she'd said something to him about ForenZics. She began to juggle times and obligations in her head, wondering who would agree to put in hours of unpaid overtime on this.

She telephoned Laurie Jarrett. 'I'd like to show Alysha a photograph.'

'Who of?'

'A man who might be an associate of Neville Clode.'

'Might be an associate,' sneered Jarrett. 'When it comes to acting *against* my family, everything's black and white. When it comes to *helping* my family, everything's "might" and "maybe". The answer's no. She's been through enough. Find evidence and make arrests, Ellen, okay?'

He cut her off. She called Jane Everard. 'Have any of the kids you work with ever mentioned the name Peter Duyker?'

'As an abuser? No.'

'Okay, thanks.'

'How's it going?'

'Slowly.'

Then Scobie was standing in her doorway. He looked wretched. 'I'm going to be grilled about the Jarrett shooting.'

'When?'

'After lunch. They're already in the station.'

What am I, everyone's mother? Ellen sighed and touched his upper arm reassuringly. 'Just play it straight, Scobie, okay?'

Desperately needing to get away from the station, she slipped out through the rear doors and got into her car. Within a couple of minutes she was knocking on Donna Blasko's door. 'Just checking to see how you're getting on,' she said.

'Pretty good, thanks,' Donna said, showing Ellen through to the sitting room.

And she did look pretty good: somehow tidier, calmer, healthier. Even the house was neater. But Katie remained close by, almost glued to Donna's hip and watching Ellen solemnly.

Ellen smiled. 'How are you, Katie?'

'She's very strong, aren't you, pet?' said Donna, kissing the crown of her daughter's head.

'Donna, could we—'

'Katie, love, I just need a few minutes with Sergeant Destry.'

'Okay.'

They watched Katie leave the room. 'We get the full treatment, you know,' said Donna suddenly, still gazing after Katie. She swung her head to face Ellen again. 'Whispers in the street, finger-pointing in the supermarket, people finding excuses to stop and say hello, when all they want is to grill Katie for the gory details.'

'That's terrible.'

'I don't know whether to put her in another school or not. I'm giving her another week at home, then I'll decide.'

'Have the counsellors helped?'

Donna shrugged. Ellen thought she understood: she'd struck it before. People like Donna were intimidated by educated, quietly spoken professionals. They'd rather struggle than admit to pain and helplessness.

'Donna,' she said slowly, 'the other day I saw a brochure on your fridge. Rising Stars Agency.'

Donna went alert, a little indignant. 'Hey, yeah, now you're here I want to lodge a complaint.'

'You paid for photos that you didn't get?'

'How'd you know that?'

Ellen explained. Donna was appalled. 'But how come Katie didn't recognise him?'

'He wore a disguise. He drugged her.'

Donna began to punish herself. 'It's all my fault, isn't it?'

Ellen stayed for an hour, trying and failing to comfort Donna, and left needing reassurance of her own. She pulled to the side of the road and took out her mobile phone.

'Hi, sweetie.'

Percussive music, punctuated by raucous shrieks, and her daughter's voice saying, 'Mum? I can hardly hear you.'

Ellen checked her watch. Late afternoon. 'Where are you?'

'A pub.'

Ellen almost said, acting on her immediate instinct, 'Shouldn't you be studying?' Instead she said, 'Everything okay?'

'What?'

'*Is everything okay with you?*'

'Fine. Why?'

'Just checking.'

'Look, Mum, today we had our last lecture before exams, okay?'

Ellen pictured the pub at the end of the airwaves that joined her to her daughter's mobile phone. Was Travis there? Would they party on later? Go clubbing? Head-numbing music, drug-and-alcohol-dazed faces, swirling lights, slender young things crammed together, some of them predators and some of them prey. 'Don't leave your drink untouched.'

'You think I'd let some creep spike my drink? Mum, get real.'

'You can't be too careful,' Ellen said, feeling like someone's old churchgoing granny.

'Have to go, Mum, love you, bye.'

'Bye,' Ellen said but the connection was dead.

The RSPCA inspectorate headquarters for the mid-north was in a town eighty kilometres to the south of Mawson's Bluff. Leaving Meg to sit with their father that Friday afternoon, Challis drove up and over Isolation Pass for the second time in a week, and an hour later was talking to the regional director, a slow-moving, slow-speaking man in his fifties named Sadler. 'Thanks for seeing me.'

'No problem.'

'Busy?' Challis asked, nodding at the paperwork on the man's desk.

Sadler leaned back in his chair, arms folded across his belly. 'Cruelty to animals never stops, and we never rest, but nor does the paperwork,' he said, with a faint air of self-mockery. He frowned, serious now. 'Two detectives are coming to see me later. Has Gavin's body really been found?'

'That hasn't been confirmed, but it's pretty definite. RSPCA uniform and badge, wallet, watch, all identified as his.'

Sadler cocked his head. 'What's your concern in this? You say you're with the Victoria Police?'

'Meg Hurst is my sister. Gavin was my brother-in-law.'

'But it's not your case,' said Sadler carefully.

'I don't want to step on anyone's toes,' Challis said. He felt stiff and sore from the drive: the Triumph's springs and seats no longer gave much support or security. 'You can refuse to talk to me. As you said, two detectives from the South Australia police will be coming to talk to you. But my sister and father are naturally very upset. Meg thought Gavin had run out on her, our father thought he'd committed suicide.'

'But it's murder?'

'Yes.'

'You think it was related to his job?'

'I don't know. What do you think?'

In reply, Sadler left his chair and crouched at a low-slung cupboard under his office window. He grunted with the effort of retrieving a large archive box and hauling it back to his desk. 'Gavin's stuff, just in case he turned up again.'

He removed several folders, black-covered notebooks, a clipboard, pens in a rubber band and a digital camera. 'Some of this was found in his car and returned to us by your sister. But I can't let you take anything away with you.'

'Of course not,' said Challis. He flipped through the pad on the clipboard. The bottom pages were blank, the top covered in handwriting that varied from the neat to the dramatic and emphatic, dark and deeply scored on the page, as if mirroring Gavin Hurst's disturbed moods. He scanned it: he saw 'Finucane' written several times and underlined, and the words 'evidence of classic long term starvation, with some pigs in poor condition and several in a ribby condition'.

He glanced up. 'He was inspecting Paddy Finucane's place on the day he disappeared?'

'Apparently.'

'How does it work? Did someone report Paddy, or did Gavin target him for surprise inspections?'

'An anonymous call, according to the log. Someone saw that his pigs were in a distressed state, no food or water.'

'Man or woman?'

'I seem to recall that it was a woman,' said Sadler. 'Listen, is this going to take long? Are those Adelaide detectives going to come in here and find me talking to you? I like your sister, I want to help, but—'

'Just a few more quick questions,' said Challis smoothly. 'So you relayed this anonymous report to Gavin?'

'Well, it is in his district.'

'Did another inspector follow it up when Gavin went missing?'

'I did, about four days later.'

'And?'

'Mr Finucane's pigs looked fine to me.'

'How were you received by Paddy?'

Sadler looked uncomfortable. 'I really don't think—'

Challis didn't pursue it. He knew that the Finucanes had short fuses. If Gavin was also on a short fuse the day he inspected the pigs, anything could have happened.

'What's Meg going to do now?' Sadler asked.

Challis widened his eyes, trying to see Sadler as a future brother-in-law. Somehow he couldn't see Meg, let alone Eve, going for it. 'What else was Gavin working on?'

Sadler drew his hands down his face tiredly. He was in his chair again, swivelling. 'Typical stuff, the sorts of things we all encounter. For example, he was trying to trace the owner of some emaciated cows found wandering on the road. He was investigating the trapping and sale of tiger snakes. He'd prosecuted a husband and wife for live-baiting their greyhounds, and again for the state of their dog runs.'

'Names?'

'I can't tell you that,' said Sadler emphatically.

It didn't matter. Challis thought it was probably Joy and Bob O'Brien, who'd always had one or two greyhounds. He'd gone to school with them. They were the kind to struggle in school but be geniuses at cheating the taxman or anyone in authority. There were families like the O'Briens and the Finucanes all over the world, including his own neck of the woods back in Waterloo.

He asked pleasantly, 'May I see what's on the camera?'

Sadler glanced at his watch. 'I'm sure the batteries are flat after all these years.'

But Challis was already trying the buttons, without success. He tipped out the batteries, two rechargeable AAs. 'Shall we try *your* camera?'

He'd taken charge of the man, the room, and the situation. Sadler's RSPCA camera sat on the windowsill. It also took AA batteries, which Challis transferred to Gavin's camera.

He scrolled through the photographs stored in the memory. Several showed bony but not starving pigs eating scraps in a cement trough. 'Are these Paddy's pigs?'

Sadler looked. 'Yes.'

'How would you rate their condition?'

'As I said, I made an inspection. I found the situation didn't warrant prosecution or intervention. The pigs weren't fat, but they hadn't been mistreated.'

Challis chose his words carefully. 'Meg said that Gavin seemed a bit zealous in the weeks and months before his disappearance—his death.'

Sadler stroked his jaw like a farmer faced with a knotty problem and not the words to express it. 'I did have a couple of complaints.'

'From whom?'

'I can't tell you that.'

Challis let it go. 'Did *you* have any run-ins with Gavin?'

'I spoke to him about the complaints.'

'How did he respond?'

'Shouldn't I be telling this to the South Australian police?'

Challis said shamelessly, 'It will help put Meg's mind at rest to know these things.'

Sadler looked angry, but answered the question. He said tensely, 'He blew up at me on the phone.'

'And?'

'Then he got tearful. Then he blew up at me again. I slammed the phone down. Then the next thing I know, he's disappeared.'

'The police spoke to you at the time?'

'Yes. I told them his mood had been up and down a lot.'

'The people who complained: did they make threats against him?'

'No. He just said to send someone else next time.'

Challis pounced. '*He?* It was a man who complained? *One* person?'

Sadler looked hunted. 'I shouldn't be telling you any of this.'

'I am the police.'

'Even so, it's not right.'

That's all Challis could get out of Sadler. Nixon and Stormare were pulling into town as he was pulling out. He saw them glance with their roving cops' eyes at his old sports car, because it didn't belong in the bush, and because it had Victorian plates, and finally because they recognised him. He accelerated sedately, watching his rear-view mirror, and saw them swing around in a U-turn on the long, dusty highway and race after him. A moment later they were on his tail, flashing and tooting. He pulled over onto the gravel verge and they pulled in behind him. A semi-trailer went by in a blast of aggrieved air. He got out. Stormare and Nixon got out. He perched his rump against his door. 'Gentlemen.'

'Inspector, you're out of your jurisdiction here.'

'Am I?'

'Don't play dumb. You went to see Sadler.'

'Yes.'

'You'll stuff up our investigation if you keep talking to our witnesses,' Nixon said. '*Sir.*'

'I'm helping my sister.'

'You're putting ideas into the heads of our witnesses,' Stormare said. 'Surely you realise that.'

Challis did realise. For all he knew, Stormare and Nixon were very good at their job and would find the killer. He wouldn't like it if they trampled over one of his investigations. But he wasn't going to lose face with them or make promises he didn't intend to keep.

'My brother-in-law was pretty unstable in the weeks and months leading up to his murder. Moody, hypercritical, even violent. Not only with my sister, but also with his work colleagues, and with the people he was investigating.'

'We know that,' said Stormare tiredly. He waited while another truck blasted past. 'Don't tell us our jobs, okay? Butt out. Sir.'

'I'm going to see Paddy Finucane.'

'Where do you think we've been?' snarled Nixon. 'There's no need for you to see him.'

'How did you hear about him?'

'Your sister, sir, in fact.'

Challis nodded. 'What did Paddy say?'

'Sir,' Stormare said, 'I'm afraid we'll have to speak to our boss, who will speak to *your* boss, if you continue to interfere with our investigation.'

Challis thought they would do so anyway. The complaint would take a while to find its way to McQuarrie. He rubbed grit from his eyes as a refrigerated van passed close to their cars, followed by a school bus, the kids waving madly, one kid baring his bum in the rear window. Challis glanced at his watch. Almost 4 pm.

'Mr Finucane has made a statement,' Nixon said.

'Stay away from him. Sir,' said Stormare.

Scobie Sutton was obliged to wait for three hours before the shooting board officers—a man and a woman, both youngish and expressionless—took him into an interview room. With a nod and a grunt, they sat him where suspects usually sat, so that he felt like a suspect and almost wanted to add his mark to the scuffs, scratches and graffiti on the tabletop.

'You want to ask me about the shooting of Nick Jarrett?' he said, trying to keep his voice unconcerned and accommodating.

The male officer, an inspector named Yeo, gave him a humourless smile. 'Correct.'

'I didn't see what happened.'

'We know that,' said the female officer, a sergeant named Pullen. 'But you were on the scene soon afterwards, you collected evidence, and took that evidence to the lab.'

'Yes.'

She, like Yeo, smiled without warmth or humour. 'We were contacted by the lab. Apparently there were irregularities in regard to the way you collected the evidence.'

Scobie swallowed.

'Are you protecting Senior Sergeant Kellock and Sergeant van Alphen, DC Sutton?'

Scobie shook his head mutely.

'We understand that there's a certain culture in this police station,' said Pullen.

'Not sure what you mean,' Scobie said, his voice betraying his nerves. He was quaking. He'd never been in trouble before. He'd never done anything to warrant trouble. An unwelcome thought came to him that this was punishment for his displeasure with his wife and the feelings he'd had for Grace Duyker yesterday. Could God act so quickly?

'Oh, I think you do,' said Pullen. 'A masculinist culture, arrogant, protective. Kellock and van Alphen are running their own little fiefdom, correct? Men like you do their bidding, protect them, cover up for them. A culture that cuts corners, that likes to get a result, whether lawfully or not.'

The whiplash words were somehow worse coming from a woman, and maybe that was the point. 'You've got it wrong,' Scobie whispered. He wanted his wife's cuddly arms around him, protective, forgiving.

'Or maybe it was tunnel vision,' said Yeo. 'You went in looking for what you expected to find rather than what was there. You all hated Nick Jarrett, after all. I mean, he was scum, killed the son of one of your civilian clerks.'

'I followed procedure,' said Scobie stiffly.

'I followed procedure, *sir*,' said Yeo.

'Sir.'

'Don't make me laugh. Rather than call in bloodstain and GSR experts you gathered evidence and then released the scene before the techs could do their job properly. We lack separate, isolated tests for gunshot residue on Jarrett, van Alphen and Kellock, for example. Too late now. Thanks to your bull-in-a-china-shop methods, we can't construct a narrative of what happened.'

'Narrative' was a new buzzword. Scobie felt a rare anger, but tried to look baffled, an expression he'd seen on the faces of the consummate liars he'd interrogated over the years.

Pullen leaned forward. 'What did you think you were doing,

bundling everything together? Didn't your training tell you about cross contamination?'

Before Scobie could reply, Yeo hammered another question home to him. 'And you let the crime-scene cleaners come in the very same morning. Why did you do that?'

'I didn't know they'd been ordered to clean up,' Scobie protested. 'The others must have arranged it.'

'We've seen the paperwork,' said Yeo. 'Your name is on the requisition: Detective Constable Scobie Sutton. Look.'

He showed Scobie a faxed form. 'That's not my signature,' Scobie said.

He swallowed and looked inwards, down long roads of fear and shame brought on by men like van Alphen and Kellock, and their schoolboy equivalents before that. He wanted to admit that he'd been intimidated. But he could picture the scorn and contempt the admission would bring. And he didn't really mourn Nick Jarrett, he realised suddenly. But van Alphen and Kellock were dangerous. They'd killed a man, after all. So he did what most people did and played dumb.

'We don't know who was doing what, or where,' said Pullen. 'We can't verify the sequence of events.'

'No narrative,' Scobie muttered.

'Are you being smart?'

Yeo leaned forward. 'Why the hell didn't you photograph the scene, at least?'

'No camera,' Scobie muttered. 'Budget constraints.'

Maybe he could lay all of this at the feet of Superintendent McQuarrie.

'Oh, that's convenient.'

A camera, Scobie realised, would have frozen Nick Jarrett in time, his position on the floor, his gloved hands, the knife before it was moved from one hand to the other. Yeo and Pullen had a point, that was for sure.

'Those cuts on Kellock's forearm,' said Pullen. 'What's that about, do you know?'

Scobie frowned uncomprehendingly.

'You didn't notice the neat grouping? Three shallow, parallel, non-life-threatening cuts?'

'Defence wounds,' Scobie said.

'Defence,' scoffed Yeo. 'I'd say van Alphen and Kellock have their defence pretty well sewn up, wouldn't you, DC Sutton?'

'Sir?'

Pullen leaned forward. 'We need your on-scene notes, DC Sutton. Now, please.'

Scobie swallowed and looked at the wall behind her and said, in creaking tones, 'I lost my notebook.'

'Lost? Oh, that's a good one.'

They kept him there until early evening. When he came out he saw Pam Murphy in the corridor. He tried to rally. 'I thought you were away on an intensive?'

She was young and bright and healthy and he couldn't stand it. 'Just finished the first week. They let us go home for the weekend.'

'Well, good luck.'

'Thanks, Scobie.'

Pam knocked on van Alphen's door. 'Got a moment, Sarge?'

He waved her in. He looked deeply fatigued.

'Heard about Nick Jarrett, Sarge,' she said carefully.

He scowled. 'This afternoon I was chewed on by a couple of shooting board dogs.'

'Everything okay?'

He shrugged. 'They've got nothing. Take a seat. What can I do for you?'

'Thought I could pick your brains, Sarge.'

'About?'

'Interview techniques.'

'Interview techniques?' said van Alphen, faintly mocking.

Normally Ellen Destry would have been Pam's first choice, but Ellen was snowed under, looked distracted, even miserable. Plus, Pam felt a little guilty because she was leaving the uniformed branch and moving on to plainclothes. She didn't want van Alphen, her old uniformed sergeant, to think that she was a snob, had no more time for her old colleagues.

'I have to write an essay,' she said. 'Worth twenty-five per cent of my marks.'

'Essay? You should be out cracking heads.'

Pam smiled at him across his tidy, gleaming desk and said, 'Well, you're a dinosaur, Sarge. Me, I'm up-and-coming. Three thousand words by Monday morning, so I'll have to work all weekend. Questioning witnesses versus questioning suspects. What to ask, what not to ask. Establishing mood and rhythm. Using psychology and body language. Etcetera, etcetera.'

Van Alphen stared at her in disbelief. His expression said that he relied on experience and instinct, techniques learned on the job, not in a classroom, and which didn't have fancy names like 'body language'.

'Murph, you know how to interrogate people,' he said. 'I've seen you in action. You're good at it. Just write what you know.'

'What I know doesn't add up to three thousand words, Sarge.'

'Then you shouldn't have gone to detective school, should you?' he said, with a sharkish smile.

'Oh, thanks a lot,' Pam said, getting to her feet.

He waved her down. 'Take it easy, take it easy. I realise you have to get on in this game, you don't want to be stuck behind a desk or the wheel of a patrol car.'

She gave him a sympathetic smile. He must hate being desk-bound. 'You'll be cleared for duty soon, Sarge, don't worry.'

His lean, saturnine face relaxed into what passed for a warm smile.

'As you say, Murph, I'm a dinosaur. Three thousand words! Jesus.'

'Exactly,' said Pam, who was accustomed to writing terse arrest reports, in which narrative flow, tone and even grammatical sentences were a handicap.

'You said psychology. It's all psychology.'

Pam wrote the word on her pad and looked at him expectantly.

'You're interviewing a suspect,' said van Alphen. 'You want him or her at a disadvantage.'

Pam nodded. She knew that but had never labelled it before. It was instinct. 'How do *you* achieve that, Sarge?'

'Little things, and you let them accumulate. For example, use of their first name, not their surname, helps to undermine them. The use of silence—let it build until they're desperate to fill it. Fire a series of answers to unasked questions at them, your tone frankly disbelieving: "So you say you don't know how the knife got under your mattress?" for example.'

Pam scribbled to keep up.

'You used the term "body language", Murph. Terrible expression, but I guess it explains what one does in an interview room. You let your face and body show contempt, doubt, ridicule, sometimes sympathy. You get in their faces, pat them gently on the wrist, exchange scoffing looks with your partner, slam your palm down hard on the table, stuff like that.'

All things Pam had done. 'Sarge,' she said dutifully.

'And you vary your approach, keep them unsettled. Kind, then cruel.'

'Sarge.'

In the corridor outside, and in the nearby offices, were the sounds of voices, laughter, footsteps, doors slamming—familiar sounds that Pam badly missed. She glanced at her watch. She'd spend thirty more minutes with the sarge, then drive home and relax in the bath. 'But what about *their* body language, Sarge?'

'What about it?'

Pam flicked back to her lecture notes. 'If they have their legs together, ankles crossed and hands in their laps they're protecting their genitals—fending off trouble, in other words.'

'If you say so,' scoffed van Alphen, rocking back in his chair and slamming one booted foot and then the other onto the top of his desk, giving her a wry look.

Pam grinned. 'If they touch their nose and lips, it means they're stressed. There are many capillaries in the nose and lips. Blood rushes there…'

Van Alphen drew his slender hands down his narrow cheeks comically.

'Arms folded across the chest is another protective gesture— protecting the heart, concealing powerful emotions,' Pam said.

'A little book learning is a fine thing, Murph,' van Alphen said. He paused. 'On the subject of psychology: you need to find out what they want.'

'Their "dominant need",' Pam said brightly. 'Respect, safety, flattery, sympathy. One should stimulate or exaggerate this need, then finally offer to gratify it in return for a confession or co-operation.'

'So why the fuck are you asking me all this?' growled van Alphen, not unkindly.

'It's questioning techniques, Sarge. I know the psychology: I just need to know how to frame questions.'

'But it's all psychology,' insisted van Alphen. 'For example, if a suspect's tired, you fire hard questions at him.'

'The *wording*, Sarge.'

'Apart from who, what, where, when and why?'

'Yes.'

'All right, try to get at motive. Ask things like: "Can you think of any reason why someone would want to kill him?" or "Did they argue over money?" or "Was she involved with another man?" Obvious, surely.'

'Sarge.'

'Psychology,' insisted van Alphen. 'Just when they think an interview is over—you're going out the door, in fact—you turn back and hit them with what's really on your mind. Or you ask a series of absurd, grotesque or mild questions to throw them off balance, then hit them with the million-dollar question. Or you give them back their answers twisted slightly, to see what corrections they make.'

Pam scribbled, her head down, commas of hair brushing her jaw.

'You throw them a series of quick questions requiring short, simple answers, then suddenly lob a difficult one at them, a trick question. Or they answer, but you look at them quizzically until they qualify it to fill the silence. It's *answers* that matter, not questions. The absences in answers, their tone, and the specifics that can be challenged or disproved or that contradict other specifics.'

'Sarge,' said Pam, still scribbling.

'You force suspects and witnesses alike to separate what they think they know from what is actually true, you help them through uncertainties and attack their certainties.'

'Fair enough.'

'And always, always, you ask earlier questions again, worded differently.'

'Sarge,' said Pam, wondering if she had enough for three thousand words. She thought she might look up old case notes and reproduce interview transcripts, generally pad out her essay in the time-honoured way of all students everywhere.

'Always get their story first,' van Alphen said. 'Get them to commit to it. Then you take it apart, detail-by-detail. You'll find that most people can lie convincingly some or even a lot of the time, but only the good liars remember exactly what they said.'

'He doesn't work here any more,' said the manager of Prestige Autos late that Friday afternoon. 'I sacked him.'

John Tankard stood there with his mouth open, feeling powerless.

He hadn't felt this bad since that time he'd shot a deranged farmer. He'd gone on stress leave for it, then returned to work and thrown himself into the job, together with coaching a junior football team, and these things had been pretty successful in staving off depression, but it was his new car that he'd been counting on most to make himself feel better.

'The guy ripped me off,' he said hotly, 'while employed by you.'

The manager, a portly older guy with furry eyebrows, made a what-can-I-do? gesture. Plastic pennants snapped in the breeze. A salesman in a sissy-looking suit was putting the hard word to a young guy who was critically but longingly circling a Subaru WRX—drug dealers' car, thought Tank sourly—while his girlfriend looked on in boredom. A bus belched past. And so life was going on unchanged around John Tankard but he himself was breaking inside. Over a car, but still.

'I was sold the car on your premises. I bought it in good faith. You're obliged by law to provide a warranty.'

The manager was unmoved. 'The salesman who sold you that car was doing so off the books. The car was never possessed by this business. I'm a victim here, too. This is bad for my reputation.'

Tank was incredulous. 'I have to feel sorry for *you*?'

'Look, son, I have no legal obligation to give you your money back.'

'I'm not your son. Anyway, this does involve you because your finance company financed the deal.'

'Again, that was done without my authority. As I understand it, your contract is with them. I think you'll find it's legally binding. It has nothing to do with me.'

'I'm out thousands and thousands of dollars,' Tank said, wiping away tears.

'Sell the car. You'll get most of your money back. You might even make a profit.'

'I can't. It's been black-flagged in all states and territories. I can't register the fucking thing anywhere.'

'All right,' the manager said slowly, 'spend a few thousand to get it in compliance.'

'Where am I going to get that kind of money?' asked Tank rhetorically.

'I could structure a loan for you,' said the manager smoothly.

'Prick.'

'There's no need for that.'

'Thousands of dollars,' John Tankard said, his mind shooting in all directions. Had anyone been cheated like he'd been cheated...? Refuse payments to the finance company...Put a bullet through his brain...

That night 'Evening Update' floated the idea that a person of interest to the police in the Katie Blasko case had possibly been active for years in Victoria and interstate. It was a good story, kept the level of moral panic raging in the community, and worth a thousand bucks to John Tankard.

But it was more than the money. Tank considered it important to keep people in the loop. Keep them vigilant against the creeps. Protect little kids like his sister. He kept telling himself that.

Scobie came home feeling so hurt and aggrieved that he was curt to his wife. 'Is this the man?' he demanded, showing her Duyker's mugshots.

'Yes,' said Beth defensively.

They were in their sitting room, Beth putting aside one of their daughter's T-shirts, in the act of cutting out the label inside the collar, which Roslyn said was itching her.

'You paid him money for photographs.'

Beth looked mortified. The house needed airing. She sometimes shut herself in for hours, trying to keep busy. Scobie often found her gazing into space, or in tears. 'I need to find a job, Scobe,' she'd say.

'By cheque or cash?' he went on furiously. He didn't like himself for it. It's the pressure, he told himself. The police shooting board inquiry.

His feelings for Grace Duyker. He was confused and lonely and unhappy.

Beth was close to tears, and that made it worse. 'Cash,' she said.

'Damn.'

'I can show you the receipt.'

She left the room and came back with a receipt torn from a receipt book that had probably been purchased in a stationery store for $2. Scrawled blue ballpoint writing. Maybe the lab could lift Duyker's prints from it, but so what?

'Beth, listen carefully, did you ever leave Ros alone with him?'

Beth went very still and turned an appalled face to him. 'Is this more than fraud? Do you suspect him of, you know, you're working on the Katie Blasko abduction and you…'

He touched her wrist to stop the panic. 'Settle down, for God's sake.'

'You have to believe I would never knowingly put our daughter at risk like that. He never touched her.'

'Did he look at her in a certain way?'

'No!'

'Good.'

'He was a bit creepy. Smiled a lot,' Beth said.

Scobie patted her forearm absently. He prowled around the house and garden, muttering, clenching his fist. He went to the back fence and pulled out his mobile phone. 'Grace? Scobie Sutton here.'

She sounded pleased to hear from him, and that gave him an absurd little lift, the kind he'd not felt for years and years and one of the first things to go in a marriage. 'I wondered if I could pop round tomorrow,' he said. 'A few more questions.'

'Of course,' she said.

That same night, Kees van Alphen went on a prowl of the beaches. He knew them all, the nude beaches, small and tucked away, known only to nudists and a few pathetic peeping toms, the gay beaches, one near the Navy base, another near the huge bayside estate—now carved into a few exclusive house blocks—of an airline magnate. He knew all of the hangouts of the Peninsula's druggies, street kids, prostitutes, gays and rent boys. He knew that a place could be one thing by day and quite another by night.

He waited until almost midnight, and then he started to make contact. Matches flared in the darkness, briefly lighting hollow cheeks. The susurrations of the sea, the moon glow on it. A drift of marijuana smoke. Feet squeaking on the sand. Somewhere in the distance a dog barked and far away a siren sounded down a long, empty road.

Fifty bucks for a blowjob.

Van Alphen said he could be interested.

Five hundred for the whole night. Or a threesome could be arranged.

He moved on. They were very young, some of them. Barely twelve, and looking younger—older, if you looked at the experiences behind their eyes.

Then he found Billy DaCosta.

'But you had a history with him, Paddy,' said Challis on Saturday morning. 'Gavin had it in for you.'

'Like I told them city coppers, I never fucking seen Hurst that day.'

They were standing in Paddy's dusty yard, which was a vast area of soil erosion stained here and there by motor oil, paint and animal droppings. Around it were rusting truck bodies, ploughshares, harrows and car batteries, standing in collars of tall dry grass, and several corrugated iron sheds: door-less sheds for Paddy's tractor, plough, truck and hay bales, a set of low-slung pig pens, a fenced dog run and a hen house. Challis had set all of the animals into a frenzy when he drove his aged Triumph into the yard.

'He was due to come here,' Challis said. 'There was a report against you.'

Paddy spat on the ground. 'I tell ya, Hal, the bugger was never here.'

Challis had gone to high school with Paddy and other Finucanes. Paddy and his siblings and cousins liked to steal from lockers, sell exam questions, run sweeps for the Melbourne Cup horse races, and taunt the young teachers. It was mostly good-natured. They were also excellent athletes, although lazy. Their fathers and uncles all had convictions for drunkenness or receiving stolen goods and were often away for short stretches.

None of that had mattered at the time. But then Challis had gone away to the police academy, returning to the Bluff as a uniformed constable, young, pimply and barely shaving. Within days he'd found himself obliged to arrest the very same Finucanes he'd gone to school with. They wouldn't struggle, argue or appeal to his better nature—they knew they'd been caught fair and square—but they would look at him in a certain way, partly mocking, partly disappointed. It was as if they—the whole district, in fact—thought he'd let the side down. Soon Challis was turning a blind eye. His sergeant, Max Andrewartha, told him to rethink his options. 'You're too soft,' he said. Pretty soon, Challis had resigned and moved to Victoria, where no one knew him. He joined the Victoria Police, eventually becoming a detective, and now was an inspector, living near the sea, not right out here in the never-never. He lived in a landscape where the rain fell and all was green.

But back here in the Bluff he was still the guy who'd gone to school with some of the locals and been a failed town policeman many years ago. He was called Hal. He wasn't some stranger.

'Hal?' Paddy said, breaking into his reverie.

Challis blinked. Paddy's face was seamed from years in the sun. He was slight, wiry, canny. He was a clean-looking man in filthy work clothes. Challis had no doubt that the clothes were laundered repeatedly by Paddy's poor, timid wife, but the oil, grease and paint were permanently melded to the cotton weave.

'Paddy, I won't bullshit you, they're sniffing around Meg.'

Paddy nodded. 'The divorce thing.'

Challis blinked. He shouldn't have been surprised. The Finucanes knew everything about everybody. 'Meg thought that Gavin had run off on her.'

Again Paddy nodded. 'Them letters she got.'

'She told the police that Gavin had made plenty of enemies those last few months.'

'Enemies like me, you mean? Mate, he was a prick from the moment he come into the district.' Paddy swept one scrawny arm over the infinite earth. 'No people skills, that's for fucking sure.' He grinned.

Challis grinned back. Gavin had always seemed an up-tight, lay-down-the-law type to him, too, on the few occasions they'd met over the years, usually at Christmas time. No one in the family had quite known what Meg had seen in him, but she'd seemed happy enough with the guy.

'Tell me about some of the run-ins you had with him.'

Paddy cocked his head. 'You sound like them Homicide blokes, you know that?'

'Well, Paddy, that's my job, too.'

'But not here it isn't.'

'True.'

'Mate, you know me; you know where I come from. We cut corners, you know that, but we're not mean or vicious.'

Challis said, with mock solemnity, 'I have it on very good authority that you rubbed sawdust in his face.'

Paddy roared, then wiped his twinkling eyes, quite worn out. 'That I did, that I did. The cunt reckoned sawdust wasn't a fit bed for dogs; it was smelly and bred fleas and disease. I picked up a handful and said, go on, smell it. Well, he didn't, of course, so I rubbed it in his face and shoved it down his neck. A mistake, yeah, I can see that, but it felt fucking good at the time.'

'What else?'

'The usual. Was I washing the shit out of the pig runs regular? Why was I keeping the sheep in an unsheltered paddock? Was I keeping water up to them? Stuff like that.'

'People reported you? Your neighbours?'

'Maybe, I don't know. All I know is, the prick liked to turn up unannounced and walk around like Lord Muck with his clipboard.'

Challis pictured it and grinned at Paddy. Paddy scuffed the dirt with the toe of his boot.

'When's the funeral?'

'Monday.'

Paddy nodded, looked off into the distance. 'I'm no killer, Hal.'

Challis didn't think he was. But if Gavin hadn't been at Paddy's the day he disappeared, who had taken the photographs? Who had made the anonymous report?

'Sadler came to see you a few days later?'

'Yep. Told me your brother-in-law left him a shitload of work to follow up on. I gotta say, he was a more reasonable bloke to deal with.'

'He didn't find anything wrong here?'

'Nope.'

'Did he take photographs of your animals?'

'Nope.'

'*Could* he have, when you were out?'

Paddy shrugged but could see where Challis was going with this. 'You think Sadler killed him? Who knows? Old Gav must have been a bastard to work with. Complaints flowing in left, right and centre.'

With a half smile, Challis said nothing.

'When them Adelaide blokes finished with me yesterday, I got the feeling they were going to see Sadler.'

Challis said nothing.

'They didn't believe me when I said Gavin Hurst wasn't here.'

'Didn't they?'

Paddy Finucane said, 'Fuck off, Hal. Look, you going to help us out?'

'What can I do, Paddy?'

'Talk to the bastards.'

Challis guessed that Sadler would have shown the photographs from Gavin's digital camera to Nixon and Stormare, meaning the Adelaide detectives would have even less reason to believe Paddy's story. With a series of minor gestures that might have meant anything at all, he left Paddy's farm and drove home to see to his father's needs, the shadows disappearing from the dusty paddocks and the sun high overhead.

That afternoon, as his father slept, Challis sat in the backyard sun with the Saturday papers, his address book and mobile phone. He'd taken the house phone off the hook, and made it clear to the reporters who knocked on the door from time to time that he had nothing to say. But they knew he was a detective inspector from Victoria. There seemed to be a story in that.

He finished the *Advertiser* and the *Australian* and then called Max Andrewartha. 'I suppose you've heard?'

'Mate, it's the story of the week—or the day, at least.'

'There's nothing in that file, is there?' said Challis, knowing his voice carried frustration and anxiety. 'Nothing I missed? Nothing we missed?'

Andrewartha was silent for a moment. 'Mate, I should tell you a guy from Homicide called me yesterday afternoon.'

'Nixon? Stormare?'

'Nixon.'

'And?'

Another silence, the quality of it making Challis apprehensive. 'He asked me a lot of questions about the case, but he mainly seemed interested in you, and in me.'

'You? You weren't here when it happened.'

'I know that. But they see us as mates.'

Challis said flatly, 'They want you to steer clear of me for the time being.'

'That's about it. Sorry.'

'Well, given that I'm family, I am a suspect.'

He'd been one thousand kilometres away at the time, investigating the murder of a man found in the sand dunes near a lonely Peninsula beach.

'Family first,' Andrewartha said.

'Family First is a fundamentalist Christian political party, Max.'

'I rest my case.'

Challis smiled slightly, enjoying the sunshine. 'I was going to ask a favour.'

'I'm fresh out of favours, Hal,' said Andrewartha warningly.

'Have you got someone I can call in the forensic lab, that's all.'

'Sorry, pal.'

As if to mark the end of something, a querulous voice called to Challis then, and he returned to the dark rooms of his father's house.

Ellen Destry's Saturday had started with a one-hour walk, the morning air almost sickeningly scented from the springtime blossom and grasses, with the result that she returned with red-rimmed nostrils and itchy eyes. A shower cooled her hot face, and she ate breakfast outside, in the low sun. No sign of the ducks, but the open slope of land beyond Challis's boundary fence was dotted with ibis and a couple of herons. She barely registered them. She and Scobie Sutton would begin shadowing Peter Duyker today. Van Alphen and Tankard were owed time off, and didn't intend to start helping until Monday.

She cleared away her cup and bowl, and drove to Duyker's house. She soon established that he was there, but he didn't stir until mid morning, when he drove to the netball courts in Mornington and watched girls playing netball. Scobie relieved her at 2 pm, thirty minutes later than he'd said he'd be. She relieved him at 6 pm, by which time Duyker had returned home. She watched until midnight; Duyker went out once, walking to his local pub and staying until 11 pm. She followed him home and saw his light go off at 11.45.

Scobie had first watch on Sunday. She relieved him at 1.30, when he reported that Duyker had gone out once, late morning, to buy bread, milk and the Sunday newspapers. She waited until 3 pm before Duyker appeared. She tailed him to a couple of popular beaches, where he watched children dig sandcastles and play with kites. He went home at 6 pm. Scobie rang her three hours later to say that Duyker was apparently watching television. She told him to wrap it up for the day.

She had extra hands to help her from Monday, and a long week unfolded. At the beginning and end of every day, she held a briefing, always starting with the words, 'So, what's our guy been up to?'

Variations on his weekend movements, apparently, and sufficient to arouse their suspicions. Ellen herself reported that she had seen him cruise slowly past a school playground one lunchtime and again at going-home time. At morning recess the next day he'd returned to the school and parked next to the fence line, where an old woman wheeling a shopping cart had stopped to watch the children at play, together with two much younger women, the kind of idle, anxious mothers who live through their children and haunt their children's schools.

'Duyker actually *joined* them,' she reported. 'You'd think that would have made them suspicious, but he seemed to be sharing a joke with them.'

Later in the week John Tankard reported that Duyker had spent the whole lunch hour watching from his van. 'Finally a teacher came out of the gate and tapped on his window.'

'What did he do?'

'Talked to her, then drove off. I asked her what he'd said. Apparently Duyker had a newspaper propped on his steering wheel and was eating a sandwich. Said he was a tradesman on his lunch break. She wasn't suspicious.'

Scobie Sutton tailed Duyker on Wednesday night. At Thursday morning's briefing he reported that Duyker had watched netball training.

'Netball again?'

Scobie looked sick at heart. 'Kids Ros's age.'

'And after netball?'

'He went straight home.'

'You're sure?'

'I removed a globe from his rear lights so I wouldn't lose him in the dark.'

'Scobie, put it back again.'

'It's just a globe.'

'I don't want some gung-ho traffic cop pulling him over and spooking him. Put it back.'

Scobie sighed. 'Fair enough.'

Ellen witnessed the next incident. At 3.45 on Thursday afternoon she tailed Duyker to a dusty lot opposite a small church hall on the outskirts of Penzance Beach. Several cars were waiting, some of the occupants leaning against their doors, talking to each other. A few minutes after 4 pm a succession of school buses pulled in, discharging kids from a range of far-flung secondary schools. One by one the waiting parents drove away until only Duyker's van was left, parked among trees and almost invisible. She couldn't see Duyker.

Alarmed, she got out, peeked in his window, looked around wildly. A sealed bicycle path wound through a scattering of nearby pine trees. On the other side of the pines it veered past a set of rusty swings and seesaws and around the perimeter of the football ground and tennis courts. There were houses after that, backing on to open farmland. It was a desolate stretch of land, choked with chest-high grass, blackberry canes and shadowy hollows. A solitary figure was walking along the bicycle path, almost one hundred metres ahead of Ellen, who recognised the uniform of Woodside, a well-heeled private school on the other side of the Peninsula. The girl wore the skirt very short, her long legs shapely but lazy under it, as she scuffed along the path. Suddenly the girl stiffened, stood stock-still in the centre of the path as Ellen hurried up behind her. Duyker was in a little clearing, barely visible in the transfiguring light. What a cliché, was Ellen's first thought, for he wore a long coat. He was hunched a little, his hands busy, but Ellen could only speculate, for the girl was obscuring her view.

Suddenly Duyker crashed away through the trees and the girl laughed raucously at his back and tossed a stone after him. 'Loser!'

'Excuse me!' yelled Ellen, out of breath.

'What?'

It was Holly Stillwell. Ellen's daughter had gone to school with Holly's older sister. 'Didn't recognise you, Holly.'

'Hi, Mrs Destry.'

'Did that man…was that man…'

'Creep!' said Holly, laughing.

'Did he expose himself to you?'

'Gross!' said Holly, still laughing. 'Pathetic!'

'I'll walk you home,' Ellen said.

'That's okay, Mrs Destry. No need, I'm all right.'

'No, I insist.'

They walked. 'How's Larrayne? I haven't seen her for like ages,' Holly said.

'She's fine. Got exams soon. Look, Holly, I need you to give me a statement.'

Holly still thought it was a huge joke. 'Forget it,' she said, as if Ellen had offered to do her a favour. 'I've seen worse. He's just a pathetic little man.'

'Still, it was indecent exposure and it's illegal.'

'Yeah, but all he did was wave his stupid willie at me. It's not the first time that's happened. I mean, it's gross, but no big deal. No big deal, get it?'

The girl was irrepressible. 'I get it,' Ellen said. 'But if it's happened to you before, was it that man?'

'Never seen him before,' said Holly.

Ellen left it at that. Duyker would be on his guard now—in fact, Scobie Sutton saw Duyker dump half-a-dozen pornographic magazines that night.

And then, at Friday's evening briefing, Ellen presented her little team with a more pressing development.

'Owing to Van's work, trawling through the files,' she said, nodding her head at van Alphen, who replied with the briefest of expressionless smiles, 'we have a very instructive cold case.' She indicated an array of crime scene photographs, tapping them with her forefinger. 'Serena Hanlon, eight years old, raped and strangled in 1996. Her body was found here, in Ferny Creek.' She tapped a wall map that showed the city of Melbourne and the ranges to its east. 'Her schoolbag was later found here, several kilometres away.' She indicated the town of Sherbrooke.

'Duyker?' said Scobie.

Ellen leaned both hands on the back of her chair, inclining her body tensely over the head of the table. 'In 1996 Duyker was living near Ferny Creek. He was working near Sherbrooke.'

'Was he questioned?'

Ellen looked to van Alphen, who said, 'No. He should have been a person of interest because he'd been questioned over an indecent behaviour incident in Sherbrooke a year earlier, but his name wasn't passed on to detectives investigating the murder.'

They all shook their heads. 'I know, I know,' Ellen said. 'One thousand suspects were eliminated in that case, two and a half thousand homes searched, one thousand cars searched, and Duyker wasn't on the list.'

They were quiet, thinking that Katie Blasko had been lucky, and wondering how many other Serena Hanlons were out there, rotting in the ground.

'He has a record for sexually deviant behaviour,' Ellen said. 'We ourselves have witnessed instances of it. What we don't have is hard evidence that he also abducts and rapes, let alone kills, little girls.

Mounting suspicion, yes. Evidence, no. Meanwhile the super, in his infinite wisdom, has cut down on our resources.'

She noticed, and ignored, the way that Kellock—the super's friend—was watching her, giving her a sardonic smile, as if she were being unprofessional. 'Kel?' she queried.

He shrugged. 'You could get Duyker for flashing that schoolkid.'

'And see it thrown out because she won't press charges? No thanks.'

'You were there, Ellen.'

'I didn't actually see his penis,' said Ellen, unable to hide her distaste for the word in this context.

'Come on, Sarge, just say you *did* see it, and arrest him,' said John Tankard.

'Thank you, constable, for encouraging me to pervert the course of justice.'

Tankard flushed and muttered.

Ellen was angry now. 'You guys just don't get it, do you? Let's say I do arrest him. He gets bail because some magistrate decides it's trivial, and immediately absconds after destroying incriminating evidence. Or, if he sticks around and it goes to court a year from now, it's my word against his because the girl won't press charges. Or if he *is* convicted he gets a rap over the knuckles or a short custodial. I don't want him to go down for a bullshit charge. I want him to go down for a very long time on charges of abducting and raping Katie Blasko and, if we're lucky or he confesses, abducting, raping and murdering Serena Hanlon and God knows who else. Understood?'

'Sarge,' they said, looking away awkwardly.

'I've got his DNA,' said Scobie shyly.

Ellen paused, her mouth open. She closed it. Someone else said, 'How?'

'The porn magazines.'

'He'd wanked over them?'

'Yes,' Scobie said. He looked around the room. 'Probably

inadmissible in court, but at least we can compare it to the samples found at the Katie Blasko scene and the murder of this other girl.'

Ellen smiled. 'True. Good work.'

It was a nail in the coffin. That's how most cases were built, a nail at a time. Even so, too much was resting on DNA matches and Ellen wanted more and better evidence than that. 'Go home,' she said. 'I've arranged half-day shifts for each of you over the weekend, and we'll begin in earnest again on Monday.'

Meanwhile Pam Murphy had come to the end of her second week of intensive study, this time at the police complex in the city. She had another week to go. Her parents had urged her to stay with them, for they lived only fifteen minutes by tram from police HQ, but they were old and frail, and she knew she'd get caught up in their lives, spend all of her free time shopping, cooking, cleaning, ironing and taking them to the doctor. They'd want to domesticate her. It was okay for her brothers to have professional lives but she'd always had the niggling feeling that her parents had assumed she'd get married and have kids.

And so she'd been commuting to the city from her home in Penzance Beach: thirty minutes by car up the Peninsula to the end-of-the-line station in Frankston, then one hour by train into the centre of the city—one hour of madly finishing essays or catching up on her seminar reading. Yeah, she felt guilty because she could have been helping her parents, and was tired from all of that travelling, but she was very glad to sleep in her own bed at night.

Like her—like almost everyone who worked at the Waterloo police station—Kees van Alphen didn't live in the town. He lived in Somerville, a town some distance away, in a 1970s brick house that was much the same as the others in his cul-de-sac between the shops and the railway line. On her way home that Friday evening, Pam went by, checking his driveway. Good, his little white Golf was parked there.

'Thought you'd like to read this, Sarge,' she said, moments later, thrusting a manila folder at him.

Her essay on questioning techniques and strategies, back promptly from her tutor, marked A+. She could have e-mailed it to van Alphen, but wanted him to see the original, with the annotations, the ticks, the big red A+.

Van Alphen looked edgy. He wore jeans and a T-shirt, his feet bare. It was odd to see him in casual clothes instead of his uniform, which always looked crisp and clean. His hair was damp; he smelt of shampoo and talc. He'd come home from work, showered and changed. Was he going out later? Did he have a woman with him? Pam realised that she knew nothing about his personal life and half hoped he'd ask her to dinner or a movie. She was attracted to him, only just realising it, her mind running with the thought. He reminded her of Inspector Challis, the same leanness, olive skin and air of stillness and prohibition. But in Challis the stillness and prohibition spelt shyness, a sensitivity that she didn't necessarily want. In van Alphen there was coiled anger, and the air of a man who took shortcuts to get results, and she found that attractive right now. He'd always been kind to her.

He didn't invite her in, and suddenly, she just knew, he wasn't alone. The confirmation came immediately, a voice calling, 'Hey, you got any vodka?'

A young guy, blue jeans, tight black T-shirt and vivid white trainers. Fifteen? Sixteen? Trying to pass as twenty, and almost succeeding, owing to the knowingness and deadness in his eyes. How was van Alphen going to explain this? 'Pam, meet my nephew'? Pam waited, hoping that her face wasn't betraying her.

'Pam, this is Billy. Billy, Pam.'

'Hi,' Pam said.

The Billy guy smiled prettily and did a little exaggerated quiver and pout behind van Alphen's back, enjoying himself.

'Anyway, I'd better go,' Pam said.

'I'll enjoy reading this,' van Alphen said, gesturing with her essay.

Billy cooed 'See ya!' at her departing back.

40

It had been a long week for Hal Challis, too. First there were the mundane tasks associated with arranging his brother-in-law's funeral. Until the state lab released the body, the family couldn't even nominate a date, and had to be content with sounding out a firm of undertakers and the local Uniting Church minister.

Then there was the old man's health. On Monday morning Challis found his father twitching on the sunroom floor, eyes badly frightened, the left side of his face and body entirely slack. He rang for an ambulance, and then for Rob Minchin, and finally for Meg.

The doctor beat the ambulance by a couple of minutes. He bent over Challis's father, his fingers nimble. 'I don't think it's a stroke, but we'll take him in for observation.'

Later, in the hospital, Meg and Challis were obliged to wait. They were finally shown to their father's bedside that afternoon. He looked weak, diminished, but gave them his old mulish, critical, combative glare. 'Stop fussing. Rob said I can go home in a couple of days.'

'But Dad—'

He lifted his frail hand but there was no frailty in it for Challis and Meg, who saw only his old sternness and lack of compromise.

On Wednesday, the old man back in his sunroom chair, Challis finally heard from Freya Berg, the Victorian pathologist, who gave him the name of her South Australian counterpart. 'He's a by-the-book kind of guy, Hal. Don't expect much joy. But I did get a bit of information out of him. The techs didn't find any prints or useful traces anywhere: the garbage bag, the body or the grave.'

'Ballistics?'

'Inconclusive. A couple of fragments, consistent with a projectile, but it must have been powerful, went straight through the skull.'

'Thanks. I'll give him a call.'

But the South Australian pathologist refused to answer questions or speculate. 'I have released the body for burial. Kindly speak to the police if you want answers.'

Challis called the Homicide Squad's office at police headquarters in Adelaide. Nixon returned his call that afternoon—from Mawson's Bluff. 'We've just taken your mate into custody.'

For a wild moment, Challis thought he meant Rob Minchin. 'My mate?'

'One Patrick Finucane.'

Challis was silent. He said, 'How solid is your case?'

'Probably less solid than if you hadn't been sniffing around. Sir.'

Challis's final calls of the day were to the undertaker and the Uniting Church minister. After some to and fro, they settled on Saturday morning for the funeral.

Ellen called him on Friday night. 'Sorry it's been a few days, Hal.'

She explained that she'd been working a lot of unpaid overtime, following one of her suspects. 'But that's not all.'

She told him about Serena Hanlon. He listened to her voice, far away, and sitting in one of his armchairs. He was listening to the meaning of her words, and listening for a sense of her face and body and personality. But the name Serena Hanlon seeped through. 'Ferny Creek? Ten or so years ago? I worked that case. It was huge at the time.'

'We think Duyker did it.'

'He was in the area?'

'Yes.'

They talked on, a kind of closeness building, and an antidote to the bad shadows of the night. She told him that McQuarrie had been ranting and raving to her about an 'Evening Update' story which had linked the Katie Blasko abduction with the Ferny Creek case.

'He doesn't strike me as an "Evening Update" kind of guy,' Challis said.

'Oh, sure. "Big Brother", "Australian Idol".'

'At one with the common people?'

'Of course.'

'Couple of jars in the pub after work?'

Ellen snorted, as if registering the image of Superintendent McQuarrie in a crowd of beer drinkers. 'Thanks, Hal, you're a tonic.'

He smiled at that.

'But you do have a leak to the media, Ells.'

'I know I do. What about you? Found your killer yet?'

'The locals think they have. They arrested a guy I went to school with, Paddy Finucane.'

'And...?'

'I don't think he did it.'

Saturday morning was like all of the other mornings that spring: mild to hot, a little dusty, the gum trees still and apt to creak as the temperature rose, the galahs and cockatoos wheeling and screeching. But the church was cool, dimly lit, with comforting gleams from the gold crosses and the stained glass. Challis was surprised to see that the pews were full, then realised that it wasn't Gavin that people had come for necessarily but sympathy for the family, dismay at the kind of death suffered by Gavin, and a break from the long, monochrome days out here at the edge of the rain shadow.

That impression was reinforced at the graveside. Everyone was aware that Gavin had been found there; the freshly turned earth was suggestive of his original resting place, not his final one.

And while the minister said his final words and the coffin was lowered into the ground, Challis for a short time did what a good detective will do. He was standing with Eve, Meg and his father on one side of the grave, and from this position had a commanding view of the other mourners, who had spread out on the opposite side. His gaze roamed among their faces, which were serious, curious, blank, dutiful. Only two faces gave away more than that: Paddy Finucane's wife, who stood at the margins of the mourners, and the RSPCA boss, Sadler. Mrs Finucane caught Challis's eye, flushed sadly and when he looked again later, she'd disappeared, but Sadler was staring intently at Meg and Eve, almost as if he wanted to rush to their aid. Then he grew aware of Challis and the expression vanished. Challis didn't see him again.

The little family was obliged to linger. Lisa Joyce was one of the last to approach them. She wore a sombre dress and shoes, her hair in a French bun, her face almost devoid of makeup, and to Challis looked the more beautiful for it. She clasped Meg's hands, then Eve's, and finally Challis's. 'I'm so sorry.'

She was frankly sad, all of her sensuality muted, and continued to grasp him, her slender fingers fierce. She was full of unexpressed emotions. He found himself searching her face, almost as if twenty years hadn't passed and he was young again, wanting to know who she really was.

Then she released him, stepped away and crossed the parched dirt reluctantly to the black Range Rover, where Rex Joyce waited. Joyce looked clean and crisp in a white shirt and dark suit, only his eyes giving his privations away.

Challis felt exhausted suddenly. A week had passed, marked by tedium, frustration and banality, but overlying all of it, for Challis, was a sense of being watched and judged and found wanting.

41

On the following Monday morning, Sasha was out and about, lunging and veering after fugitive odours, nostrils to the ground, sometimes pausing to dribble on a post to mark her passage along the side streets of this part of Waterloo. She'd slipped her lead the moment her owner had left for work that morning, then squeezed through the gap where the drunken gate failed to seal the picket fence around 57 Warrawee Drive. The neighbours all knew her; one would feed her some kitchen scraps and return her to number 57 eventually. There was almost no traffic along these little streets, so no one was particularly concerned for her welfare. Besides, she had good road sense, for a dog.

What neither the neighbours nor the owner knew was that she sometimes ventured several blocks away before returning to Warrawee Drive, and so she had a second encounter with Katie Blasko, who was being walked to school by her mother. This was a big day for Katie. She'd not been at school for the past fortnight, but both she, and Donna, knew that couldn't last. Donna was walking her. There had been a time when Katie rode her bike to school, alone, but not any more. They were both too fearful for that, and both had endured two weeks of whispering, pointing and appalled fascination. And Donna had been feeling an obscure kind of shame, these past few days. Nothing would have happened to Katie if she hadn't hired that photographer, or if she'd been a better mother instead of giving all of her attention to Justin and not enough to Katie. Then again, Katie could be a real little brat sometimes.

But not just at the moment.

They were a block from the school, Donna unfurling her umbrella against a spring shower, when Sasha bounded up to them, eyes bright, hindquarters in a frenzy. 'Sasha!' cried Katie, kneeling to hug the dog.

'You'll get wet,' said Donna automatically. Dogs dismayed her. She was a cat person. Cats minded the rain.

'This is Sasha!' said Katie, still joyful.

Donna frowned. It was great to see Katie so animated, but what was the story with this dog? 'Sasha?'

'She was in the van with me, and at the house,' Katie said. Days had gone by and this was her first unconscious reference to that terrible time.

Donna's wits were about her. She went cold and still. 'Are you sure?'

Katie flipped around the registration and ID tags on Sasha's collar. 'See? Sasha Lowan, 57 Warrawee Drive, Waterloo. I remember now. And she knows me, don't you, Sash? Oh, you're a good girl, you're such a good girl.'

Dimly Donna remembered the police asking about a dog, dog hairs discovered on Katie's clothing and in that horrible house. So horrible in Donna's imagination that she'd vowed never again to drive anywhere near the place.

She stood there in the gathering rain and got out her mobile phone. She had Sergeant Destry on speed dial.

Ellen was in mid-briefing when the call came. She listened intently, then directed a slow-burning smile around the room. 'We've found the dog.'

She sent John Tankard to bring in the dog, and Scobie to contact the owner, then packed up and returned to her office.

She was immersed in paperwork when Scobie reported back. 'Spoke to the owner,' he said, standing in her doorway.

'Is he known to us?'

'No. And he has an alibi. He's one of the opticians in High Street. Bemused to think his dog might help us.'

Then there was a commotion downstairs and Ellen found John Tankard there, surrounded by uniforms and civilian clerks oohing and aahing over the dog. Kellock was in the middle of it, clearly irritable. 'This is a police station, not a bloody lost dogs' home.'

'Do you bite?' said Ellen to the dog.

Tankard, a little smitten, said, 'Not a harmful bone in her, Sarge.'

Ellen drove Sasha up to the ForenZics lab herself, a slow journey, owing to scudding rain. To her irritation, Riggs was on duty. She was beginning to think of him as her bete noire. He was a spike-haired young guy, with pierced eyebrows, earrings and a studded belt looped through black jeans. Lab-cool, as though he'd modelled himself on a character in a US forensic policing show. He looked askance at Sasha. 'This is still a grey area. We might not be able to get DNA from the hairs found at the house. We can maybe testify that the hairs are similar, but a good lawyer will laugh that out of court.'

Ellen shrugged. She was tired of Riggs. Meanwhile, police work often boiled down to 'maybe' and 'might'. She watched him examine Sasha, who stood trembling, eyes rolled mournfully at Ellen, as though terrified that a vet with a big needle or greased finger was examining her. 'Shhh,' she whispered, fondling Sasha's silky ears.

'You're in my way,' said Riggs crossly. He elbowed Ellen aside and bent his head to Sasha's neck. 'Well, hello.'

'What?'

'Looks like dry blood on the collar.'

Ellen peered. 'Sasha's?'

'There's no injury here.' He glanced quickly over the dog. 'Nor elsewhere. She might have been in a fight. Or it's her owner's blood.'

'Or a stranger's.'

'We'll test it,' said Riggs. 'Test to see if it's animal blood, then extract DNA and compare it to database samples.'

'And that will take how long?'

Riggs sniffed. 'As long as it takes.'

'However,' said Ellen, wanting to put the guy in his place, 'the sample might prove to come from a ninety-year-old grandmother who died in a house fire three years ago.'

Riggs went tight and red. 'We've put new procedures in place,' he said.

Ellen returned to the Peninsula, Sasha asleep on the back seat, snoring a little. She went straight to van Alphen's office, but the sergeant was out of the station, so she sought Kellock, who refused to let her have a couple of uniforms.

'But I need to know if anyone witnessed the dog's movements.'

'The *dog's* movements? For God's sake, Ells.'

'It's crucial,' Ellen said stubbornly. 'There was blood on the collar.'

Kellock gazed at her for a long moment. She couldn't tell what he was thinking, or if indeed he was thinking. Eventually the words rumbled from his broad chest: 'Sorry, can't spare the troops.'

Ellen scowled. 'It's as if all the urgency's gone now that Katie's been found.'

Kellock shrugged massively. He was busy with files and barely glanced at her. 'Have you seen the roads? They're wet and slippery. We've had a spate of accidents—one of them caused by a Jarrett kid, incidentally, all of twelve years old, driving a stolen car.'

Ellen didn't doubt him, but she sensed that he'd lost interest in the Katie Blasko case. Meanwhile, where was van Alphen?

And so she took Scobie Sutton with her. Scobie got behind the wheel before she could. His usual bad driving was exacerbated by the heavy rain, which Ellen knew was stirring the patina of grease and oil into a dangerous slick on the road surfaces. She grabbed the dashboard as he rounded a corner and braked mid-way down Warrawee Drive, his hands clutching the wheel inexpertly as he checked house numbers.

'Two blocks from Katie Blasko's,' he said. 'What do you think happened? Sasha wanders off, finds herself on Trevally Street, sees Duyker's van with the door open, and somehow or other climbs aboard without being noticed.'

'Makes sense,' Ellen said, gingerly letting go the dashboard.

'But how did Sasha find her way home again? How long was she missing?'

Ellen's head snapped forward as Scobie reversed. 'Obviously Duyker brought her back here,' she gasped.

Scobie braked again. 'He'd rape and maybe kill a child, but be kind to a dog?'

'Yes.'

Scobie considered that, full of doubt. 'But why not let the dog out somewhere else? Why risk bringing it back?'

'People would wonder. They'd take her to the pound, the RSPCA, a vet, the police. That would generate a record. But if Sasha is found or released a block or two from home, no one's going to wonder about it.'

'You could be right.'

And so they began doorknocking. At 5.15 they got lucky.

'Sasha? I know Sasha. She was with the little Blasko girl, the one who was abducted.'

Ellen went cold. She regarded the speaker, an elderly woman, intently. 'How do you know that, Mrs Cooper? That detail has never been made public.'

'I heard the child's mother talking about it in the shop this afternoon.'

Curse the woman, Ellen thought. 'We need to know Sasha's movements at the time of the abduction.'

Mrs Cooper's eyes twinkled. 'You make Sasha sound as if she's a suspect.'

Ellen gave her a lop-sided grin. 'My report-writing language infects my regular speech sometimes.'

Mrs Cooper smiled. 'I was an English teacher,' she said cryptically. 'Now, let's see. I feed Sasha sometimes. Bacon rind. It's too tough for my teeth.'

'Yes.'

'So I probably saw her that day, but I can't be sure. Ask me something that happened forty years ago and I'll remember every detail.'

Ellen said carefully, 'Did Sasha have a history of jumping into people's cars?'

'Oh, yes, indeed she did! Sometimes she'd appear just as I was about to drive to the shops. She'd leap in and immediately go to sleep in the back. I always leave the window part-way down for her, whilst shopping. If it's too hot, I make her get out of the car.'

To halt the flood, Ellen said, 'How did other people hereabouts treat her?'

Mrs Cooper smiled at the 'hereabouts'. 'We all know her. Most try to discourage her. I suppose I should, too.'

'What if someone didn't realise that she'd jumped in?'

'Then they'd drive all over the Peninsula with her, maybe even to Queensland with the holiday luggage.'

'But people know where she lives. They'd bring her back eventually.'

'Of course.'

Scobie spoke for the first time. 'Can you recall any instances of people letting Sasha out of their cars?'

'Recently?'

'Yes.'

'There was a white car,' said Mrs Cooper after some thought. 'I think it was white. I think it was recently.'

'Could it have been a van?'

'You know, it was a van. I saw Sasha jump out.'

'Did you see or know the driver?'

'Oh, I wasn't looking at the driver,' Mrs Cooper said.

Van Alphen reappeared for the evening briefing, offering an explanation but no apology. 'I've been running down some leads,' he said, his voice and body giving nothing away.

It was contemptuous, and pissed Ellen off. 'I'm trying to co-ordinate an inquiry here, Van, and you're supposed to remain in the station and trawl through records.'

Van Alphen shrugged.

Ellen sighed. It was fruitless. She changed the subject, told them more about the dog. 'I just got a call from the lab: the blood on Sasha's collar is human, not animal. It will be some time before we have the DNA result.'

'Human?' said Kellock sharply. He threw down his pen. 'Even if it is, there's no way of determining how it got there. Meanwhile the procedures of that lab don't exactly inspire confidence.'

'Back to time-honoured methods, eh, Kel?' Ellen said.

Kellock looked fed up. 'Always been good enough for me.' He pushed back his chair, gathered his files. 'Have to go. I'm giving a talk at a retirement home this evening.'

Ellen was reminded again that a police station had a community role, a welfare role. Officers like Kellock went to schools, hospitals and other institutions, giving talks and assistance. It was something she hadn't done for many years and she felt chastened.

'Thanks, Kel.'

Kellock left and the briefing continued. Everyone was tired, dispirited, and finally Ellen dismissed them. But as they filed out, van

Alphen took Ellen aside. He looked sly and satisfied. 'You need a decent witness, Ellen.'

Ellen didn't bother to reply. She was pissed off with him.

'Well,' he murmured, 'I've found you one.'

'Who?' she demanded. 'What kind of witness? Witness to what?'

'Keep your voice down,' he said hoarsely. 'A street kid called Billy DaCosta.'

'What's his story?'

'Abused by several men over a period of three years, from when he was eight until puberty, when he no longer interested them. It happened at a house here on the Peninsula, but he's not sure where.'

Ellen straightened her back, feeling her old keenness returning. She looked fully at van Alphen, who was giving her his most cryptic half smile.

'Several men. Like who?'

'Clode and Duyker, among others.'

'Jesus Christ, Van. When were you intending to tell me this?'

'I'm telling you now.'

'This kid identified them? How?'

'Photos,' van Alphen said. Suddenly he stiffened, and called, 'Everything all right, Constable?'

John Tankard had been hovering in the corridor. He came in, looking embarrassed. 'Sarge.'

'Haven't you got work to do?'

'Sarge.'

Tankard turned back toward the door, looking stung. Ellen called after him: 'John, you've been a great help to this investigation.' She paused. 'I'm confident we'll see some results tomorrow.'

'Thanks, Sarge.'

When the room was clear again, van Alphen said, 'Is he our media leak, do you think?'

Ellen cocked her head. 'You've been wondering about that, too?'

'Sure.'

'It can wait,' Ellen said. 'What we need to do now is get this kid of yours to make a formal ID. Can you bring him in first thing in the morning?'

'No problem.'

'Meanwhile I'd better tell Kellock about him.'

Van Alphen grabbed her upper arm, his fingers like manacles, but his voice was mild and apologetic: 'Not yet, Ellen, okay?'

'Why ever not?'

'Look, Kellock and I go back a long way, but he's the senior officer in this station, and the eyes and ears of the superintendent. If you tell him I've found a witness, he'll be obliged to pass the information on, and I can't afford for the super or the shooting board to learn that I've been out in the field instead of desk bound.'

Ellen wasn't convinced by the argument, but said, 'Suit yourself.'

It was odd having a kid around the place again. Kees van Alphen decided he liked it. His wife and teenage daughter long gone, living up in Melbourne now, he'd spent too many years living alone in this soulless house. Sure, a teenage boy is not the same thing as a teenage girl, especially if he sells his body for a living, but certain factors remained constant—the noisiness, the irreverence, the untidiness. Van Alphen decided that he'd been too obsessed with silence, solitariness and order. Billy DaCosta was doing him good, especially with investigators sniffing around the Nick Jarrett shooting. It could be months before they reported back to the commissioner, and he didn't know if Scobie Sutton would withstand the pressure.

'You can't keep me here forever,' Billy said.

On this Monday evening they were sitting at the kitchen table, going over Billy's statement, van Alphen also preparing Billy for the types of questions he could expect from Ellen Destry and others. It was 9 pm, Billy wired, van Alphen weary. Cooking odours hung in the air: roast chicken and potatoes, salad with a sharp dressing. Billy had wolfed down the chicken, ignored the salad. He was extraordinarily thin, and van Alphen suspected that he'd slipped out during the day, maybe taken the train to Frankston and scored dope near the station.

'I know I can't keep you here forever,' he replied, 'but these are dangerous people.'

'I can handle them,' said Billy sultrily. 'Got any ice cream?'

Van Alphen went to the fridge, passing close to Billy's chair, Billy stinking a little. You can't expect a street kid to feel immediately at home and want to shower and launder his clothes regularly. Van Alphen longed to teach him these things, longed to meddle and guide, but he'd lost his wife and daughter that way, so kept his trap shut. Billy's fingernails were grimy, his jeans torn at the knee, his T-shirt funky. Billy projected a certain look to attract the punters. It was a skinny urchin look, with a touch of cheekiness and vulnerability. Van Alphen was taken by it, but not sexually—although Billy thought he was.

Billy shovelled the ice cream down his throat. 'When are we going to do this?'

'First thing tomorrow morning. Sergeant Destry's getting impatient.'

'I don't want to appear in court.'

'You might not have to.'

'I could just disappear. You'd never find me.'

That's what van Alphen was afraid of. 'Let's at least get you on record,' he said. 'Video and audiotape, and a signed statement. That, together with other evidence we have, will help nail these bastards.'

'They're not the ones I'm scared of.'

'I know,' said van Alphen gloomily.

His mobile phone rang. He only did police business on it, he never ignored it. He answered, Billy pouting prettily, playing with him.

'Van Alphen.'

'You gotta help me, Mr V.'

Lester, one of his informants. 'That's not how it works, Lester. *You* help *me*, and you get paid to do it.'

'It's me brother. He's bipolar.'

'I know that.'

'Well, he's threatenin' to kill me sister with a knife.'

'Call triple zero.'

'Can't we do this off the books? Keep the authorities out of it? I'll see he takes his meds, I guarantee it.'

No one would accept a Lester guarantee, but van Alphen was feeling in the mood to be helpful. He asked for the address, somewhere on the Seaview Park estate. 'I can't promise anything.'

'Thanks, Mr V, you're a champion.'

'Meet me there,' growled van Alphen.

'Count on it.'

You didn't count on Lester, either. Completing the call, van Alphen pointed to the papers spread out upon the table and told Billy to go through his statement and the photographs again. 'I have to go out for a while.'

Billy fluttered his eyes, hung his mouth open, spread his knees wide in the kitchen chair, and stretched to show his slender bare stomach. 'I'll wait up for you.'

'Cut it out, Billy,' said van Alphen, who had no interest in touching him. 'Don't answer the door. Don't answer the phone.'

'You're no fun,' Billy said.

At about the same time, Ellen Destry was startled to see headlights swoop across the sitting room windows and then she heard tyres crushing Challis's gravelled driveway. She checked her watch, faintly perplexed. Maybe Challis had enemies she didn't know about. Ditto vengeful ex-girlfriends. She opened the front door a crack and saw her daughter lumping bags from the back seat of her car. Larrayne saw her, and at once crumpled up her face and said, 'Oh, Mum.'

'Sweetheart,' said Ellen, rushing out.

'Oh, Mum,' Larrayne said again.

'Tell me.'

'Can I stay for a while? Maybe till after the exams?'

Ellen felt a surge of happiness. 'Sure you can.'

She helped Larrayne into the house and along a corridor to the spare bedroom, which was musty, sterile. Larrayne stood, diminished looking, in the centre of the room, her backpack over one shoulder, her laptop case beside her on the floor. 'This is so weird.'

Ellen was careful not to push or probe. 'If you'd rather go to your father's, I won't be hurt,' she said, knowing she would be.

'It just feels weird, that's all,' Larrayne said, suddenly decisive with the backpack, bouncing it down on the surface of the bed. A little dust rose, Ellen noted guiltily. She mentally retorted to Challis: *So, am I supposed to run major investigations* and *sweep and dust?*

'Dad's place is too small,' Larrayne said. 'It's right on the highway, so there's all this noise. I'd never be able to concentrate. I'm packing death over these exams, Mum.'

Ellen got extraordinary pleasure from hearing her daughter say 'Mum'. It was as though she'd not heard it for months and was parched. 'I'll show you where the bathroom is.'

'I don't have to shower with a bucket at my feet, do I?'

Challis relied on tank water for his house and garden, not mains water. In a dry season he'd recycle shower, laundry and washing-up water onto his garden. But this was spring, a season of occasional downpours, and so his tanks were full. Why hadn't Larrayne figured that out? She was a city girl through and through. 'No,' Ellen said amusedly. 'But no tampons down the loo—it's a septic system.'

Larrayne rolled her eyes. 'Whatever.'

Mother and daughter glanced at each other uneasily. 'Want me to help you unpack?'

'I'm fine.'

'Where's the rest of your stuff?'

'In the car. It can wait.'

'Hungry?'

'I ate with Dad.'

'Ah.'

Ellen wondered if 'Dad' was going to lurk in the corners of every conversation. She wondered if Challis would lurk, also, leading to snide recriminations from Larrayne.

'Tea? Coffee? Proper coffee.'

Challis had installed coffee machines at work and at home. He had a special terror of being obliged to drink instant coffee in the homes of witnesses or friends.

'Coffee. I need to stay awake.'

'You're going to study tonight?'

'Yes.'

'You'd better use the dining room table.'

When Ellen was in the kitchen, the phone rang. 'It's only me,' Challis said.

Ellen kept it short and murmured, explaining about the dog and the upcoming interrogation of Duyker. 'Larrayne has just arrived.'

'To stay?'

'Do you mind?'

'Of course not. Is she okay?'

'Not exactly,' Ellen said. 'I'm waiting for her to tell me.'

'Speak to you soon,' Challis said, and he was gone.

Ellen carried the coffee with a couple of chocolate biscuits through to the sitting room. Larrayne was pacing the room. At one point she scanned the shelves of CDs and shook her head. 'There's exactly nothing here I want to listen to.' Then suddenly she was sniffing, and looked young and small. 'Mum, Travis broke up with me.'

'Oh, sweetie, I'm sorry.'

'It's the *worst* time. Just before exams.'

Ellen hugged her. Larrayne, so unyielding for months, hugged her back fiercely.

Meanwhile van Alphen was heading down to Waterloo and Westernport Bay, ten minutes away. It was out of order for Lester to ask for his help in what was a private, not police, matter, but he had to admit that his informants didn't often ask him to intervene in their affairs. It was all about balance. As a copper, van Alphen couldn't operate without a stable of informants, registered and unregistered alike. Sure, they often fed him poor tips about small-time crimes and criminals, but now and then they came up with gold. Lester was unregistered: probably, thought van Alphen now, because the little prick enjoyed informing for several of Waterloo's finest. Lester was always playing some kind of game. He liked to be seen in public with van Alphen ('Here's my tame cop'), and take van Alphen to auction houses and pawnshops that dealt in stolen goods ('This cop's on the take'), his intention clear: *Mr V, if you ever try to break this partnership, I can make you look dirty.*

Van Alphen tolerated Lester, knowing never to sink all of his hopes in just one informant. It was impossible to know how long Lester would be useful to him, however, or even how long Lester would live. Meanwhile Lester was in it for different types of gain: to get money, or revenge, or some hard guy off his back; to feel good about himself; to divert the attention of the police away from his own activities. Van Alphen knew all of this, but he needed guys like Lester. After all, Lester had told him where on the Peninsula he'd find the likes of Billy DaCosta.

Not that Lester went in for young boys, or girls. There was something oddly asexual about the man. He lived with his mother above the betting shop they ran, on High Street in Waterloo. She fed information to van Alphen sometimes, too.

Van Alphen drove. He'd never met Lester's sister or brother. He'd heard all about them, though: the sister a single mother, on methadone, the brother a head case who kept forgetting to take his medication. A typical Seaview Park estate story...At that moment, van Alphen frowned: he could have sworn that Lester's sister and brother lived on a housing estate outside Mornington, on the other side of the Peninsula.

Still, people like that tended to move around a lot.

He entered Seaview Park estate and crept along the darkened streets. More than half of the overhead lights were out, shards of glass at the base of the poles. The houses watched him mutely, most well kept but others with old cars in the front yards, rusting inside a shroud of dead grass. No one stirred. This was a country of shift workers and young families: any noise would come from people like the Jarretts, or those who had no job or anything to look forward to but blowing the welfare payment on booze and dope every night. And so it was quiet and dark along Bittern Close, Albatross Crescent, Osprey Avenue and, finally, Sealers Road. Van Alphen wound down his window and aimed his powerful torch at the front windows of 19 Sealers Road. It was the last house in the street, deep within a corner of the estate, bound on one side and the rear by the estate's stained pine perimeter fence, and on the other by an unoccupied house, a For Sale sign on a lean in the dead front lawn. Number 19 looked dead, too, but if Lester's sister was a junkie, or a recovering junkie, she probably didn't care about the upkeep of her garden or want light pouring in.

Van Alphen parked his car and knocked on the front door. A dog some distance away barked, but otherwise there was only the wind, and the sensation of the earth whispering through space. Van Alphen had these fancies sometimes—encouraged now by the scudding clouds and the moon behind them. There was no sign of Lester's little Ford Fiesta, big surprise.

After a while he went around the side of the house, peering through windows, to the back yard, where someone had jemmied open the glass sliding door, buckling the aluminium frame and cracking the glass. He froze. He edged aside the curtain with his torch and went in, to where there was sudden movement behind him and a shotgun exploding, the sound deadened by a pillow, but not the outcome.

43

Challis completed his call to Ellen Destry feeling a little frustrated. He'd wanted to tell her that his father had been taken to hospital that morning. He'd wanted to tell her that it was maybe his fault.

It started after Gavin's funeral, when he'd argued with Meg, the argument continuing all weekend.

'Can't you see?' she said. 'Dad's worse.'

'He seems the same to me,' Challis had said.

'It's subtle, but he's definitely worse. He should go back into hospital.'

'What can they do, except observe? All that to-ing and fro-ing will do more harm than good. He needs rest.'

Saturday passed, Sunday, some bad old history informing their arguments. Eve forced them to apologise, but they were wrung out and could not do more than that. They were stubborn; it was a standoff.

And then, as if to underscore the fact that Meg knew what she was talking about because she'd stayed close to her family and Challis hadn't, the old man had collapsed after breakfast and been rushed to hospital. Challis had just come home from spending the day there.

His conversation with Ellen cut short, he felt restless and incomplete. The house oppressed him at night, and he didn't want to sit for hours in the hospital again.

Then the kitchen phone rang and he looked at it with dread. Meg's voice was low and ragged. 'It's Dad.'

At once Challis pictured it: their father in the grip of another stroke or one of the weeping fits that seized him from time to time, as though life was desolate now. He asked foolishly, 'Is he okay?'

The raggedness became tears. 'Oh, Hal.'

Challis understood. 'I'll be right there.'

He fishtailed the Triumph out of his father's driveway and sped across town to the hospital. There was a scattering of cars parked around it, but otherwise the place seemed benign, even deserted, as though illness and grief had taken a rest for the day. He parked beside a dusty ambulance and barged through the doors. Here at last were people, but no sense of urgency or of lives unravelling.

'Hal!'

He wheeled around. A dim corridor, smelling of disinfectant, the linoleum floors scuffed here and there by black rubber wheels. Meg and Eve were sitting outside one of the single rooms with Rob Minchin, who patted Meg and got to his feet as Challis approached.

'So sorry, Hal.'

The two men embraced briefly. 'I'll be back soon,' Minchin said. 'Couple of babies due some time tonight.'

Challis turned to Meg and Eve. Their faces were full of dampish misery, but uplifted a little to see him, as though he were their rock. He didn't feel like a rock. It was a lie. He was quiet and thoughtful, and people mistook that for strength. In fact, all he wanted to do was join Meg and Eve in weeping.

Meg drew him onto a chair beside her. Eve gave him a wobbly smile.

He said gently, 'What happened?'

'Massive cerebral haemorrhage.'

He found that he couldn't bear to think of it. There would have been suffering, brief, but intense. There would have been a moment of extreme fear. He didn't like to think of his father's last moments.

Meg held his hand in her left and Eve's in her right. 'It could have been worse,' she said.

They sat quietly. 'Can I see him?'

Meg released his hand and pointed. 'In there.'

The room was ablaze, a nurse and an orderly bustling and joking as they worked. They sobered when they saw him. 'Hal,' said the nurse.

He peered at her. 'Nance?'

She nodded. Another one he'd gone to school with, the younger sister of...

'How's...' He couldn't remember her husband's name.

'Oh, he's history. Good riddance.'

She took Challis by the elbow and gently ushered him to the bedside. 'We have to move him soon, but I can give you a few minutes.' She patted him and he was aware of the lights dimming and of Nance leaving with the orderly.

His father's mouth hung open, and that, with his scrawny neck and tight cheekbones, seemed to configure despair, as though the old man wasn't dead but imploring someone to help him. Challis began to weep. He tried to close his father's mouth but nothing was malleable. Maybe the old guy had never been malleable. Challis pulled up a chair, sat, and held a light, papery hand. He let the tears run until Meg joined him and he found the strength to say to himself, *Enough*. Enough for now, at any rate.

44

On Tuesday morning Scobie Sutton stared in fascination at the man who had abducted and raped Katie Blasko, possibly abducted and murdered other young girls, and also cheated a stack of people of $395 plus booking fee. Duyker, with his eyes dead as pebbles, dry, heavily seamed cheeks and neck, and patchy, tufted brown hair, did look disturbing close up. At surveillance distance he'd seemed nondescript, a tradesman on his day off, maybe, a man who favoured pale coloured chinos, deck shoes and a polo shirt. You wouldn't look twice at him. Now Scobie couldn't take his eyes off the man. He visualised Grace Duyker, sweet Grace, with her skin like ripe fruit, sitting unconsciously close to him as he'd interviewed her about Duyker. Well, the closeness was probably unconscious, but Scobie had liked it, and had 'unconsciously' moved his bony thigh closer to hers as she told him about family occasions when she was young, and the creepy way Uncle Peter had looked at her.

He forced himself to pay attention, and heard Ellen Destry say, 'You've been identified by a witness, Mr Duyker. You, Neville Clode and other men have for many years been sexually abusing underage boys.'

An equal opportunity child rapist, Scobie thought, boys and girls. Of course, Ellen was jumping the gun here. Van Alphen hadn't produced his witness yet, hadn't even come in to work yet.

Duyker, on the other side of the interview table, folded his arms and stared at the ceiling panels. Scobie looked up, astonished and angry to see wadded tissue stuck up there, as though this was a public toilet. He privately vowed never to leave a witness alone in an interview room. 'Mr Duyker?' he prodded.

'I'm not saying anything until my lawyer gets here.'

Out of the corner of his eye, Scobie saw Ellen lean back in her seat. 'Now, where have I heard that before?' she said. Scobie continued to stare at Duyker, looking for the flinch that said to keep pushing. Duyker was expressionless. The air in the little room contained an evil stink, suddenly, as if Duyker exuded contempt through his pores while his eyes remained flat and dead. Contempt for young girls, police, anything decent at all. Scobie shivered involuntarily and said a few words of prayer to himself.

'We have enough to hold you, Mr Duyker,' Scobie said. 'May I call you Pete? Peter?'

Nothing.

'Fraud, in addition to the sex offences.'

Nothing.

'You defrauded my wife of $395,' Scobie went on. 'A policeman's wife. We have a pattern here, don't we? Your record shows fraud charges in New South Wales and across the water in New Zealand.'

Duyker said flatly, 'My lawyer.'

'*He's* not helping us with our inquiries, Pete, *you* are,' Ellen said.

Scobie pretended to read a page from the file that lay before him on the chipped table, where coffee rings overlapped like Olympic logos rendered by deranged children. 'This pretend photography. It wasn't all pretend, was it? You took *actual* photographs sometimes? Little girls? Naked? Having sex with you and your mates while they were too drugged to resist?'

Scobie found himself reeling in distress at the sudden pictures in his head, of his sweet daughter at Duyker's hands, and he himself floundering, unable to save her.

Duyker sat unblinking.

So Scobie said, headlong and spiteful, 'Your DNA matches DNA found in the house where Katie Blasko was found.'

Beside him Ellen threw her pen down softly. Around him the air shifted, and a slow smile started up in Duyker's face, an empty smile but a smile.

'I don't recall giving you a sample from which to make a match. I don't recall that you asked for one. Meanwhile my DNA is not on file anywhere. Stop playing games.'

'We'll be asking for a sample,' Scobie said, going red. Ellen breathed out her disgust.

Duyker was amused. 'I wonder what my lawyer will say.'

Scobie and Ellen were silent, Scobie mentally kicking himself. *Never give them ammunition to use against you:* Challis had drilled that into him time and time again. And this interview was being videotaped: a good copper always keeps his facial expressions neutral in those circumstances.

Ellen tried to take the initiative. 'You've been identified from a photograph array as being one of the men involved in the sexual abuse of underage boys, Pete.'

According to Kees van Alphen, thought Scobie in disgust. Van Alphen had been evasive lately, supplying partial answers or none at all, and he was never in his office. Running his own investigation, as Ellen had said in frustration last night.

Then, out of nowhere, an appalling thought came to Scobie: van Alphen was running interference for this gang of paedophiles. Van Alphen had assured Ellen that his informant, some kid named Billy DaCosta, had identified Duyker and Clode from a photo array, but maybe that was a delaying tactic, or an outright lie. And where were van Alphen and his mystery informant?

Duyker was yawning. 'Are we done? Can I go?'

'You're not going anywhere,' Ellen said. 'We intend to make the fraud charges stick.'

'So, make them stick.'

'We will.'

'My lawyer will have me back on the street so fast your heads will spin,' said Duyker, showing heat for the first time.

Scobie suspected it was true. A search of the man's house had found nothing. His van was clean, apparently washed, waxed and vacuumed until it was like new. But Scobie and Ellen knew what Duyker didn't know: there was a paint smear in the rear compartment. Purple enamel, the same colour as Katie Blasko's bike, a smear so tiny that it was no wonder Duyker had missed it, amongst all of those other scuffs and scratches, obtained from years of loading and unloading. They were waiting for a paint analysis. They'd already approached the manufacturer of the bike for the composition of the paint that had been used on bikes like Katie Blasko's.

They didn't have the bike, though. 'It will be at the bottom of the bay,' Ellen had said last night. 'We might prove he had a bike on board, but not that he had Katie Blasko's bike.'

Now Scobie heard her ask Duyker to account for his movements on the afternoon Katie Blasko was abducted.

Duyker shrugged. 'Out and about, probably.' He shifted in his seat, fishing for his wallet. It was a fat wallet, the leather worn, the cotton stitches unravelling. And full of business cards, receipts and paper scraps. Scobie and Ellen watched as he leafed through it all, wetting his index finger laboriously, loving every minute of it. 'Here we are,' he said eventually.

He slid a cash register receipt across the table. Ellen poked it into position with her fingernail. Scobie peered at it with her. At 4 pm on the day Katie Blasko was abducted, Peter Duyker had been buying a photography magazine in a city newsagency, one-and-a-half hours away by car or van. 'My filing system,' he said apologetically, 'leaves a lot to be desired.'

Then Duyker's lawyer arrived and advised Duyker to say nothing more. 'Nothing more?' echoed Duyker. 'I haven't said anything to begin with.'

'How long will you be holding my client, Sergeant Destry, assuming you don't charge and remand him?'

'The full twenty-four hours.'

'Is that necessary?'

'It's necessary,' said Ellen flatly.

The door closed on Duyker and the lawyer. In the corridor outside the interview room, Scobie began to apologise. 'I'm sorry, Ellen. I wasn't thinking.'

'No, you weren't, were you? We still don't know if the DNA found on Duyker's skin mags—which might belong to someone else, incidentally—can be matched to the DNA found in De Soto Lane, or to the degraded DNA found on Serena Hanlon.'

'I thought I'd throw a scare into him.'

'Well you didn't,' Ellen said.

Perhaps she was being unfair. The truth was, she was finding it hard to get Hal Challis out of her head this morning. He'd phoned her with the news about his father, and she could still hear the desolation in his voice, the particular timbre of his grief and sadness. A hint of longing and loneliness, too? She thought so. She wanted to be with him, but could hardly do that, for he'd be too distracted, she didn't know his family, and she had important investigations to run. And so he resided in her mind.

She made for her office. Maybe DNA evidence would help solve this case, but the lab was dragging its heels, and who knew what appalling errors of procedure it was making. She cast back in her mind, Duyker sitting comfortably across from her in the interview room. No bite marks on his fingers or forearms. Maybe Sasha had bitten him on the leg.

She was leafing desultorily through paperwork in her in-tray when the lab called. 'That paint chip,' one of the technicians—not Riggs—said.

'Yes?'

'We traced it to a line of children's bicycles manufactured by Malvern Star between 2003 and 2005.'

'Yes!' said Ellen.

'We aim to please.'

Ellen pressed the disconnect button of her desk phone and sat like that for a while. She should have made a more concerted effort, sooner, to find the bike. Everything that had happened, especially finding Katie alive, had blinded her to obvious matters. She released the button and called the media office, arranging for a wide circulation of descriptions and photographs of the bike. She was in a kind of trance now. She was stepping inside Duyker's skin, not Duyker the paedophile—she 'knew' that side of him—but Duyker with an unwanted child's bike on his hands.

This Duyker would have left the bike, helmet and schoolbag in his van after taking Katie Blasko to the empty house, but he wouldn't have wanted to keep them for long. There were remote places he could dump everything, but what if he were seen by someone. Also, a newish bicycle found in the middle of nowhere is going to raise questions, especially if the police have been saying they're looking for one just like it (here Ellen squirmed in her seat). Dumping the stuff at sea would require a boat. No, she could see Duyker leaving the bike in a public place, where children played—the sort of community where claiming an abandoned bike as your own was not a matter of dishonesty but of keeping your trap shut and thanking your lucky stars. The helmet and schoolbag he could have dumped anywhere.

Her only hope now was a firm ID from van Alphen's street kid, Billy DaCosta. She went downstairs. Van Alphen was not in his office, or Kellock's. According to the front desk, he hadn't checked in yet. She made for the sergeants' lounge. Kellock was there, flipping through a newspaper, turning the pages in typical style, as if to tear them out. He looked up at her with barely controlled patience. 'Kel,' she murmured, turning to go out.

'Sergeant Destry,' Kellock roared.

She turned back.

'What is it?'

'I'm looking for Van.'

'Maybe I can help you.'

She tried not to show her frustration. 'I need a statement from his witness. I need to take it myself, face to face. I can't take Van's word for it that this kid of his can identify Clode and Duyker.'

'Kid?'

'A street kid called Billy DaCosta. Van Alphen found him and was supposed to be bringing him in this morning.'

Kellock tossed the newspaper aside and lumbered across the room to her. He spoke, a gust of coffee breath: 'Look, Van's one of the good guys, but this shooting board investigation of the Jarrett shooting has got him worried. *I'm* worried. He could lose the plot, crack under the pressure. Go easy on him. Give him time.'

'He's running around finding witnesses and collecting evidence,' said Ellen exasperatedly. 'If it's useful, great. But I can't afford to waste time on red herrings, or *fail* to act because he cries wolf once too often.'

'Leave it to me.'

'He could run into some nasty people, doing what he's doing.'

'I know that.'

Ellen cocked her head. 'Unless he's protecting them.'

She hadn't meant to say it. You always divided the officers you worked with into those who made you uncomfortable and those who didn't. You did it every time you were posted to a new station or squad. It didn't mean the men or women who made you feel uncomfortable were dishonest in the strictly legal sense, or unlikely to watch your back in a tricky situation, but you knew to be wary of them. You didn't offer them anything of yourself. Kees van Alphen had always made Ellen feel uncomfortable. Hal Challis had always said, 'Be careful of that guy.'

Now Kellock had his head on one side. 'I'll pretend I didn't hear that.'

Ellen blushed and to defuse the moment said, 'It's all a bit too murky for me, Kel, this case.'

'Leave it to me. I'll track him down and reel him in.'

'Thanks.'

She returned to her office and found Duyker's lawyer waiting in the corridor. Sam Lock was short, damply overweight in a heavy suit, the knot of his yellow tie a fat delta under his soft chins. In all other respects he was hard and sharp. 'A quick word, Ellen?'

She led him into her office. He looked around it amusedly. 'Hal Challis's office, if I'm not mistaken. How is the good inspector?'

'Get on with it, Sam.'

'I want you to let my client go. Fraud charges? A few hundred dollars here and there? Resides locally?'

'Resides all over Australia, Sam. Sure, he owns a place in Safety Beach, but he likes to travel, stay a while, rip off star-struck mothers of young children—amongst other things more serious—and move on again.'

Lock examined his fingernails. Like all lawyers, he was full of little diversions that masked or delayed his real intent. Police officers did it, too. Ellen waited.

'You think he abducted Katie Blasko?'

Ellen gazed at him, wondering how much to reveal. Sam Lock would battle furiously on behalf of a client but he also had small children, two boys and a girl. 'He had something to do with it, even if not directly. He was there in that house with her. We also suspect him of the rape and murder of a child back in 1995, and are currently matching his movements nationwide with unsolved rapes and abductions of young girls.'

'He said you have DNA.'

'Yes,' Ellen said neutrally.

'But is it his? You don't have strong enough grounds to compel a sample from him, and his DNA is not on file anywhere. I wouldn't get your hopes up even if you had a sample, and matched it, because your forensic science lab is prone to stuffups. Witness the Neville Clode debacle.'

Ellen watched him carefully. 'Who told you about that?'

Lock shrugged.

'You do know that Clode's late wife was Duyker's sister?'

'That was mentioned.'

'Doesn't it bother you? Sure, the lab has admitted instances of cross contamination, but what if there wasn't any contamination in *this* instance?'

'It all goes to reasonable doubt, Ellen. You'll need something stronger if you're going to charge my client with Blasko. Meanwhile he's going to walk on that chickenshit charge you brought him in on.'

'Meanwhile you keep your children where you can see them,' Ellen snapped.

Lock's eyes flared, then he was impassive again, and Ellen watched him walk away. Moments later, her mobile rang, Kellock asking her to meet him on the Seaview Park estate.

46

Ellen stared at the body. The blood, bone chips and brain matter had slid down the wall here and there, and were beginning to dry. A couple of flies had got into the house. The left side of van Alphen's skull had taken the brunt of the shot: massive damage that still left enough of the face intact to confirm identity. Scobie Sutton was sketching the scene in his notebook. Like Ellen, and the crime scene technicians, he wore disposable overshoes.

'I'll leave you to it,' said Kellock, grim-faced in the doorway.

They were friends, thought Ellen, and now he was to inform the super.

'Who found him?'

'I did. Went looking for him, as I said I would, and recognised his car.'

'What do you suppose he was doing here?'

Kellock shrugged. 'Doing his own thing.'

'Doing his own thing, and look where it got him. Do we know who lives here?'

'I looked through the bills,' Kellock said, indicating a shallow fruit bowl piled with papers, unopened envelopes, spare keys, a hair tie and a half packet of potato chips sealed with a clothes peg. Every house in the land has a receptacle like that, Ellen thought.

'And?'

'Rosemary McIntyre.'

Ellen cast back in her mind. 'The name doesn't mean anything. Does it mean anything to you?'

'No. I called it in and they ran it through the computer. Solicitation, twelve years ago.'

'Where is she?'

'Your guess is as good as mine.'

When Kellock had left, Ellen looked for a calendar or diary but found nothing. Then the pathologist arrived and she watched him examine the body. She realised that her mouth was dry and she wasn't feeling her customary remoteness. She was well aware that the job had desensitised her. That was necessary. She was quite able to attend an autopsy and cold-bloodedly note the angle of a knife wound or gunshot, knowing that that information might catch a suspect out in a lie ('He tripped and fell on my knife'), but right now her eyes were pricking with tears. Van Alphen was a fellow police officer. She blinked and looked keenly at Scobie Sutton. 'Your first dead copper?' she murmured.

'Yes.'

'Upsetting.'

'I regret every violent death, Ellen.'

Sometimes he could sound like a churchman or a politician. 'Come off it, Scobe.'

'He was a nasty piece of work.'

'He didn't always follow regulations,' Ellen conceded.

'He and Kellock shot Nick Jarrett in cold blood,' Scobie said, 'and more or less warned me not to investigate too hard.'

Ellen blinked. There were spots of colour on her colleague's gaunt cheeks, his stick-like figure inclined toward her, draped in his habitual dark, outmoded suit. She backed up a step. The technicians and the pathologist were looking on interestedly but hadn't heard the outburst.

'All right, settle down,' she murmured. 'There's an estranged wife and daughter, I believe?'

Scobie wiped his mouth. 'I sent someone to inform them.'

'Thank you.'

They stood for a while, watching the pathologist, who finally released the body. The local funeral director took charge then, overseeing as the body was loaded onto a gurney and taken out to a waiting hearse for transfer to the morgue. The pathologist sighed and pulled off his latex gloves with a couple of snaps.

'Time of death, doc?' Ellen asked.

'Time of death. It's always time of death with you people.'

'Well?'

'Last night. Late evening. I can't be more specific than that.'

'Thanks,' Ellen said. She paused, then muttered to Scobie, 'I want you to bring Laurie Jarrett in for questioning. Meanwhile I'll see if I can find Van's witness.'

'If he exists,' said Scobie heatedly. 'Van Alphen was probably trying to divert attention away from the Jarrett shooting. Trying to make himself look good.'

'Even so.'

'I'll come with you.'

Ellen cocked her head. Was he hoping to find a diary or journal in which van Alphen described the true circumstances of the Jarrett shooting? Before she could reply, a voice called from the front of the house, a woman's cigarettes-and-whisky voice, full of outrage. 'What are you lot doin' here? I live here, you bastard, take your hands off me.'

They heard her pounding through the house. She burst in on them, shouting, 'You got a warrant?'

Then she spotted the gore, and went white, rocking on her feet. Ellen guided her back to the sitting room at the front of the house.

The newcomer was about forty, dressed in high heels, a black, short-sleeved beaded top, a knee-length tan skirt and dark stockings. Thick, dirty-blonde hair. Plenty of gold on her slim fingers. Slim legs and ankles, Ellen noticed, but a bit heftier around the bum and chest. A good-looking woman, a woman who liked the nightlife.

'Rosemary McIntyre?'

'Who wants to know? Was someone hurt? What's going on?'

Ellen introduced herself and then Scobie. 'First, can you tell us where you were last night?'

Not so belligerent now, Rosemary McIntyre gazed about her sitting room, which was dominated by a home entertainment unit, huge white leather armchairs facing it. There were a couple of pewter photo frames and very little else. 'Out,' she said.

'Where?'

'I work up in the city.'

'Where?'

Rosemary McIntyre folded her arms stubbornly. 'Siren Call.'

'The brothel?'

'*Legal* brothel.'

'I'm not making judgements. Were you there all evening?'

'Since six yesterday afternoon. I'm exhausted, and come home to this.'

Ellen didn't doubt that her alibi would check out. 'Does the name Sergeant van Alphen mean anything to you?'

''Course it does.'

Ellen regarded her for a moment. 'That's his blood on your floor and wall.'

Rosemary McIntyre screwed up her face tightly, then relaxed it, breathed out, looking bewildered. 'Don't know anything about that. I mean, what was he doing here?'

'Well, you're the one who says his name means something to you.'

'Well, duh.'

'Explain, please. Are you having a relationship with Sergeant van Alphen?'

The woman flushed angrily. 'Are you having a go at me? Are you? Fucking bitch.'

'No, I am not having a go at you. I'm trying to piece together what happened here.'

'Van Alphen,' said Rosemary McIntyre heavily, 'is one of the bastards that shot Nick.'

'You knew Nick Jarrett?'

'He's my second cousin,' said Rosemary McIntyre, as if Ellen and the whole world should have known that.

47

Leaving Scobie to finish up, Ellen drove to van Alphen's house. The kid who opened the door looked about eighteen but he could have been as young as thirteen. Dark clothes, untidy, a little grubby-looking. Music was blaring behind him, and she had to lip read him say, 'Yeah?'

'My name is Sergeant Destry, from the Waterloo police station,' she said. 'I'm a colleague of Sergeant van Alphen's.'

His face was blank for quite a while and then it screwed up and she saw him cup one ear and shout, 'What?'

She repeated her name. A light seemed to go on in his head and he held up a finger and ducked through an archway into the sitting room. He turned the music down. Then, as though having second thoughts, he turned it off. By then Ellen was in the room with him, a room that gave her an insight into an arid life. Van Alphen owned few books or CDs. Some four-wheel-drive and camping magazines, *TV Week* and the *Bulletin* on a cheap plywood coffee table. The TV set was small, a portable tucked away in a corner. Through a further archway was a dining-room table, manila folders and a computer heaped at one end—reminding her of Larrayne, taking over Challis's table. But with Larrayne it was temporary; Ellen guessed that van Alphen had lived like this since his wife and daughter had left him.

Or maybe they'd been driven out because he lived like this.

She turned to the kid. 'May I have your name?'

'Er, Billy. Billy DaCosta.'

Either he's nervous about giving his name to a police officer or he uses a false name, Ellen thought. She had to be sure who he was. 'Billy. Are you Sergeant van Alphen's witness? You were abused by certain men when you were younger, and have been able to identify them from photographs?'

'Er, yep.'

'I'll have to ask you to come to the station with me, Billy. We need a formal statement and you may be asked to attend identity parades.'

She had her doubts about the latter, thinking that a defence lawyer could claim the identification had been tainted because Billy had already been shown photographs, by a man now dead, and not in a formal context.

'Er, Mr Alphen's not here.'

Ellen cocked an eye. Van Alphen was always called Van, or Sarge. Then, taking in Billy's curly hair and delicate features, she wondered if they'd been lovers. Did that account for van Alphen's secretiveness and evasions? Was that why his marriage had failed? How old was Billy? If he was underage, that would help to account for van Alphen's recent behaviour. What, finally, would it do to Billy to learn that van Alphen had been shot dead?

'Do you know where he is?'

'He got a phone call,' said Billy, not looking at her and apparently concentrating furiously. 'Last night. He went out straight after.'

'Last night. You weren't worried when he didn't come back?'

'Nup.'

She needed to get the kid into safe custody. She needed the controllable environment of the police station in which to break the news to him. If she told him here and now, he might bolt.

'Well, we'd been expecting him to bring you in to make a statement this morning,' she said. 'Perhaps we can do that now. It's all right, he's a colleague.'

Billy looked hunted. 'I'll get my things.'

Ellen knew enough to follow him. He went to the main bedroom. All of the intermediate doors were open. There were signs she didn't like: drawers open, cupboards ajar, papers spilled here and there. Had Billy been searching through Van's things? Was he the kind of young male prostitute who liked to set up house with an older man, then do a midnight flit with the guy's valuables?

'This way, Billy,' she said, taking him to her car.

They drove in silence to the station, where she set him up in the artificial comfort of the Victim Suite, with its DVD player, armchairs and fridge stocked with soft drinks and chocolate bars. 'I'll be in to see you shortly, okay?'

'Sure,' said Billy, putting his feet up. Spotless new trainers, Ellen noticed, at odds with the grimy black jeans.

She encountered Scobie Sutton in the corridor. 'Did you bring in Laurie Jarrett?'

'Yes.'

'Let's go.'

Jarrett was in one of the interview rooms, arms folded, at peace with the world. Ellen was faintly alarmed to realise that she could smell him. It wasn't unpleasant. His eyes were clear, his manner taut but not threatening, the narrow planes of his neat head inclined toward her half mockingly. 'Ellen.'

'Mr Jarrett.'

'Good to see you again.'

'Cut the crap, Laurie. Tell us about Rosie McIntyre.'

'Rosie's a cousin.'

'Quite a clan,' Scobie said.

Jarrett ignored him.

'Are you close,' said Ellen, 'you and your cousin?'

'Not really.'

'But you'd know her general habits,' Scobie asserted. 'After all, you're cousins and you live on the estate.'

'It's a big estate,' Jarrett said, addressing Ellen.

It is, she thought, and getting bigger. She cleared her throat. 'You'd know that Rosie works in Siren Call, up in the city. Know she puts in long hours there.'

'Is that a question?'

'Did you call her in the past day or two? Landline or mobile? Or go around to see her?'

'She looked after Alysha a couple of weeks ago. That was the last time I saw her. What's this about?'

'Did she tell you her work schedule this week, specifically yesterday?'

'Like I said, haven't seen her for a couple of weeks. She in trouble? She hurt?'

Scobie said, 'Where were *you* last night, Laurie?'

Jarrett turned at last to Scobie and snarled, '*Mr* Jarrett to you, arsehole.'

Scobie flushed. 'There's no need for that.'

'With you,' Jarrett said, 'there is.'

Ellen privately agreed. 'Please answer the question.'

He smiled. '*You* can call me Laurie. To answer your question, I was at home with Alysha until about ten. Then she started fitting and I took her to the hospital. Check it out, if you don't believe me.'

Ellen felt an unaccountable sadness. 'Fitting?'

'She's epileptic. It's manageable, except last night it was worse than usual.'

'Is she okay?'

He cocked his neat head at her. 'I think you genuinely care. Yes, thank you for asking.'

'Witnesses?' demanded Scobie Sutton.

'Oh, it's you again. Witnesses? Other than Alysha? I didn't know I'd be needing witnesses, but there will be plenty at the hospital. We were there until long after midnight.'

'We'll be checking it out,' Scobie said.

'Go your hardest.'

Ellen thought of the girl with a pang. She thought of Larrayne then, and had an overwhelming urge to phone her, to see that she was all right. She gave in to it. 'Excuse me,' she said.

Scobie, startled, stopped the tape. Ellen slipped out into the corridor and flipped open her mobile phone. 'It's only me.'

'Mum, I'm trying to study.'

There had never been anything so welcome as her daughter's brattiness just then. 'Everything okay? Know where everything is?'

'Well, Mum, I haven't searched through all of the cupboards and drawers yet.'

Ellen had sometimes longed to search Challis's house. She wondered if she'd find letters or diaries that would help to explain who he was. His wife, jailed for trying to have him shot, had stayed in touch until she committed suicide. She used to phone him from prison. Had she also written? Would he have kept her letters? Ellen's mind flashed down this unwelcome and irrelevant path.

'Mum!' shouted Larrayne. 'Is there anything else?'

Ellen jumped. 'Sorry, no, see you later. Don't wait up.'

She went back to the interview room, where Scobie turned on the tape again, and she said at once, 'Sergeant van Alphen was shot dead in your cousin's house last night. We believe he was lured there by a phone call. You have made several threats to kill him. Did you kill him, Laurie—or order it done?'

Laurie Jarrett swallowed, the only sign, and said levelly, 'I won't say I'm sorry he's dead, but I swear to you that I did not kill the prick.'

Then he asked for a lawyer.

Scobie tried to be matey. 'Lawyer? They just charge the earth and complicate matters.'

Jarrett stared at Ellen, jerked his head at Scobie Sutton. 'Get him out of here.'

Ellen stared back consideringly. 'All right, but the tape keeps rolling.'

'Fair enough.'

'Ellen!' Scobie said.

'I'll be fine. You can listen in.'

He went out grumbling. Ellen said, 'What do you want to say, Laurie?'

'Nothing about van Alphen. Like I said, I don't know nothing about that.'

'Okay,' she said slowly.

'Alysha.'

'What about her?' Ellen said, sounding harsher than she'd intended.

'There are things she's not telling me.'

'All kids do that.'

'Do you think she needs to see someone?'

'You mean a therapist? It couldn't hurt. Do you have a family doctor who can refer you?'

Laurie Jarrett shrugged.

Ellen said, 'In the meantime, maybe it's *how* you've been trying to get her to talk that's holding her back.'

'What do you mean?'

'She needs to know she's loved and wanted.'

'She is,' said Jarrett emphatically.

'At the same time, she needs to know she's not being accused of anything. That she didn't do anything bad, or wrong. That you don't think she's a bad person. That none of it's her fault.'

Jarrett stared unseeingly at the wall. He blinked. 'Am I under arrest?'

Ellen thought about that. 'No. Just a few more questions—when your lawyer arrives, okay?'

'Sure.'

After the interview, Ellen returned to the Victim Suite, catching Billy slipping the DVD of *King Kong* down his jeans.

'Billy.'

'You got me,' Billy said. He put up his wrists to be manacled.

'Billy, I'm afraid I've got some bad news.'

'What?'

'Van—Sergeant van Alphen—was murdered last night.'

Billy opened and closed his mouth, then screwed up his face in emotion. Exactly what emotion, Ellen couldn't say, but he did sigh and flop into one of the floral-print armchairs. 'Thank Christ for that.'

Ellen froze. She knew something bad was coming. 'Billy?'

Billy got to his feet again and rummaged in the refrigerator. He took out and replaced one drink can after another, finally settling on a Coke.

'Did you have something to do with his death, Billy?' Ellen said, watching him closely. 'Is that why you're relieved?'

'Me? Nah.'

'Then why aren't you more surprised or upset?'

'I was scared of the prick,' Billy said. 'We all were.'

Ellen swallowed, then sat down opposite him. 'Go on.'

'He told me what to say. Coached me in how to answer questions. I never seen those guys in the photos before, but he told me I had to say they abused me.'

48

Time passed bewilderingly for Hal Challis. On Tuesday morning he contacted the funeral director and the Uniting Church minister again, telling them he had some repeat business for them, the joke falling flat. They settled on Saturday. After that he was rarely away from the phone, or the front door, as people from the town and the district dropped in or telephoned with their condolences.

Even McQuarrie called from Victoria. 'Very sorry for your loss, inspector.'

Ellen must have told him. 'Thank you, sir.'

'Take as long as you like, but things are in a turmoil here, and we can't afford to have you running an independent inquiry in South Australia, now can we, Hal?'

Nixon and Stormare told their boss, Challis thought, who then made a few phone calls. Perhaps the super fears I'll be even more uncontrollable now that my father's dead. At another time he might have used that to annoy McQuarrie in subtle ways, but he was too tired. 'No, sir.'

The day dragged on. Needing badly to fill time, he began to bundle together his father's clothing for the local op-shop, but it was far too soon, and he lost heart. He went through his father's desk, paid some bills. That's when he found the will. The old man had no shares and only a few thousand dollars in the bank. He'd left his house to his children and his car to Eve.

At 3.30, Challis parked the old station wagon in the street outside Meg's house. He checked in with her, then returned to the car, tied a purple ribbon around it, and waited on the verandah for Eve to come home from school. She appeared at 3.45, shuffling, head down, all of her striding, knockabout humour gone. She spotted the car, and froze. Challis called out to her.

She turned, shaded her eyes as he crossed the lawn toward her. 'Uncle Hal.'

He kissed her. 'As you can see, I come bearing gifts.'

Her eyes filled with tears. She tried to hide it by turning wry and scoffing. 'You expect me to drive *that*? I'll lose all street cred.'

Challis drew himself up. 'I'd be proud to be seen in this car.'

Eve was sniffing, blinking her eyes, trying to smile. 'Mum said you lost your virginity in it.'

Challis's jaw dropped comically. Suddenly Eve was wailing, crumpling. Challis held her tight for a while. 'Hush,' he murmured.

'I know he could be mean to you and Mum, but he was great to me.'

'I know.'

They stood like that. Eve sighed raggedly. 'The Murray Challis memorial station wagon.'

'That's the spirit.'

They went inside. Meg was on the sofa, making a list of hymns for the funeral. 'How about "Abide With Me"?' she said.

They both shuddered. 'No thanks.'

They discussed the will. 'I don't want the house,' Challis said. 'You can have my share. Maybe you can live there.'

Mother and daughter were seated together on the sofa. They turned to each other in silent communication and then kissed. It was as if they had settled all doubts, and Challis, on the edges of their lives here, realised that they were going to be all right. They faced him resolutely. Meg smiled and said, 'We're happy here.'

'Then we'll sell the house and you can have my share.'

'No, Hal. Equal shares.'

'I had a word with the real estate agent. It's worth about $175,000, but he said potential buyers are thin on the ground. People are leaving the district, not flocking into it.'

'We might have better luck finding tenants,' Meg said. 'The married housing on the sheep stations around here is pretty basic.'

Challis remembered Meg's words when Lisa Joyce came to see him late afternoon. He ushered her through to the kitchen, saying, 'You and Rex don't want to buy this place for your stud manager, do you?'

Lisa gazed around her. He began to see how shabby everything was. 'Not right now, Hal,' she said, smiling kindly as though he'd made a brave joke. 'I was really sorry to hear about your dad. He was a lovely guy.'

Challis doubted that Lisa had spent more than five minutes with Murray Challis in her life, but he appreciated the compliment. 'Thanks.'

She said, with a hint of stronger feelings, 'I suppose you'll go back to Victoria pretty soon.'

How to answer that? He was feeling the little disturbances he'd always felt when he was around her. 'There's a lot to do,' he said lamely.

Her fingers lingered on his wrist as she went out. It was affection, commiseration and the gesture of a woman who had an unconscious excess of sexual energy.

He was bucked up to hear Ellen Destry's voice that evening, the kindness and affection flowing from her, but shocked to hear that Kees van Alphen had been shot dead. 'I should come back,' he said.

'You can't, Hal. Bury your father.'

'But—'

'You're better off out of it. It's become a feeding frenzy for the media. McQuarrie keeps popping up in front of the cameras. And any minute now, we're going to have a team from Melbourne down here, crawling all over us. Stay away, Hal—not that I don't wish you were here.'

'I wish I was there, too.'

The pause was awkward. It rang with implications.

On Wednesday morning Pete Duyker was released on police bail. Ellen had charged him with fraud, knowing nothing else would stick. She didn't like it, and, with Scobie Sutton, stood outside the police station, watching Sam Lock usher Duyker into his car. Lock gave them a complicated smile. Complicated, Ellen thought, because the lawyer side of him had not seen more serious charges laid against his client, and the father-of-young-children side of him was afraid that he was aiding a paedophile.

Meanwhile, van Alphen's will-o-the-wisp evidence had been thoroughly discredited. She sighed and turned away, overwhelmed. She wanted to find van Alphen's killer, she wanted to put Duyker away, and she wanted to console Hal Challis.

Scobie Sutton was saying something, one hand shading his eyes against the sun. Masses of rain yesterday, masses of sunshine today. She forced herself to concentrate, and heard him say, 'Everything's clean, including his computer.'

'Maybe he wasn't involved in the abduction,' Ellen replied, 'or someone else borrowed his van, but I bet he was at the house, I bet he made videos or took photos.'

Scobie nodded. They stood there glumly, the spring air mild and scented, imagining how the case would have played out if Katie hadn't been found but killed by Duyker and her body disposed of.

'Back to work,' Ellen said, and they re-entered the station. 'Talk to the vice squad and missing persons. We might be able to match faces in recent kiddie porn with those of children who have gone missing or been abducted or found murdered in recent years. We might also find visual clues that help identify the men involved, men like Clode and Duyker.'

'But they'd sell that stuff to Asia, Europe or the States.'

'It's global, Scobie.'

They passed the Victim Suite. The door was open, the room empty. 'Think we'll see Billy again?'

Ellen shook her head. 'He's long gone. He's either on the other side of the continent, running scared, or he's been paid off, or he's dead.'

'Has he got a record?'

Ellen had searched the databases. 'No.'

They continued on to CIU. 'Have the shooting board officers finished with you, Scobie?'

He gave her a hunted look. 'Yes.'

'And?'

'It will go on my record, failure to follow correct procedure.'

'What will their report say? They can't do anything about van Alphen now, but will take action against Kellock?'

Scobie said irritably, 'I don't know, Ellen, all right? I'm not privy to their findings.'

'Scobie, I don't want any messing up of forensics in regard to the Blasko investigation.'

'You don't have to talk to me like that,' Scobie said chokingly, and he stalked off. When she reached CIU, he was muttering covertly on the telephone.

She'd scarcely made a start on the paperwork cluttering her desk when Superintendent McQuarrie called. 'I hear you let our cop killer go.'

This aroused conflicting emotions in Ellen. She twirled in her chair, the phone held to her ear. McQuarrie was too neat and precise a man to use the term 'cop killer'. He was trying out the phrase, trying to sound tough or ingratiate himself. Also, his tone was accusatory. Did he ever praise? Would he ever praise her? Had he ever praised Hal Challis? Finally, the man had spies and cronies everywhere. She couldn't blame Kellock: it was his job to keep his superiors abreast of things. Still, McQuarrie's tone was reminding her yet again that the police force was made up of many wheels. Her own was small and barely revolved, it seemed to her. It didn't exist within, or intersect with, the wheels that mattered.

'Sir, we didn't have enough evidence to hold Mr Jarrett.'

'Gunshot residue?'

'None.'

'Then someone from his appalling family carried it out.'

'They all have alibis, sir.'

'Good ones?'

'Yes, sir.'

She was tired of calling him 'sir'.

'Jarrett could have washed off the GSR. How's his alibi?'

'Solid, sir. We have a witness who heard a shot at eleven o'clock last night and...'

'This fine, upstanding person didn't think to report it?'

'Sir, it's the estate. At the time Sergeant van Alphen was shot, Laurie Jarrett's daughter was being examined by a doctor and a nurse in Casualty at the Waterloo hospital. Laurie was with her the whole time. It checks out.'

'Convenient. What about Jarrett's wife, the kid's mother?'

'She's in a drug rehab clinic in Perth, heroin addiction, court ordered after she was arrested for burglary and shoplifting offences.'

'Divorced? Separated?'

'Never married. She left home when Alysha was born.'

'Making Laurie a heroic single dad,' snarled McQuarrie. 'It makes me sick.'

She suspected he meant the loose family arrangements you found these days. She felt like reminding him that his own family wasn't squeaky clean, that his own son had taken part in suburban sex parties—then reflected sourly that sex parties were probably seen as an acceptable aberration of the upper classes, whereas children born out of wedlock to addicts was seen as a condemnatory characteristic of the lower classes.

She cast her mind back to her interrogation with Laurie Jarrett. Deciding against a lawyer, he'd opened up finally, seeming almost genial. For the first time, Ellen glimpsed what it was like for him. He was an old-style crim, who didn't use or condone drugs. He stole to make money, an income, not to feed a drug habit, unlike his sons, cousins, nephews, de facto...He was loyal to his family, bailed them out, but sometimes that love must have been sorely tested.

'He still could have ordered the hit,' McQuarrie was saying now.

'Ordered the hit' was another expression that sat oddly in the super. 'We'll keep checking, sir.'

'You sound doubtful. In fact, you have doubtful outcomes mounting up all around you, Sergeant.'

He sounded cocky and provocative. He was the kind of man who hated and feared women—the hate and the fear being one and the same thing, really, for he hated women because they made him fear them. She said nothing, but a kind of black light suffused her. If he'd been there with her she'd have struck him. Instead, she hit him another way. 'Speaking of doubtful outcomes, sir,' she said, 'did you know that Sergeant van Alphen had been coaching a witness, a street kid called Billy DaCosta, to give false evidence against the men we suspect of abducting and abusing Katie Blasko?'

There was a silence. Then, in a constrained voice, McQuarrie said, 'Is he connected to the Jarretts, this DaCosta person?'

Ellen had checked. 'No, sir.'

'How can you be sure? The Jarretts are behind this. It's a revenge killing, of a police officer, and won't be tolerated.'

'Sir.'

'It's too big for you, for your team.'

'Sir.'

She felt oddly relieved as McQuarrie went on to tell her that Homicide Squad officers would come down from the city to take over the investigation into van Alphen's murder. 'They have the resources and the expertise.'

'Sir.'

'Leaving you free to do whatever it was you were doing before this.'

As though Katie's abduction and abuse were minor things, easily forgotten. In his mind, McQuarrie probably thought that he'd successfully undermined Ellen. She had a creepy sense of the forces at work around her.

50

The days passed and she made no headway. The urgency had gone from the investigation. Not even the van Alphen murder could galvanise anyone, for when the Homicide Squad detectives took over the case, they immediately shut Waterloo staff out. There were four of them, three men and a woman, young, sleek, educated and close-mouthed.

Commandeering one of the conference rooms, they interviewed all thirty of the staff based at the station—uniformed officers, probationary constables, Ellen's CIU detectives, collators, civilian clerks and cleaners—their manner clipped and impersonal, arousing resentment.

On Friday they interviewed Ellen. They seemed cynical with her. Doubting. Probably because she'd had charge of the investigation for the first few hours, she thought.

'I didn't really know him,' she told them.

'You had him digging around in that abduction case.'

'He was assigned to desk duties pending the inquiry into the Nick Jarrett shooting,' Ellen said. 'He wanted to be useful.'

'So useful he left his desk and operated in secret.'

They were well informed. Ellen said, 'Unfortunately he didn't confide in me.'

'Did he like little boys?'

'I have no idea.'

'He was shacked up with a street kid.'

She supposed that their besmirching van Alphen was part of a strategy. They wanted to know if van Alphen's hidden interests and activities had made him a target. They wanted people to be outraged, and talk.

'As I understand it,' she said carefully, 'he was protecting a witness.'

'Do you still understand that to be the case?'

Ellen shrugged. 'The witness claimed that he'd been coached by Sergeant van Alphen, so I don't know what to believe.'

'Hissy fits, sudden flare-ups of temper, biting, scratching and kicking. It can get quite volatile, the gay scene.'

Ellen wasn't going to let them provoke her. 'We don't know that he was gay. We don't know that he liked little boys. They're not even the same thing. Look, I know you have to examine every contingency, but why this one? It impinges on my case. Why aren't you looking at the Jarrett clan?'

'Like you said, we'll look into everything.'

Ellen watched them expressionlessly, their four clever faces staring back at her, giving nothing away. She'd scarcely registered their names or ranks. Not even gender factored here. The four detectives were interchangeable. 'I expect, or at least request, full co-operation from you,' she said firmly.

They said nothing.

'If your investigation into Sergeant van Alphen turns up anything related to child abductions or the activities of a supposed paedophile ring on the Peninsula, then I want you to pass it on to me,' she continued. 'Formal or informal witness statements, names and addresses, case notes, jottings, files, computer records, child pornography, phone numbers scribbled on napkins, anything at all.'

'And if this material also relates to his murder?'

'Then we overlap,' Ellen said. She hesitated. 'Is there anything? Have you got suspicions?'

She wanted them to articulate *her* suspicions—that van Alphen had been protecting paedophiles, hence his sloppy police work and indifference regarding Alysha Jarrett. That he'd intended to betray Billy DaCosta by claiming Billy had lied to him, which would have raised doubts about information given by *genuine* victims. That, even so, the members of his paedophile ring had killed him to shut him up. Killed Billy, too.

'Have you?' she repeated. 'Can I see it? Did you find stuff on his computer?'

'We'll let you know if we do find anything,' they said, with sharkish good will. 'But a few minutes ago you pointed the finger at the Jarretts. Now you imply that van Alphen was killed because he was doing work for you, or that you would find out about him. You can't have it both ways.'

'They are the two most logical avenues to explore.'

'Sergeant van Alphen must have made enemies over the years.'

'We all do,' said Ellen, bored and hostile now.

'This is off the record, but we understand that the police shooting board findings will exonerate Kellock and van Alphen. Perhaps the Jarrett clan sensed this, and wanted revenge for Nick Jarrett.'

Ellen was expressionless. As far as she was concerned, truth, or at least the police version of it, was never black and white, A or B, but many things together, merging, overlapping and existing simultaneously.

'If that's all?' she said, getting to her feet.

They smiled broadly and emptily as she let herself out of the room.

She found Scobie waiting. 'Well, that was fun.'

He nodded. He'd already had his turn with them.

'Some good news for you, though,' Ellen said. She told him what she'd been told about the shooting board's findings. She'd never seen a man so relieved, or so troubled. 'Meanwhile, what have you been doing?' she said.

'I tried to get in and search Van's house. I was refused permission.'

Ellen shrugged. For a long time afterwards, she didn't reflect on Scobie's remark. It was Friday. All she wanted to do was go home, pour herself a stiff drink, hang out with her daughter and call Hal Challis.

When she got home at eight that evening, she saw a familiar red Commodore in the driveway. Her husband was in the sitting room, drinking a glass of wine with Larrayne, Larrayne with her long, youthful bare legs curled under her on the sofa. Alan was in the armchair that Ellen normally chose. He raised his glass. 'The great detective returns.'

He wasn't being snide. It had been an old joke between them, back when the marriage had been tolerable. She gave her husband and her daughter a wintry smile. 'Not such a great one this evening.'

Alan nodded soberly. 'I heard they gave the van Alphen shooting to some hot shots from the city.'

Ellen poured herself a glass of wine. It was a good wine, a Peninsula pinot noir, and therefore probably raided from Hal Challis's own stock. She glanced from the label to Larrayne, who winked. 'Cheers,' she said, raising her glass. 'To what do we owe the honour of this visit?'

'Dad said he'd take me out to that new Thai place in Waterloo,' Larrayne said.

'You're welcome too, Ells,' said Alan, clearly not meaning it.

There was no way that Ellen was going. She glanced at Larrayne, trying to read her daughter, ready to step in if Larrayne wanted to study but couldn't say no to him. 'I'm fine with it, Mum.'

Ellen looked more closely at her husband. He'd lost weight. He'd dressed up: new chinos, a new shirt. 'You look nice.'

He waggled his jaw from side to side. He did that when he was hiding something. He dissembled, glancing around the room. 'So, this is the boyfriend's house.'

Ellen felt deeply fatigued. 'Shut up, Alan.'

He flushed dangerously and sloshed some of Challis's costly wine onto the hardwood floor. 'Dad, we'd better go,' Larrayne said.

It was when they were gone that Ellen remembered Scobie's remark. He'd wanted to search van Alphen's house, and been refused permission. Well, naturally, for van Alphen's murder wasn't their case. But van Alphen had been working on a case that *was* theirs, and he was a man full of secrets.

Forty-five minutes later, with a hastily prepared ham sandwich inside her, Ellen snapped latex gloves onto her hands, slid open Kees van Alphen's bathroom window catch with a thin blade, and let herself in. She'd called at the station first, going to the hardware cupboard and borrowing—but not signing for—a piece of equipment used by electricians to check if power sockets were live. A dead socket could mean that a small safe was concealed behind it.

She went through van Alphen's house swiftly; all of the electrical sockets were genuine. Then she checked behind the paintings and prints hanging on his walls, kicked baseboards, listening for tell-tale hollow sounds, looked under the dirty clothing in the laundry basket, examined tins, jars and freezer packages. She was an expert at this. Now and then over the years she'd found small amounts of cash. Sometimes she'd pocketed it. It was a kind of pathology that she should do something about, she thought idly. But she didn't want to see a counsellor or therapist. She believed that she could control it herself.

Frustrated now, she went through the house again, hoping to avoid searching van Alphen's garden shed, with its noisy tools, bins and cans, and uncomfortably close to the neighbour's bedroom window. She pulled out drawers and felt under them. She looked behind the façade at the top of his old-fashioned wardrobe. The computer had been removed by the Fab Four from headquarters, but wouldn't van Alphen have concealed backup CDs or floppies somewhere? Books. CD and DVD covers. A tissue box.

She looked at the TV set. It was small, years old, worth nothing to a junkie. She lifted it experimentally. It felt light. Van Alphen had gutted it.

She waited until she got home. The material was a thin folder of statements, forms and photographs, and she quickly saw why van Alphen had hidden it, and she was betting that he hadn't signed it out from Records. She read right through, glad that he'd been so thorough, heartbroken that the thoroughness had got him killed.

In 2005, a boy named Andrew Retallick, then aged thirteen, had approached teachers at Peninsula High School—who had contacted the Department of Human Services and Waterloo police—to say that he'd been abused by a group of men for many years, in several locations, but mainly at a house on the outskirts of Waterloo. He described the house. He remembered a spa bath and soft toys. He'd been photographed in the spa bath, naked, with the men who'd abused him. He'd been asked to suck his thumb and pose naked with the soft toys. The men varied: there was a hard core of four or five, with others whom he saw occasionally or only once. Some were dressed as policemen. The abuse had started when he was seven years old and continued for many years. He hadn't liked it but hadn't let himself think it was wrong. After all, policemen were involved. Whenever he was hurt, someone would tend to him. Going to high school had changed everything: not only was his body changing but sex education classes had opened his eyes to what had been done to him for all of those years. And so he'd told his teachers, and DHS officers, counsellors and, finally, the police. But nothing had been done, and so he'd stopped talking. He changed schools three times. He tried and failed to kill himself by cutting his wrists. That was last year.

Ellen leafed through the file, making sense of the statements and forms. The photographs of Andrew showed a small, hunted-looking boy, although in one instance he was smiling, a sad smile but it transformed his face, so that he looked sweet and exotic. Long lashes, Ellen noted, dusky skin.

Larrayne returned, looking tense. 'Mum, he's got a girlfriend. I had to sit there and hear all about her.'

So that was it. Larrayne seemed miserable, like a child who had tried and failed to keep her parents together. 'It was bound to happen, sweetheart.'

'It's not fair.'

Ellen tried to hug her. Larrayne shrugged her off. 'I'm going to bed.'

When the house was silent again under a barely moonlit sky, Ellen returned to van Alphen's case notes. She read for some time, finally coming to his summary, written as fragmentary observations in his neat, pinched hand: 'A litany of errors or wilful obstruction. Two of AR's statements missing, computer files been tampered with. Parents were urged to let matters drop. Officers interviewed Neville/Shirley Clode, owners of the house where the abuse took place, Sept. 2005. They accepted Clodes' explanation re spa room—had been set up for granddaughter. Quote: "The Clodes were interviewed and subjected to a background check. This showed them to be normal, everyday citizens, who were completely shocked by the allegations". AR's parents angry re Office of Police Integrity's decision to take no further action, despite independent confirmation that A had been abused (see report, Royal Children's Hospital's Gatehouse Centre). Parents told me the senior sergeant in charge was v. aggressive. Warned them kids often lied about being sexually abused; allegations could destroy decent families, etc., etc. Quote: "There is nothing further the police service can do for you". Meanwhile police members investigating A's allegations did not contact his psych or the Gatehouse Centre.

'Managed to speak to AR. He's unwilling to make further statements to police. Had been shown porn videos and magazines depicting him having sex with his abusers, feels deeply ashamed etc.

'Asked AR's parents if they wish to swear out a complaint against Snr Sgt Kellock. Declined. Asked AR to identify abusers from a photo array. Declined, but gave me the name of another abused youth, Billy DaCosta. Talked to a snitch who told me where to find DaC.'

Ellen felt cold all over and the dark night pressed darker around the house on its quiet back road. If only van Alphen had come to her instead of finding Billy DaCosta himself. But he'd always been a loner, despite his apparent matiness with Kellock and men like Kellock. And if he'd always considered Kellock a friend, he'd want to make pretty sure of his facts before accusing him. Perhaps he feared that Kellock would withdraw his support over the Nick Jarrett shooting, even change his story.

The fear corroded her. She called Challis, and he answered immediately, sounding alert. 'Sorry to call you so late.'

'Something's wrong.'

'We've got a rotten apple,' she said.

She told him all about it. 'What do I do?'

'Make absolutely certain of everything. Cover your back. *Watch* your back. Make multiple copies of every report, file and conversation, and secure them in separate locations. Trust no one. I'll be back as soon as I can.'

51

At lunchtime on Monday, John Tankard stood in the canteen serving line, watching but not registering the wisps of steam escaping from the stainless-steel trays of Bolognese sauce, lasagne and Irish stew. He felt wretched: another weekend, nightmares and depression, so bad that he'd barely made it through. He'd thought he'd beaten the nightmares and depression. Clearly not. He could put it down to the stress of the job, but knew better: he was bitter and sad because he'd lost his dream car.

Not lost, exactly. It was in a mate's lock-up garage, where it would never be found by the finance company.

He took his bowl of lasagne to a corner table and picked at it. Someone cast a shadow over the table. 'Hello, Tank.'

Pam Murphy sat, beaming at him across the greasy Formica. 'I'm back,' she said.

He noted sourly that she wasn't in uniform. That made him feel worse. 'Detective duties,' he said flatly.

'That's right.'

'What's the Iron Lady got in store for you?'

That's what he called Sergeant Destry, who'd always made him feel small, and more than once bawled him out over trifling incidents.

'Cut it out, Tank,' Pam said, in a tone that said 'grow up'.

She looked good: leaner, more assured, and ready for business. Somehow he knew she'd blossom in CIU and he hated her for it. He also wanted her more. He couldn't fight his body language: his eyes flicked over her with pathetic desire and longing, as of a lover left far behind, and she registered it, too, the bitch, unconsciously turning her trunk away from him, crossing her legs and shielding her breasts. One body reacting to another. He wished he wasn't so overweight.

He changed the subject. 'Shitty thing, what happened to Van.'

He saw her eyes fill with tears. 'Yes.'

'You going to the funeral tomorrow?'

'Of course. Aren't you?'

He shifted in his seat, then said, his voice imploring: 'Have you, like, heard any whispers?'

'What about?'

'You know, that he was, you know...'

He saw a flicker in her eyes. She *had* heard things, or had suspicions. 'I don't fucking believe it, myself,' he snarled.

She struggled to give him a bright, releasing smile. 'Same here. Good to see you again, Tank. Must go.'

Tank watched her leave the canteen, watched Senior Sergeant Kellock hold the door for her, big grin and a welcome back. Then Kellock was crossing the room toward him like a purposeful bear. 'Constable Tankard.'

Tank stood awkwardly. 'Sir.'

'Sit down, son, sit down.'

Tank complied, Kellock sitting where Murphy had sat. He wondered what Kellock wanted, and felt his legs turn to jelly. They know I've been selling information to the media, he thought. He opened and closed his mouth a couple of times gaspingly.

'John,' said Kellock in a kind uncle voice, 'you did the right thing last week, telling me that Sergeant van Alphen had found a witness.'

'Sir, it just slipped out. I assumed you knew, actually. I would never have—'

'Of course I knew, son. Don't fret it.'

'Thank you, sir.'

'It's important at the senior level to keep abreast. That's an important part of my job, John, making sure I keep in the loop.'

'Sir.'

'So if you ever hear anything you think I should know about—like Sergeant van Alphen's secret witness—even though I already knew—then you must tell me. Because sometimes the right hand doesn't know what the left is doing.'

'Sir.'

'You did the right thing. It's not your fault he was shot, remember that. The fucking Jarretts shot him.'

'Yeah, I know,' said Tank. 'Sir.'

There was a pause. Kellock said, 'Another thing, John—I've been looking through Sergeant van Alphen's paperwork.'

At once Tank knew what this was about, but he said innocently, 'Sir?'

'Trouble over a certain car?'

Tank blurted it out, the car, the finance company coming after him for the money and wanting to repossess.

'I mean, my car's on a black list, sir. It can't be registered anywhere in Australia, so what good is it to the finance company? I don't know why they want to repossess.'

'But you are refusing to give it to them? They do have a legal right to it.'

Tank swallowed, barely concealing the shiftiness and desperation he was feeling. 'Actually, sir,' he said, his voice not quite making the grade, 'some bastard stole it.'

Kellock put his huge head on one side. 'Incredible.'

Tank said nothing.

'How did Sergeant van Alphen get involved?'

'Sir, he went with me to the finance company. You should have seen him, sir. He told them they had no legal standing, they loaned me money on an illegal car. Failed to do due diligence. Left themselves open to investigation for their part in a car re-birthing racket. It was bloody magnificent, sir. He told them if they wanted their money to go after the caryard proprietor. Unreal.'

Kellock was spoiling his grim exterior with a small smile. 'We lost a good man.'

'We did, sir,' said Tank, welling up, his throat thick with sudden grief.

'But that's where it ends, as far as the police are concerned, understood?'

'Sir.' Tank also took that as an obscure warning not to contact 'Evening Update' ever again. 'Cross my heart, sir.'

'You have dragged us into what is essentially a personal matter. Use a lawyer next time.'

'Understood, sir.'

'Back to work, John. Bike patrol, okay?'

'Aww, sir,' Tank protested.

'John.'

'Sir.'

Tank went back to work. Bike patrol. Another of Kellock's bullshit innovations, like that road safety campaign a few months back, when he and Pam Murphy had driven around in a little sports car, rewarding courteous drivers. Bike patrol entailed zipping around Waterloo on a bicycle, an exercise aimed at keeping down bag snatching, car theft and theft from parked cars—crimes that had escalated in recent years, what with Waterloo's paradoxical growth in social distress *and* commercial activity. People were getting poorer but Waterloo also had a new K-Mart now, plus a Coles, a Ritchies and a Safeway, all with vast, choked car parks, a boon to thieving kids from the Seaview estate.

He'd barely completed a circuit of the foreshore reserve parking area when his mobile phone jangled. He dismounted, answered the call. 'The well drying up?' growled the producer of 'Evening Update'.

Tank said, the words simply popping into his head and feeling right, 'I can't do this any more.'

'Oh, I *see*. A crisis of conscience.'

Tank hated the guy's tone and fluency. 'It's…I just…'

But the line had gone dead. Feeling good, and bad, Tank pedalled across town to the Safeway supermarket, and five minutes later he nicked fifteen-year-old Luke Jarrett. Luke's car of choice was a 2004 Hyundai Accent, which was parked in a shadowy region between the side doors of the supermarket and a couple of huge metal dump bins.

'Is this your car?'

'Ow! You're hurting me. Pig.'

Luke Jarrett was dark, lithe, darting. A kid who'd seen everything in his short life. Tank didn't waste any time. He took the kid deeper into the shadows, to where the garbage stank, fluids stained the ground and papers blew about. He began systematically to punch the boy: testicles, stomach and face. He knew how not to leave bruises.

'You want to wake up to yourself, mate. Had enough?'

The kid didn't answer but was crying softly, snot and saliva smearing his face.

'Where were you intending to take the car?'

No reply. Tank beat him again. Eventually the boy said, 'Korean Salvage.'

Tank was astonished. The guy who ran Korean Salvage was the father of one of Waterloo's ace under-18 footballers. 'Get your sorry arse off home, Luke,' he said. 'Keep your trap shut and I won't arrest you. That means you do not warn Korean Salvage.'

He watched the kid run, doubled over, in the general direction of High Street, then snapped on his bicycle clips again and pedalled around to the industrial estate. He found Korean Salvage, and there he talked long and hard to the proprietor, pointing out various pros and cons, eventually coming to a mutually beneficial arrangement with the guy. In return for rebirthing Tank's hitherto doomed Mazda, the proprietor of Korean Salvage would not be reported to CIU for car theft and related offences.

Tank finished patrolling at five that afternoon, his bum sore from the saddle of the bike, his meaty legs aching, and saw Pam Murphy return one of the unmarked CIU Falcons. 'Knocking off work for the day?'

She shook her head cheerfully. 'I'll be on for hours, yet. A detective's work is never done.'

She said it jokingly. At once Tank thought of a way to wipe the joke off her face.

52

Challis was at RSPCA regional headquarters. He'd buried his father on Saturday; now it was time to finish this last thing. Sadler was in his office and not pleased to see him.

'I hear they arrested Paddy Finucane,' he said bluntly.

'Yes.'

'So why do you want to see me?'

Challis checked the outer office. It was almost 5 pm and they were alone.

'What are you doing?' demanded Sadler. 'I think you'd better leave.'

Challis closed the office door soundlessly and crossed the room, leaning both hands on Sadler's desk, towering over the man. 'Where were you?' he murmured.

'What?'

'Gavin Hurst was a liability. Mood swings. Antagonising people, *including* his work colleagues.'

'You can't...I wasn't...Paddy Finucane...'

'Paddy Finucane didn't kill him, no matter what those hotshots from Adelaide think. I know it and you know it.'

'If the police think he did it, that's good enough for me.'

'That anonymous call: you invented it. There was no call.'

'No! Check with the receptionist. She logged it. The police took a copy with them.'

'You got someone outside this office to make the call.'

'I wasn't even here that day!'

'Exactly. You were in the Bluff, shooting Gavin in the head.'

'No!'

Sadler was looking wildly past Challis, hoping for deliverance. The world outside was ticking over benignly, slowed by the springtime sun. 'You can't do this.'

'I'll ask it again, where were you?'

'Down in Adelaide.'

'Can you prove it?'

'Yes! Dozens of witnesses. My daughter's nursing graduation.'

'You got someone to do your dirty work for you, then.'

'No!'

Challis was going through the motions. He'd fantasised that Sadler was the killer, over the past few days, but now, facing the man, no longer believed it. 'Gavin's camera?'

'What about it?'

'When did you take those photos of Paddy's place?'

'The only time I was at his place was days later, and I had my own camera.'

Challis pulled a chair up to the desk. He sat, and was less intimidating. 'When was Gavin's camera passed back to you?'

Sadler, relieved but still jumpy and indignant, said, 'Weeks later. They were going to give it to Meg, but all the photos on it were work related, so it came to me.'

'Who else did Gavin have a history with?'

The question was unwelcome. 'He did his job. He prosecuted several people over the years. Fair and square.'

'But was he fair and square in the last few weeks and months?'

Sadler looked away. 'Not always.'

'Spit it out. I'm tired of this.'

Sadler shrugged. 'He might have had a couple of arguments with Rex Joyce.'

'Joyce? About what?'

'Mistreating a horse.'

'What action was taken?'

'None.'

'Why not?'

'Can you see Rex Joyce mistreating a horse? I don't think so.'

'I can, actually,' Challis said. 'He has a bad temper.'

Sadler looked hurt and astounded, as though Challis had insulted the Queen.

'Who reported him?'

'No one.'

'So how did Gavin know to investigate?'

'For your information,' Sadler said, 'Gavin Hurst liked to sneak around. He *claimed* he just happened to be driving past Mr Joyce's property and saw him whipping one of his horses with a length of barbed wire.'

'Can I see his report?'

'You may not. I destroyed it, as it happens.'

'Why the hell would you do that?'

'No merit.'

'Did Gavin tell you he was going to prosecute?'

'Like I said, the case had no merit.'

'Are you friends with Joyce?'

Sadler blinked at the shift, and stumbled. 'I don't know what you mean.'

'You were at boarding school with him, perhaps? Belong to the same Liberal Party branch? Play golf with him?'

'Now you're being offensive.'

'He's rich, right? Local gentry? Long pedigree? Therefore he can do no wrong?'

'Get out.'

'What did your pal Joyce say when Gavin charged him?'

Sadler looked hunted.

'Come on, Sadler,' snarled Challis, 'you'll be asked this in court by Paddy's barrister, so it's in your interests to tell me now, and tell me the truth.'

Sadler rubbed at a mark on his spotless desk. 'He might have said that Gavin would get his one day.'

'His just deserts, do you mean? Is that how you understood his remark?'

'How would I know? It was just talk. Rex can sound off sometimes.'

'So you *do* know him.'

'A bit.'

'He has a temper. He drinks.'

'I wouldn't go as far as that.'

'Wouldn't you? Did you tell Nixon and Stormare any of this?'

'No need.'

'Why not?'

Sadler looked for ways out and found only a couple of mealy-mouthed replies. 'I've already said too much. Nothing to do with me. Plus it seems clear this Finucane character did it. Rex Joyce does not strike me as the kind of person to...'

Do anything quite so grubby as murder another person. Challis left and buckled himself into his car, thinking that Sadler pretty well summed up the Australian national character, which was not fine and egalitarian but grovelled at the feet of men who'd gone to a private school or could kick a football or had become billionaires by being allowed to evade tax.

On his way back over Isolation Pass, Challis scraped the guardrail. He was speeding a little, distracted by tense speculations about how he should approach Lisa and Rex Joyce, eyes screwed up against the setting sun, and failed to slow for a bend called the Devil's Elbow. The car rocked and screeched in protest and he fought to get it back under control. His heart racing, he pulled into the next lookout and surveyed the damage. The chrome bumper had been torn off, one headlight mangled, the quarter panel dented and gouged. He crouched to view the passenger side front wheel. It was scraping against metal and the wire spokes and spinner were chopped about. He searched around for a fallen branch and levered the damaged panel away from the tyre. The rubber itself looked sound. He got back into his seat and drove sedately down the mountain, aware of his mortality but ready for anything.

Lisa and Rex lived in a huge stone house that dated from the 1890s. It, and the huge woolshed and stables on the grounds of the property, were on the National Trust register. There were railing yards behind the stables, the rails vivid white in the last of the sun's rays. Lawns surrounded the house itself, which looked cool and composed on a slight rise, with tall gum trees, cypress hedges and fruit trees casting long shadows and completing the general air of a long, stately history. Challis had been on the place only once before, when he was ten years old and all fifty-seven kids at the local primary school had been carted here in two old yellow buses for a tour and a talk about pioneering endeavour in the district. He could remember the occasion, not the talk. No doubt the Joyces were the heroes in the story. But there had been one enduring benefit: there was an airstrip on the property, with a Tiger Moth stored in an adjacent barn. Challis had slipped away from the group and was found two hours later, sitting in the cockpit. That had been the start of his love affair with old aeroplanes.

He thought about that now, as he crept up the gravel driveway, the Triumph clattering miserably. He was restoring a 1930s Dragon Rapide at the little aerodrome near Waterloo, but various things had happened in his life and the Dragon was mouldering away in a hangar there. He felt guilty about that. His father, who'd valued hard work and finishing the tasks you set for yourself, would have been badly disappointed. Challis could hear the old man's voice in his head and he wished he'd brought his inhaler with him.

He followed the driveway around. There were no vehicles parked near the house. No sign of life, either, until he'd parked at the bottom of the verandah steps and got out, when the huge front door swung inwards and Lisa appeared behind the outer screen door. She stood waiting for him, a hazy shape behind the fine wire mesh.

'Hal?'

Challis climbed the steps warily. 'Lisa.'

'What's up?'

'Is Rex here?'

'He's away. Why?'

Challis let some silence build. 'I think you know why.'

'Sorry?'

'Did Sadler call you?'

She didn't say 'Who's Sadler?' but frowned. 'No. Why? What's going on?'

'I've just come from him. He claims that Gavin intended to prosecute Rex for cruelty to a horse. I think Rex killed Gavin, not Paddy.'

She looked astounded. 'What?'

'Lisa, those Homicide detectives will be back eventually.'

'I don't know what you're on about.'

'Let's talk. Tell me what happened. Did Gavin push too hard? Did Rex snap? You can't go on protecting him.'

'Stop it, Hal.'

He took a step closer. She took a step back. He stayed where he was. 'Let's sit down and talk,' he said. 'Perhaps you can make me a cup of tea. I almost crashed on the Pass and I feel a bit shaken.'

'Good,' she said. 'Pity you didn't go over the edge.'

He considered the words and her mood, and realised that things had gone beyond her control and she was merely striking out to deflect her guilt or misery. 'Lisa,' he said gently, approaching the screen door and extending one hand to the knob. The hinges squeaked as he opened it, and then he could see her clearly. She was dressed in spotless riding boots, jeans and shirt, as if about to exercise her horse, but her hair was awry and her eyes red and darting.

'Hal, don't.'

He entered a cool, echoing hallway as she retreated. At the end of the hallway he glimpsed a white door, sufficiently ajar to reveal a huge black enamel kitchen range. 'Let's sit at the kitchen table and talk. Please?'

She looked sour, thwarted, but stood back to let him pass, and then followed him. They sat at a long wooden table. Lisa watched him tensely, and then her face cleared. 'Are you okay?' she asked, placing her hand on his. 'I'm sorry about your father, I really am.'

Challis withdrew his hand. 'Where's Rex?'

'Away on business.'

That irritated Challis. 'Did you make that anonymous call to the RSPCA all those years ago, Lisa? Did you set up Paddy Finucane?'

'I beg your pardon?'

'Did Rex mean to kill Gavin? I bet he didn't. There was a struggle and he went too far and when he realised what he'd done he came to you for help.'

She said sharply, 'Hal, stop it. You're making a fool of yourself. You're being offensive. Just go, all right?'

'Rex was relying on you to get him out of trouble, just as he's always relied on you.'

She gestured curtly. 'This only involves Rex in the sense that your precious brother-in-law was a pig to *every*one.'

'You're right, he was, toward the end.'

He said it gently, to encourage an admission, but Lisa said, in her hard, emphatic way, 'So why are you coming after us? Gavin harassed a number of people.'

'But only one person killed him.'

'People are saying your sister killed him. I can't say I blame her.

Now, shut the door on your way out.'

She showed her cutting profile, as if Challis were a tradesman with grubby hands. He looked at her consideringly. 'You've always had to cover for Rex, haven't you. He's a drunk. Does he hit you, Lisa?'

As a way of turning her, giving her a way out, it failed. 'The door's behind you.'

'Was it Rex's idea to make that phone call to the RSPCA? I bet he took the photos on Gavin's camera, too. Did he also drive Gavin's car out east and make you pick him up?'

'Hal, I'll call the police if you don't leave me alone.'

'Whose idea was it to bury him in Glenda Anderson's grave? You'd been to her funeral, is that it? You knew the ground was soft?'

'Hal,' said Lisa, frowning and reaching for him across the table, 'we were lovers, now we're friends, but you're spoiling everything. Please stop.'

He jerked back, his spine rigid. 'Why did you send Meg those letters? Misdirection? You've always been good at that.'

'What letters?'

'You know very well what letters. It was cruel, Lisa.'

Her face tightened. 'That's it. That's enough. You're frightening me. Please leave.'

She was unwavering. He didn't know what would make her break. He didn't let himself think that he was wrong about her. 'Where's Rex?'

'Why? Want a quick shag before he comes back?'

'When Sadler phoned, did Rex take the call, or did you?'

'*What* call?'

'Probably no more than an hour ago, as soon as I left Sadler. Rex took a call, heard something he didn't want to hear, and ran, am I right? Saved his own skin and left you behind?'

Her gaze went involuntarily to the window. Challis stood, looked out. The darkening blue ranges that sheltered Mawson's Bluff seemed to stretch forever, into the stony saltbush country where people died or disappeared. The sun was barely a fingernail on the horizon now. 'Is he running? Hiding?'

She joined him, her hip touching his thigh. She was quite small, he realised. She packed a lot into it. 'You seem determined to make yourself miserable, Hal. All this jealousy. It's unbecoming. I'm *married*. Get that through your skull.'

Challis pointed. 'Is he out there somewhere?'

She bumped his hip and with a low chuckle said, 'What's out there is a little plateau, with a ruined shepherd's hut, just a couple of walls and a chimney. That's where Rex and I had our first screw.'

It was intended to wound him, on several levels, but what it did was convince him of her guilt. Wondering what he'd ever seen in her, Challis said coldly, 'I want you to come with me. I'm taking you in. You'll make a statement to Sergeant Wurfel.'

'You're pathetic, you know that?'

He tried to grab her. She was quick, lithe, shrugging him off, almost as if they were young again and it was a Saturday night and she was rebuffing his advances in the back seat of his father's station wagon. She darted down the hallway and into one of the rooms along it. Fear grabbed him then. He was paralysed, his mouth dry. There would be firearms on the place, for shooting vermin and putting injured animals out of their misery. He called, 'Lisa, don't.'

She emerged with a shotgun and motioned with it. 'Out,' she said, 'or I swear to God…'

Challis tried to hold himself upright but his spine tingled as he passed her in the long hallway and on down to the front door and out into the gathering darkness.

Meanwhile Scobie Sutton had arrived home and found Beth getting ready to go out. She was small, round, unfashionable and always did her duty as a wife and a Christian. With a pang, he compared her to Grace Duyker, who seemed to him the kind of woman who'd admit some risk and improvisation into her life. Risk and improvisation like him, in fact. If he dared make the move. If she let him.

'Anything wrong, Scobe?'

He pushed the fingers of both hands back through his sparse hair tiredly. 'The van Alphen shooting.'

It was a good diversion, and close to the truth. The Fab Four—Ellen Destry's term, but entirely apt—had questioned him again, this time concentrating on van Alphen's role in the Nick Jarrett shooting. 'Pretty sketchy, these notes of yours, DC Sutton,' they said, and 'Perhaps you were steered by Kellock and van Alphen,' and 'It would appear that a culture of protection and containment exists in this police station.' They asked questions that the shooting board officers had asked: Why had he failed to test for gunshot residue on the hands of Kellock and van Alphen? Why had he bundled items of clothing from both men together with the victim? Why had he let them move the body, or at least before he photographed it? Why had he failed to have the blood on the carpet tested, and allowed the carpet to be steam-cleaned?

Scobie was a wreck.

'Where are you going?' he asked his wife now.

'The Community House on the estate.'

'Why?'

Beth gave him her mild, reproving smile. 'Sweetheart, I told you, the public meeting. The petition.'

Scobie remembered. The locals were trying again to have the Jarretts kicked out. Five hundred signatures from residents and local shopkeepers. Officials from Community Services and the Housing Commission would be there, together with Children's Services welfare workers and a senior officer from Superintendent McQuarrie's HQ.

'Good luck,' said Scobie tiredly, looking around the kitchen absently to see if she'd prepared something for his dinner. He could see Grace Duyker coming up with something rare and subtle, a vaguely French sauce over tender veal, a fragrant Middle Eastern dish.

'I hate to see families broken up,' Beth was saying worriedly, 'kids taken away. In my opinion this kind of pressure is only going to lead the Jarretts to *more* crime, not less.'

Scobie thought approvingly of Grace Duyker's toughness and scorn, and found himself snarling at his wife: 'The Jarretts continue to commit crime because they're evil, and because gullible people like you believe they can be saved.'

Beth stood stock still, her face white and shocked. 'Is that how you see me? Gullible?'

Scobie swallowed. 'I think you try to do good where it sometimes isn't warranted, where it won't work.'

Her hand went to her throat. 'Oh, Scobie, I thought I knew you.'

'Forget I said it. I'm sorry.'

'I can't.'

Scobie touched her upper arm, his voice gentle. 'Go to your meeting, love.'

Beth said stoutly, 'I might just vote to let the Jarretts stay.'

Scobie, punch-drunk with tiredness and strange emotions, said, 'Do what you like.'

Suddenly he was bawling. Beth, with a brave little face, said, 'You work out what's wrong and we'll talk about it when I get back. For dinner you could zap last night's leftovers in the microwave.'

Detective Constable (provisional) Pam Murphy still had to sit a Police Board interview, but she'd passed all of her core subjects and been assigned to work with Ellen Destry in Waterloo CIU, so life was looking pretty good by Monday evening.

She didn't miss the physical training, the theory or the gruelling tests. She didn't miss the Academy at Glen Waverley or the classrooms at Command headquarters, where each day she'd had to pass through the foyer with its glass cabinets displaying guns and other murder weapons. Instead, she was feeling thankful that it was all over. Sure, she'd be obliged to take a million training courses in the coming years, but none of the really gruelling stuff. God, last week she'd run into a group of guys who'd enrolled for Special Operations Group training: of the sixty candidates, only nine had survived.

Seven o'clock, clouds across the moon, so it was pretty dark out, especially at the Penzance Beach yacht club. Uniform had checked it out: a burglary, meaning it was now a CIU case. Sergeant Destry, looking edgy and distracted, had told her John Tankard had called it in. 'Apparently the manager's on the premises, waiting to give you a statement.'

The wind rose on the water, moaning through the ti-trees, and soon there was a lonely metallic pinging. Sail rigging, Pam realised, slapping against the masts of the yachts parked in the yard behind the clubhouse. She approached the building and found a door open but almost pitch black inside. She went in, one hand patting the wall for a light switch. She'd left her torch in the CIU Falcon. It occurred to her that she still had a lot to learn.

'Police!' she called.

Maybe the burglars had come back and beaten the manager over the head, tied and gagged him.

The door slammed behind her.

She spun around, thoroughly spooked now, and felt for the doorknob. It wouldn't budge. She was locked in. She looked up and around, trying to find the patches of lighter darkness that indicated the windows.

They were clerestory windows, up high, far out of reach.

She tried to swallow and her heart was hammering. She fumbled for her radio, badly panicked, the weeks of training counting for nothing.

Stay cool, she told herself, releasing the call button of her radio, her mind racing. *Think*.

Her thoughts didn't take her in the direction of burglars and burglary. They took her in the direction of rookies, probationary cops, who are always good for a laugh. It was entirely probable that everyone at the Waterloo police station was waiting to hear how she coped tonight. They wanted fear, loss of control, booming through the public address system. They'd preserve her shame on tape, burn it onto a CD, for the world to enjoy over and over again.

'DC Pam Murphy, requesting urgent assistance,' she said, pressing the transmit button.

The radio crackled in delight, 'Go ahead, DC Murphy.'

Pam gave her location. 'I'm with Constable John Tankard,' she continued. 'I'm afraid he's soiled his trousers—fear, or a dodgy lasagne at lunchtime. Please send assistance and a spare nappy. The smell is awful.'

The dispatcher snorted. 'Will do.'

'I got a peek when he cleaned himself up,' Pam said. 'I know there's a height requirement for the Victoria Police, but shouldn't there also be a *length* requirement?'

Behind her the door was flung open and a teary, angry voice beseeched her to shut the hell up.

All through that long Monday, Ellen repeated it like a mantra: *Trust no one*. It made sense. According to Andrew Retallick, not just one but *several* policemen had abused him. Kellock, presumably, but who else? Maybe even the superintendent. Maybe even Scobie Sutton. She wasn't dealing with a couple of miserable individuals but a secretive, protective and organised circle of men. She'd known from other cases in Australia, Europe and the States how powerful these circles could be. The makers and keepers of the law often dominated: judges, lawyers, cops, parole officers. These men had the clout and know-how to protect themselves, subvert justice, and kill.

At least now she knew that van Alphen hadn't been involved. That didn't mean he'd been a sensitive, caring individual: fuck, he was so blinded by hatred of the Jarretts that he'd branded Alysha a tart and liar and helped ambush Nick Jarrett. A vaunting avenger, yeah, but not a paedophile.

He'd been working for the good guys, and that had cost him his life. Who had shot him? Kellock, probably. Ellen, in the incident room on Monday evening, glanced back over her shoulder and kept misjudging the reflections in the darkened windows. Would he come for her here? At Challis's? Arrange an ambush somewhere?

She tried Larrayne again. The phone went to voice-mail again.

Where was she? Finally she tried Larrayne's mobile phone, knowing it was futile, for there was no signal in the little valley where Challis lived.

But, bewilderingly, Larrayne was there on the line, shouting, shouting because there was background noise, not a weakened signal. 'I'm in my car, Mum.'

Ellen practically fainted with relief. 'Where?'

'Just coming in to Richmond.'

Ellen pictured the old suburb, on the river and close to the inner city. Students, yuppies, small back street factories, a solid working-class core and a long street of Vietnamese restaurants and businesses. She was puzzled and concerned. 'What are you doing there?'

'Do I have to tell you everything? A group of us are having a swot session for next week's exams.'

'Thank God for that. When will you be back?'

'I left a note on the table. I'll stay overnight, work in the library tomorrow, and come home tomorrow evening.'

'Sweetie, can you stay away longer?'

Larrayne was the daughter of police officers. She said warily, 'Something's happened.'

Ellen said simply, 'Someone might try to do me harm.'

'Mum! You can't stay at that house any more, out in the middle of nowhere!'

'I know that, sweetheart.'

'Well?'

'I'll find somewhere else, I promise.'

'I don't like this,' said Larrayne, a little hysterical now. 'Van was shot. Are the same people after you?'

'Not if I get them first.'

Larrayne went into full paranoia mode. 'Text me, okay? Or send an e-mail with the details. Don't trust the phones.'

'I will, sweetie.'

Ellen finished the call and went to the head of the stairs to listen.

The station was muted but not dead. She heard voices and laughter. Suddenly Pam Murphy's voice came crackling out of the public address speaker above Ellen's head. There was an edge to it. Ellen listened tensely, realising that Pam was in trouble. But as she listened, she relaxed. Soon she was grinning. She said aloud, 'Good one, Pam,' and returned to the incident room, where she made a call.

'I need you back here now.'

'Sarge,' Pam said, 'I'm sorry about the radio business, but—'

'Forget that. I need you on another matter.'

'Sarge.'

While she waited, Ellen mused. She dipped into her store of Kellock memories, Kellock over the past few weeks. The cuts on his hands, that morning she asked for extra uniforms. Scratches? From a dog, or Katie Blasko? The briefings in which he'd discredited Alysha Jarrett. The briefings in which he'd emphasised the DNA cockups. He'd been protecting Clode and Duyker, she realised. And in murdering van Alphen, he'd been protecting the entire ring.

But how did Billy DaCosta factor into all of this? How had Kellock got to him in time? Had Kellock intimidated or paid the kid into changing his story? Had Billy acted alone, spurred by the murder of van Alphen? Or had van Alphen, a man who would help shoot dead a criminal in the interests of meting out rough justice, not hesitated to create a 'witness' to bring down Kellock's gang?

There were no women in the lives of Clode and Duyker, but Kellock had a wife. A wife who suspected something? Colluded? Knew nothing? Ellen had once investigated a case of child abduction and murder in which the killer had a wife and children. On the surface he was a decent, plausible man, who went to church and was active in youth groups. When arrested, he'd denied everything. Then he'd claimed that the child had been the instigator. Then he said the child had choked in his car and he'd panicked and buried her. A kind of accident, in other words: can I go home now? Finally, as Ellen and the other investigators pulled apart his story, he got angry. A moment later he was full of apologies—not for losing his temper, as such, but for allowed his façade to slip. Yet it was the man's wife whom Ellen remembered. She'd known nothing of her husband's hidden life, or his past convictions for indecent exposure to children. She was protective of him. She dismissed everything that Ellen had to say.

But Ellen had sown a seed. Before long the woman remembered that her husband had washed his own clothes on the day of the murder. He'd never done that before. He'd also washed and vacuumed his car, something he never did unless the family was going on vacation.

Men like him are dead inside, Ellen thought now, feeling spooked by a movement in the window. She'd signed for a service .38 and put her hand on the butt, ready to slip it out of the holster on her hip. But it was only a passing headlight—possibly reflected upwards from a raked windscreen—catching the corner of the whiteboard. On an impulse, she called Challis in South Australia.

Voice-mail.

She badly needed him here. She didn't deny it. She wanted his stillness. It was a supple kind of stillness. He was respected, and respectful, but people were wary, too, for they couldn't always read him. He was good at spotting complexities and nuances that others missed, but he also knew when to look the other way in the interests of commonsense and the best outcomes. He was a chameleon sometimes, able to connect with a homeless kid one moment and a clergyman the next. He remembered names: not only of criminals, informants and the people in the corner milk bar but also their families, friends and acquaintances.

She also liked the shadows and planes of his face. The way his backside looked in a pair of pants, too, a nice distracting thought while it lasted. But right now she needed to know what he'd do, if he were stuck in her situation. She swivelled agitatedly in her office chair.

Funny how the mind works. *Stuck in* her situation. There was that old Creedence song she'd played last night, 'Stuck in Mobile again'. Why did place names in American popular songs sound mysterious, sad, romantic? She'd also played 'Sweet home, Alabama', singing along to the words. Yeah, she could see that working in Australia: 'Sweet home, New South Wales'...'Stuck in Nar Nar Goon North again'... 'Twenty-four hours from Wagga Wagga'.

'Sarge?'

Ellen jumped.

'I did knock, Sarge.'

'Sorry, million miles away,' Ellen said. 'Close the door, pull up a chair.'

'Sarge,' Pam said, obliging.

'You had a little fun tonight,' Ellen said, when they were settled. It was now 10 pm.

Pam laughed. 'Not the first time it's happened to me. Back when I was fresh out of the academy they sent me to an address, said Mr Lyon was drunk and disorderly. It was the zoo.'

Ellen grinned. 'They sent me to the arms locker to get a left-handed revolver.'

God, that had been twenty years ago. Without wasting any more time, Ellen told Pam everything, watching the younger woman shift from perky interest to distaste and finally nervy alertness as she responded with the question uppermost in Ellen's mind: 'If they can kill Van, what's to stop them from killing us?'

Ellen felt a tiny surge of hope. Pam had used the word 'us'. It said that she saw herself as part of a team.

'We need to work fast. We need to talk to Billy DaCosta again, for a start.'

'I saw him at Van's,' Pam said, explaining the circumstances.

Ellen regarded the younger woman for some time. 'You were fond of Van, weren't you?'

Pam nodded, her eyes damp. 'I know he wasn't a paragon of virtue, Sarge, but he was on the right side.'

Ellen nodded. 'You're going to his funeral?'

'Yes.'

'Me too.'

There was a brief, fraught pause, then Ellen coughed and said, 'Here's my interview with Billy. See if it tells us anything.'

She aimed the remote control and pushed the play button. Pam watched. She stiffened. 'That's not Billy DaCosta.'

Ellen paused the tape. 'That's not the kid you saw at Sergeant van Alphen's house?'

'Positive. Completely different kid. Sure, there are vague similarities—same sort of clothing, same grubby gothic look—but that's not the Billy I was introduced to.'

Ellen was silent. They looked at each other. 'The real Billy's dead,' Pam said.

'Yes.'

'God,' Pam said fervently, 'the nerve, the ability, not only to kill Van but also substitute a witness to discredit him.'

'The substitute could also be dead.'

'Sarge, I'm scared.'

'Me, too.'

'What do we do?'

'We try to find whoever this is,' Ellen said, indicating the flickering screen. 'He might not be dead. He might be a victim whom they've turned. He might be one of the gang now, and be willing to talk.'

Pam stared at the false Billy DaCosta. 'It looks like you interviewed him in the Victim Suite.'

'Yes.'

'He's drinking Coke.'

Ellen sat very still for a moment, then went around and hugged the younger woman. 'Brilliant.'

'But the cleaners would have cleared the can away, I suppose.'

'Billy handled every single can of drink in that fridge,' Ellen said. 'No one has used the room since. We can lift his prints for sure.'

She stood and placed her hand on Pam's shoulder. 'We can't do any more tonight. Go home. We have a lot to do tomorrow.'

Meanwhile Challis had reported to Sergeant Wurfel and was waiting by the phone. The call came at 10 pm, clamorous in his father's gloomy house. 'Was she there?' he asked.

'Yes.'

The voice was disobliging. 'And?' Challis demanded.

Wurfel waited before he spoke again. Challis read hesitation, tact and a hint of impatience in it. 'Look, I questioned her as a favour to you. You were persuasive, I'll give you that. But it was a monumental waste of my time and I don't appreciate having my time wasted.'

'She and her husband are in it together,' Challis said heatedly. 'Gavin intended to prosecute Rex for mistreating his horse, and Rex lost his temper and killed him. They staged his disappearance, and created evidence incriminating Paddy Finucane, just in case.'

'So you keep saying. She denies it.'

'Of course she denies it.'

'She says you barged in on her this evening, throwing your weight around. You scared her.'

'Rubbish. She waved a shotgun at me.'

'You scared her, Inspector. She looked scared to me.'

Challis shook his head in the cheerless room. 'Check with Sadler, Gavin's boss. He'll tell you that Gavin was going after Rex Joyce.'

'Look, this is not my case. Sadler's been interviewed. A suspect is in custody. Case closed.'

'Do you think I'm making all this up?'

'Well, are you?' demanded Wurfel. 'Isn't this personal? Mrs Joyce told me that you and she had been romantically involved in the past. She said you had trouble accepting that it was over and have hassled her from time to time ever since. I advised her to file a complaint, in fact.'

'You bastard,' Challis snarled. He felt close to losing it.

'Inspector.'

Challis swallowed. 'Was Rex there?'

'No.'

'Didn't you at least ask where he was?'

'Rex Joyce is away on business,' Wurfel said flatly. 'He often is.'

'Don't tell me you're his little mate, too,' Challis said, before he could stop himself.

'Let's pretend I didn't hear you say that, shall we?'

He's going to inform Nixon and Stormare, thought Challis. They'll inform McQuarrie. And I don't care.

'I think it's worth getting up a search party tomorrow morning,' he said. 'It's possible Rex is suicidal. He could be up on the Bluff somewhere. He likes to go there, Lisa said.'

'Rex Joyce,' said Wurfel with false brightness, 'is away on business. Goodbye.'

Challis slept badly and at first light on Tuesday morning drove to the Joyce homestead and mounted the steps again.

It was a replay of yesterday evening, except that this time Lisa waited behind the screen door with the shotgun. She looked perky and rested, and said, 'Hal, I swear I'll shoot you if you try to touch me.'

He said gently, 'Has Rex come back? Let me talk to him.'

'He's still away. Look, you scared me last night.'

'Lisa, does Rex have a mobile phone with him?'

She frowned. 'Yes.'

He took out his own phone. 'What's the number?'

She shrugged, told him, and he called. Reaching Rex's voice-mail, he pocketed the phone again. 'He's not answering.'

'So? Please go.'

'He could be hurt, Lisa. Please stop the charade.'

She looked discomposed for the first time. Stared past him at the gentle dawn light on her spreading lawns and shady trees. Sparrows and starlings were busy, calling out, squabbling, nest building.

'Lisa?' said Challis gently. 'Let's go and look for him.'

She snapped into focus again and said briskly, 'He *did* receive a call yesterday. He left the house soon afterwards in the Range Rover.'

Challis nodded. 'What mood was he in?'

She searched for the word. 'Upset. Rambling.'

'Let's try the shepherd's hut.'

She seemed embarrassed. 'Because it has significance to him?'

'Something like that.'

She opened the screen door and stepped out, still holding the shotgun. She smelt of perfumed soap and shampoo, a clean, healthy woman who wore jeans and a sleeveless, crisply ironed cotton shirt that revealed toned, faintly tanned, delectable skin. Challis was repelled. He took the shotgun from her hands and rested it against the verandah. 'Let's leave this here, okay?'

'Whatever.' She pointed past him. '*That* won't make it up the Bluff.'

Challis eyed the Triumph, which sat dented, sun-faded and low-slung on the gravelled driveway. 'Oh.'

He felt uncertain. Lisa took charge. 'There's an old Jeep in one of the sheds.'

She fetched the keys. She drove.

Fifteen minutes later they were deep into the foothills and following sheep pads, the dusty erosions that scribble all over the outback, meandering along slopes, through long grass and around stony reefs. Lisa set the Jeep to four-wheel-drive, the old vehicle wallowing and pitching, climbing steadily toward high ground. Below them lay the town, several kilometres away. The sun flashed on distant windscreens, and crows and hawks wheeled above, sideslipping in the air currents.

Suddenly the Jeep powered over a hump in the ground and they were on a little plateau, startling half-a-dozen sheep. On the far side was the shepherd's hut, in the foreground the glossy Range Rover, facing away from them. Lisa braked, peered over the steering wheel. 'He's sitting in the back seat.' Suddenly she thumped the heel of her hand against the horn. 'Rex!' she shouted futilely.

To Challis there was something unnatural about the shape in the rear of the Range Rover, something wrong about the relationship of the head with the shoulders, the back of the seat and the window glass.

'Is he asleep?' asked Lisa.

'Stay here, okay?'

'I'm coming with you.'

'Lisa,' he said.

'I'm coming with you.'

They approached, drawing adjacent to the rear of the Range Rover. Rex Joyce's head lolled back; there was blood spatter on the glass beside his left ear but more on the ceiling lining above his head. Challis assessed the signs rapidly. Joyce had shot himself. The rifle was between his knees, the muzzle under his jaw. It made a certain kind of sense.

Meanwhile Lisa had gasped and moaned and doubled over, dry-retching. Challis reached out to touch her shoulder. 'Don't touch me!'

He snatched his hand back.

She straightened. 'Sorry. Sorry, Hal. I'll be all right in a minute. Phew.' She swallowed, grimaced at the taste. 'There's water in the Jeep.'

Challis let her go. He finished making his visual inspection, then followed her. He could see her shape behind the open door of the Jeep, head tilted back as she drank from a plastic bottle.

Halfway there, he stopped. He spun around and strode back to the Range Rover. First he checked the driver's seat. It sat well forward, as though the last person to drive the vehicle had been short. Rex Joyce was tall. Then he peered through the gap in the seats, noting the rifle between the victim's legs: it was long-barrelled, a hunting rifle. Too long for Joyce's arms? He couldn't be sure about that, but he was sure there should be more blood on the seat back and ceiling.

He closed the driver's door and opened the door beside the body.

He was sorely tempted to lean in and check for signs of lividity. If Rex had died sitting upright, his blood would have pooled and settled in his buttocks, the underside of his thighs and in his feet and the bottoms of his legs. Challis was betting he'd find lividity all along the body, indicating that Lisa's husband had died somewhere else, then been laid flat and transported here.

Police work had made Hal Challis an infinitely sympathetic man. That didn't mean he condoned, necessarily, just that he understood, and now he turned his patient, sorrowing gaze toward the Jeep and Lisa Joyce, even as a hole appeared in the window beside him, glass chips sprayed over his face and chest, and a slipstream plucked at the hairs on his head.

While Challis was being shot at, Ellen Destry and Pam Murphy were attending Kees van Alphen's funeral. They were surprised by the turnout: his wife, daughter and extended family, friends from Waterloo and other Peninsula police stations, McQuarrie and other top brass, and even a handful of snitches and hard men who'd remade their lives.

Back in the CIU incident room they worked the abduction of Katie Blasko and a backlog of minor crimes, using them as cover for more specific actions. Pam searched, without luck, for the missing files mentioned in Kees van Alphen's notes, and checked, and confirmed, some of his other statements. Ellen drove to the forensic science lab with all of the soft drink cans from the Victim Suite refrigerator, stopping along the way to show photographs of Duyker, Clode and Kellock to Andrew Retallick. He neither confirmed nor denied that they'd abused him, but he did flinch and look distressed.

At lunchtime they met in the lounge of the Fiddler's Creek pub, taking a corner table where they could not be heard. They ordered meals—fish and chips for Pam, chicken salad for Ellen—and compared notes. Mostly the two women were ignored, but drinkers from the Seaview Park estate were in the main bar, those with criminal records casting occasional glances at them through the archway, curling their lips to keep in training. There was a background cover of shouted conversations, jukebox music and punters at the slot machines.

'We can't go after Kellock yet,' Ellen said.

'Why not?'

Ellen drained her glass, mineral water with chunks of ice floating in it. 'There's no hard evidence. Let's look at his lack of action back when Alysha Jarrett lodged her complaint: he comes across as insensitive, that's all, not a paedo protecting other paedos. And is he the only one in the police? I don't think so, do you? Is he the only one at the Waterloo station? That's a harder question to answer. What if Sutton or McQuarrie are in on it?'

'Scobie? God no.'

'I agree, it doesn't seem likely, but Scobie's easily intimidated. He's very trusting—he probably shouldn't even be a copper. If we bring him in on this, he might inadvertently reveal the details to the wrong person.'

Their meals were delivered. When the waiter was gone, Pam said flatly, 'I can believe it of McQuarrie.'

'It doesn't matter who, at this stage. The thing is, Kellock is untouchable for the moment. We can't arrest him, can't get a warrant for his house or car. We can't seize his clothing. We can't trust anyone else. It's us, Pam.'

Pam brooded. She toyed with her food, popped a chip into her mouth and chewed it. Then she said determinedly, 'We go after Clode and Duyker, and hope one of them turns on Kellock, and we try to find Billy DaCosta.'

'The real and the fake.'

'Yes.'

Ellen looked at the younger woman as if for the first time. Pam Murphy was no longer the uniformed constable who showed initiative but a fellow detective. For a while Ellen had been her mentor, coaxing her into plain-clothed work, letting her find her potential, but now they were colleagues. Not equals—if you counted age and rank—but a kind of friendship linked them. And Ellen badly needed friends now.

'Everything all right, Sarge?'

'Just thinking. I wish Hal was here.'

Pam said, a little sternly, 'Well, Sarge, he's not.'

57

Challis risked a peek. Lisa was shooting at him from behind the driver's door of the Jeep. A semi-automatic rifle with a small clip. He guessed that it had been stowed behind or under the seats. There was a crack and a bullet punctured the tyre beside his foot. She fired again, the bullet punching through the open door. He ran around to the front of the big four-wheel-drive, glad of its bulk. His relief was short-lived: a bullet pinged off a nearby stone. He felt terribly exposed. Lisa Joyce would cripple him and then shoot him where he lay.

Then he heard her call his name.

'What?' he shouted.

'I phoned Wurfel when I saw you arrive.'

She'll present Wurfel with a self-defence story, he thought. He couldn't see any point in negotiating, or waiting, and slithered on his belly and elbows toward the shepherd's hut, using the Range Rover for cover. Lisa fired again, the bullet whining away and dust and stone chips flying.

Just then the sheep, made skittish by the cracks and echoes in the still air, broke away and charged toward the hut, passing close to Challis. He rolled to his feet and ran with them in all of their fear and exultation. Dust rose and pebbles flew and the sheep kicked and bucked. Lisa fired, a desultory shot that went nowhere.

Challis huddled behind a ruined wall. Lisa had the advantage in this engagement, while he had nothing but the hut and small deceptions in the sparsely grassed soil of the plateau. He glanced hurriedly about: only heaped stones and a length of wood, possibly a lintel or part of a window frame. He grabbed it like a club, alerting Lisa, who got off a shot that sent a stone chip into his face. Blood coursed down his forehead, blurring his right eye. He swiped at it with his forearm and another shot smacked numbingly through the wooden club. He lay afraid and very still, and then began to retreat again. If he could reach the far rim of the plateau, he might be able to try an outflanking manoeuvre.

The next shot creased his ear and he pissed his pants. None of his nerve endings would let him alone. He trembled, tics developing in his face, and the blood dripped onto the dust, balling there. He supposed he was sobbing aloud, he didn't know, but retreated in a mad scramble from the hut until he found a stone refuge, where the rocks were grey and licheny, weathered and streaked with bird shit. It was a good place. He huddled there and, in his visions, Lisa Joyce appeared above him and shot him like a fish in a barrel.

Dimly then he heard a starter motor grinding. He risked a look: Lisa was in the Jeep. That galvanised Challis. He charged forward, making for the Range Rover and Rex Joyce's hunting rifle.

Instantly Lisa stepped out of the Jeep. Challis was barely halfway to the Range Rover. He ducked and swerved, but she merely stood with her arms wide to the world. 'I haven't got any bullets left.'

Challis halted tensely. 'Then drop the rifle.'

'I haven't got any bullets left.'

'So put the rifle down.'

'It was all Rex's fault.'

'Lisa, drop the rifle.'

Challis advanced, and Lisa stood there with the rifle outstretched. 'Drop it, okay?'

'None of it was my idea.'

Still Challis advanced. He reached the Range Rover, leaned in and retrieved the hunting rifle from between Rex Joyce's legs. He jacked a round into the breech, then emerged from the shelter of the vehicle, blinking furiously to clear his bloodied eye, the rifle to his shoulder. 'Lisa, I'm warning you.'

'I suddenly said to myself, what am I doing, shooting at Hal?'

Challis stopped, the rifle aimed squarely at her, and said quietly, 'Lisa, are you listening to me? Do you understand what I'm saying? Please put the rifle down.'

Lisa grinned and deftly slapped the rifle from one hand to the other and up to her shoulder. Challis shot her legs out from under her.

She screamed and rolled in the dirt. 'Ow! You shot me!'

'Yes.'

She tossed in agony, raging at him. Challis retrieved her rifle, ejected the magazine and checked the breech. She'd had one bullet left.

'I didn't think you'd shoot me!'

'In a heartbeat,' Challis said.

She began to cry and swear and deride him. He found a handkerchief and wiped the blood from his eye, then crouched beside her. 'Shut up,' he said, tearing off one of his sleeves.

'It hurts!'

'You'll live.'

He bound her leg and then sat, depleted, not thinking about anything at all but feeling the weariest he'd ever felt. And then a surprising contentment settled in him. He tilted his face to the sun and adjusted his body to the pebbly dust as if he were part of the landscape. Finally Sergeant Wurfel's Land Cruiser appeared over the rim of the plateau like a breaching whale.

Ellen pushed her food away, barely touched. 'Let's go back and see if we have a result on Billy's prints.'

They returned to the station, taking the back stairs to CIU, checking the incident room first. Only John Tankard was there, pecking at a computer keyboard. He didn't see them.

Ellen closed her office door carefully and called the lab. 'What?' said Pam afterwards, seeing the expression on her face.

'The fake Billy is in the system. The prints we lifted from the drink cans in the Victim Suite belong to a Kenneth Lloyd.'

She logged on to her computer. She knew what she was about to do would generate an electronic record, but would Kellock be checking for that? Had he flagged Lloyd's name? She had to risk it.

She typed, her hands flying over the keys. Soon Lloyd's face and record filled the screen. 'That's him, all right,' said Ellen. 'The false Billy DaCosta.'

She scrolled down. 'Charged with inappropriate sexual behaviour when he was fifteen. Two arrests for soliciting last year.' She stopped, then looked up at Pam, who was peering over her shoulder. 'Arresting officer, Senior Sergeant Kellock.' She peered at the screen again. 'Charges were reduced. Rap over the knuckles.'

'Kellock's influence?'

'Probably.'

There was an address for Lloyd. Ellen tapped her finger on the screen. 'I know this place. Gideon House. It's a kind of shelter for homeless kids. Let's see if our boy's at home.'

Pam shuddered. 'I don't hold much hope of that, Sarge. Either Kellock has topped him or given him a thousand bucks to make himself scarce.'

'We have to try.'

Ellen used her office phone, for its number was blocked. She heard it ring, and then a voice came on. 'Gideon House.'

'Please, I'm going out of my mind,' said Ellen, her voice whiny and adolescent. 'I'm tryin' a find me brother. He's run off.'

Behind her, Pam snorted. The voice said, 'I'm afraid we can't give out the names of our clients.'

'I'm really, really worried about him. Mum's desperate. His name's Ken Lloyd. We call him Kenny.'

There was an assessing silence. 'Well, I guess it's all right. He was here, but he left.'

'Did he say where he was going?'

'Look,' said the voice, 'I'll put Mrs Kellock on the line. She's the supervisor here. Please hold.'

Ellen hurriedly cut the connection. Pam saw the tightening of her face. 'Sarge?'

Shaken, Ellen looked up at Pam and said, 'I was asked to hold for the supervisor—whose name is Mrs Kellock.'

Pam sat, her face etched in a kind of fierce concentration. 'Hell, Sarge.'

'It could be a coincidence,' Ellen said, 'another Mrs Kellock entirely. Or she doesn't know what her husband's been up to.'

'Come on, Sarge, it all holds together. That's how these guys get their victims.'

Ellen's desk phone rang. She stared at it in consternation, then answered it. 'Hello?'

A familiar voice said, 'Sergeant Destry. I was hoping you'd be in.'

'Mr Riggs, my favourite forensic tech,' said Ellen, trying not to let her tension show, and failing.

'No need to be snide.'

'Good news, or bad?' said Ellen. 'Maybe you're ringing to tell me you've sacked all of your incompetents and our DNA evidence is solid after all?'

The silence was hurt and sulky. 'Well, if you don't want to hear this…'

'I'm sorry,' said Ellen, meaning it. 'A long day.'

'Ditto,' said Riggs.

Ellen sighed. 'What have you got?'

'That blood on the dog collar.'

Ellen had completely forgotten about it. 'You have a match?'

'Kind of.'

'Let me guess, Neville Clode's, and we can't use it because you already have his *victim* sample.'

'Not Clode's,' said Riggs, 'but yes, it does match with a victim sample.'

'Who?'

'One of your officers. He was stabbed in the forearm in an altercation with a burglar.'

'Senior Sergeant Kellock.'

'Yes, for what it's worth,' said Riggs.

There were heavy footsteps in the corridor. Ellen froze. But it was only John Tankard. 'Can I knock off now, Sarge? Got some car business to take care of.'

'Of course, John.'

'Thanks, Sarge.'

Tank walked around to Korean Salvage on the industrial estate, and there was his rebirthed Mazda. 'She'll pass scrutiny?' he demanded, one sausagy hand thumping the gleaming roof.

Under the bluster he felt jumpy, uncertain. Something was going on at work and he didn't know what it was. Maybe Destry was onto him. He wanted one constant in his life—his car.

'Yep,' said the proprietor of Korean Salvage, wiping his hands on a rag.

'I mean the design and safety regulations. She'll pass any test?'

'Yep.'

The sun was streaming through the garage doors, lighting oil spills, car bodies and parts, chrome tools and Tank's Mazda. On the outside, this was the car he'd fallen in love with, sleek and red, a real head-turner, but on the inside she was a different car. He saw no irony in the fact that he was pinning all of his hopes for fulfilment on an object of false provenance.

'I don't want to take her in for a roadworthy and have the guy say she's iffy.'

'Not going to happen.'

To be doubly sure, Tank vowed to take his car to a different roadworthy tester next time. He began to feel uncomfortable. Several ethnics were standing around in the shadows, mechanics, car strippers and thieves, watching him inscrutably, some holding wrenches. He played 'Spot the Aussie' and scored only two, himself and the boss. 'Mate,' he said, hurriedly, 'I don't know what you did and I don't want to know, but I'm pumped, a very happy boy.'

The proprietor of Korean Salvage was not happy. He didn't like it that a cop had something over him. Sure, he had something over the cop, but he preferred it when it had just been him, his mechanics and the Jarrett kids who stole cars for them.

'The paperwork's solid, okay?' he said sourly. 'VIN number, engine number, chassis number, it all belongs to a legit car. It all checks out.'

'Cool,' said Tank.

It wasn't cool, but that was the price of doing business in this town, apparently. The proprietor of Korean Salvage watched the beefy young cop get behind the wheel of the Mazda and peel out of the shed. Burning a bit of oil. Maybe the engine was knackered. He took some comfort from that.

Ellen worked until late evening. She drove home under a scudding moon, the shadows tricky, especially when she came to the tree canopy over Challis's rain-slicked road. But she'd driven this road at this time of the night ever since the Katie Blasko kidnapping, and was familiar with the bends, the contours, the gaps between the roadside trees— particularly the gap where a stock gate had been set in Challis's front fence. The gate, never used now, dated from an earlier era, when the house had been part of a working farm. She liked to glance through the gap: Challis's house was set on a gentle slope, and she found it reassuring to look up and see the floor lamps glowing behind the sitting-room curtains, lights that she'd left on that morning to welcome herself home.

This time she saw a shape slip past one of the windows.

Ellen did not vary her pace but continued along the road, up and over the hill, past the farm with the barking dogs, letting the sound of her car apparently dwindle into the distance. She drove for a kilometre, and then pulled into the driveway of a hobby farm. The owner, a Melbourne accountant, was never there during the week.

She went back to Challis's on foot, avoiding the loose gravel of the road, which would announce her presence and fill her own ears with distracting sounds. Instead, she headed overland, trotting carefully through grassy paddocks, vaulting over the wire fences, until she came to the rear of the house. Behind her was another slope and another hobby farm, several hundred metres away and also empty tonight.

From here she was slightly elevated and could look down on the back of Challis's house. His rear boundary was another wire fence. She paused for a while, listening. Her eyes were accustomed to the darkness now and she was alert for all sounds and movements. She waited for ten minutes before she saw Kellock. A brief, chancy beam of moonlight caught him, just as she was about to advance on the house. It was not so much his face as his stance, his bulky alertness, that she recognised. He watched and waited, and so did she, for a solid hour. He was patient, she was patient. She could smell him, she realised, an amalgam of aftershave and perspiration. Did he sense her? Her perfume, this morning's scented shampoo and conditioner? He gave no sign of it. She was distracted by thoughts of Challis then. How would she characterise his smell? Clean, undisguised. There wasn't much in the way of scented soaps in his bathroom. No old aftershave containers. Skulking like this in the nighttime and its shadows was arousing her.

Kellock broke first. One moment he was there and the next he was gone. Ellen shrank deeper into the grass and waited, just in case he was flanking her. She thought about the blood on Sasha's collar. Of course it was Kellock's, and of course he'd got it when Sasha bit him. But a defence lawyer would have a field day with that evidence. He'd cite the discredited lab work and Scobie Sutton's balls-up at the scene of the Jarrett shooting, and propose another scenario: 'My client is in charge of the Waterloo police station. Naturally he keeps abreast of all its functions and activities. He patted the dog when it was brought in to the station on its way to the lab. The dog bit him. There is nothing sinister in his blood being found on the collar.'

Ellen tensed. She heard a motorbike fire up in the distance. It revved once or twice, idled, and then howled away. She'd wondered how Kellock had got here, and now she knew. She slipped inside the house, gathered together a change of clothing and spent the night in the Sanctuary Motor Inn, up in the hills northeast of Melbourne, where she paid cash and used a false name.

59

She drove to work on Wednesday wondering if she'd be able to control her face. She'd had plenty of practice over the years, hiding her reactions and feelings from the men around her—hiding attraction and repulsion—but she'd never had to hide something as monumental as the information she held in her head.

She used the front door, feeling almost sick, expecting to encounter Kellock.

But Kellock wasn't in his office. No one had seen him, and he hadn't called in. What did that mean? Had the lab, apologetic, contacted him to say they'd found his DNA on the dog's collar but it was all a mistake? Ellen had expressly told Riggs not to inform Kellock, but Kellock had cronies everywhere. All kinds of paperwork crossed his desk. Was he out there somewhere, getting rid of evidence? Were his mates covering their tracks?

And so she was predisposed to find significance in anything Scobie Sutton did. When she walked into the incident room and saw him hunched covertly over his desk phone, she was immediately suspicious. When he'd completed the call, she asked, 'Everything okay, Scobie?'

He looked hunted, a little sulky, and went very red. 'Just the wife.'

Then Pam arrived. She wore tan slacks and a white T-shirt under a crumpled cotton jacket. Her hair was pulled back severely from her face. She looked scrubbed, athletic, ready for action. They worked in silence and the morning passed, empty coffee cups accumulating. Ellen put Scobie to work watching videotapes from the closed-circuit security cameras; she and Pam read documents. Then, when Scobie and Pam went out to buy pastries for morning tea, she pressed the redial button on Scobie's phone.

'Grace Duyker speaking.'

'This is Sergeant Ellen Destry, of the Waterloo police station—'

The woman cut her off. 'Are you taking his side? Is that it? Now *I'm* the ogre?'

'I'm sorry?'

'Look, he's a nice guy and everything, but it's inappropriate. I'm happily married. *He's* married. I swear I never encouraged him, but he's got it into his head that I—'

Thinking rapidly, Ellen said, 'I think he understands that now.'

'I don't want to get him into trouble. I don't want him to get *me* into trouble.'

'You have my assurance on that,' Ellen said.

Pam and Scobie came in, Scobie's gaze going straight to Ellen on his phone. He looked as though he might burst into tears, but Ellen said pitilessly, feeling like a stern aunt, 'I was just informing Grace Duyker that she can rely on us to be discreet. Scobie, you'll endorse that?'

'Ellen,' he muttered, head down, while Pam cocked her head and said nothing.

Ellen watched him and pondered. His mortification was genuine: she should trust him. Still, she withheld that. She wanted a stronger indication that he could be trusted.

It came just before lunch. Ellen walked down High Street to the delicatessen, bought three smoked salmon and avocado rolls, and came back to find Pam and Scobie side by side in the incident room, deeply absorbed. She stood back to watch and listen for a couple of minutes, trying to read Sutton. He was explaining the progress and lack of progress in the Katie Blasko case. Pam was asking him questions—but she, also, was trying to read him, Ellen realised. She watched them sift through the statements, photographs and other documentary evidence, Scobie gesturing once or twice as if overwhelmed by the workload. He hadn't spotted Ellen yet. 'A ton of stuff to go through,' he said. 'Just look at it all: CCTV footage, parking and speeding fines, witness statements to check again.' He glanced at Pam, trying for humour. 'I bet you wish you were back in a patrol car.'

'No thanks, Scobe,' she said brightly. She peered at the sheet of paper in her hand. 'Rising Stars Agency,' she read. 'What's this?'

Scobie almost broke then. He told Pam about Duyker's scam, his voice catching as if he couldn't comprehend the evil that Duyker represented. 'My own daughter could have been his next victim.'

Pam was watching Ellen over his shoulder. They communicated silently, instinctively, and Pam said, 'Oh, hi, Sarge.'

Scobie turned. 'Sorry. I was just catching Pam up on some things.'

'Scobie,' Ellen said, 'there's something you should know.'

It took her ten minutes. He was shocked, now and then glancing uneasily at the door, as though Kellock might materialise there.

'Scobie, keep your cool.'

'I can't.'

'Yes you can. You'll have to.'

They ate lunch hurriedly, and then resumed work, Scobie throwing himself into it, as if work might cure his fear and agitation, and punish him because he'd felt desire for another woman and been naïve about human wickedness.

And he found salvation of a kind. 'I think I've got something,' he said two hours later. 'Duyker gave us a cash register receipt to prove he wasn't in Waterloo between three and four on the Thursday Katie was abducted?'

'Correct. A big newsagency in the city.'

'Duyker wasn't there,' Scobie said, leaning forward and tapping the monitor screen, 'but Neville Clode was. I've got him picking discarded receipts off the floor inside the main door of the newsagency that same afternoon. Five-thirty, to be precise.'

Pam and Ellen joined him. 'That devious little shit,' Pam said.

They watched Clode peruse the receipts and dump all but one into a bin. 'Model citizen,' muttered Ellen. 'Back it up, Scobie, to around three-thirty, then roll it forward to five-thirty. We need to double check that neither Clode nor Duyker were there between those times.'

Scobie complied. It took a while. 'Nope,' he reported.

'Okay, let's pick both of them up. Duyker first.'

They crossed the Peninsula in a CIU Falcon, Scobie directing while Pam drove, flicking the wheel expertly, her pacing and anticipation giving them a smooth ride. Ellen closed her eyes in the back seat and let Scobie twitch and prattle on in the passenger seat.

Finally the car slowed. Ellen opened her eyes. 'His van's here,' Pam said.

'Scobie, go around the back,' said Ellen. 'Pam, you come with me.'

She knocked on Duyker's door and the fact that it swung open, and the air was saturated with the odour of blood and the buzzing of springtime flies, told her that she was too late, Kellock had got here ahead of her and taken care of a loose end.

60

She went into action. 'Scobie, head back to Waterloo, grab a couple of uniforms for backup, and arrest Clode.'

'Will do.'

When he was gone, she made a series of calls, first arranging an all-points apprehension order on Kellock: air, sea and ferry ports, bus terminals, train stations. Then she called Challis. She didn't need his advice; she wanted to hear his voice, that's all. But his mobile was switched off or out of range, and had been since yesterday. Finally she called Force Command headquarters and asked for a team of armed response police. There was a pause when she said who the target was.

'One of ours? You sure?'

'Perfectly sure. Armed and dangerous. He's already shot one man dead.'

Another pause. 'Where exactly are you?'

Ellen gave directions.

'Take a while to get there. Hour and a half, maybe.'

'I realise that.'

'Meanwhile don't do anything rash.'

'I won't,' Ellen said, immediately taking Pam with her to Gideon House to hunt for Kellock. They'd barely reached the outskirts of Mornington when her mobile rang and Superintendent McQuarrie was barking at her.

'Tell me this is all a bad joke, Sergeant Destry.'

'No, sir.'

'Armed response officers? A warrant for his arrest? What the hell is going on?'

Ellen had to go carefully here. Everyone knew that the super used Kellock for information and influence, but did the relationship go deeper than that? She didn't say anything about the paedophile ring, or police involvement, but merely said that Kellock was apparently unhinged and had shot dead a witness.

'I hope you know what you're doing.'

There had been a time when Ellen might have said 'So do I' to herself, but not any more. 'I do, sir,' she said with some force.

McQuarrie muttered and broke the call.

Gideon House came into view, set one block back from the Mornington seafront in an overgrown garden. Once a gracious residence, and later a boarding house, it now sheltered street kids and the homeless with funding from the shire and the state government. It looked run-down, and Ellen wondered if the Kellocks were siphoning the upkeep funds into their own pockets, along with abusing the kids in their care.

That's if Kellock's wife was involved.

Ellen knocked. A shy-looking kid answered.

'Is Mrs Kellock in?'

'Er, yep.'

'Could you fetch her, please?'

A moment later, Kellock's wife appeared from the gloomy interior. She was bulky, blowsy-looking, with short, stiff, carroty hair, an affronted jaw and a hard face. She wore dressy black pants and a silk shirt, with plenty of gold on her fingers, wrists and neck. Narrow, tanned feet in elegant sandals, with bright red nails. A woman who tans joylessly all year round, Ellen thought.

'Mrs Kellock, I'm Sergeant Destry and this is Constable Murphy.

May we speak to your husband?'

The reply was guarded. 'He's not here.'

'Do you know where he is?'

'He doesn't tell me his every move. Why do you want to know? He's in charge of the station. He doesn't have to justify himself to anybody.'

It was absurd pride. Ellen said firmly, 'We need to speak to him.'

'Try his mobile.'

Ellen knew that would spook him—that's if he hadn't already flown the coop. She asked, 'Do you and your husband live here, Mrs Kellock?'

'We have a flat at the back.'

'Could he be there? Maybe he slipped home while you've been in the main building?'

'No.'

'Can you think where else he might be?'

'Why?'

Because he's on a murderous rampage, Ellen thought. She cleared her throat, suddenly uneasy: had she sent Scobie Sutton into a trap? 'We need his input on something,' she said with an empty smile.

The eyes narrowed and an expression passed across them, as though Kellock's wife knew why they were there, and that everything was about to fall apart in her life. She recovered and said tartly, 'He could be at a conference, at divisional headquarters, at one of the other stations. Check his diary.'

'We have, Mrs Kellock.'

Pam had been silent until now. 'Your husband is closely involved here, Mrs Kellock? He's close to the children who live here?'

'What's that got to do with anything? Who do you think you are? My husband is senior in rank to both of you and I want you to remember that.'

It was pointless grandstanding. Ellen said, 'Do you have another house?'

'Of course.'

'Where is it?'

Kellock's wife scowled, then muttered an address in Red Hill, twenty minutes south.

'Could your husband be there?'

'Well, why don't you go and look,' snapped the woman, stalking off around the side of the big house.

Ellen got out her mobile phone, walking around with it in the grounds of the building until she got a clear signal. 'Scobie? Thank God.'

He cut in hurriedly: 'I was just about to call you. Clode's dead.'

She breathed in and out. 'Any sign of Kellock?'

'No.'

'Same MO as Duyker?'

'Yes. Shotgunned in the groin and bled out on the floor.'

'You know the drill, Scobie. Secure the scene. We're heading for Red Hill: the Kellocks have a house there.'

She gave him the address. He grunted. 'He'll have done a runner.'

'I know that, Scobie,' Ellen said. She ended the call, jerked her head at Pam. 'Let's go.'

They sped down the Peninsula, taking the freeway south and exiting onto a road that climbed steeply away from the coast, past vineyards, orchards and little art-and-craft galleries. Red Hill was a ribbon of houses amid huge gums, with vines and hobby farms on the nearby slopes. It was a well-heeled town, home to wineries that offered costly wines and meals to weekend tourists from the city. Ellen navigated, directing Pam to Point Leo Road and finally a gravelled track that plunged between dense stands of gum trees. A firetrap in summer. Pam braked suddenly.

They'd come to a clearing, a house fronting a tight turning circle. There were two vehicles, a police car and a Toyota twin-cab, a dented working vehicle. The house, of sandy brick, red tiles, gleaming aluminium window and door frames and potted ferns, looked out of place amongst the native trees. Ellen leaned forward, one hand on the dash. 'I know that Toyota. It belongs to Laurie Jarrett.'

Both women glanced at each other then. 'I should have realised,' Ellen said.

'We need backup, Sarge.'

'Yes.'

But their arrival had alerted Jarrett. He burst from the house, pushing Kellock ahead of him with the barrel of a shotgun. 'Stay out of this,' he yelled.

Ellen and Pam alighted from the car. They did not approach him but stood behind their open doors.

'Laurie,' Ellen said, feeling futile and pointless, 'put the gun down.'

He was coiled and powerful behind Kellock, who looked soft, depleted, in shock, his shirt hanging out and blood around his nose. 'I'm doing what you lot should have done a long time ago,' Jarrett said, prodding Kellock closer to the Toyota.

He had something in his free hand: a rolled magazine. To distract him, Ellen said, 'What have you got there, Laurie?'

'Have a look.'

He tossed it deftly; the magazine fluttered then fell like a stone. Ellen emerged cautiously from the shelter of the car and retrieved it. She was now about fifteen metres from Jarrett and Kellock, who were beside the Toyota. She straightened the pages of the magazine. It was printed on glossy paper, with plenty of pale, defenceless flesh on show, the children otherwise dressed in Little Bo Peep outfits, nurses' uniforms and schoolgirl tunics. It was called *Little Treasures*.

'What am I looking at, Laurie?'

His face burned with a kind of exultation. 'What the fuck do you *think* you're looking at?'

There was silence while she flipped through the pages. Then she heard him snarl, 'No you don't, sweetheart.'

Ellen glanced up: he was gesturing with the shotgun. She looked back over her shoulder. Pam had moved away from the car, her hand on her holstered .38. 'Both of you,' Jarrett said, 'guns on the ground. *Now!*'

'Do it, Pam,' Ellen said.

She placed her own gun on the gravelled driveway, watched Pam follow suit, and then she returned her attention to the magazine. A moment later, she found Alysha Jarrett. Laurie's daughter had been allocated a four-page spread. Her smiles were mostly empty, but there was pain in the emptiness.

Feeling sickened, Ellen looked up. Laurie was watching, still burning. 'Now you know,' he said.

'Yes.'

'Look closer.'

Ellen forced herself to comply. Hairy groins, but no faces, no way of identifying the abusers. Then she froze: she'd almost overlooked a bare foot with a birthmark like blood spilt across it. And there was Clode's spa bath. She looked up again. 'Taking care of business, Laurie?'

'Yes. First Clode, then Duyker. Clode told me about Duyker, snivelling piece of shit. They *both* told me about Kellock.'

'Don't make it worse, Laurie. Let Mr Kellock go, so that DC Murphy and I can arrest him.'

Kellock struggled. He still hadn't spoken. Jarrett clubbed him with the shotgun, a meaty thud. 'Fuck that, Ellen,' he said savagely. 'The police will protect their own, just like they always do.'

'No. There's too much evidence against him.'

Kellock looked at her then, as though relieved to think that she might sway Jarrett. She felt nothing for him and looked away. 'Mitigating circumstances, Laurie. The judge will understand. No one should have to bear what you've had to bear.'

He seemed to be listening. She went on: 'We failed to protect Alysha or punish her abusers, we hassled your family, we blamed you for shooting van Alphen—that wasn't you, I take it?'

He shook his head.

'And Kellock and van Alphen killed your nephew.'

There was a twist of pain on Laurie Jarrett's face. He shook his head as if to clear it. 'Killing Nick was the only good thing they did,' he muttered.

Ellen and Pam exchanged puzzled looks. 'I thought you hated them for that,' Ellen said, while Pam asked, 'What do you mean, Mr Jarrett?'

Laurie Jarrett looked from one woman to the other. The pain outgrew him as they watched, his voice and manner breaking apart. 'Don't you understand? Ellen, I took your advice, really sat down and talked to Alysha. Know what she told me? Nick and the others had *sold* her to Clode.'

Ellen gulped. You thought you'd seen the worst, and then someone would go one step further. 'Oh, Laurie.'

She ran the shooting of Nick Jarrett through her head again. She'd never doubted that Kellock and van Alphen had ambushed him, but she'd always seen it as a case of rough justice. Now she could see that Kellock had an additional—or different—motive: he feared that Nick Jarrett might have learnt about his involvement with Clode and Duyker. Nick Jarrett probably wasn't part of the ring—Clode was merely a source of ready cash—but he might have known about it. Clode might have boasted about his other activities and acquaintances.

'Laurie, let him go.'

'I should've realised what was going on,' Jarrett said, his distress growing. 'I can't bear to think about it.'

Kellock twisted violently as if he knew it was his end. Jarrett clubbed him again. Ellen cringed at the meaty sound of it. 'Laurie! Listen to me! Did Clode owe money to Nick? Is that why he was beaten up?'

He blinked. 'What?'

'Did Clode owe Nick money?'

'Who fucking knows?'

'We need details, Laurie. We need to speak to Alysha. We need you there. Come on, put the gun down.'

'You must be joking,' Jarrett said, bright and unequivocal again, as though his heart had never broken. He struck Kellock's kidneys with the barrel of the shotgun. 'Get in.'

Kellock hauled his huge mass over the driver's seat and across the gearstick to the passenger seat. Jarrett climbed in after him, first motioning the shotgun at Ellen and Pam. 'We've leaving now. You two won't try to stop us.'

Ellen said, 'Don't do this, Laurie,' and Pam began to circle around him.

In answer, he shot out the tyres of their car. They froze, their insides spasming, pellets and grit spitting and pinging. He said again, 'You won't stop me.'

Ellen glanced around at Pam, who gave her a complicated look. 'We won't stop you,' she murmured.

The Toyota threw gravel at them as it started away but it wasn't speeding. It moved sedately through the trees, exhaust toxins hanging in the still air, and they heard it pause at the main road above, and turn right. Waterloo lay in that direction, where the land levelled out to meet the sea. But before that there were many other roads, and back roads, full of secret places known to men like Laurie Jarrett.

61

After finding Neville Clode's body—Clode bent in a foetal position in a pool of blood, his private parts perforated from a shotgun blast—Scobie Sutton secured the scene, putting a senior constable in charge, and then sped away to help the girls in Red Hill. He hated to think of them going up against Kellock. Kellock scared him. He hated Kellock.

He was driving a police car, there being no unmarkeds available. He rocketed through Bittern and turned onto Bittern-Dromana Road, which had a reputation for a couple of dangerous intersections. If you were drowsy or inattentive, you were alerted by a series of speed humps. Not short stubby ones, like in a suburban street, but broad shallow ones. They didn't harm your suspension but they sure made you jump and take notice.

He was mentally mapping his way to Red Hill when he heard the dispatcher warn all personnel to be on the lookout for a white Toyota twin-cab, registered owner Laurie Jarrett, last seen in the Red Hill area. Jarrett was believed to have a hostage and be armed and dangerous. Oh God, Scobie thought. He accelerated. He was still down on the coastal plain, fifteen minutes from Red Hill. Frantic, he thumbed the speed dial on his mobile.

'Ellen! You all right?'

'I'm fine, Scobie.'

'I'm on my way there now.'

She got a little short with him. 'No need. Go back to Clode's. But keep an eye out for Laurie Jarrett. He's taken Kellock hostage. It was Jarrett who killed Clode and Duyker.'

Her voice unnerved him, it was so matter-of-fact. But he supposed it always would be and always had been. She broke the connection. Distracted, he tossed the phone onto the passenger seat, and so was unprepared for a sudden and dramatic series of percussions under the car. Warning humps: he was approaching one of the dangerous intersections. He braked. The car swerved, alarming a motorcyclist. His face went red, his palms damp: Ellen had never hidden the fact that she considered him a bad driver.

He came to a halt at the stop sign. A white twin-cab was approaching from the opposite direction. It also stopped. Scobie peered intently: dimly through the windscreen he could see Jarrett, one hand on the steering wheel, the other holding a shotgun under Kellock's jaw.

He fumbled for the siren. He hadn't been in a patrol car for fifteen years. Not that he needed a siren. It was unmistakeably a police car that he was driving.

Jarrett accelerated through the intersection and swept past. Scobie made a wild U-turn and went after him. Afterwards he wondered if he should have done that. It panicked Jarrett. He was later told that Jarrett would have killed Kellock anyway, but right then Scobie's job was to save Kellock and arrest Jarrett.

He put his foot down. Both cars flew along the stretch between Balnarring and Coolart Roads, through undulating farmland, spring grasses tall in the ditches and the roadside trees heavy, sombre and still. Up the gradient and there was Coolart Road and another stop sign and warning humps. The Toyota hit the first one at speed, and Scobie was told later that Jarrett's finger must have tightened involuntarily on the trigger of the shotgun. All he knew now was, the rear window of the Toyota was suddenly messily red, opaque, and the vehicle was slewing across the road and into a tree.

It was several hours before Pam Murphy could go home. She went to her little house in Penzance Beach—weatherboard cottage under pine trees, ten minutes walk from the beach—wondering if she'd participated in something that would alter her perception of the job, and of herself. She went home wondering if she and Ellen Destry could have affected the outcome in any way.

Pros and cons.

On the pro side, their .38s were on the ground and Laurie Jarrett was holding a shotgun on them. Plus, he'd shot out one of their tyres. Plus, they'd done the right thing and formally reported the incident, alerting the police of several local jurisdictions and calling for roadblocks.

On the con side, they hadn't called it in with any urgency. There had been an air of inevitability about their actions after Jarrett had taken Kellock away. The inevitability had been in the air even before that. Jarrett was going to kill Kellock and they couldn't stop him. But they hadn't tried very hard.

On the pro side, Kellock was a killer. He also abused children sexually, procured them for sexual abuse, and stood by and watched and encouraged the sexual abuse of children. He was a police officer. You could argue that he deserved to die.

And Laurie Jarrett was entitled to get his revenge.

On the con side, I am a police officer, thought Pam. So is Ellen. We have protocols to follow, standards to meet. We have a duty to save and protect, just as much as we have a duty to exert justice.

On the pro side, there had probably been nothing they could have done about any of it.

And so Pam went home, showered and poured herself a big, strong gin-and-tonic. 'My body is my temple,' she said wryly to the hollow air of her sitting room. Normally she went for a run or a long walk on the beach after work, but that could wait until tomorrow. She didn't want cheering up, necessarily, or even to wallow in misery. She wanted to think. She wanted to think about ethics, responsibilities, chance and fate. She played a Paul Kelly CD. His wry take on things suited her perfectly just then.

Scobie Sutton went home to his wife all twitchy. To his way of thinking, he'd precipitated a violent death that afternoon.

'Oh, you poor boy,' Beth said when he told her all about it. She took him to the sofa and perched there, holding his hands in her lap.

'There was nothing I could do.'

'Of course there wasn't.'

'It wasn't my fault. He was holding a shotgun to Kellock's head.'

'It's okay, love.'

'This has all been such a mess.'

'I know it has. And I haven't exactly been a help to you, with my moods.'

Well, that was true. Scobie felt a little aggrieved. But at least she was there. The sensations of her were familiar and welcome, her warm hands and the press of her breasts against his arm.

'Things will get better, you'll see,' she went on.

That's what his mother had always said. That's what he and Beth always said to Roslyn. 'I hope so,' he said in a small voice.

She said perkily, 'I've got a job interview.'

'You have? That's wonderful.'

'A short term contract with the shire, but better than nothing.'

With the shire that sacks its workers via e-mail. 'Exactly,' said Scobie in his bucking-up voice.

As he saw it, his and Beth's way was modest. A woman like Grace Duyker had a different way. That wasn't to say that one was right and the other wrong, he didn't think, just so long as he kept telling himself that.

Ellen didn't go home. At 11 pm she was still in her office writing up her notes. There was no urgency, she didn't have to do it now, but the world outside was mad and in CIU it was quiet. She put down her pen, swivelled in her chair and looked out on the purple night. After a while, she went to the incident room and began to dismantle the displays of maps, charts and photographs. So much paperwork. She'd once worked an investigation of six months' duration. It generated over fifty boxes and folders, containing thousands of search warrants, extradition documents, interview transcripts and field notes.

Well, this was going to be another big one. It wasn't over yet. Kellock might not have been the end of it: there were surely more men involved, some of them possibly his colleagues in the police. And what of the women? Was Kellock's wife part of it? And who would look after Alysha now, stop her going off the rails? Most of her abusers were dead but there were various cousins and siblings who'd profited from her abuse. Ellen vowed to see them into jail. That, together with a possible life sentence for Laurie, would dismantle the Jarrett clan. Peace would reign on the estate for about five minutes.

'Sergeant Destry.'

McQuarrie stood in her doorway. 'Sir,' she said, standing but not scrambling about it.

He'd come from some function. He was wearing his full dress

uniform, with plenty of ribbons and patches—all earned from staying in power, not merit or achievements. She realised from his voice and manner that she was in trouble about something. She didn't know what, but if McQuarrie was the kind of policeman to get such a thrill out of dressing up, he'd hate being called away to do actual police work, so she was probably in some deep shit.

'Hell of a mess.'

'Yes, sir.'

'Unbelievable.' He shook his well-combed head. 'If you hadn't let Jarrett go, this would never have happened.'

Ellen flushed. Her old blackness built in her head, a dangerous blind pressure. 'As I told you, *sir*, we had nothing to hold him on.'

McQuarrie took a step back. He looked very fine in his uniform, if short. 'I don't like your tone. And what's this I hear about a circle of paedophiles? Tell me it's all a huge mistake.'

'No mistake, sir,' and she laid it out for him. She was harsh and careless; she wasn't going to spare him. She also said, 'I know he was your friend, sir,' to see what he would do.

The colour drained from his face. He swallowed and recovered. 'Is that how you see me? One of them?'

She was pretty sure that he wasn't part of Kellock's ring. It had been a useful speculation, though, back when she was afraid and the men around her seemed sly and creepy.

'Of course not, sir,' she said evenly. 'But there may be others, and we have to root them out.'

She could see him thinking, the murky lights going on in his head. The pressure looming, the top brass and the press and the government leaning on him.

She decided to push it. 'Oh, another thing, sir, regarding that private lab you hired for our forensic testing. The press are getting wind of their sloppy procedures: shall I refer all calls to your office?'

McQuarrie said nothing but sat slackly, his uniform not quite so immaculate now. Ellen sat with him. And then, out in the car park, there was a familiar rattle, an old, tappety British motor.

'That would be Hal,' she said, beaming at the super. 'Home.'

He must have driven night and day. She felt a little dizzy and apprehensive. She'd left dishes in his sink, and hadn't replenished his stash of office coffee, and the subject of where she would live now hadn't been discussed. At the same time, she felt buoyed by her achievements, and by an old, familiar stirring in the pit of her stomach.